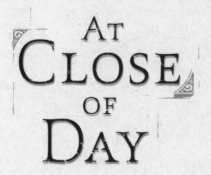

AT CLOSE OF DAY

JOSEPH BENTZ

At Close of Day

BETHANYHOUSE
MINNEAPOLIS, MINNESOTA

At Close of Day
Copyright © 2003
Joseph Bentz

Cover design by Lookout Design Group, Inc.

Published by Bethany House Publishers
11400 Hampshire Avenue South
Bloomington, Minnesota 55438
www.bethanyhouse.com

Printed in the United States of America by
Bethany Press International, Bloomington, Minnesota 55438

Library of Congress Cataloging-in-Publication Data

Bentz, Joseph, 1961-
   At close of day / by Joseph Bentz.
     p. cm.
   ISBN 0-7642-2209-0 (pbk.)
   1. Parent and adult child—Fiction. 2. Father and child—Fiction.
3. Secrecy—Fiction. I. Title.
PS3552.E6 A8   2003
813'.54—dc21
                                               2002152600

For

The Niños

JOSEPH BENTZ is a professor at Azusa Pacific University. He is the author of *Song of Fire, A Son Comes Home,* and *Cradle of Dreams.* He holds degrees in English as well as a Ph.D. in American Literature from Purdue University. He and his wife have two children and make their home in Southern California.

"Old age should burn and rave at close of day;

Rage, rage against the dying of the light."

—Dylan Thomas

1

JACKIE:
THE WAY I SEE IT

The problem began two nights ago, in the aftermath of Dad's latest stroke, when he got all talky and confused. I wasn't there when he let slip some "confessions" that have thrown the whole family into an uproar. My sister Pam says it's just the irrational chatter of a sick old man and we shouldn't pay any attention to him, but I don't agree. I think we should get to the bottom of it right away. Pam begged me not to bring it up with Dad right now. She said she doesn't think he's aware of what he said, and if we confront him about it in one of his clearheaded periods, the shock of it could "send him over the edge," meaning kill him.

I don't agree with that, either, but I'll tell you what. If I did try to squeeze the truth out of him, and then he died even a few weeks after that, I'd get the blame. The way this family operates, I'd never live it down. I'd always be known as the one who killed Dad.

Of course, Mom could have ended this whole thing right away if she had simply insisted that Dad was lying or hallucinating. He has certainly said enough other things that were easy to pass off. Dad had his stroke five days ago, and on the first night I came to visit him in the hospital, he looked up at me and said, "I'm tired. I been laying tile all night."

"Laying tile?" I asked. "What's that supposed to mean?"

He rolled his eyes and let out this huge sigh like I was the crazy one. "Don't you know what tile is, for heaven's sake?"

"Of course I know what tile is."

"Floor tile."

"I know what floor tile is, Dad, and any other kind of tile you could mention, but you haven't laid tile for years. You had a stroke. You're in the hospital. Don't you remember?"

"Oh," he said, and he leaned back against the pillow, his face all cloudy with confusion. He looked away from me, embarrassed, and mumbled, "Feels like I been working all night. That's why I can hardly keep awake this morning."

"It's not even morning, Dad. It's seven at night."

"Night?" he whispered in that raspy voice, lifting up his head and squinting at me as if to see if I was toying with him.

"Do you even know who I am?"

"Of course," he shot back, offended.

"Who?"

"My daughter," he growled.

"Which one?"

"Juh . . . Carol . . . I mean . . . Pam. What are you—?"

"You were on the right track the first time. Jackie."

"I know who *you* are."

Now, every time I visit, I make him tell me who I am, which bugs him no end. I also test him with other questions, like what day it is or what year it is. Last night he retaliated by pelting me with questions the minute I walked into the room. He really loved it. You could see him perk up the minute he saw me. "Who's the president?" he yelled so loud they could hear him all the way down the hall. "What month is it? What planet are we on? What's the square root of seven hundred? When was the last time you had a bowel movement?"

Even though he was doing it to annoy me, I just laughed and yelled my own questions right back at him. It was fun for us, to tell you the truth, but the ones who got annoyed were Mom and my sisters. They don't like him yelling like that. I guess they think it might throw him into another stroke or something. But I think what really bothered them was the embarrassment of other people hearing us. Mom hasn't talked above a whisper the whole time Dad's been in the hospital, like she thinks we're in a funeral home or a library or something.

When Dad and I played our little question game, Mom waved her arms back and forth to try to quiet us, but we ignored her. Then my sister Pam stepped in to take Mom's side. Pam doesn't usually like to mess with me directly, so she turned to Dad instead and said, "Settle down, Dad. The doctor said you're not supposed to get all riled."

"He's not allowed to *talk*?" I asked.

"Bellowing down the hall is not talking," Pam snipped.

Mom said, "Don't you know there's sick people in this hospital? You don't have to create a ruckus."

That should tell you something about my family. Talking out loud equates to "creating a ruckus."

My other sister, Carolyn, was there, but she didn't want to get involved. Carolyn operates in one of two modes: hysteria or passivity, and last night she was hunkered down next to Dad's bed like she was just about to crawl underneath it. She was so embarrassed by our little bit of fun that you would have thought I had pranced down the hall naked, singing the national anthem.

I love Carolyn, and I think she's well-meaning, but I have to say that, in my honest opinion, she is turning into a muddled mess of a person. I've been noticing lately that she's even started to walk different, a little stoop-shouldered, like her body's begging the world not to notice her or not to pile any more burdens on her back. She's only forty-three, but that stoop makes her look even older than me. I'm forty-five, the oldest in the family, but I honestly don't think I look it. It's my weight that ruins me. If I could drop twenty-five or thirty pounds, and if I could find a hair stylist anywhere on this earth capable of taming my frazzly mop, I would look pretty good.

Not that I'm heavier than Carolyn. I'd say she's got ten or twenty pounds on me. Plus, pardon me for saying so, but I honestly think I carry my weight a little better than she does. I stand up straight and don't look ashamed to have a few extra pounds.

Carolyn, on the other hand, looks like she's searching for a hole in the ground to crawl into, and she acts that way, too. Her apartment is a perfect example of her rabbit-hole existence. It's the darkest home I've ever seen. She never opens her drapes unless somebody asks her to. She has a balcony but never uses it. She likes to burrow into her big old couch and, with only one faint light bulb burning, lose herself in the weirdest combination of reading material I ever saw—tabloids like *Star* and the *National Enquirer,* magazines like *People* and *Vanity Fair,* self-help books, religious devotionals, mystery novels, even the Bible. All those books and magazines are scattered out across the room like a library that's been hit by a tornado.

I'm not trying to criticize her. She's had it tougher than most of us, especially after she divorced her jerk of a husband who was having an affair. She's trying to raise Brandon by herself, and I give her credit for that. I know Carolyn resents me a little bit because she thinks Dad likes me better than her, but the problem is she has just never known how to deal with him. He senses she's weak (she practically wears a *sign* on her chest that says so), so he feels free to take out his frustration on her, especially now that he's sick. I don't even know if he realizes he's doing it half the time. She won't fight back. She just scrunches down and waits for his little verbal thunderstorms to pass. If she takes any action at all, it's to flee from the room and cry.

That's why I know that whenever it comes time to make any decisions about Dad's future, Carolyn won't be any help at all. I'll have to take the lead. Carolyn acts like Dad's strokes are nothing more than a little touch of the flu that he'll get over after a few days of rest. She'll never be able to confront the fact that he might die or he might never be well enough to live at home again.

I'm not even sure that Pam will be strong enough to sit down with Mom and Dad and make them face the facts. Even though she's a few years younger than Carolyn and I, there was a time when we would have looked to her to decide what to do. If these strokes had happened five years ago, Pam would already have planned what the next step would be, and she'd probably have the house up for sale and an apartment picked out for them and all the rest of it. She lived with Mom and Dad until she was almost thirty, and they're a lot more likely to listen to her than to any of the rest of us. Even after she moved out and got married, she still kept running over there all the time once their health started declining and they got so needy.

But now she can't do it. She's got a three-year-old and a one-year-old and a husband and a house and a part-time job. With all that on her mind, she's gone a little soft when it comes to Mom and Dad. Now she's more likely to go along with Carolyn's more passive approach to them. When I asked Pam what she thought Dad should do once they released him from the hospital, she said, "I guess they'll send him to the rehab center."

"But that's only for a few weeks," I pointed out. "What then?"

"I guess he'll go home."

"Pam, he can't *walk*," I said. "He can barely stand up. How's he going to live at home? How would he even get from the bedroom to the bathroom?"

"He could use a walker."

"Even though he can't walk? You expect him to not only cross the rooms but also maneuver a walker up and down those steps?"

Mom and Dad have a very old house, and to get from their bedroom to the bathroom, he'd have to go up one step into this narrow hallway, then down a step into the living room, then up another big step by the upstairs landing, and then a step down in front of the bathroom. Impossible for him right now.

"Well," said Pam with a big old tired sigh, "Mom will have to help him."

"She can barely walk, either!" Mom is very weak. Every time she totters across the room, I'm just sure she's going to tip over headfirst onto the floor. There's no way she can manage Dad. He'll crush her!

"Well," Pam drawled again, "we'll have to cross that bridge when we come to it."

I wanted to scream, "The bridge is just a few feet away! It's swaying in the wind! It's cracking! It's going to collapse!" But it's pointless to push Pam when she gets that way.

I'd give anything if I could have been there the night Dad started blabbing. The way Pam tells it, she and Carolyn and Mom were in the room, and Dad had been pretty sick. The first night he was in the hospital, we were afraid he wouldn't even live through the night. But on this particular evening, it was close to eight o'clock, and Dad happened to ask them when he could go home. There was nothing unusual in that. Almost from the time the ambulance dropped him off at the hospital, when he was barely able to move or talk, he was griping about being ready to go home. Pam says she told him he wouldn't be going home for a long time, maybe a couple months.

That got him all agitated. He yelled, "I can't stay in the hospital for two months! I can't afford it! The insurance will run out and I'll be paying off this bill for the rest of my life. I won't go bankrupt just so you can keep me locked up in here."

That's how he talks. As if the stroke was *our* idea. As if we *like* spending every night of our lives visiting him at the hospital and listening to him bellow.

So Pam explained that he won't be in the hospital that whole time, but that when he's released he'll have to go to a rehab unit and stay there till he's able to walk again, till they can see if he's strong enough to live on his own.

Well, that "if he's strong enough to live on his own" sent him off on another tirade against poor Pam. If they tried to put him in one of those rehab places, he vowed he'd walk right out of it and send Pam the bill. He'd been through that before and would rather die than spend another month in there. On and on he went, the same old stuff we've heard many times before. Pam just let him talk, knowing that, by the time he got well enough to go to rehab, he wouldn't even be able to remember that this conversation had taken place.

Then he got real quiet, and she figured he was worn out from his little tantrum and was going to give everybody a rest. A few minutes later, she walked up to him to straighten his pillow, which had almost fallen off the bed while he was yelling. As soon as she leaned over to help him, he muttered, "I'm not going."

"Let's talk about it later," Pam told him. "Just rest."

Then he leaned back into the pillow and smiled, which is pretty unusual in itself. Then he said it. "I'll call my other family to come and get me."

"What other family?" asked Pam, at first thinking he was talking about me or one of his nieces or nephews.

"Never mind," he said, still wearing that sneaky little smirk.

"Do you really think Jackie—or who else, Sandy? Billy?—is

going to go against the doctor's orders and take you home when you can't even walk yet?"

"I can too walk," he said.

"Dad, you haven't taken a step since you got here."

"But I don't mean Jackie or any of them. I know they're in cahoots with you."

"Who then?"

He didn't answer for a few seconds. He gets like that sometimes now. You'll be talking to him and suddenly he'll fade out in the middle of a conversation. Then real quiet, like he was talking to himself, he said, "I have a son in California. He's a businessman in Los Angeles. He'll take me out of this place."

Like I said, the strokes make Dad say crazy things all the time, so normally we would have dismissed this as just more chatter. But Mom's reaction brought everyone to a halt. As soon as the words "son in California" registered, she sprang forward in her chair (which is unusual) and spat out the words, *"Shut up, Hugh!"*

Now, for lots of people, "Shut up, Hugh" would not be a shocking thing to say. But I do not remember even one time in my life when Mom has ever said "shut up." And I would bet my whole life savings that she has never said it to my dad. Not only that, but she rarely even refers to him as Hugh when it's just family around. She usually refers to him as Dad or, if she's in a really good mood, Honey.

What happened (or should I say didn't happen) next doesn't make a bit of sense unless you know how dumb my family can be. If I had been there—and I would give a whole month's salary to have heard Dad say he has another family and to have heard Mom tell him to shut up—I would have closed the door and sat everybody down and gotten to the bottom of it.

Carolyn, of course, sensing danger, crawled into her little turtle shell and refused to utter a peep. But why didn't Pam force Mom or Dad to tell her what was going on? She claims she tried but that she was too stunned to know what to say. I would have known what to say. Nobody would have left the room until it was all out on the table. But Pam just said some weak little thing like "What's he talking about?" and Mom turned red and shook her head and refused to talk. Pam said Dad clammed up real fast, too, after Mom's "shut up" jolted him back to reality.

So finally Pam dropped it and decided she'd bring it up later once she'd had a chance to think it through and once Mom and Dad were back to normal. Big mistake. That delay gave them time to build up their defenses and get their stories coordinated. Now Dad says he doesn't remember saying anything about another family, and Mom's being just as evasive. She says the only reason she told him to shut up was that her nerves were shot and she couldn't stand to hear him get started on another bunch of nonsense.

The first time I saw Mom and Dad in person after the episode was last night, and I was determined not to leave that hospital without getting to the truth. I waited for over an hour before I mentioned anything, and then all I said was, "Mom, I need to talk to you."

"I'm busy with your dad," she said, even though Dad was lying there half asleep and she was sitting in a chair at the end of the bed doing nothing. Pam was sitting on one side of her and Carolyn on the other. Pam looked as tired as I've ever seen her, kind of dazed, with her head propped up against her hand.

"This won't take long," I said.

"Don't start," Mom shot back.

Pam jumped up out of her seat as if she had suddenly remembered something and said, "Come down to the cafeteria with me."

Before we got halfway there, I looked back and saw Carolyn puffing her way down the hall after us, head tilted down toward the floor like she was afraid to be seen. Pam told me all about Dad's health problems of the day, and she said Mom was feeling pretty lousy, too. Mom's arthritis was bad, and her stomach was bothering her, and I don't know what all. Pam said, "That's why I wanted to get out of there for a while. I didn't want to get anything started in there tonight. I don't feel so hot myself."

Carolyn caught up with us in line, and once the three of us got our Cokes and sat down, I said, "So what else have you found out?"

"Nothing," said Pam.

I let out a little huff of frustration, which I thought was more restrained than actually saying something, but which offended Pam anyway.

She looked at me sideways with that annoyed expression and said, "There's nothing *to* find out. It's just another of his hallucinations. Remember his stroke last year? He kept telling me to get all those paint cans out of his hospital room. There was nothing in there that looked the least bit like a paint can, but he kept insisting that the paint smell was giving him a headache."

"This isn't paint cans, Pam," I said. "This is a *son*. And the thing is, he was so specific. I mean, a *businessman* in *Los Angeles*. Where would he get that?"

"How could he have a son? When? He and Mom have been married for over forty-five years!"

"Well, maybe he had an affair, or—"

"Dad? No way. He would never do that to Mom. And she certainly never would have stood for it."

Carolyn, who had been staring off toward the condiments counter during this whole conversation, as if none of this applied to her, turned her gaze back to our table and said, apparently to the napkin holder, "I think he was telling the truth."

That brought the conversation to a screeching halt. It's very unusual for Carolyn to state a blunt opinion, particularly when

Pam and I are still arguing about something.

"Why do you say that?" I asked her. "Do you know something we don't?"

"No," she said, real quiet and mysterious, still not looking directly at us. "But I know people. I know when they're telling the truth."

I couldn't help letting out one of my big sigh-groans, which made a couple people at the next table look over at us, and which I feared might send Carolyn scurrying back inside herself.

"Keep it down, Jackie," scolded Pam.

"Well, I can't help it," I said. "She makes it sound like she has some information, and then all she comes up with is, 'I *know* when people are telling the truth,' like she's something off the psychic hot line."

"When we were growing up," said Carolyn, ignoring my comment, "didn't you ever suspect that Mom and Dad were hiding something?"

"No, I didn't," said Pam. "Like what?"

"Like why did we always seem to know more about Mom's life before she met Dad than we did about Dad's life before he married Mom?"

I had never given this much thought, but once she mentioned it, I knew in my gut she had a point. Even though Dad had never exactly *refused* to talk about his life before Mom, the details of those years had always been shrouded in a hazy lack of specifics.

"I know all about Dad's life before he met Mom," Pam claimed. "After high school he got drafted into the military, right? It was at the end of World War II. When he got discharged he came home and got a job as a house painter in La-fayette, and then when his father died, he moved in with his mother for a while and hired on at the Brantwell factory in Indianapolis. Then he met Mom and they got married. Then they started having us. So what's so mysterious about that?"

"He graduated from high school in 1945, right?" asked Carolyn. "And he and Mom got married in 1954, when he was twenty-eight years old. So there's almost ten years there between graduation and his marriage to Mom that are basically unaccounted for."

"They're not 'unaccounted for,'" said Pam. "I just told you what he was doing during those years."

"We know just the barest details," said Carolyn. "There was plenty of time in there for him to have a relationship with some other woman—even a marriage—and to have had a son who is now a businessman in Los Angeles, just like he said."

Pam scoffed at this, but you could tell from her face that she believed it was possible.

"Well, there's one way to find out," I said. "We can march right back in there and corner the two of them and not let anyone leave until we get it nailed down."

Pam was shaking her head no before I even finished the sentence. "Listen, Jackie, I know you like to charge in and take control of the situation, but you just can't do that this time. I'm telling you, when Dad brought this whole thing up, there was *panic* in Mom's face unlike anything I've ever seen. She's already on the verge of cracking up over what's happening to Dad. Now is not the time to back either of them into a corner. If there's anything to this story, which I doubt, then there'll be plenty of time to talk about it once they're safe at home."

"I agree," said Carolyn. "Dad's too sick. I'm not even sure he's going to *make* it home this time."

It took every ounce of restraint in my body to keep from lifting the table up and slamming it back down. I settled for tapping my fingers like a maniac, causing Carolyn to stare at them as if I were performing some feat of athletic prowess. I knew my sisters were joining ranks against me and I'd never be able to get them to go along with me even though what they were saying was stupid. Didn't it occur to Carolyn that if Dad really was going to die, then this might be our last chance to find out the truth? I wasn't suggesting that we *torture* Mom and Dad, just that we ask them for an explanation. But I know my sisters well enough to know that any logical argument I would have made at that point would have only made them more determined to fight me.

While I was thinking this through, Carolyn said, "I think he wants to tell this anyway, so there won't be any need for a show-down. Let him tell it his own way. I think the son's gonna show up someday soon."

"What! What has he told you?" I asked.

"Nothing. But if Dad knows that this guy is a businessman in Los Angeles, then he must have heard from him. It only makes sense that the son would visit if he'd go to all the trouble to track Dad down."

"You're getting way ahead of yourself," said Pam. "Right now we don't know a thing. So can we just drop it for the time being until Dad's out of danger?"

They both looked at me.

"Jackie?" said Pam. "Will you promise me that?"

"All right," I agreed, and they shot each other a glance, as if they had pulled something over on me.

They weren't as smart as they thought they were. I agreed to keep quiet for the moment, but I have plans of my own. I know I can visit early or late one day soon and get in the room with Dad alone. If I catch him in one of his talky phases, I can get the truth out of him myself. Then I'll decide from there what to do with the information.

What if we *do* have a brother? At first, I thought that might not be such a bad thing. I was actually kind of curious to see what he'd look like. Would he act or sound like any of us? Would it be obvious that he was our brother, or would he seem like a complete stranger?

But the more I thought about him, the more worried I got. Why is he popping up now, when Dad's probably on the verge of dying? Could he be after Dad's money? Are we going to get tricked out of what little inheritance we have coming to us? Why is Mom afraid of him? Pam and Carolyn are too squishy to think about things like that, but I don't intend to let some stranger march in here and steal everything we've got. I intend to find out the truth.

2 CAROLYN: MAY I CHIME IN?

Dad never dies when you expect him to.

I can't talk about that to anyone in the family because they'd think it sounds like I *want* him to die, but that's not it. The thing is, Dad had a heart attack that almost killed him over ten years ago, and another slight one about a year after that. Then he had the stroke six months ago, and these other two over the last couple weeks. So altogether, we've been on a kind of deathwatch for him for about a decade.

I remember that right after his first stroke, one of his doctors made it clear to us that he didn't think Dad would make it to the end of the week. That stroke made Dad compliant, almost like a little kid, looking up at you with big eyes and talking nice or just smiling, completely unlike his regular personality.

I actually sat with him and had long talks that week—normal conversations where he would listen and smile and ask me questions. He wasn't mean at all. He didn't berate me or give me stupid advice about what I should do with my life. He didn't remind me fifty thousand times about some little chore he wanted me to do for him. I kept thinking how strange and sad it was that the best talks I had ever had with my dad were not happening until he was on his deathbed with his brain ravaged by a stroke.

I didn't exactly *want* him to die then, but I have to admit that I thought about how comforting it would be to remember him this way, all serene and loving. I dropped all the anger that I usually carried around toward him and actually felt guilty for how disappointed he had always been with me. I even started reminiscing with him about the good times we had together when I was a kid, something I'd never done before. In fact, until then, I probably would have said I didn't *have* any good memories of him from my childhood.

Most of the stuff I was telling him didn't come to mind until I was opening my mouth and starting to say it. I remembered him carrying me on his shoulders around the backyard when I was three or four years old. I can't believe such a memory came back to me. I had never thought about it before. But as I told it to Dad, I could feel what it was like to be perched up there above his head, taller than everybody, thrilled but also a little scared as he bounced around the yard and—this part is a little vague—sang some little song. I can picture the top of his head, hear his voice, see the green lawn spinning beneath me as he trots around.

Dad remembered it, too. He said, "The problem was you never wanted to get down. If I put you down too soon, you screamed your head off. You'd want to keep going until my back was aching and I was gasping for breath."

I also remembered a few times when Dad took only me and none of the other kids somewhere. I remember one trip to the hardware store when I was maybe five or six. I was so proud to be sitting next to Dad in his truck while my sisters had to stay home. We went to the hardware store and picked out some paint that Dad was going to use on one of the bedrooms. I can still see the man mixing the paint; I can see the machine shaking the can back and forth as I stand watching by my dad. When it stops, Dad teases me by asking me to carry the can out to the truck for him, but it's too heavy. Then he picks it up and pays, and I follow him out to the truck. On the way home, country music fills the cab as my dad hums along and occasionally whistles.

As an adult, I have never felt as close to my dad as I did during those conversations after his stroke. If he had died right then, I would have remembered those final conversations and could have told myself that that was my real dad. He loved me. Even though I spent most of my life believing he considered me a disappointment, at the end we had a true connection.

But Dad didn't die that week, and he didn't stay nice. The more he recovered, the meaner he got. I came to visit him one night at the end of that week—Pam and Mom were in his room—and before I even said hello, he started in on me. That night he decided to insult my home, which is a common theme for his harangues. "When are you gonna move out of that dinky apartment?" he bellowed. "It's no good for Brandon."

"The apartment is not dinky, Dad," I said. "It has two big bedrooms and one of the biggest living rooms I've ever seen in an apartment complex."

I immediately regretted taking his bait. The best thing to do when he gets like that is to ignore him. Otherwise, he makes a contest out of it and keeps pounding you until you finally surrender in exhaustion.

"That's no place to raise a child," he growled.

"Why not?"

I couldn't help myself. Even though it was a no-win argument, I felt this need to play it out. That's how I am with Dad sometimes. Part of me is a victim who wants to flee from his words, but another part of me is an onlooker, fascinated by the spectacle, analyzing it as it unfolds.

"A kid needs a yard to play in," he said.

"He has a yard. He has a whole playground. Besides, Brandon is a teenager now. He doesn't even need—"

"Not a playground!" he snarled. "A yard. A yard of his own. Aren't you ever gonna buy a house for him to live in?"

Dad knows I'm divorced. He knows I can barely afford our next meal, let alone a down payment on a house. But this criticism of my finances is a recurring theme in his nagging.

"If you give me the money," I said, already embarrassed that Pam and Mom were sitting there overhearing this, "I'll be glad to buy a house for Brandon. I'm sure he'd be thrilled to have that gift from his grandpa."

"If you'd learn how to manage your money, you wouldn't need me to bail you out all the time."

"When have you ever—"

"You've frittered it all away! You've wasted every cent you've ever made."

Pam jumped up out of her chair at that point and stood right over him and said, "Knock it off, Dad. This is not the time or the place to have another stupid argument."

"I'm not arguing," he said. "I'm just—"

"Just stop!" she yelled, right in his face. "If you start this tonight, we're all gonna walk right out of here. Carolyn came to visit you. She doesn't need you jumping all over her the minute she walks through the door."

That shut him up for the moment. Pam knows how to deal with him better than I do. Her methods don't always work, but most of the time she can get his attention and derail him from his tirade. He let out a painful sigh and stared off with that vague look he gets, as if he had been alone in the room for a long time.

Pam, acting like Dad wasn't even there, said to me, "You've got to ignore his meanness, Carolyn. It's the stroke talking, not him."

I nodded, but then I realized, if that meanness isn't really him, then that earlier kindness wasn't really him, either.

The minute I heard Dad say he had a son in Los Angeles, I knew it was true. It's hard to describe, but it felt like I wasn't even hearing the news for the first time. It felt more like I was *remembering* something I had known years ago but had forgotten. It was like being reminded of some acquaintance I knew in high school but had never thought of since. I can't say that I ever really *suspected* that Dad had a son. I mean, I never would have come up with that fact on my own, but when he let it slip, it certainly fit with all the evasions and the hazy descriptions he had always given us of his early life. And Mom, with that horrified expression, might as well have screamed, "It's true! It's true!"

My sisters would jump all over me if I ever said this to them, but I'm actually glad to know that we have a brother. I'm even starting to know what he looks like. I know that sounds strange. I know my family would make fun of it, but I do actually know things in ways that are different from other people. I don't yet have a complete picture of my brother, but I have an outline and a few details. I see brown eyes, like my dad's. I see myself looking into these eyes. I see a thin man, wearing jeans and a sweat shirt, a man who is older than us but who looks about our age. Wavy hair, brushed back in some of my visions of him. But the eyes are what I really have down. They're looking at me. They're interested. We have an instant connection as brother and sister. We'll be friends. He'll like me and trust me more than anyone else in the family.

I'm afraid of what Jackie might do. She never thinks about anything before she blurts it out, and she can be so belligerent that I'm afraid, if she gets the chance, she'll ruin any kind of meeting we can set up with our brother. She'll think she has to prove herself to him by fighting him or putting him on the defensive. She'll have to show him who's boss, like she does with everybody else. That's why, if possible, I want to find out about him first, before Pam or Jackie does, so that I can contact him somehow and warn him what kind of weird family members he's related to.

But first I have to find a way to make Mom and Dad feel comfortable telling us the truth about this. That's another place where Jackie could really cause problems. If she charges in there and tries to force Mom and Dad to spill their guts about something they've managed to keep quiet our whole lives, then I'm afraid they'll get all defensive and clam up for a few more months or even years. I know she promised Pam she wouldn't say anything for now, but I don't trust her to keep that promise.

The best solution is for me to find out the truth before anybody else, so that I can do some damage control ahead of time. Then, once the story does come out, the best way for me to fight Jackie will be to get Pam on my side. But I don't know what Pam will do. She's clinging to her denial that this brother exists, even though deep down she must have some sense that he's real. So when he does appear, will that denial turn into suspicion and make her side with Jackie against him?

I know I'm jumping too far ahead. My first priority has to be to get Dad or Mom to talk to me before Jackie gets to them. One fact I wish I knew is whether Mom knew before she married Dad that he had a son. I sure hope he didn't hide it from her until sometime later. If she did know about it before their marriage, then I don't feel so bad for her, because she knew what she was getting into. And in that case, I don't see why we shouldn't know the whole truth, too.

I'm tempted to skip Dad and go right to Mom to find out. If

I got her alone, and in the right mood, she just might talk. And then I could take the next step and contact my brother. I don't even know his name! What will his voice sound like? What will he say when we're talking on the phone and he hears, "This is Carolyn. Your sister. I'm so happy to finally talk to you." He'll be happy, too. I just know it. I can't wait to meet him. I could use another friend in this family.

3 HUGH:
THE OLD MAN SQUEEZES IN
A FEW WORDS

When I was young—in my twenties and thirties—I figured that by the time I got to be as old and feeble as I am now, I would pretty much be ready to die. I figured I would look back on my life and say something along the lines of, "I've lived a long and happy life and have experienced most of the good things that people long for. I've had lots of bad times, too, but I survived them. Now I'm ready to go."

But now that I actually find myself one of those cadaverous old geezers who can't even make it to the bathroom half the time without peeing on myself, I find that I am not at all ready to die. My daughters hover around my bed at the hospital, as warily as vultures, and when they speak to me, it's with that pityingly sweet tone that says, "I know this might be the last time I talk to you, so I want to be nicer to you than I ever was when you were healthy." It makes me so mad I want to use what little strength I have left to lash out at them. I want to push them out of the room and yell, "Get away from me! I'm not dead yet! I refuse to die according to your schedule!"

To hear them tell it, most of what I say to them is pretty mean anyway. I can hardly ask for a glass of water without being accused of yelling at somebody or abusing them or demanding that everybody live according to my dictates.

I'm not nearly as bad as my daughters like to paint me. But I'm willing to admit that I've sometimes gone overboard in things I've said. I've become, I'm afraid, something else I never could have imagined when I was young—a grouchy old man. The sad thing is that I have as wide a range of thoughts and emotions as I ever had, but only the grouchier ones seem to come out. I wish I could stop myself, but I just get so furious! I could help my daughters if they would only listen, but they won't. Because I've become this skeletal shell of my former self, and because it's a struggle for me to simply walk across the room or lift a fork to my mouth, they assume I've lost touch with reality. They talk to me in the patronizing tone usually reserved for two-year-olds and patients of an insane asylum.

"Would you like some more peas, Dad?" they ask in that fluty little simper. "Here, let me mash those up for you."

If I point out to them that my mouth is still perfectly capable of mashing a pea without anyone's help, they yell at me for being mean and for not showing enough gratitude for all they do. I'm supposed to nod and smile and slurp down their mushy mess without complaint. Never mind my own humiliation. I'm an old man now. I'm supposed to passively accept my role as the grinning idiot.

If you saw me from the outside, you'd see a feeble, inarticulate wreck, but here where I'm speaking from, deep inside myself, I am unhindered by the horrors that have been inflicted on my body and mind. Those around me don't realize that deep within, I am still my essential self, still the whole man that they assume no longer exists.

Of course, these strokes do temporarily throw me into confusion. Sometimes it feels like my brain has been dunked in a whirlpool and my thoughts are swirling crazily around my head. I can get ahold of individual thoughts, but I can't always grab the exact ones that I need. I know I'm forgetful. A detail that I have a pretty good grasp on one second will pop right out of my brain in the next, and for the life of me I can't get it back.

To me, the worst part of this memory loss is the embarrassment. The other day, I asked Pam how her husband was doing (his name slipped my mind). I thought I was being nice. I felt good about making polite conversation even though I felt lousy enough to die at any moment. But Pam looked at me with this irritated scowl as if I had just asked her to recite the alphabet in Chinese.

"Dad," she scolded, "that's the fourth time you've asked me. He's fine."

That was certainly a conversation stopper. What could I do but sit there in belittled silence, feeling like the senile old fool I'm sure she thinks I am. I didn't remember asking about her husband more than once, but I couldn't really deny it, either. It sort of *felt* like she might be right, once I thought about it. That's the way it is with my memory these days. Even when I can't remember something outright, I'll sometimes have a vague outline or hint of the idea once somebody jogs my thinking. But whether Pam was right or wrong about me saying it four times, I was irked that she had to be so rude about it. Whatever happened to respect for your parents? I never would have talked to my own father the way my kids talk to me. I wouldn't have talked to *any* older person that way, for that matter. But you see, if I had complained to her about her rudeness, then suddenly I'd be the bad guy again. Mr. Grouch. Mr. Why-Don't-You-Hurry-Up-and-Die.

Another thing I don't remember, but that I guess I did, was

letting something slip about my son, Danny, in Los Angeles. Vonnie, my wife, told me I said it right in front of the girls. Pam and Carolyn, that is. Not Jackie, thank God. It's hard to tell what she would have pumped out of me if she had been in the room. Vonnie was furious, let me tell you. That's why I believe I must have done it, even though I've never let anything slip like that before, no matter how bad a condition I've been in. Vonnie said she tried to pass it off as just some more of my idiotic rambling (I don't get much respect from her anymore, either), but she thinks the girls are suspicious and will probably keep probing until we tell them more.

I could kick myself for blabbing about Danny. If they press me to the wall on this, I can't even imagine how I could begin to explain the fact that I have a son they've never known about. That also happens not to be the only thing they don't know. I also have a daughter they don't know about, Donna, who is now about fifty years old and who I have not laid eyes on since she was a little child. I was also married to the mother of these children for four years, before I met Vonnie.

When I think of having to look into the faces of my daughters and tell them this, I honestly have to say that the possibility that I'll die before it all comes out doesn't sound so bad. I almost welcome that way of avoiding this horrible showdown. There is no good way to tell it. I mean, it may sound like I'm making excuses for myself, but to reduce the story into a summary that you could squeeze into one conversation oversimplifies it. It ignores the complexities. It overlooks the fact that these were peculiar circumstances that unfolded in a particular time and place, with certain unfortunate occurrences, and it doesn't make half as much sense now, looking back on it, as it did living through it.

Now, can you imagine me trying to explain that to Jackie? "What a load of garbage," she would say. "Don't talk to me about 'complexities' and 'peculiar circumstances'. Get to the point. Tell me the facts."

Not that I blame her. I'd have the same reaction. She inherits her "garbage detector" from me. But I'm telling you, in this case, the facts don't speak for themselves. Not that I justify my own actions. Every day of my life I feel the wrongness of what I did. The only hope I had left was that I would get to the end of my life without ever having to explain. I've prayed to God for years that He would grant me that one request. I still think we'd all be better off if we could leave the past buried and live in the reality we've created in the present.

But I sense now that I'm not going to be let off that easy. After all these decades, I am going to be held accountable. I am going to have to *pay*.

Even though I was stupid to let that slip about Danny, that little disclosure wasn't what really got this whole mess started. This whole part of my past was resurrected last year when, for the first time ever, I got a letter from Donna. I can still picture the long blue envelope with my name on it, written in neat black handwriting, with a name on the return address that I didn't recognize: *Donna Pryce,* her married name. When I opened it up and read, *Dear Father,* I thought I would have another heart attack or stroke right then and there. I almost hoped for it.

Fortunately, Vonnie was asleep that afternoon when the mail came, so she didn't see me open the envelope. She was dozing in her armchair right across the living room from me. I stuffed the letter back in the envelope right away and took it into the bedroom before Vonnie woke up.

You might expect that when I got to the bedroom, I ripped that letter open again and read it as fast as I could. I didn't. I could barely stand to think about it, let alone read it. I opened the drawer of my nightstand and buried it deep under the receipts and medical papers and other junk that I keep there.

Vonnie wouldn't look there in a million years. Then I went back to the living room, sat down in my recliner, and started opening the rest of the mail. I guess you could say I'm not a very emotional man, but I had to sit there for a couple of hours hardly moving a muscle while waves of some emotion I can't even name—fear, regret, panic, dread—washed over me. We got this advertising catalog from a clothing store that day, and I opened it on my lap and stared at it without seeing a thing for almost two hours. Vonnie woke up in the midst of this, and eventually she noticed me staring at this catalog, from which I have never bought anything and which I normally toss aside without a glance.

"Are you planning to buy some pants out of there?" she asked.

"I just might," I lied.

"I thought you always like to try things on before you buy them."

"Well, I don't know," I said. "I'm just looking."

She knew something was wrong and kept a close eye on me for the rest of the day, but I didn't tell her anything.

It was the next day before I could bring myself to read Donna's letter. Even now it's hard for me to think about it. I went into the bedroom and got it while Vonnie was taking her bath, which fortunately is a long process now that she's getting so feeble. I put the letter inside the owner's manual for our VCR as I read it, just in case Vonnie happened to come into the room.

The letter had a sophisticated look to it, handwritten in perfect script on pale blue stationery. She told me in the letter that she's an English teacher in a high school, which might help explain the good handwriting. She told me that she found out about me two years before, right before her mother died.

I dropped the letter at that point. *So Barbara's dead. My first wife.*

I didn't feel grief exactly, but I felt lightheaded. *Barbara. Barbara. No longer in this world.*

Memories swirled around me, my head faint. I pictured her face. I imagined her standing in our house around 1950, laughing, her lipstick blaring red. Her skirt twirls a little bit as she bounces around the room—doing what?—listening to the radio as she carries the dinner dishes from the dining room to the kitchen.

I picked up the letter and tried again. It said that when Barbara told Donna about me not long before she died—*What did she die of? How long had she suffered? What was her life like in those final years?*—she begged Donna never to contact me. She actually made her promise that she wouldn't.

For two years I kept that promise, wrote Donna, *but now I feel compelled to break it.*

You should have kept your promise! Don't you see? Barbara was right. She knew the chaos that could be unleashed by breaking open the past. If she had known you would do this, she never would have told you!

Why, Donna reasoned, would her mother have told her the truth about her natural father if she didn't think that at some point they would meet? Besides, after thinking it over for a long time and talking to many people she respected, she had come to the conclusion that the decision was not her mother's to make. She had the right to decide for herself whether or not she would contact her own father.

The right! She sounds just like my other daughters. Sweep aside what your parents say and do what you want. Who are parents, anyway, just troublesome old fools keeping you from your rights.

Donna had also talked to her brother, Danny, who is a businessman in Los Angeles.

Tell me more about him! What is he like? Does he have a

family? What kind of businessman? Why is that the only phrase she uses to describe him? Why would she say so little? She's toying with me. She's trying to build up so much suspense that I'll have no choice but to contact her to find out more.

> *Danny agreed that getting in touch with you was the right thing to do. Both of us want to meet you, but we both decided we would respect your wishes. We will not call you or come to your home without an invitation, but we ask you to please understand this from our perspective. We want to know our father.*

I put the letter down again and tried to relax a little, catch my breath, not overreact. I thought, if she really means what she says—that she won't call me or come to see me without an invitation—then I could tear up this letter right now and things could go right back to the way they were before. My silence would respect and confirm Barbara's wishes that Donna and Danny never know me or see me again. Ending this now would also fulfill my long-time promise to Vonnie that our marriage and our own children's lives would never be burdened with this.

Telling myself that I was free to rip up this letter whenever I wanted to made it easier for me to pick it up and finish reading it. Now I was reading only out of curiosity, not out of an imminent threat. The rest of the letter wasn't very revealing. In her English-teacher tone, Donna told me the various ways I could reach her or Danny. She included a home phone number and a cell phone number for herself, and a home phone number for Danny. She also left an e-mail address for herself. She included her own home address but not Danny's. Once again, I felt like she was playing games with me. She left endless questions unanswered. Is she or Danny married? Do they have children? What happened to Barbara's husband? How did she get my address? How much does she know about me?

She also didn't include any pictures, which she should have known I'd be intensely interested to see. I could almost hear her say (in her mother's voice!), "If you want to know more about us, you'll have to call us." It gave me a strange feeling to look at her address and realize how close she was. She lived in Carmel, Indiana, just half an hour from my own home in Indianapolis. If I wanted to, I could drive up there and find her house and at least catch a glimpse of her. If she has kids, my grandkids, I could see them go in and out of the house.

On the other hand, she might have done the same with me. Has she driven by this house, seen me walking to the mailbox, getting in or out of the car? Has she followed me to a restaurant or a grocery store and been tempted to come up and introduce herself? Or maybe she has actually spoken to me at some time or other without telling me who she was.

I didn't know what to do. As I sat there thinking about it, the phone on the nightstand rang, nearly knocking me off the bed. Was it Donna? There was no reason it should be, but I was so absorbed in thoughts of her that I expected her to stride into the room at any moment and demand that I talk to her. I answered the phone, trying to sound unfazed. It was Pam wanting to talk to her mother. I hid the letter in the VCR manual, stuffed it down into the papers in the drawer, and went to see if Vonnie was out of the tub.

About an hour later the phone rang again, and I couldn't help but be startled. Is this how it's going to be from now on? Every time I hear a phone or a knock at the door, or every time someone of Donna's age looks at me in a crowd, I'll worry that it's her? If she was so willing to break her promise to her mother never to contact me, what's to keep her from simply showing up on my doorstep one of these days? I wonder if I would recognize her if she did.

Little Donna. The last time I saw her, she was a five-year-old girl in a pink dress and shiny black shoes. Offering me her half-eaten cookie. Saying "Bye-bye, Daddy. Come home with us." As her mother pulled her away. "Bye-bye, Daddy." Not knowing, not imagining, what the words would mean. *Donna-girl. Donna Banahna.*

In the letter, Donna said that once she found out about me, she could vaguely call up memories of me from when she was little. She even thought she remembered calling me Daddy. She said they had convinced her as a child that I wasn't her real daddy but just a close family friend with that nickname. Eventually, she had put me out of her mind.

I stewed over the letter for three days, and then I decided to tell Vonnie about it. I remember her grim expression as she sat at the dining room table reading it that afternoon. By watching her, you might have thought she wasn't even reading the paper in front of her. Her eyes, her face, did not move. It seemed an eternity before she put one page down and read the next. When she finally finished, she folded the pages neatly and put them back into the envelope. Only then did she look up at me as I sat across the empty table from her.

I did not dare ask any questions of this face of stone. Let her speak when she's ready, I figured. Her eyes didn't appear to see me any more than they had seen the letter. I almost wanted to glance behind me to see what she was staring at. Her expression was impossible to interpret. Was it anger? Contempt? Resignation? In the next room a clock patiently ticked.

"What do you plan to do?" she finally asked.

"I have no idea," I said. "That's why I showed it to you."

"Do you think she'll keep insisting on contacting us if we don't respond?"

"It's hard to say."

Vonnie gripped the edge of the table and pushed herself up, letting out her little *O-o-h*s that she moans when her legs or back are hurting her. She stood upright, and as she walked out of the room, she shook her head and said, "I just want to be left alone."

"What?" I asked, not because I didn't hear her, but because I didn't understand whether she meant she wanted me to leave her alone right then or whether she wanted me to make sure Donna left her alone.

"Just want to be left alone," she repeated unhelpfully.

I left her alone, and she didn't speak of it again until two days later. That was an agonizing two days for me, let me tell you. I kept watching her expression, wondering whether she would suddenly blow up or burst into tears or whether she planned to just keep up this silent act for the rest of her life and pretend that I never showed her any letter. But finally at lunch on that second day, she calmly said, "I haven't forgotten about that letter, but I just don't feel right doing anything about it right now. I can't bring myself to."

"All right," I answered reluctantly. "So when—"

"I don't know when the time will be right, but it isn't now, so I want to leave the subject alone. She said she wouldn't call us if we didn't want her to, right?"

"She said that, yes. But—"

"Well, then let's leave it at that for now. All right?"

"All right," I said. It really wasn't all right, but I knew it would be better to get my thoughts together before I challenged her. The more I thought about Donna and the letter and Danny in Los Angeles, the more I thought I might like to talk to her, at least on the phone. For me, the hardest part had been telling Vonnie about the letter. After that, I actually began to hope that she'd tell me to go ahead and call if I wanted to.

I had this conversation with Vonnie in the middle of the week, and at the end of the week, on that Saturday, I had my first stroke. I nearly died from that one, and it put any thoughts about reconciling with Donna and Danny on the back burner. For the next couple months I had to concentrate on survival.

As the weeks went by and my thinking cleared up, I kept coming back to the letter. Before long, even with my memory as bad as it is now, I practically had it memorized. I found myself filling in all the gaps that her letter had left about what Danny was like, what she was like, what their families were like. What I really wanted to do was drive up there to Carmel and sit and watch her and then decide whether to get out and talk to her. But they won't let me drive anymore. So then I thought about calling her without telling anybody, but they almost never leave me alone in the house, either. So I let things slide, and Donna never wrote again, and Vonnie never mentioned it.

Finally I had these latest strokes, and then I made that slip-up about Danny. So I don't know where we go from here. Short of lying, I don't see how we can avoid telling the girls the whole story. But I won't say anything until Vonnie's ready. I owe her that much.

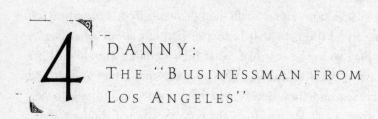

4 DANNY:
THE "BUSINESSMAN FROM LOS ANGELES"

I'm feeling that urge to quit my job and move away.

That urge has hit me more times over the years than is good for me, but this time it was triggered by a specific incident that left me feeling old.

I was driving home from the office when I pulled up to a stoplight a few blocks from my apartment. In the lane next to me was this young blond woman, a real beauty, wearing a purple dress and gold necklace and earrings and probably going home from work, sitting alone in her car and smiling as she tapped out a beat on her steering wheel. She didn't see me looking at her. I wasn't *ogling* her or anything, it was just a quick glance at a pretty woman, and it made me happy for a second that I shared the road with her.

But then I heard it. The booming, disturbing noise. I rolled down my window to hear it a little better. Her car was shaking with the most raucous, incomprehensible rap music I have ever heard. Do they still call it rap music? I don't even know the terminology anymore, much less understand the sound itself. Some angry voice, like a demon from hell, was screaming profanities at this lovely girl, accompanied by "music" that sounded more like a recording of a building being demolished. And there she sat, *smiling* about it, tapping her *fingers* to it. I wondered how this radiant young woman could subject herself to such trash. Why would she voluntarily listen to it?

The light changed and she drove away, her car pulsing with the ugly rhythm. I was so distressed that for a moment I sat there and stared at the space where her car had been. The car behind me tapped its horn, and I drove away, forgetting for a few seconds where I was headed.

When I got home, I sat on my sofa for a full hour feeling depressed. I remembered that when my father had heard the rock music I listened to as a teenager, he had said, "That's not music. That's just noise." I had never wanted to be like him. For years, even into my forties, I had kept up with the latest groups and recording artists. The music I had listened to was *not* noise. It was beautiful, soaring, bone-shaking *music!*

But what was that sound coming out of that girl's car? It really *had* sounded like noise. It made me angry that the world was now listening to music I could no longer identify with or understand. It made me angry that it wasn't obvious to these young people that that stuff was hideous.

The next day, as if to counteract the barbarism that was encroaching on my world, I went out and bought a stack of CDs that I could play loud on my own car stereo. Billy Joel. Bruce Springsteen. Boston. Pink Floyd. Sting. U2. The Eagles. Fleetwood Mac. I decided I would fill the world with good music once again. I would show these young people that they didn't have to listen to someone abusing them with that chaos!

I played those CDs loud in my car for a couple weeks,

leaving my windows open so everyone could hear, but it still wasn't enough to lift my gloom.

I thought, maybe playing these groups is not enough. Maybe this society has become so crass that I'll have to go even further back into musical history to counteract it. I bought a Frank Sinatra CD. Sinatra is not even my music. He's more of my father's era, but still, it comforted me to hear him singing "That's Life" and "New York, New York." So civilized. Let the young barbarians hear that as they drive down the street.

After a few days of Frank, I started feeling too much like my father again and put that CD away. Then I bought Neil Diamond. That was about the time I started to realize the futility of my project. I could play those oldies till they shook my car to pieces and those young people wouldn't care any more than I would have cared if my father had blasted his big band music at me as he drove down the street. I was playing to an audience that wasn't listening. I was trying to stop time by shaking my fist at it.

In other words, I was growing old.

As crazy as that may sound, that's when I decided it was time to break out of my rut, move away, try something new. And that's also about the time my sister, Donna, started trying to talk me into moving to Indiana.

I'm not sure what brought it on, but Donna's going through this phase where she wants to gather all the family around her as often as she can. For the last couple years she's started having these big Christmas Eve bashes with all the extended family, some of whom I barely know. She bugged me all last year to come for Christmas, even though it meant flying from Los Angeles and taking time off work. And she still has this idea that we should try to get together with our "real" dad, even though he hasn't bothered to respond to that letter she wrote him (not to mention the forty-some years he had ignored us before that). She even thinks we'll eventually get to know our "brothers and sisters" of his second family. Of course, we don't even have the vaguest information about these people, such as how many there are. Chances are they don't even know we exist and wouldn't want to have anything to do with us even if they did, but Donna's already worrying about whether they'd be willing to come to her Christmas party. Last time I talked to her on the phone, she asked me, "Do you think I should invite them to the Christmas party first, or should I have a separate get-together before that just for the brothers and sisters to get to know each other?"

I said, "You mean with all of us sitting around some huge dining room table, holding hands, while this father we don't even know sits at the end carving the turkey?"

"Why are you so cynical?"

"Why are you turning all Norman Rockwell on me?"

"I don't see what's so strange about wanting to get acquainted with my own family members."

"They're not *really* family members," I said. "Not in the sense that—"

"Yes, they are *really* our family," she insisted. "We share the same father. I do believe that makes us related."

"Well, these people may not be so thrilled that we've found them—assuming that we do find them. They might see us as a threat."

"Why would they? I don't understand your attitude. When Mom told us that our father had remarried and had more children, the first thing I thought was that I'd like to meet them. Why wouldn't they feel the same way? I think they would."

I said, "Remember that it's just possible that they've known about us for years. In that case, they haven't seemed too eager to get in touch."

"I don't believe they know. Mom said her agreement with our father was—"

"I wish you'd stop calling him our father. Dad is our father."

"Well, what am I supposed to call him? Our birth father? Hugh? Mr. Morris?"

"Any of those would be fine."

"Well, as I was saying, Mom said her agreement with our birth father was that the children were never to be told."

"Yes, and she broke that agreement, so it's likely that he did, too."

"I don't believe he broke it."

"How would you know? You don't even know him!"

"I think that agreement with her is the reason he didn't respond to my letter."

"I don't buy that," I said, "but if you're right, we'll never meet him, and we won't meet his kids, and you won't have to worry about inviting them for Christmas."

"I still don't understand why they'd see us as any kind of threat," she persisted, following her lifelong habit of never being able to let anything drop.

"Put yourself in their shoes," I said. "You've lived your whole nice cozy life thinking you know your father, and then suddenly, when he's in his seventies, you find out he had a whole family before yours. A wife and children he abandoned—"

"He didn't *abandon*—"

"And then out of the blue this new 'sister' invites you to her Christmas party."

"In the first place," said Donna, "I wouldn't do it out of the blue, and in the second place, yes, if I found out I had a sister and she invited me to her home, I would graciously accept and go to meet her. Wouldn't you?"

"You've got to realize we're the outsiders in this situation. We're the ones landing on their father's doorstep, demanding to be recognized. These kids of his will very likely be suspicious and wonder what claims these people think they have on Daddy. What will they try to get out of him? Why did they have to surface in our lives? Why couldn't they have kept to themselves? Why do they even have to exist in the first place?"

"Well, I'm sorry to hear you talk like that," she said. "I thought I could count on you to help bring the two families together."

"Donna, let's be blunt about it. This father walked out on us forty-something years ago and never looked back. He hasn't answered your letter, which I think makes it clear he doesn't want to be reminded of us, and I don't think his children do, either."

She was quiet for a moment and then she said, "He didn't walk out on us exactly. That isn't what Mom said. She left him first, remember?"

I let out a weary sigh, hoping it would make her change the subject.

"Family is family," she said, and I let her have the last word.

Anyway, as I said, these "brothers and sisters" are not her only obsession. Regardless of what happens with them, she's also convinced that I belong near her in Indiana, and she's doing everything she can to get me there. Once or twice a week she sends me want ads from the *Indianapolis Star* with all the jobs she thinks I'd be interested in circled in black marker. The best plan, she says, would be for me to come out and stay with her and Phil and the kids while I look for a job. They have plenty of room for me, and the whole family is dying for me to come, she claims. If I'm skeptical about moving permanently, I could leave my stuff in California and commit to only a few weeks in Indiana. Call it a vacation. Then I could look for a job, meet all her great friends she's been telling me about, go to her church a few times and get acquainted with people, and then decide if I want to move there for good. If I do, I could move in with her, or if I want to be stubborn and independent as she suspects I would be, I could pick out a place of my own. She said she's certain that if I give Indiana a try, I'll fall in love with it and will want to get out of California as soon as I can.

"I grew up in Indiana," I remind her.

"I know," she says, "but that was a long time ago. It's different now. And so are you. Let's face it. What do you have to keep you in California now, with all that's happened?"

By "all that's happened," she's referring to my divorce, three years ago. It wouldn't hurt my feelings if she said the word "divorce," but Donna almost always prefers to refer to it indirectly. From the moment Terri and I split up, Donna had this image that the rest of my life would consist of me wandering around in my boxer shorts in some broken-down apartment, which would be empty except for a couple TV trays and a lawn chair. She's been trying to rescue me ever since. I wish her image was further from the truth than it sometimes has been, but still, as I try to tell her on the phone, I do have some semblance of a life. I have a job. I have friends. I have a son who I still need to be close to.

She doesn't embarrass me by challenging each of these statements, none of which could stand up to much scrutiny. She only mentions Alex, my son. He's almost sixteen and lives with his mother and stepfather in northern California, far enough away that I have to fly up there or he has to fly to L.A. for me to see him. Donna says, "If he has to get on an airplane anyway, he could fly to Indiana almost as easily as he could fly down to Los Angeles. It's a little more expensive, and it would take a couple more hours, but who cares? And if he came out here to see you, at least he'd be surrounded by family. He could get to know his cousins. You might even be able to talk him into going to college out here, which would keep him closer to you and to us, too."

Donna is starting to remind me of Mom more and more in the way she latches on to an idea and then doesn't stop pushing it until she either convinces you of the merits or else wears you down so much that you just give in and do it her way. I'm always noncommittal when Donna brings this up, but her idea does have some appeal. Not necessarily for the reasons she tries to press on me. I certainly am not interested in moving just to meet this "dad" of ours or his second set of children. And I'm not so sure Alex would think it's such a great idea. But it would offer me a way to strike out toward something different. Dropping everything and moving to Indiana would at least be bold. A new home. New friends. New job. New prospects.

Beyond all that, oddly enough, what most attracts me about moving is the idea of the long drive to get there. Earlier in my life that probably would have been the least attractive part. Twenty years ago I probably would have *flown* to Indiana and hired movers to hassle with hauling my stuff across the country. I would have seen such a drive as a waste of time. But now I feel this need to look around for a while. It's hard to explain, but right now, if I didn't need to make money so badly, I'd be content to just drive around the country for a few months on my own and sit in coffee shops and talk to people. I long to drift, to sit and stare. I don't want to see tourist attractions. I don't want to stay in fancy hotels, or camp out, or go white-water rafting or mountain climbing or anything like that. I'd just like to drive from town to town, heading vaguely east, and stay in whatever motel is handiest whenever I get tired at the end of a day. In the morning, I'd like to eat a big breakfast in the local hangout, read the town's newspaper, listen to the people's voices, strike up conversations, maybe stay another day or two if I like it, and then head out to the next place.

I realize that this desire to drift around is not the best motivation for making a major life move from one city to another. It would make more sense to do the trip as a vacation, as Donna suggested. The only problem is that the hospital where I work as an accountant is not offering vacation time for anyone in our department. The unspoken reason for this is that the hospital is going bankrupt. It's possible that the place will close down in a matter of months, or a year at most, unless there's some big unexpected infusion of cash. We've been having trouble getting reimbursements from some of the big health insurers. If we work that out soon it could give us a little breathing room, but no one is sure that money will arrive in time to save us. Even if we go bankrupt and have to close, my supervisors have hinted there might still be work for me for quite some time. They're vague on this, of course, since they're not even supposed to be admitting that bankruptcy is likely. But I'm not sure I want to be around that long. Let somebody else bury the corpse.

Although this may be a strange admission, I have to say that working for a hospital that is going down the tubes has been strangely comforting to me. The place is in even worse shape than I am. Unlike with most of my other jobs—and there have been many—I know that I'll probably walk away from this one unscathed, while the institution itself will crumble. Usually it's the other way around—I limp away and the company goes right along as if I had never touched it. I also have the consolation of knowing that the hospital is not suffering because of anything I've done. It was doomed before I even got hired, due to forces beyond my control—changing demographics, bad government policy, and on and on. I have done my job well, and I'll be able to walk away with a clean conscience. I won't have to deal with that regret I usually feel when I leave a job, that sense of *if only I had stuck with it a little longer, if only I had applied myself and not daydreamed so much and not let my restlessness and discontent get the best of me, this job might have been the one that I could have stuck with for thirty years, the way Dad did (the dad who raised me), and I could have built up a secure retirement and taken care of my family better and given my ex-wife less of an excuse to berate me for being fickle and irresponsible.*

But that gets me off on a whole other tangent. The question is, pretty soon I'll have to switch jobs anyway, so do I want to simply find another one here in L.A., or do I want to use this as a reason to refurbish my life overall?

I try to picture the life I might have in Indiana, but it's hard to get a sense of it. Would it be like the scenes that Donna tries to paint for me, all those cozy evenings with family at the dinner table, wearing sweaters and drinking hot chocolate? Throwing the football around the backyard on chilly fall afternoons? Going to after-church dinners and joining a softball league? Would I be welcomed into her group of friends and maybe even fall in love with one of them, remarry, get Alex out there, find a steady job, buy my own house, and settle down as if California had never happened?

Or would I move out there and immediately feel like I was in the way? Would Phil and the girls resent me for taking up their space? Would they count the days until I found my own apartment and got out of their hair? Would Donna's friends at church look at me with suspicion and say, "What's this fiftyish man doing here anyway, unattached, jobless, homeless? Is he one of Donna's pitiful relatives, some charity case she hopes to reform?"

Would I miss the warm California weather, the chance to walk the beaches? Would I end up feeling cold, snowed-in, bored, frustrated, angry with myself for buying into such an unlikely pipe dream? Would I resent Donna for interfering? Would I alienate Alex even further by being so far away from him?

I don't know what to do yet. So I do nothing. I drift in place and help to manage the hospital's slide into dissolution.

5 CAROLYN:
BREAKING THROUGH

I finally squeezed some information out of Mom, but it wasn't easy. The whole thing still amazes me. I could hardly get to sleep last night. I kept imagining all these scenes of Mom and Dad's past. I tried to picture them back there in the '40s and '50s, so young, falling in love, making stupid decisions, running scared, spinning out their lives with a passion that I would never associate with them now. This is all so bizarre! It's like having your parents walk in and tell you that they aren't really earthlings, that they emigrated here from some far-off planet before you were born and have had to live deep undercover.

I got the chance to talk to Mom after I took her home from the rehab facility where they took Dad a couple days ago. He was in the hospital for a week before they transferred him over to this new place. He hates it, of course, and it was all we could do to convince him to go there instead of going home. They're supposed to help him learn how to walk again, using the walker, and they're hoping his mind will clear up a little more, I guess, and that he'll regain some of his strength overall. He insisted he didn't need any rehab and that he was ready to go home. The truth is he can only take a step or two, and he's incontinent. Part of the time he's confused, too, and he says the same thing over and over until you're ready to scream. The last time I saw him at the hospital, which was a couple days before he left, I had to sit on this little footstool because the other chairs were taken. Dad said, "Why don't you ask that nurse to bring you in a chair?"

"No thanks," I said. "This is fine."

A moment later, he said, "Don't you want a chair? Ask that lady to bring you one."

"I'm fine, Dad. This is comfortable enough."

Not thirty seconds later, he said the same thing, as if this was the first time he'd thought of it. To keep from tearing my hair out, I decided to make a game of it by secretly counting the number of times he told me to ask for a chair. Nine times in the first half hour. After that, I finally did pull in a chair from the next room just to keep him quiet.

I wasn't around when they talked Dad into going to this rehab place. Pam said Jackie finally had to get tough with him and say that the doctors were either going to send him to rehab or to a nursing home, it was up to him. She told him that "by law" they were not allowed to let such a sick man go home. She said they'd be sued if they released him, so he had to make a decision. I doubt this is the truth. I don't think there's any law that can force a stroke patient to go to rehab, but it worked. "Nursing home" is the most dreaded term in the English language for Dad, so I figure that, in his confused state of mind, he believed Jackie's threat and opted for rehab as the lesser of two evils.

To me, there's not that much difference between this place and a nursing home. It's certainly not as nice as the hospital. At least they try to make the hospital look a little more cheerful with colorful carpeting and wallpaper and pictures and things.

And there's lots of activity all the time, which gives you a hopeful feeling that maybe all these doctors and nurses and technicians running around will be able to actually restore the patients to health. The rehab center, on the other hand, is deathly quiet, at least when I was there. They also keep it quite dark, for reasons I don't understand. I guess there's a lot more going on during the day, but when I was there in the evening, it almost looked like the staff had all left and the patients were on their own. The atmosphere is cold, with tile floors and beige walls.

Dad has not been the most cooperative patient. Every time one of the physical therapists or doctors talks to him, he says he's fine, he's ready to leave. He ignores the fact that he can barely stand up. He hasn't even made it across the room yet, even with the walker. The one time he tried to walk the length of the room, he peed all over himself and then gave up.

We don't know how long they're going to let him stay there, but we're hoping it's as long as possible. The next step is what we're all dreading. Unless he has some drastic improvement, which doesn't seem too likely, it's hard to see how he can keep living in that house, especially with Mom so weak and hard of hearing and with such a bad heart and all her other ailments. None of us kids could handle him in our homes, so what alternative does that leave?

Pam is looking into some possibilities that aren't exactly nursing homes but that are supposed to be nicer. An assisted-living apartment is one possibility. That's one of those places where you live on your own but meals are provided and people check on you every day. Mom and Dad could live there together. Then there are board-and-care facilities, where the people have their own room and go down to a cafeteria to eat and so on, and they're more independent than nursing home patients. That sounds good, too, but it's expensive. Pam said either option would cost a lot more than what Mom and Dad could afford, so

the house would have to be sold. Mom would have to be talked
into moving into somewhere like that with Dad. Dad would have
to consent to the whole thing. Probably none of this will happen.
So what do we do?

This is the dilemma that was on everyone's mind when I visited Dad last night. As soon as I walked in the door, Jackie
pushed me back into the hallway and started hitting me with all
this stuff about where Dad was going to go after he got released.
This was even before I knew about the things Pam had been
looking into. I had no idea what to tell her. She was right up in
my face, saying, "He can only stay here two weeks! We have to
have a plan! We can't just dump this all on Mom to deal with!
We're all going to have to pitch in."

"Pitch in and do what?" I wanted to ask. I don't know why
she attacks me like that. Does she really think I'm going to have
some instant answer? Is she trying to make me feel guilty? If so,
guilty for what? Does she think I can take Mom and Dad into
my apartment? More likely, she'd really like me to offer to move
in with Mom and Dad and take care of them. Since I'm single
now and don't own my own house, everybody in the family
assumes that I don't have much of a personal life. But how am
I supposed to fit all our stuff into that house and take care of
Mom and Dad plus take care of Brandon plus work full time? I
can't do it.

So right off the bat that night I was a nervous wreck and
wanted to do nothing but run out of there. Then when I went
back into Dad's room, Jackie told Dad to identify me by name
even before I had a chance to walk over and say hello to him.
Names are not his strong suit right now. Even though I'm pretty
sure he knew who I was, he stammered around trying to say my
name and got all annoyed (at me, not Jackie!) because he
couldn't think of it. Then he got off on some tangent about why
hadn't those people brought his laundry back yet, because he

had been wearing the same pair of pants for a week (not true). Instead of giving him an answer about this, Jackie kept on him about my name until finally I said, "It's Carolyn, Daddy. How are you feeling?"

Having accomplished what I assume was her goal of getting everybody riled up, Jackie finally sat down, and we settled into our visit. If there was one night when I wished I could have had Mom and Dad to myself, it was this one, because I wanted to get Mom alone to find out some things. But wouldn't you know it, this was the one night when not only Jackie and Pam were there, but their husbands were, too! The husbands don't visit Dad very often, so I don't know what the occasion was. Maybe they thought this was the deathbed scene and they better come and see him one last time. It's not that the husbands don't like Mom and Dad or that they have *refused* to come around, exactly, but over the last few years they have just kind of *faded* into the background and let us daughters deal with our parents.

Anyhow there they were, Pam and Cliff on one side of Dad's bed and Jackie and Tony on the other. There were no more chairs left for me. Mom was perched on the edge of Dad's bed, where she liked to sit even though, as short and stooped as she is, it made her look like she was about to tumble forward onto her face.

No one offered me a chair, so I sat on the end of Dad's bed. The TV was blaring one of the evening newscasts, which Dad is obsessive about watching, and everybody was involved in this story about this audio CD you can buy that simulates the sounds of other people living in your house. If you're lonely because you live by yourself, you put this on your stereo and you hear the sounds of somebody putting away groceries in the next room, somebody vacuuming the carpet, somebody taking a shower. There's about an hour and a half of these sounds. They interviewed this older lady who had bought one of these recordings after her husband passed away, and she said she felt comforted by it.

Now, Jackie would mock me for saying this, but I know my family members so well that if I could have frozen time in the instant that this news story ended, I could have written down a prediction almost word for word of what each person in that room was going to say about this CD.

No one surprised me. Pam, as I could have foreseen, was sympathetic. She's always been the most softhearted sister, the one who could never stand for anyone in the room to be sad or lonely or neglected, the one who sobbed at movies, the one who as a girl most willingly gave up her toy or dessert so that someone else didn't feel left out. She said, "That's one of the saddest things I've ever heard. Can people really fool themselves with a recording like that? If they're lonely, why don't they at least get themselves a dog or cat or something?"

Jackie, of course, had a harsher attitude. She said, "I don't feel sorry for anybody willing to blow their money on something so stupid."

Pam responded, "I would think having a CD like that would only make you more lonely. I picture coming home at night to some big empty apartment and turning that thing on while the whole time you're wishing that it could be a real person making those noises."

Jackie's husband, Tony, chimed in next. Tony is a beefy, red-faced man who always looks like he's about to bust out of his clothes. Last night he had on jeans, work boots, and a flannel shirt whose buttons were straining to hold him in. At one Christmas dinner one of his buttons actually did pop off, which you might think would give him the idea that it was time to change shirt sizes, but he never has. He has a flattop haircut with some of the little spikes missing in the balding parts of his scalp. He makes up for those blank spots with plenty of extra fur on his back and neck. Tony laughed out loud and said, "You might as well go out and buy a blow-up doll for companionship."

"Are you speaking from experience?" asked Jackie, and the two of them had a good belly laugh.

Then it was Cliff's turn to speak. He is Pam's husband, and about as opposite of Tony as you can get. He's a high-school history teacher, skinny, quiet, usually dressed in khaki pants and a button-down oxford shirt or something similar. Even though he's been married to Pam for years, he still approaches our family like he's meeting us for the first time, like he has to be extra polite to make a good impression. He has the manners of a foreign exchange student who hasn't been in this country very long. But he's a nice guy if you get him off by himself and get him talking about something he cares about. His reaction was exactly what I would have expected from a brainy introvert. He said, "Personally, if I lived alone I'd just enjoy the quiet. I can't even remember the last time I came home to a quiet house. Having a few hours to read or think would be like paradise to me."

Mom, predictably, was off in her own world and didn't express an opinion. Dad, as usual, was off the topic: "Those laundry people have probably already gone home for the day, don't you expect? I probably won't get those pants till tomorrow now."

"Would you stop harping on that laundry?" said Jackie. "There's nothing wrong with the pants you've got on. If you have an accident, we still have one more pair in the closet."

"They picked up those pants a week ago! How long does it take?"

"It wasn't a week ago, Dad," she said. "You've only been here for two days."

His eyes squinted and his face took on that skeptical expression he gets when a fact is trying to break through his confusion. Jackie sat back looking pleased with herself for having put him in his place, and I glanced at my watch hoping it was getting late enough for some of them to leave so I could talk to Mom.

Jackie inadvertently saved the day about a half hour later by asking if I'd mind dropping Mom off on my way home. By no stretch of the imagination is Mom's house on my way home, as Jackie well knows, so I'm sure she was testing me, but I tried to hide the glee from my voice as I agreed to take her.

Mom is so hard of hearing now that I didn't even try to talk to her in the car. The engine noise makes even the most basic conversation impossible. When I got her inside the house, she had a couple chores for me to do, as usual, so that gave me the excuse to stay awhile and talk. Once I finished helping her get a couple of her bills ready to send off in the mail, I said, "I need to talk to you about something."

"Huh?" she said, suddenly getting even more deaf than she normally is. I was sitting right next to her on the sofa, so there was no reason she shouldn't have been able to hear me.

I was so nervous that I almost decided to just give up right then and talk to her some other time. But instead I yelled, "I need to talk to you about something!"

She stared at me, unresponsive. She obviously was not going to make this easy. Maybe she sensed what was coming.

I took a deep breath and said, "You know what Dad said that night in the hospital about having a son in Los Angeles?"

"What?" she bellowed, but the stricken look on her face let me know she had heard me.

"You know when Dad said that night that he had a son in Los Angeles?" I screamed. Yelling was not the tone of voice I preferred to use for this conversation. When I had rehearsed it in my mind, I had envisioned a quiet heart-to-heart chat.

"Oh, that. He was just . . ." She waved her hand back and forth in a gesture that was supposed to wipe away Dad's words as nothing but hot air. She started to get up off the sofa.

I took hold of her arm and nudged her back down. "I know that what he said was true," I declared in a loud voice.

She stared at me again, for a long time now, and I could practically read her mind. Was I bluffing, or had I really found out some facts? Was it safe for her to keep denying the existence of this son, or did I know enough to nail her? She squirmed around in her seat, as if looking for a place to hide. Even in the best of times, Mom quite frankly looks pretty pitiful these days, with her shoulders bent over and her hair a wispy mess and her whole body shriveling up like a raisin. She uses that look to her advantage when she needs to. She tries to give the impression that she is physically and emotionally incapable of handling the slightest strain and that even the most innocent question you could pose will amount to elder abuse. She perches on that sofa as if she's sitting on the edge of a psychological precipice and anything unpleasant you say might be that final puff of wind that pushes her into the abyss. Finally she said, "You girls are going to kill me with this, don't you realize that? Why are you all trying to dredge things up?"

Who else is dredging things up? I wondered. We all promised we wouldn't say anything until Dad was better. Of course, I was breaking that promise, so maybe Pam or Jackie was too. Probably Jackie, if anyone. Had Mom already told her anything? I dreaded that possibility.

Mom whined, "Not one of you cares about my feelings about this. You're like vultures, picking away at things that shouldn't be touched."

"We *do* care how you feel about it, Mom. But how can we—"

"Huh?" she rasped.

"WE DO CARE!" I yelled, the tone completely contradicting the sentiment.

"Your dad is just as bad," she said. "I never know from one day to the next what he's gonna do. He tells me he won't ever call this woman, but how am I supposed to know that when he's having one of his confused spells he won't just pick up the phone and do it when I'm not there? Or that you and Jackie won't try to talk him into something?"

"Wait a minute," I said. "What woman?" Either she was completely misunderstanding what I was asking about or this story was even more complicated than just a son in Los Angeles. Could the woman be the mother of this man? I was breaking out in a sweat.

"What?" cried Mom.

"You said Dad might call a *woman*. I don't know who you're talking about. I'm talking about his son in Los Angeles."

"It's not the son who worries me so much," she said. "It's the daughter."

"What daughter?" I screamed, not so much because of Mom's deafness this time but because I was genuinely shocked.

Mom let out a ponderous sigh, as if I were asking her to repeat something she had explained a thousand times. "I thought you told me you knew," she said.

"Dad said he had a son. You're telling me he also has a daughter?"

She nodded yes, scowling the whole time.

"Well, who are these people?" I asked, not knowing where to begin.

"You don't know a thing, do you?" Mom demanded. "You're just trying to trick me into telling things. You're just like Jackie."

"Jackie tried to trick you?"

"Not me so much as your dad. She knew I wouldn't play along. But your dad told me she's been bugging him about this son. I told her not to do it anymore. You girls are gonna kill him if you keep it up."

"She promised she wouldn't say anything until he was out of danger! That makes me so mad."

"Well, how's she any different from you?"

"I think you know how Jackie's different from me. Do you really want her to be the one to find out about all this first? Do you want Jackie to represent our family and be the first one to call them? She's so unstable it's hard to tell what she'd say."

"I don't want any of you calling them!" Mom insisted. "That's the whole point. It's none of your business, and you shouldn't be pressuring us like this."

"Mom, if Dad has a son and daughter, then don't you see that means that we have a brother and sister?"

"Half."

"Half. Whole. What difference does it make? How could you keep a secret like that from us for all these years? For our entire lives? How could you?"

"It was a long time ago. You could never understand. People your age like to blab everything. It was different in my day. People maintained some dignity."

"Maintained dignity! You *lied* to us all this time."

"No. No, we . . ."

"So what's the story? When did Dad manage to have two secret children?"

She pursed her lips and stared at the drapes as if they might contain some hidden message that would save her. "It's not my story to tell. Let your father tell it if he must. But he promised me he wouldn't."

"It's too late for that, Mom!" I shouted, loud enough so she couldn't help but hear it. I put my hand on her shoulder until she finally looked back at me. "Do you really think we're gonna just forget about this and say, 'Oh well, I guess we have a brother and sister, but we really don't need to know anything about them'? You know that the whole story is eventually going to come out. So you might as well tell me and get it over with. It won't get any easier."

In a quiet voice, as if she were merely talking to herself, she said, "I'm afraid your dad is going to call her. He said he wouldn't, but I can't guard him twenty-four hours a day. And with Jackie pressuring him, he just might do it. Or even worse, he might let her do it."

"So let me help you," I said. "Let me get to them before Jackie does."

Mom sat there lifeless for a moment, and I was just about to jog her out of it by yelling my comment again when her face brightened and she turned her whole body toward me.

Finally she meant business.

"If I talk to you about this," she said, "you have to promise me one thing."

"What?"

"You've got to promise to help me keep this girl away."

"Well, Mom," I said, stalling for time, "how could I do that?" The truth was that keeping this sister away was the last thing I wanted to do. I couldn't wait to meet her!

"Don't you realize the trouble she could cause? Bringing up all the ugliness from the past? It's you kids who would be hurt the most. I won't be around much longer no matter what happens. But you kids are the ones who will have to keep this girl and her brother from taking away everything Dad and I have worked a lifetime to leave you."

This comment was wrong on so many levels that I didn't even know where to begin. In the first place, what were Mom and Dad really going to leave us? We (mostly Pam and Cliff) have been helping them pay their bills for years. Dad did almost nothing to prepare for retirement, and his pension from the factory is surprisingly paltry considering all the years he worked there. He and Mom have almost no insurance, probably not even enough for a funeral and burial. There's the house, but it has deteriorated so much that I think we'll have a terrible time trying to sell it, and even if we do, it'll have to be split three ways after the bills are paid off. Maybe I should be more worried about this "inheritance" issue, but I just don't see that there's all that much at stake. And besides, I can't really see Dad suddenly signing everything over to these kids that he hasn't even seen in who knows how many decades.

I said, "So what demands is she making?"

"Nothing right now. She's just asking to visit. She wrote a letter to your dad several months ago."

"Well, maybe she does just want to visit. I mean, if he's her *father* . . ."

Mom squirmed around all agitated and said, "Well, of course she's not going to start making demands in her first letter. But if you let her worm her way into the family, then she might start—"

"Now, back up a minute. First of all, this letter she wrote. Is this the first time she's ever tried to contact Dad?"

"Yes."

"So did she just recently find out about him, or what?"

"Her mother finally told her about your dad not long before she died. She had promised she never would, but she told it anyway. So now this girl thinks she can waltz right in and ask for whatever she thinks she's got coming to her."

"But you said she wasn't asking for anything," I pointed out. "And if she just found out who her father is, naturally she'd be curious. How old is this 'girl,' anyway?"

"I don't know," said Mom, but the way she turned her head away when she said it made me think that she knew exactly how old she was but didn't want to say. "In her early fifties, I suppose."

"And who was her mother?"

Mom looked right at me again, stone-faced, and I was afraid she was going to pretend she didn't hear the question. "You're not going to help me keep her away, are you?" she said.

"You've kept us all in the dark about this our whole lives!" I shouted. "I need to know the facts before I start making promises. I want to meet these people and find out what they're like before I assume that they're evil people out to strip us of all our riches. I mean, it's not like we're some millionaire family. Maybe these people have a lot more than we do and wouldn't even *want* anything we own. Maybe they would even want to help Dad out!"

"Help how? We don't need any help!"

"Ha!"

Mom scrunched down a little farther inside herself, and her eyes filled with tears. I tried to prevent her from disintegrating into some pouting binge by asking, "What are the names of these kids, anyway?"

"Donna and Danny."

"And both of them live in Los Angeles?"

"No, no," said Mom. "I wish they did. Donna lives right around here, in Carmel. That's the problem. She knows our address and could pop in any minute."

"You two didn't respond to her letter in any way?"

"No."

"Well, this is ridiculous. Somebody needs to contact this woman and see what she's like. I think I should be the one to do it. I think it should be obvious that we don't want Jackie doing it. And I'll promise you this. If she seems bad, I'll do what I can to keep her away from our family."

Mom slumped back in her chair, as if to surrender. "Let me think about it," she said. "I'm tired and I don't feel good."

I knew that meant she would go along with my plan, even though it might take her another day or two to resign herself to it. I also knew she wanted to stop talking about this topic, but I couldn't resist asking one more question.

"So, Mom, just tell me how on earth did Dad manage to have

two kids that we never knew about?"

"He was married to another lady before I met him," she said. "They had two kids and then she left him. That's all I can say right now. I mean that. If you push me any more tonight, it really will kill me."

I decided not to press for more information. Now that the basic story is out there, I don't think it will be that hard to get at the details later. I was so overwhelmed by the magnitude of what Mom had told me that, when I drove away from her house, I had to pull over to the curb about a block away and sit there for a while to let it sink in. *Dad married to another woman*. Amazing! And this woman left him. Why? What drama must have been involved? What arguments and accusations and broken hearts—all those emotional entanglements I could never have associated with Mom and Dad. I felt like I was finding out not only about a new brother and sister but also a different Mom and Dad than I had ever known! Now I just have to get Donna's phone number from Mom, and then I'll make the call. I'm so nervous I can hardly stand it.

6
PAM:
STUCK IN THE MIDDLE

I'm beginning to dread the ringing of my own telephone. Jackie called yesterday morning, sounding conspiratorial, telling me how she's been trying to squeeze information out of Dad about this "son" of his. She hasn't had much luck, but she said she wanted to be sure that I knew and understood what she was doing. I think the real story is that she was afraid she was going to get caught breaking her promise not to bug Dad about this until he was better. I guess Dad reacted pretty angrily to her, so I think she's afraid he'll try to get me to make her leave him alone. She told me she couldn't bear to sit back and let some unknown relative march in and "steal Mom and Dad blind when they're practically on their deathbeds."

"Are they on their deathbeds?" I asked. "Is Mom aware of that?"

"You know what I mean, Pam," she said. "Neither of them have long to live, probably, and neither of them are exactly at the peak of their intellectual capabilities."

"You think they're stupid enough to hand everything over to

this son—if he even exists—even though they haven't even seen him in oh, say, fifty years? I mean, this 'kid' could be on his own deathbed for all we know."

"Please, Pam, if anyone in this family could face reality, I was hoping it would be you. It's hard to tell *what* Mom and Dad are capable of right now. Dad doesn't even know whether it's day or night half the time. Mom is stone deaf at certain moments but can hear a whisper clear across the room if it's something you're trying to keep secret from her. Who knows what they're doing behind our backs. They could be in touch with this guy and not even have told us about it. This could be some kind of scam where this guy has *convinced* Dad he's his son even if he isn't. Dad could already have been talked into some deal that will leave us with nothing but misery and debt once he and Mom pass away."

"Well, since Dad refuses to talk about it, I don't know what you expect me to do."

"I'm not asking you to do anything! I just need you to back me up when the time comes."

"Back you up with what?"

"If all this turns into a big mess. And please, don't tell Carolyn any of this. If she gets involved, we'll really have problems."

To me, it looked like Jackie was the only one creating a mess, and as for Carolyn, she has as much right to be involved as anyone. But I wasn't about to step into the rivalry between those two.

"We'll just see what happens," I said. "Besides, right now I'm more worried about more immediate things, like what we're gonna do with Dad once they make him leave this place he's in."

"I know," she groaned. "I'll work on that problem, too."

That remark irked me, as if Jackie is the suffering saint bearing all the weight of the family's burdens while the rest of us sit back and relax. If Jackie had her way, she would make all the final decisions about Mom and Dad while Carolyn and I simply carried out her orders to make phone calls and do all the other legwork concerning their medical care and living arrangements and all the rest of it.

"What do you plan to do?" I asked.

"I don't know. Weren't you looking into some kind of retirement home or something?"

"I got some information on some places, but how will we ever convince Mom or Dad to *visit* one of those facilities, let alone move there? Yesterday Mom told me she was perfectly capable of taking care of Dad at home herself."

"She told you that? She told me just the opposite a few days ago. She said she couldn't handle him anymore."

"Mom's idea is that we should get a nurse to come to the house to take care of Dad, but I don't know what that would cost or what Medicare would pay, if anything, so—"

"It would have to cost thousands of dollars a month! Five or ten thousand, probably, if it's somebody 'round the clock. No! She's got to see that we don't have that kind of money. He can't go home."

I had the kids by myself when Jackie called, and I had left them in the family room to play while I took the cordless phone into the kitchen to talk. Sarah, our eighteen-month-old, had finally followed me in there and was now standing at the counter screaming for a cookie from the box that she saw but could not reach. I gave her a cookie while Jackie was talking, but then Sarah wanted me to pick her up.

"Just a minute, honey," I said to Sarah. "I'm on the phone with Aunt Jackie." Then to Jackie I said, "Well, we might have to just let him go home and face catastrophe. Then he and Mom will see why we're pushing for them to move. They might even *ask* us to help them move."

"I doubt that," said Jackie as I strained to hold on to the

phone and pick up Sarah at the same time. Still hungry, Sarah started a whiny refrain of "Nana. Nana. Nana," meaning "banana." Matthew, our three-year-old, ran in from the family room, not wanting to miss out on his own chance to grab a snack. Jackie said, "No, I don't like that plan. I don't want to be responsible for cleaning up whatever disaster Dad might create. No, if the time has come for us to blast them out of that house, then let's do it."

Matthew started his own repetitive squeal: "Juice! Juice! Juice!"

"I'm going to have to go," I told Jackie.

"All right," she said. "Call me."

I hung up the phone and had just gotten the kids settled down in the family room when the stupid phone rang again. I was sitting on the floor helping put together a puzzle, and both kids let out loud protests of "Mama! Mama!" when I stood up to get the phone.

It was Carolyn this time, and I knew from the minute I heard her voice that I was in for something big. Whereas Jackie tends to yell when she gets excited, Carolyn gets this high-pitched, slightly hysterical tone, as if she might hyperventilate.

"Pam, it's true!" she squealed. "It was all I could do to keep from calling you after I got home last night, but it was late and I didn't want you to get mad at me for waking up Matthew and Sarah. And just now I've tried to call you about *five times* but the phone was busy. What have you been *doing*?"

As if I have nothing else to do but sit by the phone and make sure the line's clear for one of her outbursts.

"I had another call," I said, not wanting her to know it was Jackie. "*What's* true?"

"What do you think?" she asked sarcastically. Carolyn assumes everyone shares her obsessions. "Dad's other family. It's true! Mom confessed it all last night."

"So Dad has that son?" I asked, my stomach twisting with dread.

"Even better! A son and a daughter!"

"What?"

"He has a daughter who lives in Carmel! Can you believe it? We have another sister who practically lives in the same town!"

Matthew and Sarah chose this moment to run screaming into the kitchen. Sarah had taken her brother's little stuffed Donald Duck, and Matthew was wailing as extravagantly as if she had chopped off his nose. He was chasing her, and Sarah, running as fast as she could with Donald held high in her triumphant hand, was alternating her own screams with her version of a duck's quack—"Gock, gock, gock." The kids drowned out Carolyn for a minute, and I had to tell her to wait while I put the phone down and resolved the Donald Duck problem. Trying to give the duck back to Matthew only sent both kids into renewed spasms of outrage, so I took it away from them altogether and led them back into the family room to try to distract them with something else.

They were too upset to calm down quickly, especially Matthew, who was shrieking with all his might and still reaching for the duck in my hand. I didn't want to keep Carolyn waiting, and my head was still spinning from what she had told me, so the only thing I could think of to do was to turn on some cartoons. Fortunately, Scooby-Doo was on, which they love, so finally they settled down enough that I could go back to Carolyn. The wait had only heightened her frenzy.

I said, "So what did Mom—"

But Carolyn quickly cut me off with her own frantic words. "Can you believe they kept this secret from us for all these years?" she screeched. "I feel so stupid now! I should have known!"

"Well, how could you possibly—"

"I should have figured it out! There should have been some hint. Mom and Dad had to have slipped up at least a time or two while we were growing up, and we missed the clues! This sister and brother of ours are like fifty years old! How could we not know? Think of all our relatives who must have kept this from us! How could they?"

"Settle down, Carolyn. You're worse than the kids." I could hear Matthew and Sarah revving up their argument again in the next room, and I knew I had only seconds before they would come screaming to me to resolve it.

"You've got to help me," said Carolyn.

"Help you how?"

"We've got to call Donna before Jackie finds out about her and scares her off."

"Donna?"

"Our sister!"

Matthew charged toward the kitchen, now in full-throated cry, with Sarah not far behind, yelling something indecipherable. Within seconds they surrounded me, their arms reaching toward me to pick them up.

"Now stop this fighting!" I commanded. "Go back in there and be good. I'm on the phone with Aunt Carolyn." My words didn't slow them down a bit. Carolyn kept talking, but I couldn't understand her. Matthew renewed his earlier call for juice, which had gotten overlooked in the previous uproar, so I pulled out one of his cups of juice from the refrigerator and gave Sarah one of hers, too. "Now go watch Scooby-Doo."

"What?" cried Carolyn.

"Scooby-Doo. Not you, Carolyn. Go on."

Sarah, tired of tormenting her brother, ran off toward the family room, but Matthew stayed by me, sucking on the sippy cup with all his might.

"I'm gonna have to go," I told Carolyn.

"Well, wait!" she screamed, incredulous that I refused to join in her hysteria. "What are we going to do?"

"I don't know," I said. "Like I told you before, this all just seems so bizarre to me, and I'm still not sure I really believe it, and even if it's true, we've got a lot bigger things to deal with right now than—"

"Are you out of your mind!" she yelled. "Bigger things to deal with than a new brother and sister? And it *absolutely* is true. Haven't you been listening to me? Mom confessed! She—"

"So this woman, Donna, is claiming that—"

"She's not *claiming* anything. Dad was married to her mother!"

"Married?" I said, and for the first time that morning I felt a little light-headed.

"Yes! Can you believe it? I mean, can you actually picture our father married to someone else?"

"For how long?"

"I haven't found that out yet, but long enough to have two kids with her. I keep trying to imagine him with this woman, sharing a house, raising two children, walking hand in hand, sitting together eating dinner in the evenings, going—"

"All right, Carolyn! I get the picture." I didn't want a play-by-play account of Dad's entire previous marriage. The whole idea was so shocking my hands were starting to shake. Matthew grasped my legs and moaned, his voice mirroring my own rattled thoughts.

"And then she left him," Carolyn said. "Mom hasn't told me why yet. Mom would only go so far with this story, and then she clammed up. There must be tons of stories we haven't heard! And the whole thing might have stayed secret except that Donna and Danny's mother told them the truth right before she died, which must have been recently. She told them not to contact Dad, but Donna wrote to him anyway. Dad hasn't answered her, at least as far as Mom knows. But I think we should. We've got to get that phone number from Mom right away and call Donna before Jackie finds out."

"Without Dad knowing about it? That doesn't seem right."

"Dad's in no condition to have a rational discussion about this right now."

"That's exactly my point. We owe it to him to wait until he's better."

"No!" she screamed. "We've been waiting for our whole lives already."

"Then what difference will a few more weeks make?"

"He should never have hidden this from us."

"Maybe he has reasons we don't know about. We at least have to give him a chance to explain."

"No way. One way or another, I'm calling my sister, and none of you are gonna stop me."

"You did agree to wait on this till Dad was better."

"We're past that now."

"And we can't leave Jackie out of it. This is her brother and sister, too."

"Just till we make the first contact and let Donna know we're friendly!" Carolyn insisted. "Jackie will charge in there bullying and threatening and then we'll never get to know them. Even Mom realizes that."

"Then go ahead and make the call. You don't need me to do that. I can't stand all this sneaking around behind each other's backs. I'm more worried about Dad right now."

"And you think I'm not? I care about him just as much as you do."

"I know that." I certainly had no desire to get into a debate over who loves Dad the most. Sarah saved me from further conversation by bounding back into the room and chasing Matthew around the kitchen. Even though they were both happy, they were squealing loud enough that I could plausibly say, "I really have to go check the kids real quick. I'll call you later. Bye."

I hung up before she had time to protest or say "one last thing." To me, this is not the time to get Dad and Mom all upset by trying to embrace these so-called family members, especially if it means going behind Dad's and Jackie's backs to do it. I'm not going to let Carolyn recruit me into her scheme. But I'm not going to enter into Jackie's paranoia about them, either.

All I know is this: a new brother or sister is about the last thing I need. I can barely handle the ones I already have.

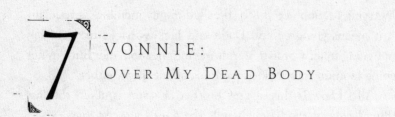

7 VONNIE:
Over My Dead Body

It's all falling apart.

It's not enough that Hugh is dying and so am I. Now our own daughters are acting like private detectives, prying into things that are none of their business.

This is not the old age I had envisioned for myself. It's hard to believe there was actually a time when I looked forward to this phase of life. Thirty or forty years ago, when I envisioned myself the age I am now, I saw myself robust and healthy, baby-sitting my grandkids, hosting big pitch-in dinners for the family on Sundays after church, taking an occasional leisurely train trip somewhere with Hugh, putting new curtains or new carpet or other improvements into the house every once in a while to keep it looking nice.

I pictured Hugh retired but still strong, puttering around in the yard or fixing things up around the house, maybe leading a Sunday school class at church, maybe taking up some new hobby like woodworking the way he always wanted to.

Almost every mental picture I had of old age back then

included my house filled with people. At least every few days Hugh and I would be surrounded by one of our daughters and her husband and kids. We would have them over for dinner, or they would surprise us by just showing up in the evening, bringing a big pizza or a plate of lasagna or offering to cook something on the grill. The kids would want to stay overnight every once in a while and have me make waffles for them in the morning. Hugh and I would proudly watch our kids raising this new generation, and as we watched them grow we would feel content with the part we had played in their lives. Our kids would be following the Lord and raising their own children in Christian homes. Hugh and I would be happy for the chance to be with them in our old age, and they'd be grateful we were still among them.

Needless to say, now that I've finally made it to my golden years, the reality is nothing like what I had hoped for. Hugh and I are a couple of worn-out old wrecks, and the house isn't much better. We can barely keep it habitable, much less decorated in the latest styles. Every time one of the girls comes over, she reminds me of how trashy it looks, and to my embarrassment, I know she's right. But I don't even have the strength to run the vacuum cleaner anymore, and the girls aren't willing to do that sort of work for me very often.

The girls claim I wear them out with all my requests for them to take us to the doctor and buy groceries and do other little errands. I do feel bad asking them to do anything, but the truth is I don't ask them to do one thing more than is necessary to keep us alive. If I asked them to do even half the things I wanted, the list would double or triple. I'm embarrassed that the neighbors have to see how our house has declined. Before all these crises hit, we made it a point to make sure our house was one of the neatest in the neighborhood. Now the gutters are loose and filled with leaves and the paint is peeling and the shutters need replacing and the trees need trimming and on and on.

We could hire this work done, and sometimes we do, but lately even that has gotten harder. For one thing, we can't afford much, mainly because of all the hundreds of dollars we spend on medicines every month. And another thing is I don't even know how to hire reliable help to fix anything anymore. It seems like as soon as these guys see how old and helpless we are, they think they can get away with not doing a very good job. They think we'll be too senile to notice or that we'll be too weak to do anything about it. They're a lot like our daughters in that way, if you'll pardon me for saying so.

I try to look back and find the turning point for me and Hugh, the moment when our lives slid into this downward spiral from which we'll almost certainly never recover. Probably Hugh's first heart attack marked the beginning of our decline. We certainly didn't think so at the time. The doctors were all optimistic, saying he could make a complete recovery. At that time we still hoped for the good old age we had dreamed of. And back then Jackie's kids were little and sweet and so was Carolyn's little boy, and we took care of them a lot. Pam was still living with us for a while before she got married, and she was a big help. I guess my optimism didn't dim completely until Hugh started having these strokes. It wasn't until then that I feared I was about to lose everything—Hugh, the house, my independence, my own health.

The final blow—the one I had come to believe God would spare me from—was the sudden intrusion of Hugh's daughter into our lives. Why now? How on earth could we have gone so many years without having to face this, and then suddenly, when I'm least prepared to deal with it, the past pops up like a coffin bubbling up out of a flooded cemetery?

I had stopped worrying about Hugh's previous family. They

had almost ceased to be real in my mind. I mean, the years when we were most at risk of this story breaking out into the open were twenty or thirty years ago, when there were still lots of people around who had known Hugh before we got married. That's when I had steeled myself against having to explain to my daughters that their daddy had been married to a woman before he met me and had produced two children with her before she dumped him. But lately, I mean the past ten or fifteen years, it felt like the danger had passed, as if we had reached some unspoken statute of limitations and were now in the clear.

When I sat at the dining room table across from Hugh that day and held that letter from Donna in my hands, all I could think was, *I have lived too long. I should have died before this letter arrived.*

Even though it wasn't until several months later that Hugh blurted out his comment about his son in Los Angeles, I knew from the moment I held those blue pieces of stationery in my hand that those other children would somehow have to become part of our lives.

I dread them. Carolyn acts so thrilled about all this, as if we're all going to be able to stage some emotional TV-talk-show reunion and blend into one big happy family. I don't expect Pam to react much differently. Jackie might not join in the celebration over these people invading our lives, but I certainly can't trust her to take my side and protect me against them, either.

It wouldn't occur to any of my girls to stop and think why facing these other kids would be painful for me. Does Carolyn really believe we can all sit in a room together and casually chit-chat as if the last fifty years never happened?

I've imagined all kinds of scenarios, none of them pleasant. Will Danny and Donna blame me for stealing their father from them? What did their mother tell them about me? Even though Donna wasn't hostile in her letter, is that nicey-nice tone sincere, or was it just her way of getting us to respond so she can swoop in and start blaming me for things and trying to get whatever it is she wants out of Hugh? Even if she doesn't want anything, how much damage is her sudden appearance going to do to my relationship with my own girls, after all these secrets we kept from them? How can they ever fully understand our decision—made so many years ago in such a different world—to cut off contact with Hugh's other kids? And how can I sit in a room with Donna and Danny and my own children with all these questions swirling around the room? How can any of them?

Still, I know it will happen. I know that no amount of pleading on my part will keep my daughters from trampling over my feelings and forcing me to endure whatever heartache their meddling might inflict. Restraint is out the window in this generation. My kids will think nothing of stripping away my dignity and hauling me in front of these people just for the fun of it, just to see the fireworks.

I know this will sound morbid, but sometimes I really do wonder whether it wouldn't have been better if Hugh and I had died a couple years ago, right before the worst of our setbacks started hitting us. (This is the point where, if I were saying this out loud, one of my daughters would scold me for being so negative and would shut down the discussion immediately.) I don't want to be a cranky old cynic, and I know my statement makes me sound that way. I want to be the loving grandmother that I always envisioned, and I do think even now I fit that description to some extent. And I *am* grateful for my family and a good husband and the many good years I had. I do wish I could restore my faith in God and be a pillar of strength for my children and a support for my husband. So when I suggest it would have been better for me and Hugh to have died a couple years ago, I don't intend it in some morose or self-pitying way. All I'm saying is, since our lives have to end sometime, wouldn't it have been better to have happened when we still maintained our dignity rather than now, when we can do nothing but crawl pitifully and help-lessly into the grave?

On the other hand, even while part of me feels like my life really ended a couple years ago, another part of me rises up and shouts, "It's not over yet, so don't assume you can toss me aside like yesterday's garbage." I'm still in the battle, and nothing brings out the fighting spirit in me like this bright idea my kids have come up with to sell our house and ship us off to a nursing home. I guess since we haven't had the courtesy to go ahead and die soon enough for them to sell off our things and haul away the loot, they've decided to hurry us along a little bit. If they can't push us all the way into the grave, they can at least get us halfway there, into a place that I consider nothing more than a holding pen at the cemetery's front gate.

What they don't realize is they'll have to kill me to make that happen. I've lived in this house more than forty years, and I don't intend to leave it now. I've never told anybody this, but long ago, soon after we moved into this house, I had a kind of premoni-tion, or a vision, or whatever you want to call it, that I would die in this house. In a strange way, I've always been comforted by that. It allowed me to truly settle in and feel at home, knowing that this place would be the backdrop for my entire life.

So I will fight to keep it, and I have no doubt a fight will be required. The problem is, even my body has turned against me in this struggle, making it hard for me not only emotionally but also physically to do battle. Not that I want to punch or slap anybody, of course. That's never been my way of dealing with my kids or anybody else. It's just that because I *look* like a shriveled-up old insect, my family believes they have the right to treat me like one. They think they can swat me away and go on to the next thing. They can't imagine I would ever stand up to them and simply refuse to have anything to do with their plan. No, in their eyes, I'm a weak little soul who will give them no more trouble than a child.

I know I've become rather ridiculous looking over the last several years. I'm all stooped over, and my hands are gnarled, and I shuffle rather than walk. Even worse than that, I can't see too well, so it's harder to read people's expressions, and that puts me at a disadvantage when they all gang up on me in an argument. Then there's my hearing, which is getting worse all the time. I hear more than they think I do, but I lose parts of every conversation, which makes me look as if I'm not just hard of hearing but also confused or not bright enough to grasp what's being discussed.

So it will take some effort to show them I mean business when I say I will not sell this house and move to a nursing home or anywhere else under any circumstances. Furthermore, I am still perfectly capable of taking care of my husband, thank you.

Despite the fact that I'm a withered old crone, I do still have a few resources at my disposal. I've hidden some important papers about the house, so my daughters needn't think they can swoop down and sell it out from under us while we're not looking. I can thwart them in ways they would never imagine. Their tactic with me on most big decisions is to do whatever they want and then come and try to convince me they had no choice. They figure I might squeak out some protest at first but then eventually go along with whatever they've decided. I can picture them trying that with this house, but it won't work this time around. I am an adult, and I am in my right mind.

Strange as it may sound, even though I dread this fight in one way, in another way it makes me feel younger than I've felt in years. I'm not dead yet! And my daughters are going to have to come to terms with that.

8 DANNY:
TEST DRIVE

I came one step closer to going to Indiana today. I bought the perfect car for it. I hadn't intended to buy a car right now, especially with things so shaky at the hospital and the prospect of unemployment hovering over me every day. But Pete, my supervisor, was selling his car. Even though it's only a few years old, he found this SUV he wants instead. I guess when you're at his level on the salary scale you can afford those kinds of impulses; although if the hospital goes bust, he and I will both be making the same amount: zero.

It's not the flashiest car, probably wouldn't have been my first choice if I were buying it new. In fact, since I bought it, I've been stabbed several times with horrible moments of doubt—I bought a car that only an old man would love! I'm planning a trip to break out of my stodgy lifestyle and here I go and prove what a fuddy-duddy I really am!

In spite of my misgivings, as soon as I sat behind the wheel, I knew—this is my car. This is the car that will carry me across the country, through deserts and plains and back to the corn-covered Midwest of my childhood.

It's a red Buick Regal, six cylinder, gray leather seats, and all the gadgets. A beautiful stereo system. A ride so smooth it feels like it's driving itself. Pete takes good care of his cars—I know that for a fact. He offered a good price, too, a couple thousand dollars less than what I had expected.

My other car is twelve years old and way beyond its prime. With the help of Jesse, my mechanic, I've managed to keep it going, but now it keeps wanting to stall at intersections for reasons that even the amazing Jesse can't figure out. It's to the point now (I tell myself) that I'm going to be spending more money to maintain the old car than a new car would cost. And one of these days something big is going to happen to it—the transmission or something will go out—and I'll be putting thousands of dollars into a piece of junk.

As you can see, I'm trying to rationalize making such a big expenditure even though I won't have my job much longer. Should I be pouring so much of my savings into this?

Out in the parking lot of the hospital, just seconds before I told Pete I would take the car, my ex-wife, Terri, suddenly screamed, *"Are you crazy? You can't afford that! Why won't you ever grow up?"*

She didn't *literally* say this, of course. She wasn't there. But even though we've been divorced for three years, she often invades my thoughts uninvited, usually to berate or belittle me. Whenever I'm on the verge of taking some bold step (or when I'm about to do or say something stupid), I can count on Terri to be right there to jump all over me.

My answer to her outburst was calculated to stoke her rage. "I'm not the one buying this car—Buster Flapjaw is buying it. This was *his* idea."

I should explain that Buster Flapjaw is a . . . Well, let me just say that he has been in my life since I was a kid. He takes the blame for things I would rather not have to deal with. Terri thought he was funny when we first got married. She would play right along when things happened that she didn't like. She would say, "Oh, it looks like Buster Flapjaw left the milk sitting out on the counter again instead of putting it back in the refrigerator." Or "I see that Buster forgot to pay the phone bill." Whenever we inexplicably went over budget for the month, we would both readily agree that it was because Buster had spent the extra money. He also took the blame when things around the house were missing, or when I was late for some appointment, or when various promises went unfulfilled.

Before long, Buster began to say things that I didn't want to say to Terri directly: "Buster was wondering whether you're really into watching this movie or whether it might be possible to switch channels and watch the football game he's been waiting all week to see." Or "Buster was wondering how you could afford those two new pairs of slacks considering the clothing money ran out a couple weeks ago."

Eventually, the novelty of Buster Flapjaw faded for Terri, and she made it clear she wanted to hear no more from him. He stopped talking to her (for the most part), but he didn't disappear. He went underground. Now, since the divorce, his main responsibility has been to protect me against Terri. If she pelts my brain with too many nasty zingers, I send Buster to talk to her.

When I wrote the check for the car, Terri started in again, flooding my mind with so many recriminations that I had to stop for a second, my pen poised in the air, while I let the bitter storm of words tear through me.

I sent Buster after her.

"*Quit trying to hold him back!*" Buster Flapjaw yelled. "*He doesn't owe you anymore. He has paid and paid. He is paying still. He doesn't have to become a beggar in the street just to pay the penance you'd like to squeeze out of him. He . . ."*

Buster kept going along those lines, but I stopped listening. I finished writing the check and gave it to Pete. Now I own the automobile. I'll sell my old one for what little I can get for it, and then I'll have to decide whether I've bought this car to take me on a two-thousand-mile trip or whether I've bought it to take me ten miles back and forth to work each day.

Part of me—the part that's been feeling kind of old and worn out—wants to call Donna and tell her to forget the whole idea of me coming out there. There's too much about it that makes no sense. It's too disruptive to my life and hers and her family's, and I should just stay here and save money and look for a new job. I'll probably end up back here anyway, so why put myself through something that has so little chance of working out?

But another part of me—the part that gets so restless in the office at around two every afternoon that I can hardly force myself to keep sitting there—says that I have no choice but to go. It says that the trip alone would be worth it and may even be necessary to my sanity.

Financially, even with buying this car, I would still be all right without a job for a couple months. I live a very Spartan lifestyle, partially in preparation for just these kinds of circumstances. Terri got the house and almost all the furniture in the divorce, and when I moved out I bought very little to replace it. I live in a cheap studio apartment, not because I can't afford more but because as a single man I like my life as simple as possible. My place is tidy and uncluttered, like an army barracks.

Beyond what I spend on bills and what I set aside for Alex, I save a good portion of my salary every month, and I've done so for years. I invest a lot of what I make toward my retirement, but I must admit that I've raided my retirement money many times, especially since the divorce. Fortunately, some of that money is invested in ways that it's hard for me to get at it, so I still should be able to retire at sixty-five or so if all goes well. But my original goal was to have saved enough to retire by fifty-five. Oh, how I wish I could have stuck with that plan! If that had happened, I would now have only a few years to go, and then I could have wandered around the country at will. But too many circumstances intervened, so now I have to make myself content with the fact that at least I have enough money to tide me over between jobs.

The truth is I have trouble keeping a job. Not because I'm not good at what I do. Not because I'm lazy or don't care. One thing I can honestly say is that when I work for a place, they get more than their money's worth out of me. Only once in my career have I ever been fired, and even in that case my conscience is clear—I earned every penny I got from them.

The problem is I just get too restless. It's hard to describe. It's kind of a daydreamy state of mind that I fall into once I've been in a certain routine for too long. It usually doesn't hit me when I'm new in a job or when there's some big challenge to keep my mind occupied. But when I'm into the routine of a job, say three or four years after I've started working there, I start finding it harder and harder to push myself through each day. I sit at my desk and get lost in a kind of trance for a couple of hours. It seems like everything is in slow motion. Even if my eyes are focused on a page and my hands are typing on a keyboard or writing with a pen, I start feeling almost disembodied, as if I'm floating above this person who is me, this office slave sitting at his desk going through the motions of work.

On the days when I fall into one of these states, I usually end up having to stay later into the evening to get my work done, which cuts into my personal time away from work and which makes me even more restless. Each day it gets harder and harder to force myself to get into the car and drive to work to face the torment. Eventually, I simply drift away from the job, finding some excuse as to why I have to quit.

The frequent job changes were no problem when I was a younger, single man, but they didn't work too well when I was married and raising a son. I tried to curb my compelling desire to drift and daydream and flee. With several jobs I forced myself to keep going back day after day for months, not knowing each morning how I could possibly survive until five or six o'clock.

Terri had no sympathy with my frustrations. "Every job has aspects of it that a person won't like," she said, quite reasonably. "You can't quit every job just because you start to feel a little bored."

Whenever I did quit, she resented it, chalking it up to mere irresponsibility. I never went without work for more than a few months, and it never put us in deep financial trouble, but we never really got ahead, either. And some of the goals she cherished most kept getting postponed as these job transitions ate into our savings.

What I never could get Terri to understand is that I have this great need for the secret place, the separate place that has nothing to do with work. Sometimes I go to work in the morning thinking I'll be all right that day. I feel almost like an actor playing the part of an accountant. I have my smiling work mask securely fastened, my tie neatly accomplishing its subtle strangulation. I answer the phone, race through projects, and chitchat with co-workers as easily as if I had been born into the corporate life. But then around two in the afternoon, as if some invisible medicine has worn off, I feel an almost irrepressible urge to flee, to run off by myself and think and stare at the countryside.

One afternoon, when I was working at a car dealership in L.A. not long after my divorce, I couldn't stand it anymore and I told my boss I was feeling deathly ill. It was almost true in a way, I felt so desperate. I stumbled out of the building, got in my car, and started driving. Before long, I found myself on the

10 freeway driving east, not sure where I was headed. At first this little adventure gave me a sense of guilty pleasure. I enjoyed the drive and felt a momentary relief.

But by the time I got to Palm Springs a couple hours later, I felt worn down and foolish. I sat in a restaurant asking myself what I was doing there. I suddenly felt lonely. I worried about the work that must be piling up on my desk. I dreaded the traffic and the drive home.

For a long time after that, I resisted the urge to flee, but the impulse still flared up in me every week or two. By the time I quit that job a few months later, the urge was hitting me every day, and afternoons were hell.

I'm nearly fifty, and I know it won't get any easier to find new jobs at my age. I know I should get with one company and stay there until the end of my career and build up a good retirement fund. Like Terri always says, I should grow up.

But will I do that here or in Indiana? I want to call Alex and see what he thinks. If there's one person I never want to let down again, it's my son. Among my many Indiana fantasies, the one that burns brightest is the one where Alex is moving into his bedroom in my new house in Indianapolis, which I share with my new wife, who has finally brought me lasting contentment. I hesitate to even let my mind dwell on that because when I do, Terri pops up and practically howls with derision, and Buster has to work himself half to death to shut her up.

9 PAM:
GETTING CHEWED OUT

The discharge coordinator at the rehab center called today and all but accused me of parental abuse because I haven't yet arranged for where Dad's going to go after he gets released. I told her I've been working on it but I haven't been getting any cooperation from anybody. I practically begged her to keep Dad for at least another week, but she said they were just about at the end of what they could do for him, which hasn't been much, if you ask me.

He still can't really walk across the room on his own, even with the walker. He doesn't like the walker, either, and complains that it just gets in his way. But of course without it he'd plop right down on his face. He's incontinent and has to wear one of those diapers, which embarrasses him. He's confused much of the time, thinking that Mom is *his* mother and asking her to bring him oatmeal with raisins in it, which he must have eaten as a child.

Even before they started trying to get Dad kicked out of this place, this lady warned me that Medicare would stop paying for his care if he didn't start being more cooperative. He's been refusing the physical therapy on most days, saying he doesn't feel good enough and that he's afraid he'll puke if they make him walk—it happened once. I tried to get across to him the fact that he had to do what the staff told him or Medicare would cut him off, but I didn't have much success with that.

"I don't have the strength for all this walking," he told me. "I feel too wobbly."

"That's the point, Dad. How are you ever going to build up strength if you don't do the exercises?"

"I need more time to work up to it."

"Well, you can't go home until you're able to walk across the—"

"I'll go home! Don't start in on me about that. This has nothing to do with going home. There's no physical therapy at home. I can sit in my recliner and be just fine."

"But how can you get from that recliner to the bathroom or—"

"Don't you worry about me going to the bathroom! I've been finding my way to the bathroom since thirty years before you were born. You get me home and I'll take care of the rest of it myself."

Sometimes when he talks that way, I'm tempted to just say, "All right, then, forget it. Just go on home. See you later. I have some other things I need to do."

I *do* have other things that I need to do, too, for the kids and for Cliff and for my job. It's bad enough to have to work all this out for Dad and Mom, but it's even worse that I have to fight them every step of the way to help them.

Of course, as soon as I have thoughts like that, I immediately feel guilty. That's not the kind of attitude I want to have toward my parents. I love them dearly. I know that a terrible thing is happening to Dad, and I'd give anything if I could restore him to health and get him out of this rehab facility and take him home for a big celebration with the whole family. Every day I pray for a miracle of healing.

One of the ways Dad has been complicating things at the rehab place is that every day he tells all the staff members that he's going home "tomorrow." He insists every day that he's about to be released, and if any of the nurses or anybody challenges him about it, he gets all huffy and tells them they can't keep him there against his will and he'll walk out of there whether they like it or not and blah, blah, blah. So it's no wonder they want him to go. And whenever the doctor talks to him, Dad says he's fine. No complaints. No ailments. With us he complains non-stop, but with the doctor he acts like he's in perfect health and these strokes have all been a big misunderstanding.

So now it looks like I've got a week at most to figure out what to do next, and I don't see how that could be enough time even if Mom and Dad were cooperating and the house were already sold and we were already packing!

This discharge lady got all snippy with me and said, "I gave you the phone numbers of all those places. Haven't you bothered to call any of them?" As if this process is as simple as calling to reserve a hotel room.

What she gave me was this directory of nursing homes and assisted-living complexes and retirement homes throughout the state. I called three or four and had them send me their brochures and price lists, and I asked some questions on the phone, but everything seems so expensive and confusing, and some of it sounds like it would take so long to set up that I don't know where to turn. Some of the apartments look so beautiful and offer so many amenities that I wish I could move into them myself.

One of the places is not far from where Dad is now, so I'm going to try to set up a tour for Mom in the next couple of days and see if she'll consider it. I don't know how we'll pay for it before the house is sold, but if I can just get her to agree to this, maybe we'll find a way.

The only other option I see, which I'm not going to tell Mom about yet, is some kind of in-home nursing care. One problem with that plan is that I think it has the potential of being the most expensive possibility, and the money just isn't there. I'm trying to find out whether insurance would pay for some of it, but I haven't been able to get a straight answer yet. The reason I'm holding this option back from Mom is that I know she would seize on it as a way of avoiding having to move, and I don't want to get her hopes up if this is something we would only be able to afford for a month or two. Like Cliff said to me the other day, we've got to face the fact that no matter what happens in the next couple weeks, my parents are reaching the place where they can no longer live on their own in that house. Why not take this opportunity to get them settled somewhere now rather than send Dad home and then have to go through this all again when he's even worse off?

Of course, Mom may not see it that way. So this tour will be the first test of her flexibility.

You might think I'd have my sisters to help me work through this, but Jackie and Tony and the kids went to Florida for a week. What a week for her to choose, just when I need her most! She said she would leave a number where I could reach her, but she didn't. I'm not surprised. She's done that before. When she's on vacation, she refuses to be bothered. If Dad were to die this week, I don't know how I'd get ahold of her.

Then there's Carolyn, who's certainly in town but who's not much more helpful than Mom and Dad at the moment. All she cares about is this "secret family." She gets so wound up every time I talk to her that she can hardly breathe. That sounds crazy, but it's true. I almost always have to spend half the conversation calming her down. The latest is that Mom, after confessing the basic details of the story, is refusing to say anything else until Dad is back home and feeling better. This has just about driven Carolyn wild. She's still determined to track down this "sister" on her own, before Jackie can get to her, but I tried to point out that we don't even know her name.

"Her name is Donna, and she lives in Carmel," said Carolyn when she was over at my house the other day.

"Oh, well, that'll get you real far," I said. "What are you going to do, go through the phone book and call every Donna with an address in Carmel?"

"I might," she said. "I mean, how many could there be?"

"Carolyn, please, don't make a fool of yourself over this."

"What are you talking about? I'm making a fool of myself just because I want to talk to my own sister? I've even been thinking of searching through the house when Mom's gone to try to find the letter."

"Don't do it!"

"Or I thought about calling some of the older relatives to see what they'd be willing to tell me."

"I'll kill you if you do!"

"Why? I can't believe you're not the least bit curious about Donna and Danny. It's bizarre to me."

"I'm curious," I said, "but we've got bigger problems to deal with right now. I think Mom's right to wait on this. We don't need any more stress right now. Help me get Dad settled somewhere, and then I'll help you, all right? We need Mom in a cooperative mood right now, and you know how sensitive she is about these other kids. If you go to other relatives and start talking about this, she'll be so embarrassed she probably won't even speak to us anymore. And then how will we get her to even consider the next step with selling the house and finding another place to live and all that. So stop this, Carolyn. You're driving me crazy with it. There's no reason why it can't wait a few more weeks."

Carolyn sat silent for a minute, pouting. Then she said, in a voice tinged with whininess, "I bet *Jackie* won't let it rest for a few more weeks. There's no telling what she's up to behind our backs."

"Well, she's not gonna get any further with this than you have, so don't worry about it."

"I think Mom's just holding this over our heads so she can force us to bring Dad home instead of making him move somewhere else. She keeps emphasizing she won't tell me anything else until Dad is settled *at home*. I feel like I'm being blackmailed."

"Well, maybe so, but if we shut up about this whole topic for a while, she won't have it to use as leverage against us. So please, Carolyn, I know you're obsessed with this, but I'm just going to have to refuse to talk about it anymore until we work out our other problems."

She has only called me once since then, and it was a short and unhelpful conversation. When I try to get her opinions on what we should do with Dad, I might as well be asking my three-year-old. She agrees to every possibility I raise, but she seems incapable of analyzing the pros and cons of anything without getting off on some tangent. If we talk about selling the house, for instance, she'll be with me for a few minutes and then she'll get caught up on some detail like what we would do with this old dresser she had in her room as a kid. "I just hate the thought of giving that away," she told me. "I know it's a little beat up, but I've thought about having it refinished someday. Do you think we could store it somewhere?"

"I don't know," I snapped. "Can't we just take it to your apartment if you like it so much?"

"No, I don't have room. I need to get rid of some of my furniture as it is."

"So *anyway,* Carolyn," I said and tried to steer her back on course, but after a few more minutes I gave up. I had tried to get her opinion on the financial problems we're facing no matter what we decide to do, but it was a waste of time. Money issues make her head spin. The most I can hope for is that she doesn't try to block whatever plan we finally come up with.

My friend Margo at church said she'd be happy to take me and Mom on a tour of the place where her own mother lives. Her mom is in her eighties and lives in one of the assisted-living communities. She has her own little apartment and eats most of her meals at the cafeteria down the hall, but the facility is set up so that if she gets too frail to manage on her own, she could move to a room where she would get more extensive care. Margo said at first her mom didn't want to move there, but now she loves it. Maybe if my mom would talk to her and see what a nice place she's living in, it would get some of these images out of her mind of some depressing urine-smelling nursing home littered with babbling old skeletons in wheelchairs. I'm going to try to set that up before I arrange any tours anywhere else.

What a relief it would be to me to have them in a place where someone would be checking on them regularly, so I wouldn't have to worry that they're taking the wrong medicines or that Dad will fall and kill himself. I really do believe this move is inevitable. If only I can get through to Mom!

I've been so stressed out over this the last few days that I've even been feeling this tightness in my chest. I pray to God for help every day, and I've got some friends at church praying. Margo said she'd ask the pastor to talk to Mom and Dad for me if I wanted. I told her I'd think about it. I'm not sure I want to put him in the line of fire, even though Mom and Dad both know him and like him.

In the meantime, I'd better figure out why both my kids are crying in the other room. I don't know which segment of my family is driving me the craziest, the really old ones or the really young ones. Some days I don't feel capable of handling either of them.

10 HUGH:
THE PAST COMES
CALLING

Danny called last night from Los Angeles and asked if I could come and visit. He said he'd arrange for me to come out by train, which he somehow knew was my favorite way to travel.

Either I got that phone call or I dreamed it very vividly. I can't remember.

My mind has been playing tricks on me lately. Even my mother has come to visit me in this torture chamber they've got me staying in. Three times over the last few days she has walked in, just as real as my wife and daughters, and offered me hot chocolate like she used to do when I was younger. Yesterday she stood there with a big white mug of hot chocolate in her hand. She had on that blue apron she wore for so many years. She walked across the room in a hurry, like she wanted me to take that mug right away so she could get back into the kitchen and get some for everybody else. She didn't look surprised to see me. Then right when Mom got up to me, Vonnie stepped in front of her and started messing with my pillow, the way she always does.

"What?" Vonnie was saying.

"Huh?" I said, trying to look around her to see Mom.

"What are you going on about?"

Mom wasn't there anymore. Never had been there, I suddenly realized. Been dead for thirty-five years. "Quit fussing with that pillow," I said.

"Apron," said Vonnie. "What's that you said about an apron?"

I tried to let my mind clear. I felt a little dizzy.

" . . . think I was wearing an apron?" Vonnie said, the first part of her sentence lost in the fuzzy atmosphere. She sat down in the chair beside me, eyeing me like I was an escapee from an insane asylum.

"Women don't wear aprons anymore," I said lamely.

"Not too much."

"When I think of my mother, I always picture her with an apron on. Seems like she almost always wore one around the house."

"I remember."

"You used to wear aprons, too."

"Years ago," she said. "Are you feeling all right, honey? Do you want me to get you some—"

"Why did you stop?"

"Why did I stop what?"

"Wearing an apron. Why is it that for the whole first half of my life or more almost every woman I knew felt the need to wear an apron around the house, and now no one does? Did food suddenly stop splattering? Did women suddenly not care anymore whether they got stains on their clothes when they cooked?"

Vonnie laughed. "It's like hats," she said. "Men's hats. Women's, too, I guess."

"What do you mean?"

"I remember a day when any man who wore a suit also wore

a hat on his head. And most women wore hats, too, when they were dressed up. And then suddenly, no hats. Do you think most men under age sixty even *own* a hat that could be worn with a suit? So why did everybody think they had to have one? I don't know. Things change."

I groaned, shifting around to relieve some pressure on my right leg, which was aching.

"What made you think about aprons?" asked Vonnie.

"My mother."

Fortunately, she didn't ask what made me think of my mother.

"I gotta get out of here," I said. "This place is doing strange things to me."

"Won't be long."

"That's what you've been saying ever since I got here. I still don't see the point of being kept prisoner here. This is not a healthy environment to live in. I could recuperate just as well at home."

She nodded in agreement. "It would be a lot easier for me to take care of you at home than it would to go through all the effort to get here every day. I'd rather be doing things myself than to always have to be fussing at these nurses and aides to do it."

"Well, tell the doctor I'm going home, then."

"You've told him a hundred times, hon."

"Tell Pam, then. Maybe she could—"

"You've told *her* a thousand times. I don't think you should keep—"

"She hasn't visited me in two weeks!"

"She was here last night. Now, it doesn't do any good to keep arguing with Pam. The girls have their own ideas about what we should do, and we're never gonna be able to convince them otherwise. So the best thing to do is keep still until you get released, which that director lady told me might be any day now, and then we'll just quietly go home whether anybody likes it or not."

I was trying hard to remember Pam's visit. The last few days were a little hazy. I also couldn't recall arguing with Pam or telling her a thousand times that I wanted to go home.

I wanted to find out from Vonnie whether my talk with Danny about the train trip to Los Angeles was real or imaginary, but if it happened not to be true, I didn't want to upset her or make her question my sanity. I was sure that at least part of it had to be true. How could my brain make up a whole detailed phone conversation and then convince me it really happened? I mean, I remember his *voice*. And if he's really going to get me on that train and take me out there, I want to get myself ready for it.

"I've been thinking about taking a train trip," I said, hoping she would say something like, "Well, of course, don't you remember setting that up with Danny last night?"

Instead, Vonnie scowled and didn't say anything at first. Finally she asked, "Where to?"

"California."

She sighed and shook her head. Not much help.

Trying a different approach, I asked, "Who was that who called me last night?"

"I don't know. Who?"

"It's not a riddle! That's what I'm asking you."

"Don't get testy. Nobody called you last night. I don't remember. You were in rare form yesterday, I can tell you that much."

"What do you mean?"

She waved her hand back and forth, as if that answered the question.

"Maybe somebody called before you got here," I ventured. "Do you remember me telling you anything about it?"

"What time did they call?"

"I don't know what time they called!"

"Well, I was here last night from five-thirty till about nine, and nobody called during that time unless—" She stared down at the floor as if maybe there was some kind of phone log written there.

"Unless what? Did somebody call or not?"

"Maybe Carolyn? I don't remember. Seems like the phone did ring. Why? Who do you think it was?"

I didn't want to answer. By this time I was sorry I had brought it up. "I thought maybe my girlfriend would've called me," I joked, hoping to change the subject, since Vonnie obviously wasn't going to be any help. If Danny did call, I must not have told her about it.

Vonnie said, "Well, if it had been your girlfriend, I would have handed the phone right over to you. What do I care? Two can play at that game."

"I know it," I said. "There's no telling what you've got going on at home while I'm stuck in here."

"Oh, Hugh," she said with a smirk. "Please."

The more I think about it, the more I'm afraid maybe Danny didn't call, even though I would recognize his voice if I heard it right now and even though I could repeat every word of the conversation we had. That's the way my memory is. The things that are the most vivid are not always the most reliable. I don't remember Pam's visit yesterday, which supposedly happened, but I have a flawless memory of Danny's phone call, which more than likely did *not* happen. The thing is, why would he suddenly call, considering that I don't even know him? How would he even know to find me here? And why would he invite me to come all the way to Los Angeles before he has ever even met me? But still, I can't get it out of my mind.

A few days ago, I woke up and could have sworn that I was waking up in the house on Green Street. I haven't lived in that house since I was married to Barbara, but when I opened my eyes, everything at first looked exactly like our bedroom in that house. It's probably the dinginess of this awful place that made me connect it to that old house. I can never think of that house without thinking how dreary it always seemed, no matter what we did with the lights or how we painted it or how brightly we tried to decorate it. "Dingy inside and out," Barbara always said about that house. The whole place appeared to be designed to block out light. The roof hung low over the front porch, so that cut off some sunshine, and most of the windows were small. The neighbors' houses on either side of us were awfully close, and in front and back we had these big oak and maple trees that hadn't been trimmed much and that blocked a lot of sun.

Barbara tried to make up for the lack of sunlight by keeping lamps blazing in every room both day and night, but even so, whenever I think back to that time in my life, I think of semi-darkness, always wishing there was one more shade to pull up or one more light to switch on.

My life has never recovered from what happened in that house. I still find myself dividing my life into two halves, before Green Street and after it. Before it was my childhood, the army, my life as a single man, the good times with Barbara, the births of Donna and Danny, the breakup. After Green Street came everything that people now know me by—my marriage to Vonnie, my three daughters, my forty-year career at Brantwell, my thirty years of activity in our church, my heart attacks and strokes, my current pathetic condition.

I have to admit that I have sometimes fantasized about the life that I might have had with Barbara and our two children. I've been thinking about it a lot lately, if for no other reason than because Barbara keeps showing up and Danny keeps calling! And Donna's letter—which I know for a fact I really received—got me thinking about Barbara a lot, especially when I read that she had died. In one way she had long ago ceased to be real to me. Barbara and my first two kids had come to seem more like characters out of an old movie than living human beings. I'm not proud to say that, but it's true. When you go for decades without seeing or hearing from someone and are forbidden even from talking about them, you eventually get the sense that maybe they exist only in your head.

Until recently, the only times I ever let myself ponder Barbara were after a few bad arguments with Vonnie, when I felt like she didn't respect me and that we were pulling apart. I think Barbara's death jolted me because in the back of my mind, even though I never would have admitted it to anyone, I always expected I would see her again. Isn't it odd that while in one way she barely seemed real, in another way I always anticipated one more showdown, one more summing up of all that went sour? I dreaded that encounter, but some part of me also wanted it to happen. Over the years, my mind had collected snippets of imaginary conversation—mostly recriminations—that I would have taken a perverse pleasure in delivering during a final talk. I also had this idea that no matter what she said, I could have told by the look in her eyes whether or not she harbored any regret for the way our marriage had fallen apart and the way I had been separated from my children. If she had it to do over again, would she have treated me differently?

My more rational side tells me that Barbara was wrong for me from the beginning and that our marriage was probably always doomed, but I have to wonder. What would have happened if we had never moved into that house on Green Street? Would she have left me anyway? If we had bought another place, far away from my meddling family, would a different side of Barbara—and a different side of me—have emerged, and would we have formed a bond that would have stood the test of time? It's pointless to speculate about this, but even fifty years later I find myself asking why it had to happen the way it did.

At first the chance to move to Indianapolis had looked like the answer to all our problems. It was a few years after World War II, when good housing was hard to find. Barbara and I were living in a dinky apartment in a house near Lafayette, about sixty miles from my parents, who lived on Green Street in Indianapolis. After I got out of the military in 1947, I had moved to Lafayette partly out of rebellion against my family. My father was working at Brantwell Corporation, which made engine parts for tanks and other military vehicles during the war and made engines for trucks and buses after the war.

Dad had always wanted me to come home from the army and get a job there, but that idea didn't appeal to me. I was a young man full of so much energy I could barely sit still, and to me the idea of coming home to punch the clock at Brantwell every day sounded like a prison sentence. I associated the company with my father, so getting a job there would have been like throwing away my youth to *become* him, trudging through my workdays and then plopping dead tired into the recliner every evening. I couldn't stand the thought of it. I didn't know what I wanted to do, but I knew it wasn't that.

Another reason I went to Lafayette was to avoid Mom and Dad's scrutiny of some of the bad habits I had picked up in the army—drinking, smoking, running around with women. Mom and Dad, as members of the Church of the Nazarene, followed a strict conservative Christian lifestyle from which I had broken away. Even though I'm sure they must have sensed that I had lapsed as a Christian, I wanted to avoid for as long as possible their knowledge of the details of the kind of life I now lived. I couldn't bear the thought of them watching me put a cigarette to my lips. Lafayette was far enough away that I could get away with visiting them only once or twice a month.

It was in Lafayette that I met Barbara, and dating her was

like going out with a tornado. Whenever I think back to those first three months of knowing her, I get this spinning sensation, as if we didn't sit still for five minutes that whole time, as if we were propelled by some whirling force that was beyond our control.

I was working for a guy painting houses. I wasn't making much money, but I would spend my whole paycheck taking Barbara out on the town. Sometimes my money would be gone by midweek, but that didn't stop us. We somehow found a way to keep going. Whenever I had a day off, we'd run down to Indianapolis or up to Chicago, which was a lot harder to do back then than it is now. I have to say that, while it lasted, it was probably the most fun I've ever had in my life. Barbara and I fed off each other's energy. It's strange to say, but during those days when I was with her, I felt almost superhuman, as if she embodied some supernatural power that sustained me through sleepless nights and turned me into an addict of her very presence.

Barbara was a good-looking woman—petite, with the most delicate white skin, a shapely body, thick brown hair, and lips that were always coated with the red lipstick that women favored back in those days. I loved her. I was so captivated by her that I would have done whatever she wanted.

She did want something, and that was for me to marry her. I'm not sure why. Not that I questioned it at the time. Back then I thought of our marriage as inevitable. I couldn't imagine that either of us could ever again be content outside of each other's presence.

It's *now* that I wonder why she so much wanted to marry me. The life of a housewife, which is what most married women were back then, was never for her, certainly not then. How could she possibly have thought she could settle into a routine of taking care of children all day and cooking meals at regular times and keeping an apartment clean and all the other expectations placed upon a wife in the 1940s?

Barbara declared that's what she wanted, but nothing in her life up to that point indicated those desires. She grew up in a family that was strictly religious like mine, but she had moved out on her own when she was eighteen, a bolder move for a single girl in those days than it would be now. She worked in a factory during the war and was working in a department store when I first met her. She shared an apartment with two other girls but spent no more time in it than she absolutely had to. From the time she was a teenager she had never been without a boyfriend or two to take her wherever she wanted to go. She had quickly grown bored—I found out later—with all of these guys and had tossed every one of them aside as if they were nothing more than one of her old pairs of shoes that had gone out of style. Never had she seriously considered marrying any of them.

So why marry *me*? Even now, even after all that happened, I can't help but think that there *was* something special about our relationship. People who knew her would say I'm naïve. They'd say I was merely one in a series of men in her life, and it's just a coincidence that she happened to be with me when she decided the time was right to get married. Sometimes I think she saw me as the man who might change her, who might make her content enough to finally settle down. I also think that her family was pressuring her to marry somebody, even if I might not have been their first choice. They wanted her to lead a more respectable life, and although she acted as if she couldn't care less what they thought, I think she did want to please them.

Anyway, whatever her reasons, Barbara wanted to get married, and she wanted to do it immediately. I was in no mood to ask questions or to rationally analyze the situation. The woman I loved more than life itself wanted to marry me. Was I going to put her off? Was I going to tell her to wait until we knew each other better or until we were more established financially or all those other things people say?

My family didn't want me to marry Barbara. I took her to meet them only a couple of times before we got engaged. They were polite to her, but she clearly was not the nice, conservative Nazarene girl they had in mind for me. Now I see that they probably also sensed the almost inevitable disaster that would result from the union of two people so unsuited for marriage. They sent my oldest brother to Lafayette as a supposedly discreet envoy to talk me into at least postponing the wedding. The only phrase I remember from our brief conversation in a downtown diner is "cooling-off period." This was his awkward way of describing the benefits of a long engagement. The expression outraged me beyond all reason. "Cooling off" from what? Did he think this was some kind of strike negotiation at the factory? I loved Barbara. I planned to marry her. I planned to never cool off about it.

Barbara and I got married one month after our engagement. The wedding, in the backyard of Barbara's aunt's house, was a cheap affair that her parents paid for, griping all the way. My family came, smiling politely and staying at the reception only as long as they thought courtesy demanded.

Two months later, Barbara was pregnant. We had debts. We were broke.

By the time Donna was born, we had moved from the tiny room where I had lived as a single man into the one-bedroom apartment in the upstairs of an old lady's house. To avoid bankruptcy, we tried cutting back on how many times a week we went out. You might have thought that pregnancy would have slowed Barbara down, but it didn't until the last couple of months. We should have had no problem paying our bills. Even though I didn't make a whole lot, it would have been plenty for a frugal couple to live on, and Barbara kept her job at the department store until a month before the baby was born.

Unfortunately, pregnancy did not bring out the best in her. She was sensitive about her appearance. She acted irrationally surprised by the fact that the pregnancy was changing her figure. She constantly stared at herself in the mirror and asked me whether I thought she was gaining too much weight. "You're probably not gaining *enough* weight," I told her. "There's a baby inside you, remember? Your body has to feed it. You're its *mother*, remember? This baby can't stay invisible. It's going to show."

She didn't like my attitude. She got very moody during the last few months, and the only way she could make herself feel better was to go out and buy whatever new clothes she thought made her look less pregnant or at least made her body look less "grotesque," as she described it. "You're not grotesque at all," I tried to convince her. "You are a beautiful, plumply healthy mother-to-be. Countless women would give anything to look the way you do. Think of how fortunate our baby is to be growing up in that body."

"So you admit I'm plump," she'd say.

"Healthy."

Then she'd go out and buy another outfit. We could have opened a maternity store by the time she was done. Some of those outfits she wore only once. A few of them she never got around to wearing. She started buying lots of baby supplies, too. You'd have thought we were having triplets. Some weeks she'd end up owing her whole paycheck, and then some, to the department store. When she finally quit, she still wanted to keep on buying, so all those purchases were piled on top of our other debts.

I was too young and immature to rein her in. Maybe this is how married couples operate, I thought. Maybe once she has the baby, she'll settle down and we'll get these bills paid off. I started working overtime. Once she quit working, Barbara felt so bloated and miserable that I would come home to find her doing nothing but sitting slumped on the sofa staring at the ceiling or the closed curtains. I tried to get her family and a couple of friends to come and stay with her, but she usually sent them away. "I feel like even more of a blob than I look," she said. "I don't feel like sitting around talking about booties and diapers. If I feel like the baby's about to come, I'll pick up the telephone. There'll be plenty of time for people to visit once it's born."

So then Donna was born, and I thought maybe everything was going to be all right. Barbara perked up at first and took an interest in the baby. She liked all the attention, and the apartment was always full of people bringing presents. But after three or four weeks, Barbara started getting more sullen again. She acted as if she resented the baby crying so much and waking us up at night, as if she had figured that stage would only last a week or two. The visitors dropped off, and Barbara was itchy to get out of the apartment. She started talking about going back to work at the department store a few days a week and leaving the baby with her mother. I didn't like that idea for lots of reasons, one of them being that I was afraid that being in that store all day might set her off on another one of her spending binges, which would have ruined us.

When the baby turned two months old, Dad had his heart attack and died. I guess I must have inherited his heart problems, but at least I've been fortunate enough to outlive my heart attack by over ten years. Dad wasn't so lucky. He came home from the factory one evening, had dinner, and then collapsed about an hour later in the hallway between the living room and his bedroom. Mom said he made a "horrible noise" in his throat, a detail she dwelled on for days, and then he fell hard on the floor. She called an ambulance and shouted out the window to one of the neighbors, but Dad was dead before anyone made it inside to help him.

Even before Dad's funeral, my brother Neil—the same one who had tried on behalf of the whole family to prevent me from marrying Barbara—tried to talk us into moving to Indianapolis and staying with Mom. I immediately rejected the idea without even discussing it with Barbara. I didn't think she'd want to get involved with my family at any level, let alone live with them. Mom certainly was devastated by Dad's death and was eager to be surrounded by family, but I didn't think it was the right move for us. Neil and my other brother, Jim, had two kids apiece at that point and didn't want to move in with Mom, and my sister lived in Ohio with her husband and daughter and had no intention of moving, either. None of them wanted to have Mom come live with them, and Mom probably would have refused anyway.

I considered the matter dropped, but on the way home after the funeral, Barbara shocked me by turning to me and saying, "So what would you think of moving down there with your mother?"

I figured Neil must have talked to her directly when I wasn't looking. "So he tried out that idea on you, too?" I asked.

"Not he," said Barbara. "Your mother. After the funeral, when she and I went out in the backyard and I fed the baby, she invited us to come there and live if we wanted to. She said it would be a big help to her, and the baby would be a comfort."

"And you would want to do that? I didn't think you even liked my family. I mean, after things they've said."

She sighed. "I know I wasn't their first choice as a wife for their precious Hugh, but now that we're married, they've all been pretty nice to me. Especially your mom. I think she likes me now."

"And you'd really be willing to live there?"

"It'd be nice to have our own house—in a sense our own— at least more than the apartment is. And your mom said she'd love to help with the baby. I might even be able to go to work a few days a week."

Free baby-sitting. I was beginning to see the appeal of this for Barbara.

She said, "And we'd save a lot of money. Your mom made it clear without me even saying anything that she would refuse to let us pay any rent. So we could pay off our bills."

And have more money to spend on clothes. And have more money for nights out on the town while Mom watched Donna. Already, just a year into my marriage with the woman of my dreams, I calculated her motives in such unflattering terms.

"I don't know. I'd have to find a job."

"It wouldn't have to be much of a job to be better than what you've got right now," she said, stabbing at my pride. "I'm sure Indianapolis must have more opportunities than Lafayette does."

"Let's think about it for a few days. We don't want to jump into anything we'll regret. Once you're an adult, it's not always that easy to live with your mother. She's never even seen me smoke a cigarette. And you know she won't allow a drop of alcohol in the house."

Barbara brushed off those objections with a wave of her hand. I could tell she had made her decision. She was probably already rearranging Mom's furniture in her mind. We were moving to Green Street, and I would be expected not to put up any obstacles. I notified my boss I was quitting as a painter, and three weeks later we moved.

It was a disaster from the beginning. The first problem was this idea that Mom would look after the baby whenever Barbara needed her to. Barbara was picturing something like a full-time nanny, I think, but Mom had no intention of watching Donna every time Barbara felt like going shopping for a few hours or spending half the day getting her hair done and her nails polished. Mom declared she was "too nervous" to watch the baby for more than a couple hours at a time. I remember watching Barbara almost quivering with anger and frustration the night Mom made that announcement at the dinner table. It was the first of many disappointments for my young wife in that house.

Later, trying to calm her down, I said, "Don't worry. She'll gradually feel more comfortable with the baby. After all, she raised all of us, didn't she? I mean, it's not like she isn't experienced with kids. And she's looked after my brothers' kids."

"She tricked me," said Donna rather loudly, which worried me since our bedroom was right next to Mom's.

"No."

"Yes she did. She lured me down here with the promise that she'd help me with Donna and that *her* house would become *our* house, but now that I'm here, she expects me to be nothing but her slave."

"That's not true," I said, but as the weeks went by, I began to see some signs that she was right. The only time Mom offered to watch the baby was when she had some "little favor" she needed Barbara to do, like running to the store for her or taking something to the post office. (Like so many women of her generation, Mom never learned to drive a car.) Occasionally I could talk Mom into watching the baby while Barbara and I went out on a Friday or Saturday night, but only if I promised we'd be back before nine, which was Mom's bedtime.

The evening meal was another source of tension. Mom apparently assumed that Barbara was responsible for making dinner for all of us every evening. Barbara swore that Mom had promised to do all the cooking. Because I was gone all day, I never learned the details of how this daily conflict was resolved, but some days I came home to Mom's meal, some days to Barbara's, and some days to nothing at all. On the days when the table was empty, Barbara would point to the door as soon as I walked in and say, "We're going out to eat tonight." Then she would grab her purse, pick up the baby and the diaper bag, which would already be packed, and we would head off on our own, leaving Mom pouting in the living room.

The rest of my family didn't help the situation. When my brothers and their families visited, they often thanked Barbara for being there to "take care of" Mom, as if Barbara were merely her nurse. The fact is Mom didn't need to be "taken care of." She was in her sixties and healthy and strong. Yet she quickly withdrew from as many household chores as Barbara would take over, from housecleaning to laundry to tending the garden.

We didn't pay rent, but Mom made it clear that she expected a certain amount of payment in this other form. Unfortunately, she never said so directly. One of the problems with living there is that we rarely discussed these disagreements with Mom. I don't know why. If I had it to do over again, I would have laid this all out on the table with Mom from the start. The only explanation I can give is that things were different back then. Even when people were adults, they were a little more reticent about challenging their parents. Certainly we never would have dreamed of talking to my mother the way my daughters talk to me.

I don't want to give the impression that living with Mom was nothing but misery. For several days at a time Mom and Barbara could set aside their tensions and be nice to each other. Mom really did love Donna, and as long as she didn't have her alone too long, she was always willing to help take care of her. She also liked to buy her toys and clothes, and she gave us a break on several nights by staying up with Donna when the baby was sick.

When I look back on it from the age I am now, I can understand Mom a little better. From the more self-centered perspective of our youth, we couldn't understand why Mom was so finicky and difficult about everything. But I think we didn't stop to realize how much Dad's death had undermined the stability she had known for decades. She grieved his loss deeply for the rest of her life, but mostly silently. She relied on her strong faith in God to get her through each day. Even though she probably invited us to live with her in order to fill the gap left by Dad's absence, she underestimated how disruptive it would be to have us there. The last thing she needed was for us to come along and throw her life into even more turmoil by adding new baby-sitting responsibilities and upsetting her quiet routine. I see that now, but at the time, she came across as merely a fussy old woman.

After we had lived with Mom for a couple months, Barbara got the idea we'd be happier there if we could remodel the place to brighten it up. We didn't have much money for that, but Mom resisted even the modest ideas we did have. Barbara would try to talk her into putting in new drapes or new wallpaper or an extra table lamp, and Mom invariably said no to each idea. A few times she would change her mind later and say it would be all right, but Barbara was hurt and disheartened to see how little we were able to do to make the home cheerful and make it feel like it was our own. The aspects of the house that we considered gloomy, Mom considered "homey." She liked everything kind of dark and subdued, as if the house were her cocoon.

Once we had lived in Mom's house for about a year in this kind of emotional standoff, Barbara got pregnant again. For some reason I was hopeful that this second child might calm Barbara down a bit and bring her some contentment, but she was just as antsy during this pregnancy as she had been during the first one. From all outward appearances, we had plenty to be happy about. Living with Mom had helped us pay down much of our debt, we had a beautiful daughter and another baby on the way, I was making a decent living, we were young and healthy. But the truth was, I hated my job, Barbara felt like a prisoner in our house and hated being pregnant, Mom had mixed feelings at best about us being there, and all of us felt as if we were on the verge of some ugly emotional eruption.

After Danny was born and was about three months old, Barbara came to me in our bedroom one evening with a surprise. Little did I realize then that her decision would be the beginning of the end for us.

"I got a job today at a shoe store downtown. I've got to get out of the house."

"What about the kids?"

"I'll only work three days a week. Mrs. Greiner said she'd watch them for me."

Mrs. Greiner was our neighbor down the street, a nice lady whose husband had just retired and who had four grown children of her own.

I said, "Do you want me to work some overtime instead? I don't want to see you have to go back to work. That was part of the point of moving here, so you wouldn't have to." There was more of a stigma in those days about women working if they had small children. Some men considered it a challenge to their ability to be a good provider, and I was one of those men.

"You know it's not the money," she said. "I can't stand sitting here day after day. I'll go insane if I can't get out. You know this hasn't turned out the way I expected."

"Let's go back to Lafayette. I'll call Stu and get my job back, or I'll get a better job, and we'll get our own place."

"No," she insisted in that tone of voice I recognized as meaning her mind was made up. "I will never go back and be humiliated in front of my family."

I didn't understand that comment exactly, but I had picked up hints that early on she had bragged to her parents and her sisters about how much my family was going to do for her—giving her a house, watching the children anytime she wanted, and so on.

Now this brings me back to what happened the other day, when Barbara "visited" me here in this nasty room of mine. I "woke up" in the house on Green Street, and it was the evening when that conversation about the store took place. I wish I could get across how real it was. It wasn't like I was *remembering* that evening, I was *living* it. But the thing is, I changed it all around from what really happened. My brain made it turn out the way I wanted it to, the way that might have saved our marriage and avoided the catastrophe that destroyed us.

Barbara's voice was the first thing I heard. She was in the other room, and through the closed door of the bedroom I could hear her singing a hymn. That was one of the funny things about Barbara. She wasn't a Christian, but when she sang to herself or to the kids, she often sang hymns. The sound was far off, and I strained to catch the words. It was "When We All Get to Heaven." This continued for a few minutes, and then Barbara walked in with the baby—almost asleep—in her arms. Donna must have been in the other room with her grandma.

Barbara was so beautiful that when she first walked in, I stared at her without saying a word. That's how things always were with us. No matter how bad things got between us, I never tired of looking at her. Even when we were arguing, there was a part of me that was adoring her through the barrage of harsh words. She was wearing one of her favorite dresses—a deep green color, tapered down at the waist in a way that she thought made her look thinner. By today's slouchy standards she probably would have looked quite dressed up, but back then women took a little more pride in their appearance, and Barbara almost always looked nice.

I was lying on the bed, and Barbara walked over and put the baby in my arms. I rocked Danny lightly up and down the way he liked, and his eyes got narrower and narrower until he finally fell asleep. Neither Barbara nor I spoke until the baby's eyes were closed. Barbara lay down beside me and sort of curled up into my side, the way she liked to do.

After we lay quiet for a while listening to the baby's peaceful breathing, Barbara said, "I've been offered a job at a shoe store downtown."

"Why were you looking for a job?"

"I wasn't. That lady across the street, Mrs. Forrester, recommended me to her son, who's the manager of it. She sang my praises to him so much that she convinced him he couldn't run the store without me. Then when she invited me over to her house this morning for some coffee, there he was, visiting, and he offered me the job."

"What did you tell him?"

"I said I didn't think so, but that I'd talk it over with you. We could use the money, and I wouldn't mind getting out of the house more often."

"Living here hasn't been what you hoped for, has it?"

"It's had its good moments, but I don't think it's the best thing for us as a family right now. We need our own home."

"Do you want to move? Go back to Lafayette?"

"Yes," she said. "If you wouldn't mind too much. I think that even if we had to go to a small apartment at first, we could pay off the rest of our bills and save up and do just fine. And your mom doesn't really need us here and would probably even be relieved if we were on our own, especially now that we have two kids."

Barbara stood up and walked over to a chair in the corner, where there was an extra blanket. She picked up the blanket and said, "If you're going to lie there with the baby, maybe I should cover you up. This room's a little chilly."

I was so happy that Barbara was willing to move away from Indianapolis! A fresh start for our family would set everything right.

As she placed the blanket over me, she said, "What? What are you talking about? Move where?"

And I glanced up again and saw that it was Vonnie standing there.

I broke out in a sweat. What had I said? How much had Vonnie heard? Had I used the word "Barbara"? In all the years of our marriage, I had never slipped up and called Vonnie by the wrong name.

Vonnie adjusted the blanket and stared at me. She said, "I thought you didn't want to move. I thought you were going to tell the girls—"

"Quit fussing over me," I said, pushing her hand away from the blanket, my brain awash in confusion, hovering between two worlds. "I'm not moving anywhere. I'm going home tomorrow."

"Oh," said Vonnie, sighing. She sat down in her usual chair by the bed. "So it's going to be one of *those* days."

At least her casual response meant that I must not have said anything incriminating—or if I did, she was too deaf to hear it. For the rest of the day, I kept going over and over that conversation with Barbara. For a while I couldn't remember whether the version Vonnie interrupted was the true memory or whether the other version, where Barbara insists on taking the job at the shoe store, was true. I was so caught up in those thoughts that I could barely speak to anybody for the rest of the day. This room in rehab seemed like the bad dream, and the house on Green Street seemed real.

Slowly it dawned on me that somehow my mind had changed around that whole conversation from fifty years ago. The reality was that Barbara had taken that job at the shoe store, which seemed innocent enough at the time but which ended up opening the floodgates of disaster.

This episode has convinced me that I have to get out of this place as soon as possible. If I stay here, I'll lose my sanity completely. I'll start talking to Barbara all the time without realizing it, or I'll howl at the moon, or who knows what.

If that hopeful conversation with Barbara wasn't true, then the phone call from Danny must not have happened, either. I really wish he had called. I'd give anything to be able to get on a train and travel out to L.A. That would teach them all a lesson about what I still can do.

I'll give my girls a few more days to get me out of here, and then if they don't, I'm going to pick up the phone while nobody's here, call a taxi, and walk out of here on my own. I'm finished with being treated like a child.

I've made one other decision, too. When I get out of here, I'm going to call Donna and Danny and come to terms with them before I die. I've kept my agreement with Vonnie for almost fifty years, but that solution is not going to work anymore. My wife would tear my head off if she heard me say this, but I have a feeling God won't release me from this life until I make peace with my other children. I won't go behind Vonnie's back, but I'll do whatever it takes to convince her it's the right thing. I wish I could have gotten out of this mess more easily, but I know now that this is the one big thing I have left to do.

11

JACKIE: THE MINUTE I TURN MY BACK

I should have known that if I left town for even a few days, I'd find a mess when I came back. As soon as we got home from our little vacation, I tried calling Pam, but she wasn't there, so I made the mistake of trying Carolyn next. She was practically hysterical. That shouldn't surprise me after all these years, but when I get away from it for a while, I sometimes let my guard down and forget what my family is really like. This time she was on the warpath against *me*.

"Where have you been?" she shrieked in response to my "Hi, Carolyn, how's it going?"

"It's nice to talk to you, too," I said.

"Why didn't you leave a number where we could reach you? Don't you know how bad off Dad is? He could have died and been buried in the two weeks you've been gone, and how could we have gotten ahold of you?"

"Now wait a minute. I was gone nine days, if you want to tell the truth about it, and my neighbor Jessica knew where I was, because she was watching the house, and Pam knows her and could have called her if Dad had died. So don't—"

"Pam did not know how to reach you! How was she supposed to know to call your neighbor? You didn't tell us where you were going or when you'd be back."

"I did so! Pam knew where I was. Did she tell you she didn't know? I gave her the exact dates, and now I'm back just like I said I would be. Can I not even take a little vacation without being screamed at the minute I get home? And you wonder why I didn't leave a number? You really think I want to listen to this yelling the few days a year I get away from this family?"

Carolyn didn't answer. She just breathed these little angry puffs into the phone. She must have been saving up that tirade against me for days.

I said, "So I assume Dad *didn't* die, right?"

"No thanks to you."

"Forget it," I said. "I don't have to listen to this. I'll just wait and talk to Pam. Bye."

"Don't you dare hang up on me!" she wailed. She had caught her breath again and was back on the rampage. "Do you expect me and Pam to take care of all this with Mom and Dad by ourselves?"

That did it. Now she was making *me* hysterical. I wanted to reach my arm through that phone line and strangle her fat neck. The only thing that saved her life in that moment was that she wasn't within striking distance.

"What do you mean 'by ourselves'?" I said. "What have you ever done to resolve the situation? Have *you* arranged for a place for Dad to go? Have *you* ever made a single phone call to a doctor or hospital or rehab unit or assisted-living facility or nursing home or anywhere else on Dad's behalf?"

"Well, for your information, he's not going to any of those places. Dad's going home tomorrow."

"You mean *home* home?" I asked, too surprised to believe it.

"Of course 'home home,' " she said, sarcastically. "What other home is there?"

I was hoping she meant one of those retirement homes or something like that. "No," I said, "Dad is not going back to his house."

"Yes he is."

"Well, what lamebrain came up with that idea?"

"The rehab people say they can't do anything else for him, and we don't have anywhere else for him to go, so he has to go home."

"I thought Pam had a place almost arranged. Where her friend's mother lived. Wasn't she going to take Mom on a tour and then—"

"Mom wouldn't go."

"Why not?"

"At first she said she would, and Pam had everything set up, but then at the last minute Mom canceled—said she was perfectly capable of taking care of Dad at home and had no intention of moving into some old folks' home where there'd be nothing to look forward to except death."

I sighed. "I should never have left town."

"That's right," she shot back.

"Well, excuse me for trying to take a few days to live my own life! I didn't know that was a crime. So is Dad any better?"

"A little. Not much."

"Can he walk at all?"

"Sort of. He still doesn't cooperate with the physical therapists too well. He hates the walker, would rather hobble along holding on to the walls and stuff."

"He'll kill himself within a week."

"It's Mom I'm worried about. I keep picturing him falling on top of her and crushing her to death. Plus he's still incontinent, so he'll be making a mess all over the house."

"How can his doctor let him go?"

"I don't know. Dad's determined to do it, and I guess there's not much way to stop someone unless they're just—you know, really off their rocker or whatever."

"And he's not?"

She didn't answer.

"This whole family's crazy if you ask me," I said.

"Well, you're part of it. So therefore—"

"How's he getting home?"

"I'm taking off work tomorrow afternoon, and Pam got a baby-sitter for the kids, so we're gonna take him. We could use your help."

"I have to work."

"Well."

"It's my first day back!"

"Go to work, then," she said. "We can manage." She wasn't saying this in a nice way, as in, "I understand your problem, so don't worry about it." She was saying it like, "Oh, sure, you've just taken a long, exotic vacation, and even when you get back, you can't be bothered to take a few hours to give your family the least bit of help. Go ahead and work instead of pulling your share of the burden. We martyrs will be happy to cover for our lazy, selfish sister."

"What time are you taking him?" I asked.

"We're meeting there at three."

"I'm supposed to go in at four," I said. "Maybe I can call and see if I could go in an hour or two later. But that won't look too good since I'm just coming off vacation."

"Do what you have to do," she droned, but I knew that if I wasn't there the next day, I'd never hear the end of it.

I did call and get my hours adjusted for the next day, but my manager, Lucy, milked it for all it was worth. She hemmed and hawed and made it sound like they'd practically have to shut the place down (I work at Wal-Mart) if I wasn't there for those two hours. I was tempted to ask her how the store survived without me for the nine days I was off, but I figured, since I was asking her for a favor, now was not the time to be a smart aleck. So I let her make a big production of it, and finally she said yes. I know she'll expect me to remember this someday soon when she calls at the last minute to have me fill in for somebody. So be it. I could use the money after all we spent in Florida.

When I got to the rehab unit, Dad was sitting on his bed fully dressed and wearing a jacket even though it was hot outside. He reminded me of a little boy waiting to go to his first day of school.

He was in a pretty good mood when I first started talking to him, but he had the idea that I had visited him the night before. I didn't bother trying to tell him that I hadn't seen him in almost two weeks. Unless it's crucial information, I no longer expend the time and energy to challenge these bizarre ideas he gets. Once Pam and Carolyn got there and the staff got him ready for release, he was pretty agitated, and he kept barking out nonsensical orders, like, "Just bring my car around front. I can drive it if you just help me in there."

"You don't even have a car anymore, Dad," I said.

He stared at me as if I was trying to pull some trick on him, and then he got quiet, apparently remembering that he can no longer drive. His memory is so bad that he repeats even sensible requests so many times that you want to scream. In the half hour before we left, he reminded us at least five times, "Now, don't forget my suitcase in the closet. It's got my new pants in it." He used exactly the same words each time he said it. You could tell he wasn't meaning to nag, but each time he thought it was the first time he said it. Finally I put the suitcase right next to him so that he'd quit worrying about it.

Getting him into the wheelchair and out to the car wasn't so bad because we had some of the staff there to help us. But when we got home, it was another story. For some reason related to the stroke, Dad tends to puke sometimes when he moves around too much, so he had one of his accidents on the way home. We had him in the front seat of Pam's car, and fortunately she was prepared. She had put an empty popcorn bucket in his lap, and he let loose in that, dribbling only a little on himself. I won't even talk about the smell. It was a sad sight, and I know that Dad, even in his confusion, is totally embarrassed by things like that.

Then when we finally got him home, we had a terrible time getting him out of the car. You wouldn't think this would be so difficult, but he couldn't seem to swing his feet out the door and onto the driveway so that we could lift him a little to get him in the wheelchair. Pam had parked a little too close to the hedges on that side, so it was hard for me to reach in and take Dad's feet and swing them around to where they needed to be. And, of course, he wasn't helping the situation, yelling for me to leave him alone and let him do it himself.

Once we finally got his feet into position, we had to lift him up, which was about as easy as lifting up the entire car. It must have been a comical sight, with Pam pushing him from inside the car, Carolyn and I tugging on both of his arms from the outside, and Dad yelling and complaining the whole time. Mom had to be out there fussing around, too, of course, and we about knocked her down two or three times.

Finally he was in the wheelchair, and we were all sweating like pigs. I had to take a little break before we did the next part, and Dad never stopped chattering the whole time. "This wheelchair's a waste of time," he said. "It's just gonna make it harder to get me into the house. Why don't you let me just walk up there? Stand on either side of me and I'll be fine."

"Sure, Dad," I said, "and after that, why don't we all just jog around the block together?"

It was not the time for sarcasm. A look of panic flashed on Dad's face, as if for a second he thought he really *would* be expected to jog.

The next challenge was the step up into their enclosed porch. It's only one step, and I've been going up it and down it my whole life without ever giving it a thought, but I never realized it is really quite high. I thought we'd be able to kind of lean the back wheels of the wheelchair against it and push/pull Dad up without any problem, but the stupid thing just would not go. We'd get him lifted up a couple inches, and then the chair would slide right back down. We thought about standing him up and letting him climb the step on his own legs, but that option carried its own hazards. Finally Carolyn and I lifted the chair from the sides while Pam pulled with the handles in back. Accompanied by a chorus of Mom and Dad's nonstop commentary, we finally made it.

That left only one more step to get over. This one was from the porch into the living room, and it was only half the height of the first one. Unfortunately, in all this commotion, Dad had peed his pants. The wheelchair was all wet, he was all wet, and he was yelling at us to get him into the bathroom. Pam had tried to get him to put on one of those diaper things before he left the rehab place, but he had refused. Her mistake was to have actually used the word "diaper" when she suggested it. It's too humiliating for him to consider wearing one of those unless you call it something else, like "one of those pads." We were going as fast as we could and couldn't do anything else to rush him to the bathroom, which it turned out he didn't need to use anymore anyway. We sent Mom off for some other pants and some things to clean him up with, which at least got her out of our hair for a few minutes.

Finally we got him up the step and over by the recliner. Then he actually made us leave the room while Mom helped him clean up and get his pants changed. That was fine with me. I was exhausted and headed toward the kitchen to get something to drink. Pam and Carolyn followed. As we drank some ice water, I told Pam, "We're gonna have to get Cliff and Tony to help us if we have to take him out of this house again. I'll have a stroke myself if I keep doing this."

Her face looked drained and sweaty. She opened her mouth to say something, but then she started to laugh. She leaned against the kitchen counter and let the laughter pour out of her.

"What's the matter?" I said.

"Oh, I don't know. The three of us in here together. For some reason I was thinking about that time when we were teenagers and Mom made us do the dishes and you knocked that big pot of chili all over the floor."

"Well, you didn't think it was so funny at the time."

"What made you spill that, anyway?"

"I thought it was empty, so without really looking at it I tried to lift it with one hand, but it was so heavy it slipped out of my hand and onto the floor. Crash! And then there was a whole big blob of chili oozing across the tile."

"And I remember you begged us not to tell, so when Mom yelled in to ask what was wrong, you said you dropped a pan but nothing spilled, and then we frantically scooped up all that chili and stuck it back in the pot."

"Yeah, and we had Carolyn make sounds that would make Mom think we were still doing the dishes like normal. We had her run the water and rattle things around while we scooped chili."

"Mom never did find out about that, did she?"

"I never told her."

"And we ended up eating the rest of that chili, too, didn't we?"

"Yep. I was scared to death she'd find some dirt in it from the kitchen floor, but she never knew the difference."

"We should tell her about it sometime. She might think it's funny now."

"Well, maybe, but not today."

"No. Getting Dad settled is plenty for one day. I'm hoping he won't need to leave the house much now, except for doctor's appointments. And haircuts. He's so picky about his hair now for some reason."

Carolyn said, "Maybe we could get someone to come in here and cut his hair."

"When's his next doctor appointment?" I asked.

"He doesn't have one scheduled," said Pam. "I haven't told you yet, but the lady at rehab has arranged for a visiting nurse to come in and check on him at least three days a week. She said Medicare will pay for it, so at least he'll get that amount of care."

"That's good," I said, "but I still don't see how they're going to make it."

"Neither do I," said Pam, "but what choice do we have?"

Carolyn said, "I'll try to come over on most of the days when the nurse doesn't come. I can bring some food on those days, and the rehab lady said they might be able to get Meals on Wheels, which would give them a hot meal for lunch."

"I talked to Mom about that," said Pam, "and she doesn't want it."

"Why not?" I asked.

"She said she can fix Dad's meals herself. She doesn't want all these strangers running in and out of her house every day."

I shook my head and groaned. "Well, she doesn't mind making *us* run around all the time doing things for her. If she's going to insist on staying here, she should at least take advantage of the help that's available. You should tell her that, Carolyn. You should tell her that you won't bring over any more food unless she at least helps you out by accepting Meals on Wheels for one meal a day."

Carolyn just shrugged, which I took to mean that, as usual, she had no intention of standing up to Mom.

"I have to get to work," I said. "Let's get him in the recliner."

"I don't think they're done yet," said Carolyn. "Mom said she'd yell when she was ready."

"Well, I don't have time for this. My shift will be over with and I'll have been fired before she manages to get those pants on him. Now let's go."

"We can get him in the recliner without you," said Carolyn. "Why don't you just go on out the back?"

"I'm not going out the back," I said. "This is ridiculous." I walked back into the living room, and Dad had his pants around his ankles and was trying to stand up so that he could put them the rest of the way on. Pam and Carolyn followed me in there, and we got the pants on him and plopped him into the recliner.

You should have seen how pitiful all of them looked once I started to leave. Dad was panting as if he'd die any minute, even though all he had done was put his pants on. Mom was sprawled kind of sideways on the couch, breathing heavily and moving her mouth in this kind of old-lady chewing motion that she's been doing a lot lately, and Pam and Carolyn, sweaty and exhausted, looked like rag dolls that had been tossed onto the love seat. All the windows and curtains were closed, which is how Mom keeps it most of the time unless you just insist that she let some light and air in. I was happy to be leaving for work.

I said to Pam, "What kind of rehab place was that, anyway, to think that this man is cured enough to go home?"

"The lady told me they don't keep them until they cure

them. They just keep them until they've made all the progress that they can reasonably be expected to."

"Well, I wish I could get away with those kinds of excuses where I work. Speaking of which, I won't even have a job anymore if I don't get out of here. Bye, everybody."

The two zombies on the love seat groaned, Mom waved her hand, and Dad didn't say anything. With my family, you don't exactly get a hug and kiss.

12 VONNIE:
MIGHT AS WELL GET IT OVER WITH

My legs are killing me. They've been swollen for several days, and on the day before Hugh left rehab, one of his nurses noticed them and told me I should go see a doctor.

"I see doctors all the time, honey," I told her. "I take even more medications than my husband does, and they don't do me a bit of good."

"Do you have shortness of breath?" she asked.

"Yes, and about a hundred other problems I could tell you about. You don't want to get me started on that. You'd never get to your other patients."

"Well, when the doctor comes to check on your husband, you have him look you over, too. You hear me?"

"All right," I said, but I had no intention of telling him a thing. I'm afraid something really is wrong with me—I feel so deadly tired in addition to all my other troubles—but now is not the time to complain about it.

My first goal was to get Hugh home, and now I've done that.

My next goal is to keep him here. If I had told the doctor I was sick and he had put me in the hospital, that would have been the end of Hugh's chances of coming home. The girls would have used that as a perfect excuse to put him away somewhere. Even now, if I end up hospitalized, it's hard to tell what kinds of tricks the girls will play. Hugh will likely not be here when I get back.

So I'll stay strong for my husband. Whatever years (or months or weeks or days) we have left, I want to spend them in this house. I have prayed to God to at least let me have that. I don't care what happens to me anymore. If Hugh died, I wouldn't care if I died the very next day, just so I could do it in this house. I want to be here with him to see that he concludes his life with at least a shred of dignity.

I made a big decision a few days after Hugh came home. I decided I was going to go ahead and contact his daughter, Donna, myself. Carolyn and Jackie made me realize I have to do this, even though that was the opposite of their intention. They had stopped bugging me about this topic toward the end of when Hugh was in rehab, and I was hoping they had decided to let it slide until we were ready to deal with it, but the day after Hugh was released, Carolyn was over here badgering me about it again. "I don't ever want to pressure you about this, Mom," she began, and then she started pressuring me. I derailed her by telling her how sick I was and by trying to convince her she was just about to push me over the edge. She stormed off in a huff.

That's the kind of sympathy I get from my children. They think I make up all my health problems just so I'll have an excuse to not do the idiotic things they want me to do. One of these days I'll really die, and then we'll see how that changes their tune.

The day after my run-in with Carolyn, I overheard Hugh talking on the phone with Jackie, and I had the feeling he was trying to hem-haw around with her about the same issue. When he hung up and I asked him what they'd been talking about, he said, "Oh, nothing much in particular," and then I knew practically for a fact that she had been asking about those other kids.

I don't know whether Carolyn and Jackie are conspiring together on this or whether they're working against each other. It's curious that Carolyn seems to talk only to me about it and Jackie only picks on her father. I don't know where Pam stands on this. She's never said a word about it, and I'm grateful for that, at least. But after seeing all this maneuvering to find things out about Donna and Danny, I decided it would be better for me to take control of the situation. If my daughters went behind my back and called Donna without telling me, who knows what kind of commotion they could cause.

My thinking was that if I talked to Donna and found out what she really wanted, then I could take care of it without having to involve the rest of the family. For instance, I thought if this was one of those situations where she wanted to meet her father just one time out of curiosity, for "closure" or whatever other kind of nonsense they talk about on the TV talk shows, then I could invite her down here, she could have her meeting, and that would be the end of it. I could politely ask her not to bother us or our children anymore, and then we would simply refuse to discuss it ever again with the girls.

First I had to talk to Hugh about it, which I dreaded, not because I thought he would go against my plan, but simply because this whole topic floods my whole system with this nauseating sense of doom. I waited until morning, when Hugh's mind is clearest, and I told him I thought it would be best for us to call Donna and have a private meeting with her before the girls somehow got in touch with her. He didn't say much about it but kept nodding and pursing his lips as if he was trying to come to a decision.

"What do you think?" I asked him.

"All right," he said softly. "If that's what you want to do."

I was hoping for a response that was not quite so passive, but these days I'm just relieved when he can follow my train of thought at all. I also hoped he would remember our conversation for more than five minutes and that he wouldn't suddenly change his mind an hour later or a day later.

"I'll need to get her phone number," I said. "Can you tell me where the letter is?"

"What letter?" he asked, and that got me worried. If he had lost that letter, then I had worked up all this courage for nothing, and it was anyone's guess how this thing would end up.

"The letter Donna sent you several months ago."

"Oh, yeah," he said, and then he looked back toward the TV, as if he thought I had been asking him merely to *remember* the letter rather than to help me locate it.

"Do you know where it is?"

"Wherever you put it, I guess," he said, his stock response whenever some little thing is missing around the house. Then his face took on that murky expression that means he knows he should know something but can't quite bring it to mind.

"I haven't had the letter, hon," I gently reminded him. "You put it somewhere, and I need to look at it to get her phone number. Otherwise how can I call her? Did you put it in the desk with some of your papers?"

"There's no tellin'," he said distractedly, as if he had already started thinking about something else.

"Hugh—"

"Let me think about it!" he barked. Then, quieter, he added, "It'll come back to me. It's been a while."

"All right," I said. "Just as soon as you remember, you tell me, and I'll call her."

It took him an entire day to remember where that letter was, and that was after several reminders. Before he finally told me where it was, part of me had started hoping he would never remember so I could forget this whole plan. I was getting nervous about it. Maybe I would die before the girls dug up anything else, and then I'd never have to deal with this. But I didn't want that, either. Part of the reason I wanted to call Donna was that if I pass away before Hugh does, I don't want him to have to face this alone.

Anyhow, he did remember and he told me where the letter was—in the VCR manual, of all places. It makes me wonder where he hides other things. So I went and read it again and had that same sick feeling that it gave me the first time. I put it away in my own little hiding place, in this old Kleenex box way in the back of the cabinet underneath the bathroom sink, and I decided to wait another day before I did anything. That was a rough night. I had pains all over, especially in my legs, and I couldn't sleep, and it felt like I was suffocating, too. Also, Hugh was jabbering some nonsense that night and was feeling lousy and had an accident on the floor that I had to clean up.

The next morning I felt brave again, and while Hugh was dozing I decided to quit making excuses and just pick up the phone and get it over with. So I dialed the number, not even giving myself any more time to plan my words, and I heard one ring, then two, then three, and I was about to hang up when I heard, "Hello." It was Donna. I had no way of being *certain* that it was her, but something inside me knew it was her voice.

I absolutely could not move a muscle. That may sound like an excuse, but I'm telling you that even if my life depended on it, I could not have let out a squeak, let alone formed words and sentences. For a second I thought how bizarre it would be if I stopped breathing and died right there on the line with her.

Donna said hello again, and this time I was able to open my mouth to speak. Nothing came out. I heard her put the receiver down, and finally I managed to hang up my phone and stagger over to my chair. *Why have you placed this burden on me, God? I* prayed. *Why now, when I'm at death's door? Why couldn't I be allowed to peacefully fade away? Is it so important to you that I be punished?*

As I was sitting there feeling sorry for myself and trying to catch my breath, the phone rang. It startled me so much I let out a little yelp, which woke up Hugh in the next room (the ringing phone itself doesn't even faze him). I immediately suspected that Donna must have one of those phone services where you can punch in a couple numbers to call someone back if they've hung up on you. Hugh and I have talked about getting that ourselves, because whenever anybody hangs up on me, I always spend the rest of the day trying to guess who it must have been.

I let the phone ring a few times, but my little whoop had startled Hugh so much that he was bellowing, "Vonnie! Are you all right? Do you need me to come in there?"

So I couldn't very well let the thing ring and ring without having him get up and try to come and rescue me and probably fall on his face in the process. And if her phone had my number, she'd probably keep trying until I eventually answered. I know that's what I'd do. So I yelled in to Hugh that I was fine, and then I picked up the phone.

It was Carolyn. I could have wrung her neck.

"What's the matter with you?" she said. "You sound funny."

"I've been busy taking care of your father. What do you want?"

She didn't want much of anything, from what I recall. Not that I was paying much attention to what she said. I was too rattled.

Anyway, I managed to have some kind of forgettable conversation with Carolyn, and then I hung up and went back to my chair to recuperate for a while. I certainly couldn't call Donna back. If I did, she would suspect that I was the one who had hung up on her, and what kind of fool would I look like then? She doesn't hear from us for forty-five years and then I hang up on her?

I wasn't able to work up the courage to try again until that night, after I got Hugh settled. Hugh can stumble around the house a little bit now, as long as he either has me or a wall or both to hang on to. He should practice walking more than he does, but I'm tired of nagging him about it. In order to reduce the number of steps, we have him eat meals at his recliner, and he sleeps there most nights, too. So I mainly have to help him get back and forth to the bathroom. He fell once, and we both strained and groaned for almost an hour before we got him back on his feet. Even when he's doing his best, I have to keep reminding him not to lean too heavily on me because I just can't take the weight.

So after his final trip to the bathroom for the night, I went into the bedroom as if I was going to bed, and I made the phone call. This time when Donna answered, I heard myself ask, "Is this Donna?" It really did feel like someone other than me was starting this conversation. I felt like I was standing there waiting to find out what this other me would say next. I was so nervous I thought the receiver would break beneath my grip.

"Yes," said Donna. "Who's calling?"

She said it kind of short, like she expected I might be selling something. I would have suspected the same thing.

"My name is Vonnie," I said. "I'm Hugh Morris's wife."

I had to say "Hugh Morris." I couldn't bring myself to say "your father."

"Well, for heaven's sake," she said. I couldn't quite figure out her tone—there were several emotions mixed up in it—but she sounded mostly friendly.

"We got your letter," I said, and then I felt stuck. Where should I begin? Should I try to explain why we hadn't called her for all these months? How could I even sum it up?

"Good. Good," she said, and I could tell she was just as nervous about this as I was. "So. How are you and Hugh doing?"

I appreciated her letting me off the hook like that, not making me explain why we were just now getting around to calling her. "Well, we're not doing well. Your . . . Hugh . . . had a stroke right after we got your letter—the letter had nothing to do with the stroke, of course—and with one thing and another, we had to set everything else aside and try to get him better."

"Oh, I'm so sorry to hear that. So is he better now?"

"No, I'm afraid to say he isn't. A few weeks ago he had another stroke—two, actually, one right after the other—so he was in the hospital and in rehab, and now he's back at home. But he doesn't walk too well, and he's awful forgetful, and he has other kinds of troubles." I wasn't about to say, "And he's also incontinent and tends to poop and pee at the most inconvenient times and places." Hugh would never have forgiven me if I had embarrassed him by giving out too many details.

Donna said, "Well, I imagine you must keep pretty busy taking care of him. How are you holding up?"

"Honey, you don't even want to hear about all my troubles. I'm a wreck, if you want to know the truth."

She laughed and said, "I'll bet you aren't. Well, it's awfully nice of you to call. After I sent the letter, I wondered—"

"Yes, I know that. . . . Well, it's been a difficult situation, and . . . I don't know . . . things that happened so many years ago are sometimes hard to . . . Well, you know people do the best they can given the circumstances, and years ago things were different."

I was well aware that I wasn't speaking coherently, but it's hard to boil everything down to a simple explanation.

"Oh, I know," she said. "When my mother first told me all about Hugh and the whole situation back then"—I clenched my teeth at the mention of Barbara—"she kept telling me, 'You can't think about this the way it looks now. You have to think about it the way things were then. It was different.'"

"Well, she's right about that," I said, surprising myself by agreeing with any comment my husband's first wife had made.

"So I'm not really expecting . . . I guess what I really wanted was simply to get to meet the man who fathered me. I'm not really expecting to resolve more than forty years' worth of questions."

"Well, Hugh would like to meet you," I said, hoping to find my way to the solid ground of the here and now. "I'm calling because I wanted to invite you to come here and see him. Especially considering the shape he's in now. Because none of us can predict the future."

"That would be absolutely lovely," she said. "I would love to come and visit."

"And your brother, Danny, is welcome, too," I said, "if he's able to come to Indiana. And, of course, your children? And your husband? Hugh wondered whether you were married and had kids and what they must be like."

"Well, I am married, and we have two children," she said, and then she starting telling me about each of them, how old they were, what grade they were in, what they liked to do, and all that. And she told me all about her husband. I had trouble hearing her some of the time, but I caught most of what she said. I felt like writing some of it down, because I knew Hugh would want to know, but I figured she could tell him herself. Before long, to my surprise, I was no longer nervous talking to Donna. I had built up such a dread of her that I expected her to be more . . . I don't know what, exactly, but certainly not so friendly. After she told me about her family, she asked me about mine, and before I knew it we had been talking for almost forty-five minutes.

Before she said good-bye she told me Danny was still in California, but that he had decided to move to Indiana. "I think he'll be here in about three weeks," she said. "I'd really like us to be able to come together to meet Hugh, but would you mind if I waited that long?"

I felt like saying, "After all these decades, do you really think three more weeks is going to be too long to wait?" But all I said was, "Three weeks is fine. We'll be here."

"Great," she said. "I'll call you before that to work out the details."

I can't even tell you the amount of relief I felt once this call was over. For the first time since we got Donna's letter all those many months ago, I had the feeling that everything might work out all right. Now if I can only keep the girls off my back long enough to have this meeting in private and then get our lives back to normal. There's no reason why the girls need to know that Donna and Danny are coming, and I have to find a way to make Hugh keep his big trap shut about it.

I'll need to try to get the house clean before they come, which these days is a minor miracle. And I'll have to plan it on a day when those nurses aren't scheduled to be here, if we haven't gotten rid of them altogether by then. The girls think I should be so happy to have those nurses to "help" me, but I feel they're more like spies than helpers. I know they call Pam the moment they leave here and report everything to her as if all they were hired to do is gossip. They tell her all kinds of things that are none of their business, like how messy the house is, and how Hugh had accidents on the floor that I haven't cleaned up very well, and how they think we shouldn't be living on our own anymore. Who asked them!

One day I told that big nurse flat out that I didn't appreciate her calling and blabbing everything to my daughter, but she just smiled at me like I was a two-year-old who was not quite bright enough to understand the ways of adults. I try to hide everything I can from her and get her out of here as fast as I can on the days she comes, but for her, even fifteen minutes would be long enough to fill her notebook full of horror stories for Pam. And I don't think she does Hugh a bit of good medically.

The next battle I've got on my hands is to keep Carolyn and Pam from sending those Meals on Wheels people here. That's about the last thing I need—more strangers traipsing through here to spy for my daughters. I don't care what the girls say. I'm drawing the line there. I may be a broken-down old bag of bones, but let me tell you, I can still cook.

13 DANNY:
St. Louis Blues

It was exactly four weeks ago today that I bought the car from Pete. Now I'm sitting in a stuffy room at a Ramada Inn near St. Louis feeling like a fool for ever leaving L.A.

Not that these doubts will keep me from pushing on to Indianapolis tomorrow. My feelings have fluctuated wildly during this trip. At certain moments I've felt this wild hope that this move will be the turning point I've been waiting for, when I'll finally be able to shake free of the past and put together a life I'll be proud of. At other times I've been near despair at the thought that running is futile and that by fleeing to Indiana I'm throwing away whatever slim chance I had of establishing a happy post-divorce life in Southern California.

Right now part of the problem is the atmosphere. Even though I've got the air-conditioner on, the air is sticky with humidity. It's nothing unusual for the Midwest in the summertime, but I'm not used to it anymore. It's stifling, as if somebody's trying to suffocate me or slowly stew me. I look out my third-story window onto a parking lot. The gray sky occasionally spits out little bursts of lethargic rain, as if even the weather can't work up enough energy to provide a refreshing storm.

It's early evening, the loneliest time of day for me on the road, the time when I picture "normal" people with families sitting down to dinner, or playing with the kids, or reading the newspaper, or watering the lawn and chatting with the neighbors. I sit alone next to my suitcase in a sterile room with artless prints on the wall. An unwatched TV, which I keep on solely for the purpose of hearing human voices, blares behind me.

I realize that I chose this trip for myself and have no one else to blame. And it hasn't been all bad. My favorite part was the first several days, out West, driving across the desert. As I looked out onto the cactus plants and the endless sand and rocks, and as I stood at the isolated rest stops and felt the heat of the sun baking down on me, I felt like an adventurer. I was leaving my easy life in civilization and heading out for new territory, like some fearless cowboy in an old western.

But then, as I worked my way farther east and the landscape got more tame and green, with more towns and billboards and fast-food restaurants, my mood shifted. I was no longer Indiana Jones. I was a failure slinking back to my midwestern boyhood home after flopping in California.

I didn't have much time to plan this move. I gave my two-weeks notice on my job just three days after I bought the car. Pete said, "I never would have sold you this car if I'd known it would make you quit."

But he didn't try hard to stop me. He knows the ship is sinking. The closer it got to my actually leaving, the more envious he sounded. When he walked by my desk and saw all my maps and tour books from the auto club, he picked them up and looked through them as if he were planning to go with me. He traced his finger across the whole route I was planning to take across the country.

My department threw a little farewell party for me at lunchtime on my last day, gave me a Cross pen as a parting gift, and then I was out of a job again, adrift, heading into the unknown.

The manager of my apartment building let me have a little moving sale on the front lawn of the complex, and people started showing up at six on a Saturday morning to buy up my sorry collection of furniture and old clothes. What little remained I eventually crammed into a little storage unit and gave a key to my friend Jeff, who said he'd be happy to arrange to have it all sent out to me in Indiana whenever I wanted it. In a way it doesn't make any sense to leave anything behind, but I think of it as my little foothold in L.A. If things don't work out at Donna's, I still have this tiny bit of California space that is my own. I still have "my stuff" to return to.

Even though I haven't even made it to Indianapolis yet, I've already messed up Donna's plans. She made contact with our "other family," and my "father" and his wife want to see us. Donna oh-so-kindly refused to meet them without me. I've been on the road for ten days, which is almost twice as long as I thought the trip would take, so we've already missed our appointment with them. I guess "Dad" might as well know from the start that I'm the irresponsible son he never raised. When I talked to Donna on the phone, I tried my best to talk her into going to see them without me, but she refused.

Last time I talked to her, she said the whole thing had taken a "weird turn," but she wouldn't explain what that meant. It's already weird enough if you ask me, so I can't imagine what else could have happened. She said she'd schedule another meeting, but I don't like this whole thing. I may not even go. Donna will kill me if I back out, but I have a choice between facing her anger and facing the intense embarrassment I'd feel if I had to go to these people's home to meet them. I imagine them looking me over and telling me how much I look like "Dad" or Uncle

So-and-So or like one of my "sisters," who will probably be there, too. I don't know if I can stand it.

One reason I'm so late getting out here is that I got stuck at the Grand Canyon. On my first day out of L.A., I drove to Flagstaff, Arizona, found a motel, and planned to spend a few hours the next morning at the Grand Canyon before driving on about midday. It was a stupid plan. You can't spend just a few hours at the Grand Canyon. Some people could, I suppose, but I think that even people who are a lot more schedule driven than I am would have trouble simply glancing at that magnificent place and then speeding off.

I had never been there before, and even though I've known for a long time, like most people, that it's one of the most beautiful places on earth, I had no idea it would have such an impact on me. I had thought that seeing it for a few hours would pretty much give me the essence of it and that looking at it any longer than that would simply be more of the same. But I found myself mesmerized by the intricacy of the formations of the cliffs and crevices and fascinated by the colors and the movement of light and shadows on the rocks. On that first day I hiked the trails along the South Rim like a madman, wanting to see as much as I could as fast as I could. The changing sunlight made the canyon look different every hour of the day, so I quickly abandoned my plan to leave that day and decided instead to stay until the light had disappeared from the horizon.

I had already checked out of my motel room that morning, so I drove back down the road to Flagstaff that night with nowhere to stay. The whole region was packed with tourists, and it took me a few hours to finally find a vacancy in an overpriced, broken-down motel way outside of town. I booked the room for two nights, which was the longest time that even that junky place would give me.

On my second day at the canyon, I slowed down a little,

picking one spot for a couple hours at a time and soaking in every detail my eyes could pick up. *This is why I made this journey,* I thought as I stood in the midst of all that beauty. *This is why I quit my job and left Los Angeles. No matter what happens after this, at least I've had this moment.* The day flew by in what seemed like just a few hours, and I reluctantly headed back to the motel.

On the third day I came back and did it all again, and that night I went searching for another motel so that I could extend my stay. I didn't care if I never made it to Indianapolis. I was prepared to stay at the Grand Canyon until all my money was gone and I had only enough gas in the car to get me back to Los Angeles. Problem was, there was no room for miles around. I searched for hours. Finally, after midnight, I got on I–40 and headed toward Gallup, New Mexico. Around three in the morning, not yet to Gallup but so tired I could hardly keep driving, I finally found a motel with a vacancy, so I took the room and slept there until noon that day. When I woke up, I realized how foolish it would be to drive all the way back to the canyon for just a few hours of daylight before I'd have to start another search for a place to stay. Reluctantly, I got in the car and headed east.

I moved along pretty swiftly (for me) for the next couple days, and then I got stuck again in Oklahoma City. This wouldn't make any sense for most people, but just outside of Oklahoma City, I found the perfect restaurant for sitting and watching people and picking up an occasional conversation. It was a little Chinese restaurant, not exactly the cuisine I would have associated with Oklahoma City. Unlike the Chinese restaurants I'm used to in Los Angeles, which are run by people from China, in this place I saw only one Asian face the whole time I was there. That face belonged to the cook, who, on my second afternoon there, came out from the kitchen and introduced himself, thanking me for my enthusiastic reception of his food.

The owners of the restaurant—A Taste of China—were Dick and Vilma Spalding. When I showed up at lunch that day, thinking I'd grab a quick meal before heading up the road a few hundred more miles, Vilma greeted me at the door. Vilma is a large woman with wide hips, a lumbering walk, big oval eyeglasses with blue plastic frames, and black-and-gray curled hair shaped like the top of a mushroom. She welcomed me as warmly as if she had been waiting all day for me to show up. She led me to my table, told me about the day's specials, and then asked me where I was from. When I told her Los Angeles, she went out back and got Dick. He had a cousin who lived near me, in Anaheim. You would have thought I was a personal emissary from this man, whose name they gave me but who, of course, I didn't know. Dick had visited him (without Vilma, for some reason) in Anaheim once, and he told me all about his impressions of the place and how much he had enjoyed going to Disneyland. In honor of my long journey from California, Dick ordered that a free egg roll be added to my combo plate.

A few minutes later some of the regular customers started arriving, and Vilma introduced me to each one of them. They were mostly older couples and a few old men by themselves. Most of them had some connection to either California or Indianapolis, which they quickly learned was my destination. I had been starved for conversation for so many days that I had a great time talking to these people. They all knew each other and had their own tables where they always sat. They ate their meals slowly and spent most of their energy talking and laughing with each other and with me. Vilma and Dick waited on the tables and acted as hosts. I stayed for nearly three hours before I finally stood up and said that I should hit the road again if I was going to get anywhere that day.

"You should stay in town tonight and look around," said Vilma. "What's your hurry? You said you're already a few days late, so what difference will one more day make? You could come back tomorrow for an early lunch, and we'll get you out of here by one o'clock."

"I'll throw in another egg roll," said Dick.

"I *am* awfully tired of the road right now," I said.

"Sure you are," said Vilma. "What is it, two thousand miles or more that you're traveling? All by yourself, with no help driving? You take the afternoon off, come back tonight for dinner if you want—there's a whole other crowd that shows up then—and find yourself a hotel to rest up in. I know the manager of a place not far from here. She'll give you a good deal."

I decided to stay. Armed with one of Vilma's business cards, I got a discounted room at her friend's hotel, went shopping for a couple books, sat in a park and read for a while, and then came back to A Taste of China for dinner. It was the most enjoyable evening I've had in months, meeting a whole new set of people and talking to a few of the lunch regulars who had also returned.

The next day I checked out of the hotel, spent some time reading, and went to Dick and Vilma's for lunch. As promised, Vilma made sure I was finished by one o'clock. The cook, Benny, came out and shook my hand before I left, and then all the regulars said good-bye and wished me well. Vilma made me promise I'd stop in again if I ever came back to town.

I left Oklahoma City happy, but the trip was pretty lonely after that. Throughout Missouri, my self-doubts and insecurities started popping out all over the place. The car was buzzing with arguments between my ex-wife and Buster Flapjaw.

Terri would screech out things like, *"Running away again, huh? What's your son supposed to think of this? What if you get out there and can't find a job? What if every employer realizes that you've been too irresponsible to ever keep a job? What if they see that you're over the hill? Too old to bother investing in when chances are you'll just quit or retire on them as soon as they get you trained? How long do you think Donna and Phil will put up with you staying with them and sponging off them? Do you think their teenage daughters really want you there? How will they explain you to their friends? What's the point of this move, anyway?"*

That's only a sampling of Terri's harangues. She could go on like that for a long time, but you get the idea. Buster tried to defend me, of course, by pointing out the positives. He said I was taking a bold step toward starting a new life. I'd be surrounded by people who loved me. I'd have new job opportunities. Maybe a new life for Alex if things worked out. Maybe even a new wife.

I know he threw in the part about a new wife just to get Terri riled. As much as she dislikes me, she never could stand the idea that another woman might fall in love with me.

In spite of Terri throwing Alex in my face, I did talk to him about this move. As with so many other things during his teenage years, he was noncommittal. He didn't seem to mind, and he did say he would come out to visit as soon as I could arrange it. As long as Terri doesn't block him. I haven't told Alex about his new "grandparents" yet. Things are complicated enough already. Maybe I'll explain the situation when he gets out here so I can gauge his response in person.

So for the last part of the trip, I've felt pretty restless, and even though I've tried to stop at places and relax and enjoy the trip, I can never get settled down for very long. I'll grab a quick meal or just look around for a while and then feel compelled to hit the road again.

Donna is expecting me for dinner tomorrow night. She already has a job interview set up for me for next week. It's an accounting job at a company that one of her friends at church owns.

I'm not sure that I want another accounting job, to be quite honest, but what else could I do?

The fact is I have big vague Other Plans for my future, but as always, there's a grating, Terri-like voice in my head whispering that all my hopes will turn to ashes.

14 JACKIE:
READY TO LET LOOSE

I know I'll be the bad guy again, but who cares? If I waited on the rest of my namby-pamby family to do anything, we'd all be in trouble.

It started when I went to visit Mom and Dad last week. I hadn't been over there much since he got out of rehab, and it's just as well. Every time I go, it's a miracle I don't end up having a stroke myself.

The reason I went over there was that Pam had called and asked if I would mind staying with Dad while she took Mom to the doctor. Now that we've finally got Dad settled in for the time being, Mom is starting to fall apart. It happened to be my day off, so I told Pam I'd do it.

When I asked Pam on the phone how Mom and Dad were doing, she said, "I think they're discouraged."

"Well, I'm not surprised, considering all that's wrong with them. Wouldn't you be discouraged?"

"I wish we could get back to how it used to be, when we could get together with Mom and Dad and really *talk* to them and have some fun and laugh and joke around. Remember when they used to enjoy the kids and we all actually *wanted* to get together? The other day Mom said she's not even sure we love them anymore."

"Of course we love them! Look at all we do for them. Look at how we arrange our schedules around them. Look at all we put up with from them. Would we put ourselves through all that torment if we didn't love them?"

"That's obligation," she said. "That's not love."

"Well, we can't pretend things are like they used to be. And they probably never will be. I mean, even the simplest conversation is a challenge now, with Dad so confused and forgetful and repetitive and Mom half deaf and—"

"I know, but I hate this feeling that they think we're pitted against them and that we don't really care—"

"We love them! We love them! They know that. We'd like to wring their necks half the time, but our underlying motivation is love!"

So I went to visit them. Out of love, in spite of what Pam says. And I also have to admit that I thought it might be interesting to get Dad alone to see what he might say to me about his son in Los Angeles. We've hit a brick wall on that topic, and my sisters haven't been much help in pressing for information. I was surprised Mom was willing to even let me be in the house alone with Dad. She usually hovers around him like a guardian angel whenever I'm there, afraid of what he might blurt out.

The visit sent my blood pressure skyrocketing from the minute I walked in. Pam was already there, and she and Mom were arguing. Mom was telling her that she had called the home-health company that the nurse works for and told them to either send a different nurse from now on or not to bother sending anyone at all.

"She's nothing but a nosy, gossipy spy," said Mom. "There's

not a thing she does that I can't do better myself."

"Oh, really?" said Pam. "Can you check his blood? Can you check his pulse? When did you get your nursing degree?"

Go, Pam! That sounded more like *my* sarcasm than hers, but I know she's been getting pretty exasperated with Mom's opposition to every attempt we make to help her and Dad.

Mom said, "That woman has only one goal—to get your dad out of this 'unsafe' house. And me, too, while she's at it. That's all I hear about the whole time she's here. I'm fed up with it."

"Mom," said Pam, "don't you realize that if that nurse stops coming, you'll have no help at all? Medicare is paying for this. It's a perfect opportunity for you to get free medical care, and you're going to mess it all up."

"Hello, Jackie. Nice to see you. Thanks for coming over. Would you like to sit down? Could I get you something to drink?"

You might have thought that by this point someone in the room would have acknowledged my presence in some way, with a hello or a wave or at least a nod. No one could be bothered with those little courtesies. Dad was in his recliner in the corner, but I don't know how much he was taking in. Every once in a while he'd kind of groan and say, "Oh, Lord." I don't know if he was really praying to the Lord or whether he was just using the expression. With Dad these days, you can't tell. I have actually seen him praying since this stroke, which I hadn't seen him do for years before that.

"That nurse is very insulting," said Mom. "I can't stand it anymore. She doesn't even think my meals are fit for him to eat. I may not be a genius, but I can still cook for my husband, I assure you."

"That's not what she said at all," said Pam, directing this at me, her first indication that she knew I was in the room. "The nurse called me and told me about the food thing."

"Spy!" Mom blurted out.

"Not a spy. I am his daughter! What she said was that she notices that Dad sometimes has trouble swallowing. That's a side effect of the stroke, because sometimes the stroke weakens the muscles and the patient can't swallow very well. So she gave Mom this powder that she's supposed to add to Dad's liquids to thicken them up so he doesn't choke. That's all it was."

"It's disgusting!" said Mom. "She put it in his coffee while she was here and made this thick, gooey mess of it. Who in their right mind is going to drink something like that?"

"Well, it's better than having him accidentally pour hot coffee down into his lungs because he's too weak to swallow!" said Pam. "That's the danger. If he doesn't swallow right and closes off his . . . windpipe or . . . whatever, he could choke to death if something went down the wrong way. That's how I understood it. It's only temporary, until he gets stronger."

"Your father can drink," said Mom.

"Teresa's a good nurse, and you should listen to what she says. If you want to keep living here on your own, you have to face some realities like Dad's choking and—"

"I *do* plan to keep on living here," interrupted Mom. "And I don't need her permission or anyone else's to do it. Another thing she said that offended me—and I told them this when I called—was this thing about bedsores. She's worried that if your dad stays here, he's gonna get bedsores. As if people in nursing homes don't! It's in places like that where you hear about people getting bedsores, not at home. Your father doesn't have any. He doesn't even lay in bed that often! He's in that recliner all day long."

Pam let out an exasperated sigh and said, "Here we go again. Are you just deliberately misinterpreting her? What she said was—"

"I know what she said!"

"What she said was, she doesn't think Dad is walking around

as much as he should. When he was in rehab, they *made* him walk every day, and the doctor wants him to walk around the house to regain his strength, but Teresa's afraid he's not doing it. And if he doesn't—if he just sits there for hours on end without moving—then there's the danger that his skin will break down and he'll get sores."

"Well, I don't know what I'm supposed to do," said Mom. "If he walks around too much, they're afraid he'll fall and break a hip or something. But if he just sits there, then they say he'll keep getting weaker and lose the ability to walk, plus he'll get bedsores."

"Well," said Pam, and she paused a minute—I knew she was weighing whether she should answer Mom or just keep her mouth shut. "Don't jump all over me, but that's why everybody's been trying to get you to consider moving to an assisted-living apartment or something like that—not a nursing home—so that Dad can get the help he needs."

Mom brushed this comment aside with a wave of her hand. She said, "Now Teresa's bugging me about my own health problems, which she's not even supposed to be worrying about."

"You should be grateful to her," said Pam. "That's partly why we're going to the doctor, isn't it? Do you want her to ignore what she sees and just let you die? She thinks you have symptoms of congestive heart failure. That could kill you."

"I don't have anything of the kind," said Mom. "It's just my legs are always swollen."

I finally jumped into the conversation and said, "Did I come over here just to listen to you two argue?"

They both glanced over at me as if they were surprised I had the ability to speak.

"Don't you have a doctor's appointment to get to?" I asked.

"You all just want me out of the house," said Mom, and I didn't know whether she meant we wanted her out right then for the appointment or whether she was back to this nursing home obsession.

I said, "Well, I'll be happy to turn right around and go home if that's what you want. I have plenty of things I need to do."

"No," said Mom, "I don't want him here by himself."

"Let's go," said Pam, and Mom started her little piddling-around rituals that she always has to go through before she leaves the house. Much of this activity centers on her purse. She gets money from various parts of the house, such as behind picture frames and underneath vases on the fireplace mantel, and wraps it up in envelopes using rubber bands. Then she has separate envelopes wrapped in separate rubber bands for her insurance card and some other medical documents, and then she takes along two or three pill bottles, which of course have to be wrapped together with rubber bands and covered, for some reason, with tissues. She of course can never do any of this before you get there. You have to sit there through the slow torture of watching her do it, and she won't let you help her even though her arthritic fingers can barely manipulate the rubber bands anymore.

Then when the purse is ready, she has to go around checking things. Is the coffeepot off? Are the burners of the stove turned off? Are the lights off in the bedroom? Not that any of this mattered, since Dad and I were going to be there, but we've learned to just let her go through it and not say anything. Fortunately, it's summertime, so we were spared the winter routine of picking out just the right coat and scarf and gloves.

On her way out the door, Mom told me, "Don't pester your dad with a lot of talk. He's pretty tired today. He needs his rest."

"Okay," I said, knowing full well what she was really worried about. I could only guess at the tongue-lashing she must have given him before we got there to try to keep him from blabbing.

As it turned out, I didn't have to push Dad for information.

He led me right where I wanted to go. He leaned back his head and sighed when Mom and Pam left, as if he was relieved not to have to try to pay attention to them anymore. He asked for one of his water bottles, so I brought it to him and sat on the couch across from him.

"Where did your mother go?" he asked, having already forgotten.

"She went to the doctor, Dad," I said. "Don't you remember?"

"Oh, that's right." He rubbed his forehead and furrowed his eyebrows in what had become a familiar sign of confusion. "What are you doing here?"

"I came to visit you."

"Is your mom coming back?"

"Of course! Where else would she go?"

"She's been awful worried lately."

"What about?"

"This whole nursing home thing."

"What do you mean?"

"She thinks you girls are gonna cart us off to a nursing home. I hope Pam doesn't try it."

I laughed and said, "Well, I promise you Pam is only taking her to the doctor. She wouldn't trick her into moving to a nursing home. You think we'd leave you here alone like that?"

"You better not try to trick us. We're not going anywhere!"

His voice was getting edgy, so I wanted to get him off the nursing home subject, which I knew was pointless to discuss. But before I said anything, he said, "Our daughters can't get away with it. Vonnie and I have talked about ways we could prevent them. You can't just sell somebody's house without their permission. I've even thought about asking Donna if she would help us block them."

Since he was talking about his daughters in the third person, I figured he had either forgotten that I was sitting there and was thinking out loud, or else he was confused about who I was.

"Who is Donna?" I asked.

"My daughter," he said.

I laughed and said, "No, Dad, I'm your daughter. My name is Jackie, remember?"

"My other daughter."

"You have two other daughters. Named Pam and Carolyn. Not too sharp today?"

He glared at me with this furious expression, and I was pretty sure he didn't know who he was talking to. He shouted, "I'm talking about my daughter Donna! From years ago."

I would have laughed this off again except that the "from years ago" stopped me cold. My mind reeled with possibilities too amazing for me to accept.

"Now hang on a minute," I said. "You're saying you have a *daughter* named *Donna* from years ago?"

He didn't answer.

"I thought the story was you had a *son* from years ago. A 'businessman from Los Angeles.' What happened to him? Surely his name's not Donna."

"No, his name's not Donna," said Dad, shaking his head as if he were talking to an idiot. "His name's Danny. Donna's his sister, and both of them are coming to visit, and I'm going to see to it that they prevent my daughters from tricking us into selling this place."

I could hardly breathe. A son *and* a daughter. Was it possible? *Could this be another hallucination, like his visions of his mother or his stories that he had been painting all night or laying tile or installing a new sink in the bathroom? I mean, how many other kids could he possibly have?*

"Now listen to me, Dad. I'm tired of all these little hints and stories that don't make any sense. I want to know the truth. You have two children named Donna and Danny, and they're planning to visit you?"

"That's right."

"You've already arranged for them to come out here from Los Angeles?"

"No," he scoffed. "Donna lives in Carmel."

"Carmel? Right here in Carmel, Indiana?"

"Yep. And Danny's moving here."

"Why?"

"What do you mean 'why'?"

"You mean he's coming here just to— He's coming to stop us from doing anything with the house?"

"I don't care what he thinks about the house. We're not selling it."

"When are they coming?"

Dad looked at me for a long time. I waited. There's something about the way his expression changes when I know he recognizes me, and as we sat there, his face lost that hostile expression and took on the look of more calm awareness. He knew who I was again. He looked away and scratched his head.

"I can't tell you when they're coming," he said. "Your mother made me promise I wouldn't."

His news was so stunning that I had to stand up and storm around the living room for a few minutes to try to come to grips with it. "Unbelievable," I whispered over and over. When I glanced over at Dad, he looked distinctly uncomfortable, squirming around in his chair the way he does when he's getting ready to stand up and walk.

"Now wait a second, Dad. When you say that this son— Danny—is moving *here,* do you mean here in this house, or—"

"No, not in this house," he scoffed. "To Indianapolis. He's gonna stay with Donna awhile. They might have us over there for dinner."

"I thought they were visiting you here."

"They might, if we don't feel like going out."

"And they're planning this secret visit to try to prevent us from selling your house—which, by the way, we have no plans to do?"

"This is none of your business. Don't say anything to your mother." His voice was pleading. He was realizing he had spilled the beans and would have to pay the price for it with Mom.

I said, "It certainly is my business if these people are planning to show up here behind our backs to plot against us."

"Nobody's plotting against anybody—unless you and your sisters have something up your sleeve that I don't know about. Now, I don't want to hear any more about this, and I don't want you bothering your mother with it. This is hard enough for her as it is, and she's sicker than people realize. Get me?"

I didn't know whether I'd confront Mom or not. I felt dizzy.

I sat back down, and both of us were silent for a few minutes, too shaken by the gravity of what had been revealed to know how to move forward.

After a while I couldn't stand it any more, so I said, "So are you sure this woman is your *daughter*?"

"Of course I'm sure," he growled.

"Her name is Donna Morris?"

"No, but that doesn't mean anything. Your name isn't Morris anymore, either, but you're still my daughter, aren't you? Danny's last name isn't Morris, either. His mother had their last names changed once . . ."

He trailed off, and I was afraid he would clam up for good. "What was it changed to?" I asked.

"Logan."

"So her name's Donna Logan?"

"No, Pryce," he said. "It's her married name, for heaven's sake. Now will you leave me alone? I'm not going to talk about this, and I don't want you badgering me anymore. Please. Your mother is very sensitive about this, and she'd be mad if she knew I said anything. I can't have you upsetting her. When she comes home—"

"I won't say anything when she comes home," I assured him. He had given me the information I needed for the moment. I knew the woman's name, and I knew where she lived. Before I said anything else to anyone in the family, I intended to track her down and find out what she was up to.

I tried out a few more questions on Dad just to see what he'd say, but he was through talking. I changed the subject to more trivial topics because I wanted him in a good mood when Pam and Mom got back so they wouldn't be suspicious. We started talking about how the Chicago Cubs were doing, which he used to keep track of pretty closely, but before long he veered off into one of his stories about the army that I had heard a hundred times.

As soon as I got home that afternoon, I called Information and asked for Donna's number. With my luck, I figured it would be unlisted, but it wasn't. I wrote down the number and called her right away. The more I had thought about it after talking to Dad, the more worried and mad I had gotten about the whole situation. How dare these people sneak in and try to see our parents behind our backs! And did they really think it was their place to try to prevent us from selling Mom and Dad's house if that's what it came to? Did they expect us to sit back and let them take control of our parents' lives and not say a word?

I also don't like this idea of them coming to get Mom and Dad and taking them to their house in Carmel. They don't realize how frail Dad is. A trip like that could kill him! Not to mention that Mom's not too steady on her feet, either. And now the nurse thinks she might have congestive heart failure and might have to take more medicine—on top of the dozen or so pills she already takes—to get it under control. They're in no condition to be hauled around town, and what's the point of it, anyway?

So when I got this Donna on the phone, I have to admit I wasn't in the friendliest mood.

"This is Jackie Berg," I said.

"Oh, hi," she said, but it was in kind of a fake-friendly tone, like she thought she probably should know who I was but couldn't place me.

"Hugh Morris is my father."

"Oh, *hi*," she said again, and this time the nicey-nice was turned way up. "So you're Jackie. Let's see, you must be the middle . . . no. . . ?"

"I'm the oldest one."

"Well, it's so nice of you to call. I've been wondering when I'd get to meet any of you."

"We've been wondering that, too, but not for very long, since I didn't even find out you existed till today."

"Really? Even after Hugh and Vonnie got my letter, they didn't tell you?"

"What letter?"

"I wrote them last year, six or seven months ago."

"I guess we've been kept in the dark about everything," I said. "That's why I'm calling. Before this thing goes any further, I think we have a right to know who you are and what you're planning to do."

That threw her off for a second. She could tell this wasn't the "long-lost sister gets blubbery and sentimental" call. She let out a surprised laugh and answered, "Well, as far as who I am, I recently found out that Hugh is my father."

"Can you prove that?"

"I don't think he's denying it, dear."

The "dear" made me want to strangle her, but I let it go. I

said, "I'm told that you were planning to secretly visit Mom and Dad."

"No," she denied. "As far as I'm concerned, it's no secret. My brother is driving out from California right now, and Vonnie invited us to come over to her house next Thursday evening. If she hasn't told you that, then you'll have to ask her about it. I'm not doing anything in secret. Danny and I are not trying to cause anyone any problems. I wrote my letter and left it up to your parents to decide whether they wanted to contact us. They did, so now we're going to meet. Do you object to us coming?"

"Well, " I said, "I'm just concerned about how all this is happening behind our backs. We don't even know who you are. I'm forty-five years old, and now suddenly I'm supposed to believe that my father had two other kids before I was born and I never heard about it?"

"I was just as surprised as you are. I don't know why they kept it from us, but I guess they thought it would be—"

"And then I find out you're having this secret meeting and that you also might try to take Mom and Dad out to Carmel, which I think is very dangerous because of their frail health. It's hard enough to get Dad out the door, let alone—"

"Now wait—"

"—let alone haul him clear to Carmel, and Mom, too. So I do object to that. I don't think you realize what bad shape they're in. They can barely survive in that house by themselves. Dad's confused half the time, and he can barely walk, and he has accidents on the way to the bathroom, and all kinds of things. So eventually we'll probably have to face the decision of where they're going to live, and if they move to a retirement home or something, that would involve selling the house. So if you have any idea of trying to block that—"

"Whoa, now. Slow down, please. I think you've got some bad information. I mentioned to Vonnie that we'd be happy to have them visit our house sometime, that's it. It was just a—"

"They can't go. I'm telling you."

Donna got quiet. I know she was getting irritated with me, but at least I was getting through to her. I didn't want to be mean, but I wanted to make it clear that she wasn't dealing only with Mom and Dad, she was dealing with me, too. And I wasn't about to let her waltz in and hatch some scheme.

After a pause, she said, "As far as trying to block them from selling their house or anything like that, I don't have the slightest idea what you're talking about. I've only talked to Vonnie on the phone a couple times, and I promise you nothing of the kind ever came up. Maybe I should talk to her again. If our visit is going to cause trouble, maybe this isn't the time to do it."

"Well, I certainly think that if you come, one of us should be there. No offense, but we don't know you, and our parents are very vulnerable right now, and—"

"I'll talk to Vonnie," she snapped. "I'm sorry you've taken it this way. We only wanted to meet Hugh. I didn't think that was so much to ask, but maybe it won't work out. Thanks for calling. I have to go now. Good-bye."

So that's where we left it. That was two days ago, and I haven't heard from Mom or anybody else yet. I assume that she or Carolyn or Pam will call and try to chew me out for getting involved, but I don't care. I still think this whole thing could be a scam, and if it is, then maybe Mom will eventually understand that I'm stepping in here for her own good. Not that she or my sisters will ever admit that or thank me for my efforts. That's not how they operate.

15

CAROLYN: IF ONLY PEOPLE WOULD LISTEN TO ME

Mom was crying when I got to the house. Not crying hard, but just that silent little cry she sometimes does, with the handkerchief covering most of her face. She had lured me over there without a clear explanation of what had gone wrong.

Our conversation on the phone had been brief. "I should have known I couldn't trust you girls with the truth about Donna and Danny. I should have known you'd stick your noses in and mess everything up."

"What are you talking about?"

"Huh?"

"What are you talking about!" I shouted.

"You mean to tell me you're not part of what Jackie did?"

"No!" I answered, my heart racing with panic. "What did she do?"

"She called Donna and told her off. Now I don't know what's gonna happen. If you had just let me—"

"Mom!" I shouted. "How did Jackie find out about Donna?"

"I assumed you were all in cahoots."

"Wrong! I never said a word to her about Donna. Jackie *called* her? What did she say?"

"Do what?"

"What did she *say*?"

"I don't know exactly. That's what I was calling you to find out. I didn't want to talk to Jackie. I'm mad at her, and I don't feel like putting up with the kind of tongue-lashing she gave Donna. But I guess I'll have to call her if you don't know anything about it."

"No!" I yelled. "Don't call her yet. I'm coming right over. We'll figure out what to do."

Mom's hearing problem is a little easier to deal with in person than on the phone, and she's also less evasive when I'm staring her right in the face. When I got there and finally pried her face out of her handkerchief, I told her I'd make her a cup of tea, which she likes in the evening. Then I led her into the dining room so we could talk without disturbing (or being interrupted by) Dad, who was dozing in his recliner.

When she sat down and I got the water going for the tea, I told her, "Now tell me the whole story, from beginning to end."

"I already told you the whole thing," she said and put the handkerchief back up to her face.

"No you haven't, Mom. Now, I need you to stop crying and talk to me."

I wasn't trying to be mean, but I wasn't completely buying the weepy routine. I think Mom sometimes uses her tears, just like she uses her hearing trouble, to keep people from asking the tough questions.

I said, "Now tell me how Jackie found out about Donna. That makes me mad. I've been trying all this time to find out about her, and here Jackie gets her phone number and calls her!"

"I don't know how she got that number," said Mom. "I think

your dad might have let something slip about Donna—he pretty much admitted that—but he says he didn't give any number. I believe him, too, because I put Donna's letter in a place he doesn't know about so he wouldn't get confused and pull it out and show it to somebody."

"So how did you find out that Jackie told off Donna?"

"Donna called me. I had called her a few weeks ago to see if she and Danny would want to come and meet Hugh alone before—"

"Mom! You promised you'd let me be the first one to contact her! Here I've been waiting patiently all this time—"

"I didn't *promise* anything," said Mom. "I decided to call her myself to prevent the exact situation we find ourselves in right now—misunderstanding and bickering between the two sets of kids. I thought that if Donna and Danny came and met Hugh and got that idea out of their system, we could all go back to normal and forget this."

I slammed my hand down on the table. "Well, I hope you've learned that all this secrecy and sneaking around is not the way to handle it anymore!"

"What I've learned," said Mom, "is that when you girls get involved, there's going to be trouble."

"That's because *Jackie* called her instead of *me*! So now Donna called you and said what?"

"That Jackie had called and been very rude to her and had accused her of things and told her that she did not want Donna visiting unless she was present."

"Unbelievable! Who does Jackie think she is?"

"And Donna said that Danny was running late anyway—he's moving out here from Los Angeles—so she thought that, for the time being, it would be better if she just canceled their visit. She said she'd give me a call later to see if things have changed. So now I can't get this thing over with like I wanted to. She could call anytime and want to pop in, and who knows what kind of scheme you girls will dream up. Now I wish I'd never even called her. I wish we had stuck with our agreement from years ago to never say a word about this. It's only going to bring heartache—I know it. Look at what it's caused already."

"No, Mom. The *secrecy* brought the heartache. You can't just lie to somebody their whole life about who their family is. So the whole truth is coming out now, one way or another, and neither you nor Jackie nor anyone else is gonna prevent it."

"And your dad was so disappointed when I told him Donna and Danny weren't coming. He's really been looking forward to it. I didn't even have the heart to tell him the whole thing about Jackie. I just told him Danny was running late and the scheduling wasn't working out yet. Your dad thinks they'll still come once Danny gets here."

"You might as well tell Dad the truth," I said. "The problems always come when you try to hide things. Maybe if Dad knew the whole story, he'd be a little more careful what he says around Jackie."

"Well, if you want *everybody* to know *everything*, then why shouldn't he blab it all to Jackie, too?"

"I'll make an exception when it comes to her."

I went and got Mom's tea and tried to figure out what to do, while she retreated into her handkerchief.

When I came back out, I set the teacup and saucer in front of her and said, "Here's what I think our next step should be. I want to call Donna myself—like you agreed to let me do before!—and I'll try to straighten things out with her. I'll tell her what Jackie's like, as if she hasn't figured that out already. We can tell Donna that Jackie was speaking for herself alone and that nobody else in the family feels the way she does. We can invite her and Danny for another visit and promise her that Jackie won't know about it and won't be there."

Mom took a sip and then shook her head. "I don't think she'll go for it."

"Why not?"

"Huh?"

"*Why not?* Do you have a reason, or are you just being pessimistic? Donna didn't say she would absolutely never come under any circumstances, did she?"

"No. Unfortunately, she didn't. If she had, I wouldn't have called you. I would have just put the whole thing behind me."

"See, you're being pessimistic. Now listen, Mom. I hate to say I told you so, but if you had done it my way in the beginning, then I would have been the first one to talk to Donna, and we wouldn't be in this mess. So go get me her number right now."

I tried to act all nonchalant after I said this, as if my request was no more significant than asking for a napkin, as if I took it for granted that Mom would jump right up and get that number. In fact I was holding my breath, knowing this could easily go either way. Mom can be pretty stubborn about things like this. She had been hiding Donna and Danny from us for so long that it was hard for her to voluntarily give us access to them, even if it was the only solution that made sense. But she *had* called me, so part of her must have wanted my help.

Mom stared into that teacup as intently as if it contained the answer to life's mysteries. After an agonizing silence, she propped her hands against the edge of the table, heaved a big sigh, and pushed herself up to a standing position. As she walked away, she said, "I'd like another cup of that if you wouldn't mind. And why don't you fix one for yourself, too?" Then she tottered off toward her bedroom, more stiff and bent than I've ever seen her.

I knew she was going to get the number, and I was so happy I wanted to clap my hands and then run up and give her a big hug, but I knew better. She might mistake that for a sign that I was gloating over talking her into something, and I didn't want to create any more resistance in her.

I went to the kitchen and made some more tea. I was hoping Mom would bring out Donna's letter so I could read it, but no such luck. Instead, she handed me a piece of an old envelope that said *Donna Pryce* and had her phone number on it. I wanted to raise it high over my head and cheer as if it were an Olympic gold medal, but instead I just stuffed it in my pocket.

Once she had handed over that piece of paper, Mom relaxed, and the tension in the air evaporated. I knew she wanted to put aside that whole topic as she settled into her second cup of tea, but I had one more thing to say.

"Unless Jackie brings it up, I don't think we should even let her know that we're aware of her call to Donna. Let's keep her off guard. Then once we've met Donna and Danny in person and see how nice they are and everything, then Jackie will just have to get over it and accept them. All right?"

Mom waved her hand through the air, a resigned gesture that meant "Handle it however you want to. I'm tired of fighting."

After that, we did manage to have a pleasant talk. When you get Mom alone, and she doesn't happen to be obsessing over some particular worry, she can still show flashes of her old self, when she was stronger, happier, funnier. One thing she did not want to discuss was her health, which in a strange way worried me. With Mom, when she *does* want to complain about something that's wrong with her, it's usually not that serious, but when she *refuses* to talk about how she feels, that means she's probably hiding something bad.

I didn't stay too long because I thought I might call Donna as soon as I got home so that I wouldn't have to keep worrying about it. But by the time I got home, made a snack for Brandon, who hadn't eaten much dinner, and got some laundry in, I didn't feel like I had the emotional strength necessary to make the call.

The next day at work I fretted about that phone call all day, to the point where it was hard for me to concentrate. My problem is that when I start thinking too much about a conversation like that, my imagination dreams up so many frightening possibilities that I can easily scare myself out of doing it. One thing my brain ran wild with was what Jackie must have said to Donna. I wish Mom had been more specific about that. I conjured up scenes in which Jackie called Donna names like "con artist" or "liar," or told her she'd beat the daylights out of her if she ever came near Mom and Dad, or bullied and bellowed in a dozen other ways that Jackie is capable of.

What if their disagreement had been so bad that Donna would take it out on me and scream and yell the way Jackie had done? The thought of it made me break out in a sweat. It can take me years to get over somebody yelling at me like that. I'm not kidding. I still shudder with embarrassment when I relive the time my third-grade teacher yelled at me in front of the whole class for talking during quiet time and then sent me out into the hall.

Another thing that began to worry me about Donna was that she lives in Carmel. Most of the people I've heard about who live there are rich. What if she turns out to be some wealthy snob who'll be appalled by the way we live? What if she sees us as some trashy family that it will be a disgrace to be related to?

And what about Danny? If he's a businessman in Los Angeles, does that mean he's rich, too? Is he like some big Hollywood studio executive who lives in a mansion and has servants and boats and pools? Why is he moving to Indianapolis? Is he one of those rich guys who owns homes in several cities?

And what will they think of us now that Jackie came along and insulted them? Will that only confirm in their minds how crude and uncivilized we are?

By the time I finished this line of thinking, my mind had

painted us as barefoot, inbred, tobacco-spitting Beverly Hillbillies, while Donna and Danny were fabulously wealthy socialites who sat around their mansions sipping martinis and would laugh their heads off about their new hick relatives once they finally met us.

I couldn't call her from work, not with all those fears swirling around my brain. On the way home, knowing that Brandon would be at softball practice that evening and wouldn't need me, I sought a little comfort before I went home to face the phone. Jackie likes to make fun of this, but for me, one of the most relaxing things to do is to walk the splendidly stuffed aisles of Wal-Mart. Not *her* Wal-Mart, of course, but the one closer to my apartment. It's almost hypnotizing for me to walk up and down looking at all the clothes and cards and CDs and coffee-pots and toys and food. I don't buy much, but occasionally I'll put some little item that I need into my cart. Then when I'm in the checkout line, I buy three or four magazines and newspapers—the *National Enquirer, Star,* the *Globe, Vanity Fair, People.* On the way home, I go to some drive-through for a quick bite to eat. Then at home, I get my food ready and settle down on the sofa and eat and read. I've followed that routine dozens of times, and even though I know it's not exactly champagne and the opera, to me it's a perfectly relaxing evening.

I made the mistake of telling Jackie about it once, and she still torments me about it. If I ever mention something I heard on the news, she'll say, "Oh, which tabloid did you get that out of, the *Star* or *Weekly World News*? Was that right beside the story about the alien abductions?" Those tabloids aren't the *only* things I read, but occasionally I like to get lost in them for an hour or so, just to see how the celebrities live, what they're wearing, what they're fighting about, what crises they're facing. Sometimes it makes me feel not quite so bad about how messed up my own life is.

Jackie likes to make fun of me for the "trash" that I read, but she never reads anything. I doubt if she's read a book clear through since high school, and maybe not even then. She doesn't have the patience for it. She can't stand the quiet for that long, and she can't sit still long enough to even read a magazine. She can barely sit through a movie, and even when she does, she can't keep herself from *talking* through most of it.

Anyway, on the way home that night, I went through my Wal-Mart, Taco Bell, *National Enquirer* ritual, but it wasn't enough to calm me down. It's not every day that you call your sister who's been kept secret from you your whole life. One of those magazines should write about me. Finally, when seven-thirty came and I realized Brandon would be home pretty soon, I decided to pick up the phone regardless of how nervous I felt.

Needless to say, having built up all these insecurities, when I finally got Donna on the line, I could barely squeak out a hello. After I got that word out, the rest of what I had planned to say popped right out of my head, and I blurted out something like, "This is Carolyn. I'm the daughter of your fa . . . I'm the sister of your . . . I'm the daughter of Hugh Morris."

"Oh, *Carolyn,*" she said, but her tone was something along the lines of, "How many wackos does this family have?"

I hurried up and added, "I want to make it clear that I know Jackie called you, but I haven't talked to her personally, so I don't know exactly what she said. I know it was probably rude, and I want to say that she was speaking for herself alone and not for anyone else in the family. None of the rest of us were even aware that she knew your name or planned to call you. I want to apologize for anything she said to offend you."

Donna laughed then, and it's hard to describe that laugh, but it was so carefree and friendly that it said to me, "No harm done. I don't take myself too seriously. I'm not the kind of person to let things like that get me too upset." Even before she said another word, I knew everything was going to be all right between us. I almost burst into tears with relief.

Once she set me at ease, I was able to get my words back, and we had the friendliest conversation you can imagine. She immediately started asking me about my work and about Brandon and Mom and Dad, and I asked her questions about her family. She's an English teacher—not a rich snob at all—has two girls and a wonderful husband, is real active in her church, and likes to throw big get-togethers at her house. I love her already.

Later in the conversation I told her, "You have to understand about Jackie. She doesn't realize how she comes across, and she usually goes barging into situations and making a fool of herself before she thinks about what she's saying. She sees herself as bold and blunt and thinks of everybody else as passive little wimps."

"Every family has a range of personalities," said Donna diplomatically. "It's the same way with us."

"Well, I'm afraid to say that with our family, the range is a little wider than I'd prefer. So what about Danny? What's he like?"

"Oh, he's a real free spirit," she said, and that sent a twinge of happiness through me, even though I didn't know exactly what she meant. "He's coming out here, you know. He's on his way right now, but he's taking his time driving out from California. He stopped at the Grand Canyon and some other places to sightsee on the way."

"Does he have a wife and kids?"

"He has a son, Alex, the sweetest teenager you'd ever want to meet, but Danny's divorced."

As soon as she said that, I *knew* I was going to get along with him. Not that I'm *glad* he's divorced, but at least in a strange way it will be something we have in common. I won't feel like such an oddball around him. He knows what it's like to go through the destruction of a marriage.

"Does he have Alex with him?"

"No. Unfortunately, Alex is in northern California with his mother. But I'm hoping that if Danny can get established out here in a new job and a new life, eventually Alex can come and visit him a lot or maybe even move here or go to college here. But it's too early to tell."

I had a million more questions I wanted to ask, but Donna said she had to get off the phone in a minute to go pick up one of her daughters. I had to get to the point pretty fast.

"Mom and Dad and I really want you to come and visit," I said. "Mom was really worried that Jackie had scared you off, but she wants me to ask you if you'd consider setting up another time to come."

"Sure," said Donna. "The only thing I don't know is Danny's schedule. But why don't we set a date and then see if it works out."

"Great," I said, and we talked about some possible dates and finally settled on a Thursday night two weeks off.

I gave Donna my phone number and told her to call any time she wanted to talk. I was hoping to hear how she found out about us and what the story was between Dad and her mother and all the rest, but there wasn't time. I was tempted to ask her whether I could call her back after she got home that night or the next day, but I didn't want to be a pest. Jackie has already made our family look bad, so I don't want to come off as pushy in another way. I have a feeling we'll have plenty of time to dig into the past.

I've decided not to tell anyone ahead of time about Donna's visit. Not even Pam. I'll tell Mom, of course, but unless she really presses me, I'd like to not tell her until just a few days before Donna comes. That way she and Dad won't let it slip out to the wrong person named you-know-who.

Jackie may have thought she pulled one over on us by being the first one to get to Donna, but I'll show her! I'd love to see the look on her face a few weeks from now, when she finds out Donna and Danny have already come to see Mom and Dad and I've already met them.

16

HUGH:
NOW WHAT?

It took me a long time to work up the determination to call Donna and Danny and try to settle things with them before I die. Then, before I got the chance to actually do it, Vonnie gave me one of the biggest shocks of my life by telling me she wanted to call Donna herself! She said she knew there was no way to avoid this meeting, so the best she could hope for was to have it happen quickly before our daughters jumped in and complicated everything.

At first I was relieved that Vonnie had changed her mind about talking to Donna. My biggest worry had never been facing Donna. It had been talking Vonnie into letting me do it. And then when Vonnie told me that her talk with Donna had gone well and that Donna and Danny were coming to see me in a couple weeks, I was overjoyed. It was a miracle. I know that call required every ounce of courage Vonnie possessed.

My undiluted happiness lasted for about a day, and then new fears crept in. I had focused so much of my energy on how I was going to get Vonnie to understand my desire to contact Donna that I hadn't spent much time thinking through what would happen if Danny and Donna actually appeared in my home. Donna's letter was friendly enough, but what if that had simply been her way of getting in the door? Once she was here, would she fling accusations at me? Would she blame me and hate me?

The one question I wish I had the answer to is how much did Barbara tell Donna and Danny about me? I'd give anything to know why, after so many decades, she broke her silence and told them anything at all. What was her frame of mind at the end? Was she a tired old woman who simply wanted to crawl into her grave unburdened by any secrets? Or was she a spiteful ex-wife who seized an opportunity for revenge?

I can't help but wonder whether she ever considered contacting me near the end to tell me that she planned to tell the kids about me. It must have crossed her mind. Throughout all the deplorable circumstances leading up to the divorce, she had tried so hard—at such cost to all of us—to expel me from her life forever. I can't imagine what could have changed her mind about it. That's what makes me think it might be a trick. Was she afraid to confront me herself, so she decided to stab me one last time by sending the kids to torment me?

One thing I could have kissed Vonnie for is that, at first, she set up the meeting so that it would only be her and me and Donna and Danny. That way, no matter what Donna or Danny said, my girls wouldn't have to hear it.

Anyway, after Vonnie told me they were coming, I imagined this reunion every possible way it could go, from angry to sappy to forgiving. Maybe they'd let me off the hook. Maybe they'd feel sorry for me and embrace me and shake their heads in pity at what a broken-down old geezer I am. Or maybe they'd take a lighter approach and just chitchat and laugh and marvel at the unexpected turns that life takes.

After I had done everything I could to prepare myself for

whatever this appointment might bring, Vonnie came in and told me Donna had canceled her visit, or at least postponed it.

"Well, did she cancel or did she postpone?" I asked.

"She canceled, but she said it might work out another time."

"Why'd she cancel?"

"Well, for one thing, Danny isn't here yet. He's still moving out to Indianapolis, but it's taken him longer to get here than he expected."

That explanation didn't sound too likely to me. Why would Danny not know how long it takes to get here? Do they not sell maps in California? Is he coming by covered wagon? Is he with Lewis and Clark, riding in a canoe?

"What's the real reason?" I asked.

"That's it."

I knew she was lying.

"If it's a matter of him being a few days late, why don't they pick another day to come?"

"Maybe they will. But for now, she left it open."

So either Vonnie didn't know why Donna changed her mind, or else (as I suspect) she knew and just didn't want to tell me. That's another side effect of the stroke—everybody thinks I need to be protected from unpleasant information. Vonnie was also mad at me for hinting to Jackie that Donna might be coming, so Vonnie might have been punishing me by withholding details that I might let slip out. I don't know why I said anything to Jackie. As soon as I said it, I knew it was a mistake. But she got me so flustered, and . . . I don't know, sometimes I get so lost in my own thoughts nowadays that I say things without realizing it.

That cancellation must have happened a week or two ago (I have a little trouble keeping exact track of time). Then yesterday Vonnie pops up and says, "You need to listen close, hon. I have some news. Donna and Danny are coming after all."

I swear, I really *will* have another stroke if my family keeps yanking me around like this. I'm in no condition to play these kinds of games.

"When?" I asked.

"In two days."

So now I've spent the last forty-eight hours working up my courage again. I've hardly slept at all. This time around, Carolyn is supposed to be here when they come.

"How did *she* find out about it?" I asked.

"It's too complicated a story," said Vonnie, who might as well have patted me on the head like I was a little boy asking where babies come from.

"I can't talk about these things in front of Carolyn," I said.

"Talk about what things?"

"I can't rehash the past in front of her. It's one thing with Donna and Danny, who didn't know me after the divorce. But with Carolyn . . ."

"Now listen, Hugh," said Vonnie, and she walked over and put her face close to mine. "You don't have to rehash anything with anybody. Do you hear me? That's not what this is about. They're coming here to *visit* you. To say *hello* and get *acquainted*. We're not going to relive things that happened more than forty-five years ago. It's too late—"

"I tried hard," I said.

"To do what?"

"To make things different. When I married you, I swore I would die before I let myself get dragged back down again into—"

"And you've lived up to that! They won't dare accuse you of a thing, or I'll shut down the conversation right away. No. This is a get-acquainted session. That's it."

I only wish I could count on that.

I really meant what I said about trying to make things different. No matter what else anybody might blame me for, nobody could have tried harder than I did to set things right so that my second family wouldn't collapse the way my first one did. Take any area of life you want. Take work. Take the church. When I met Vonnie, through some of my mother's friends at church, she was a strict Nazarene Christian young woman. She wouldn't even go out on a regular date with me until we had gone to church together several times. Everything was proper about our courtship. There was no drinking, no sex before marriage, none of the kind of carelessness that had started Barbara and me down the wrong path.

Before I even proposed to Vonnie, I joined the church. That's what she wanted, and that's what I did. I went down to the altar and prayed and confessed and asked forgiveness and gave myself to God. I admit that my faith was never as strong as Vonnie's. I mean, I encountered Vonnie and then became a Christian at the lowest point of my life. The catastrophe with Barbara had weighed so heavily on me that I had barely been functioning for a year or more. I loved Vonnie, but I was still a mess, still hurting, still working out the Barbara details in my mind.

I felt too tainted, too guilty to fully enter into the Christian faith. I never said that out loud. I know the people at church would have jumped all over that and said that God forgives everything. Forgiveness is the whole point. Why would we need salvation if we hadn't sinned? On one level I knew that. But my kids—Donna and Danny—were still out there. I felt like I couldn't fully enter into forgiveness until their status was resolved. Barbara and Vonnie and I had come to our agreement about them, but it still didn't feel finished to me. I kept expecting that by some miracle, my children would end up back in my home, in my arms, and then I would turn to God a second time for true forgiveness.

In the meantime, I did the best I could to change. I gave up alcohol immediately, and I gave up smoking after about a year of trying. I threw myself into the work of the church, and for the next thirty years or so, no pastor could have asked any more from a member of the congregation than I gave.

Our church was growing during those years, and we had two big building programs while I was on the church board. The first one was to build a brand-new church on a bigger piece of land several blocks away from the old building, and the second project was a big addition to that new building about ten years later. I was in charge of fund-raising for both projects. I got the pledge cards printed, I oversaw production of the brochures that told about the new buildings, and I chaired the committee that came up with clever ways of keeping the building programs in front of the congregation. I built the frame for this little playhouse church that we put on the sanctuary platform, and we added a brick to it every time so many dollars were pledged. Week after week we saw that little building go up, until finally one Sunday our pledge goals were met and we were able to place the steeple on top.

I insisted that all our kids go to church, and we almost never missed a Sunday morning or Sunday night. We often went to Wednesday night prayer meeting, too. I was a strict dad; I admit it. I expected the girls to dress a certain way and behave a certain way all through their growing-up years. They were always testing me, trying to wear their skirts too short or their makeup too heavy or trying to stay out too late or go to places we didn't approve of. I tried to raise them right. I wanted them to serve the Lord. I wanted them to have the right values. I know they resented me at times and tried their best to push the limits of what I would tolerate. I tried to be a good role model even though, with all my pre-Vonnie past sealed away but not forgotten, I still felt that I could not fully become a believer.

For almost fifteen years I was in charge of our bus ministry for kids. I made the arrangements for us to purchase that first old junker of a bus, and I drove the first bus route through the neighborhoods around the church. We picked up kids whose parents wanted them to be in church but who didn't want to go themselves. I understood that attitude, and I took their children back and forth Sunday after Sunday. It was the ideal way for me to witness to others about Christ, which we were always being called on to do. I didn't feel comfortable telling people about salvation in words, but I could take them to church where they could hear it.

I know that all the preachers we had over the years would say that service to the church is no substitute for true and complete forgiveness from God. They would say God is not impressed by what we do for Him. We all fall short, and we all can do nothing more than fall down in front of Him and ask for His mercy. I believe that, and I always believed that someday all the obstacles would be swept away and I would be able to stand before God and receive His salvation in the name of Jesus Christ.

I gradually fell away from the church after my first heart attack, when it became easy to use my health as an excuse not to go. But I'd still swear that my faith is not dead. I still feel deep down that God has not swept me aside or given me up for lost.

Anyway, the point I'm trying to make is that the man I have been for the past forty-five years is entirely different from the man Barbara knew. But which man will I be allowed to be tomorrow night? What weapons might Barbara have armed these children with to threaten me with in front of Carolyn? How might the things they say corrupt her opinion of me forever?

I guess I'll find out tomorrow. I wish Carolyn wasn't going to be there. I only hope that my mind is focused while they're here. I've been getting better lately, or at least it seems to me that I have. But they're coming in the evening, which is not always my sharpest time. And I hope I don't have any accidents on the way to the bathroom. What humiliation to have to worry about such things. I'm even tempted to wear one of those diapers, just in case.

Even in the best of circumstances, when my brain is functioning and my body is clean and dry, I know I look like a corpse that wasn't given a very good job of embalming. There's nothing I can do about that, but it seems a cruel time of life to have to face these children.

I guess if they're coming with good intentions, my looks shouldn't make that much difference. And if they're coming to attack, I guess they'll figure it serves me right to look like I've been put through the wringer.

Barbara, Barbara. I can't help thinking you're somehow peeking in on this and laughing at me. Is there no end to your vindictiveness? Do you have to keep assaulting me even now, when you're rotting in the grave?

17 DANNY:
STEPPING OUT

I don't know what I expected exactly, but Hugh and Vonnie weren't it. Donna had told me all about Hugh's strokes, so I wasn't surprised that he was so frail, but Vonnie looked almost as bad. She's bent over and has this creaky walk that makes you think each step might be the one that topples her onto her face. She's hard of hearing, too, so sometimes her daughter, Carolyn, had to shout things we said two or three times into Vonnie's right ear before she caught it. That certainly slowed down the conversation, and it was embarrassing at times, too, because we'd get stuck on comments that were nothing more than inane bits of small talk that didn't bear repeating even once, let alone being shouted two or three times.

At one point, for instance, when I was answering one of Hugh's questions about my trip across the country, I mentioned that it rained in St. Louis. Vonnie, who had just hobbled back into the room from helping Carolyn with the dessert dishes, said, "You're going where?"

"He's talking about his trip, Mother," said Carolyn, who

rolled her eyes and looked embarrassed almost every time Vonnie spoke.

"Where's he going?" asked Vonnie.

"He's not going anywhere!" shouted Carolyn. "He's talking about his trip to Indiana. He said it rained in St. Louis!"

Vonnie stared at her, confused.

"Rained in St. Louis!" Carolyn yelled again.

"Oh," said Vonnie, and she smiled at me and nodded. "Yes, it rains there a lot."

"I'm sure it does," I said.

"What?" asked Vonnie.

Carolyn sighed and yelled, "He's sure it does! It rains a lot there!"

Vonnie smiled and nodded again, and we all sat quiet for a moment and contemplated the precipitation in St. Louis. I was reluctant to say anything more for fear that Carolyn would have to translate it.

I had gone with Donna that evening only on one condition. I told her, "When I say it's time to go, we go."

I didn't want to go even under those circumstances, but the one possibility I found completely unacceptable was that this little encounter would turn bad and Donna would want to stay and see it through anyway. She's like that. Whereas I would want to get out of there as fast as I could if it got too weird, Donna's the type who would want to stay long enough to fix it, to confront the problems and try to make everybody feel good about it before the night was over. I love her for that in many situations, but with this, I wasn't heavily invested enough in it to care whether it worked out or not. I had lived without knowing my "father" for almost my whole life, so as far as I was concerned, I had managed to adjust just fine without him.

Donna agreed to my condition. "Will you do the same for me?" she had asked. "If I feel the need to get out of there?"

"Of course."

Donna told me about the unfriendly phone call from one of the daughters, Jackie. This hostile daughter's big worry is that we're going to swoop in and take over her parents' lives and squeeze her father for whatever inheritance we can get out of him on his deathbed. Donna made it sound like the daughter was afraid we might be running some kind of scam. I pictured her showing up and making a big scene or trying to make us prove that this man really is our father.

The daughter's paranoia made me imagine that maybe this was a family with lots of money. But if they do have money, it certainly isn't on display. Their house is small and dilapidated. It looks like it was built back in the forties or fifties and probably hasn't had any work done to it for fifteen or twenty years. On the outside, it needs paint and a new roof. Some of the pieces of wood trim on the closed-in porch have rotted and need to be replaced. The gutters are battered and about to fall off.

Inside, everything looks old, from the furniture to the drapes to the paint. Even though it was a hot evening, they only had a couple windows open, and they have no air conditioning. Even so, Vonnie wore a sweater. The house even *smelled* old inside. It had that musty old-clothes smell, mixed with what smelled like an overflowed toilet.

I might not have noticed all this about the house except that Hugh kept drawing my attention to it. The strange thing about this evening was that no one talked about the central fact that had brought us together—no one mentioned that Donna and I were Hugh's long-lost children come to see him after half a century. Anyone looking in on this scene might have imagined we were merely former neighbors or acquaintances who had dropped into town and were paying a courtesy call.

Hugh was embarrassed by how he looked and how his house looked, and in a sense, he apologized for those appearances all night. Never did he apologize for or even acknowledge walking away from us when we were kids. He offered no explanations. Instead of taking on the big issues, he focused on paint and plumbing. He said things like, "Sorry I couldn't get the place fixed up before you came. You probably noticed when you came in that the porch screen is rotting away." (I had not noticed it.) "I used to keep this house shipshape, but now it takes me forever to do anything. I'm no good with a hammer at all now. Those strokes took away the strength in my arms. So this place is in almost as bad a shape as I am."

Hugh is a broken-down old man in many ways, but he doesn't look like the kind of stroke victim I had pictured. The people I've known who've had strokes have had that drooping face on one side and slurred speech, and Hugh isn't like that. He's weak, but there's no paralysis in his face. He had trouble gripping his water bottle and spilled some crumbs of pie onto his lap, but he managed to eat without any help. He never stood up while I was there, so I don't know how he is with walking. We were told that he sometimes gets confused and even hallucinates, but he showed no sign of that. We were also told he's forgetful and often repeats himself, and that was true. Seven or eight times he asked me, "So how was your drive from California?" and each time you could tell he thought he was asking it for the first time.

I had been curious to know whether we looked like Hugh, and I immediately saw some of Donna in him—the same mouth and chin and smile. I don't think I look much like him, but Donna said afterward that she was astonished by some of the similarities in our expressions and even in the sound of our voices. Carolyn also said she thought I looked a lot like her father, and she spent much of the evening staring at me in fascination.

We originally were invited for dinner, but I vetoed that idea, not wanting to be confined to sitting through an entire meal if things went badly from the start. Instead, we came after dinner, and they served us pie and coffee. The only times I got to talk to Hugh alone was when the women went to the kitchen to get the food ready to serve and then when they took the plates and cups away again later.

As soon as we were alone, he said, "I know it smells a little funny in here right now, but I've had some trouble with my floor in the bathroom. We've had lots of plumbing problems the last few years, and the floor around the toilet is kind of caving in. I'd fix it myself, but I don't feel up to it right now. You can't hardly find a good plumber anymore. They either want to fix something quick, or else they want to charge you a fortune. But we'll end up paying it, I guess. And then if I can get him to put a new floor in, I'll have to replace the tile. But what else can you do? This place is crumbling to bits all around me."

"How long have you lived here?"

"Forty-five years, almost," he said. "We bought it brand-new. I did some of the work myself. Like that closed-in porch. That was mostly my work."

"Oh really? Did you do that kind of work for a living?"

"No, no. Back then people did things for themselves. You didn't just hire everything done like people do nowadays. Men knew how to use their tools to build things."

I laughed and said, "Well, I guess I'm closer to the newer generation. I couldn't build a porch like that if my life depended on it. Of course, since my divorce, I've been living in apartments, where all you have to do is call the manager."

Hugh looked at me closely, and if I had to guess what he was thinking, I would bet he was trying to decide whether it was appropriate to ask me about the divorce. He didn't. He said, "Well, you're a businessman, see, so you can afford to hire things done. We didn't have so much money back in the old days. What kind of business are you in, anyway?"

"I'm an accountant. My last job was working at a hospital in Los Angeles. It was going bankrupt."

"Because of your bad accounting work?" he asked with a smile.

"No. By the time I got there, no accountant on earth could have saved the place."

"Well, excuse me for saying it," said Hugh, "but considering the hospitals I've been in, some of them deserve to go bankrupt."

"So what kind of work did you do, Hugh?" I asked.

"I worked at the Brantwell Corporation here in Indianapolis. Have you heard of it?"

"Oh, yeah. They've been here for as long as I can remember. I lived in Indiana for a lot of my growing-up years, you know."

Hugh paused and gave me that penetrating stare again. Maybe he *didn't* know where I had grown up. Maybe he knew nothing about me after he left us when I was a baby. I was tempted to drop all the get-acquainted talk and get right down to business. *Exactly what was the arrangement that you and my mother made about me and Donna? Why did you never see us again? How could you have done it? How can you sit there a generation later and not feel the enormity of it?*

But just as I was working up the courage to change the conversation in that direction, Carolyn came fluttering in, followed slowly by Vonnie, who was leaning on Donna's arm for support. The next hour was filled with more chitchat, mostly about our families—Donna's girls and husband, Carolyn's sisters and their families.

Carolyn was friendly enough, even though she acted awfully nervous around me, like a teenager meeting a rock star. She told us about her son, Brandon, who is about my son's age. He wasn't there because he was playing softball. I gathered that Carolyn is divorced, though she never said so directly. She showed lots of patience with her parents, especially Hugh, who kept telling her to offer us this and that to eat and drink, even though she had already done so. Each time, she would say something like, "They already had coffee, Dad," and that would quiet him for the moment. Carolyn is a little overweight, and I think she's sensitive about it. She kept tugging at the bottom of her shirt, as if she wished she could shrink a little inside it.

After dessert, Vonnie said little and probably heard little. She mostly kept her eyes warily on Hugh, as if she expected him to suddenly collapse or explode. After a while, he leaned back in his chair, let out a big sigh, and groaned, "Oh, mercy."

"You all right, hon?" asked Vonnie.

He stared at her blankly, seemingly unaware that he had called out.

"He gets overwhelmed," Carolyn whispered to us in a tone of apology.

"Well, it's late," said Donna, "and we'd better be going."

I stood, and Hugh said, "Do you have to go? I wish you could stay and talk."

"We'll get together again sometime," I said.

I was hoping to keep any future visits vague for the moment, but as we headed out the door, Carolyn and Donna started making plans.

Donna said, "Maybe we could have all of you out to our house for a cookout this summer. It wouldn't be that far of a drive for Hugh, and once we get there, we could easily wheel him around in our house—there aren't as many steps as you've got here—and we could let him sit out back on the deck, too, if he wants. I'd love to meet the rest of the family, and I'd like you to meet my girls and Phil."

"We'd love that," said Carolyn. "Just let us know when would be good. Are you thinking a Saturday—"

"Maybe a Saturday afternoon in two or three weeks. Our

house is set up for teenagers, so I'm sure Brandon could find things he likes to do. We have a pool table, and Danny can't get enough of it! I'm sure he could teach Brandon if he's interested."

Donna and Carolyn looked at me, and I nodded politely but said nothing. I wasn't yet sold on the idea of a full-scale family reunion. I wanted time to think it over. Another person who was obviously cool to the idea was Vonnie, who stood with her arms folded and her expression stone-faced. Hard of hearing though she may be, I'm pretty sure she caught most of what Donna and Carolyn were saying. Her only comment was, "We'll have to see. Hugh's not really up to much travel right now."

As for Hugh, I don't think he was aware that we were still in the house by the time this conversation took place. He was leaning his head against the palm of his hand and looking toward the empty fireplace.

Carolyn and Donna were not deterred by our lack of enthusiasm. They tentatively chose a Saturday a few weeks off and said they would talk to their families to see who could come.

I kept quiet for about the first half of our trip home and let Donna spill out her impressions of the evening, which she thought went very well. She was surprised by Hugh and Vonnie's frailty, but she thought they and Carolyn treated us graciously. "They already seem like family," she said. "I think it's going to work out fine, even if Jackie's still suspicious of us. What did you think?"

I sighed and said, "I'm not satisfied."

Donna shook her head and smiled, not surprised by such skepticism coming from me. "Why not?"

"If we're going to have meetings like this, I'd at least like some answers. We found out nothing about Hugh and Mom, like why they split up or anything. From what he said tonight, you couldn't even tell that he knew we were his kids."

"Well, it's gonna take time. Look how hard we pressed Mom,

and she hardly told us anything. I didn't expect him to lay out the whole story the first time we saw him."

"I did."

"You can't start off that way. I don't think you'd like it if somebody came up to you out of the blue and demanded, 'So tell me why you and Terri broke up.'"

Terri suddenly awakened in my brain and screamed, *"Because you're a self-absorbed, irresponsible child!"*

"And you know nothing about love!" Buster Flapjaw shot back. *"Look at that couple we saw tonight! See what Vonnie is willing to endure for the man she loves! Did she run away from him at the first sign of trouble?"*

Donna continued, "You need to go back there and spend some time alone with him, just the two of you. Everybody was on their best behavior tonight. Nobody wanted to make anybody else uncomfortable. But if we're going to move forward as a family, we're going to have to spend time together and let some of those defenses fall."

"I'm not sure I want to."

"Well, that's what you'll have to decide. For me, the choice is easy. These people are my family, and I want to know them, in spite of whatever may have happened in the past. If Hugh made mistakes when we were kids, so be it. I'd like to know his side of it. I managed to grow up all right, and my life and my faith in God are secure enough that I can forgive him and take it from there. If Jackie doesn't like us, so be it. She doesn't have to come and eat my cheeseburgers. But I refuse to sit around and do nothing until this man is dead and it's too late. That's what I would regret."

"How could I meet with him alone even if I wanted to? I can't just call and say, 'I'm coming over.'"

"It would be easy to arrange. If I called Carolyn and told her you wanted to see Hugh again, she'd set it up in no time. You know she would. I think you should do it."

"We'll see," I said.

"I think it took courage for them to invite us tonight," said Donna. "I think they'd appreciate your making the effort to go again."

"We'll see."

I didn't want to show too much interest in the idea because I didn't want Donna bugging me about it in the days ahead. Before I went that night, I never would have dreamed I would want to go back again. But now I had to admit that I was curious to see what else Hugh might have to say. I also had to admit one other surprising thing. I kind of liked him.

18 VONNIE:
Maybe I Should Go Ahead and Die

I got through Donna and Danny's visit all right, but after they left, I felt absolutely terrible and didn't sleep all night. "You're just nervous," Hugh told me, and when I called Carolyn the next morning, she told me the same thing.

What I didn't tell them was that I'm not sure if I took the right medicines during the three or four days leading up to Donna and Danny's visit. My brain was so addled during those days and I was so busy getting the house ready and taking care of Hugh that I honestly can't say whether I took double doses or no doses of some pills. I have such a big collection right now that it's confusing even when I'm feeling my sharpest. I don't even know how many different prescriptions I have. Ten or twelve, probably. Some are morning only, some are morning and night, and some are more often than that.

I especially get confused about this newest one they gave me for my heart problems. It looks a lot like one of my other pills, and I have the two bottles sitting side by side on my little tray.

So one morning I was about to swallow one of those new pills, and then suddenly I felt like I had already taken it. I had been thinking about other things, and for the life of me I just couldn't remember whether I had swallowed one or not. I didn't want to kill myself with an overdose, so I didn't take it. The next day the same thing happened as I was about to put that pill in my mouth. This time I did go ahead and take it. Then that evening I think I forgot to take my night pills altogether! I was so concerned about getting Hugh to take his night pills that I forgot my own. But I don't know for sure that I forgot.

I thought about calling the doctor, but what would I tell him? That I took too many, or not enough, or maybe the right amount? That wouldn't help him treat me, so I kept my mouth shut. Anyway, whatever the case might have been with the medicine, on the day after Donna and Danny came, I felt like I could die at any moment. The worst thing was I could hardly breathe. It wasn't nervousness. I could tell something was really wrong. My legs were all swollen again, too, but that could have been because with our company there, I hadn't been able to prop them up the way I usually do at night. I tried to sit and rest all morning to see if I'd get better, but finally I couldn't stand it anymore. I had to see the doctor.

Carolyn would have been my first choice for a ride, but I knew she was at work, so I tried Pam instead. The problem with Pam is the kids, who are too little to be able to sit still through one of my doctor's appointments. But sometimes we try it anyway. Pam wasn't home, so I left her a message to please call me as soon as she could. I felt desperate. I didn't want to call Jackie because she lives the farthest away and is usually the least sympathetic, but I tried her anyway. She was home.

I described my symptoms, and she sighed with annoyance. She went through a long list of all the things she had to do that day. Kevin had to be taken somewhere. Band practice or something like that. Kara would be with her. They were planning to go shopping while they waited on Kevin. Then Jackie had to work that evening starting at five. She threw in a few other details I didn't quite catch. Meanwhile I was wheezing and miserable.

"Have you called the doctor to see what he thinks?" asked Jackie. "Could he even get you in today? You might have to have an appointment for tomorrow or something. Even if he wanted to see you, by the time I got there, it would—"

"Forget it," I said. "I'm sorry I even mentioned it. Maybe I'll just stay here and die so you girls won't have to be bothered."

She huffed big. "Don't make it any worse than it already is, Mom. Sarcastic comments don't help."

As if *she's* one to complain about sarcasm!

"I have to go," I said. "I'll call a cab if necessary. Bye."

I hung up and went in to Hugh, who was calling for me to bring him some water. I got the water out of the fridge and tried to decide what to do. As I stepped out of the kitchen, the phone rang. I figured it was Jackie, feeling guilty for how she had treated me.

When she said, "What's up, Mom?" I said, "Hi, Jackie."

"It's not Jackie," she yelled. "It's Pam. What's wrong?"

I told her the whole story, including the part about the medicine, which she eventually dragged out of me. She asked if I had called the doctor, and I told her I hadn't because I wanted to make sure I had a ride to get there first. She said she would call him and get back to me.

A couple hours later she was at my door, with the kids in the car and the car running, ready to take me to the emergency room. I protested that she was overreacting, but she insisted on taking me because that's what the doctor wanted. I worried about Hugh staying alone, but she said she'd work on getting somebody to come and stay with him if they admitted me.

I regretted having called her. I didn't want to end up in the hospital—I only wanted a quick doctor's appointment. I should have just suffered in silence. Pam wouldn't even come inside the house because she didn't want to bother with getting the kids out of the car seats and then putting them right back in again. She's afraid of having them in my house lately anyway because right after Hugh came home from rehab, Matthew found a pill on my floor and brought it up to his mommy and said, "What's that?" And then he started to put it up to his mouth before she grabbed it away from him. Anybody could accidentally have a pill on their floor, but to hear her tell it now, you'd think those pills were so thick on our carpet that you can't take a step without crunching them.

So she wanted me to hurry up and come out to the car. Sarah was out there screaming her head off, wanting to get out of the car and come see me. I'm not a hurry-up kind of person in the first place, and before I leave the house, I like to check through things so I don't forget and leave the coffee on or leave the milk out on the counter or something like that. And now with Hugh not feeling his best, I had to make sure he had some water bottles nearby and some snacks to eat. I also had to explain to him where I was going.

All that took a few minutes to do, and in the meantime Pam was standing in the doorway of the porch, looking out at the kids and then looking in at me, hurrying me along and making me so nervous I couldn't think straight. Hugh wasn't having one of his most clearheaded days, so he wasn't helping matters. I told him I had to go to the hospital to be tested, and he kept wanting to ask one question after another. I was going from room to room trying to get ready, and he was sitting forward in his chair, following me with his shouts. "What?" he yelled. "What are you doing? What's wrong with you? I want to go, too. Where's Pam? Pam?" On and on he went like that.

Just as I was about to finish my hasty preparations and head out the door, Pam blew her stack. She's normally the kindest of my girls and the most patient, but I've noticed that since the kids came along, her fuse has gotten pretty short.

All I was doing was putting some money and some insurance paperwork in my purse. I like things organized, so I was wrapping each thing in its own bundle with rubber bands the way I always do. Am I supposed to run out of the house without my purse?

Pam could see me from her place in the doorway, and suddenly she bounded inside, hovered right over me, and demanded, "Come on, Mother! We don't have time for the ten-thousand-rubber-bands routine today!"

To be precise, I was using four rubber bands, and if she had left me alone, I would have been finished in about another minute. Pam's the one who's going to have heart trouble if she doesn't learn to calm down.

"I've almost got it," I said.

Right then, even with my bad ears, I heard the chorus of wailing from the car. Matthew had joined his sister in bawling his head off.

I couldn't believe what Pam did next. She scooped my things up off the chair where I had laid them in a neat row, *stuffed* them into my purse, and practically *dragged* me out the door. I was too dumbfounded to say anything. What has gotten into her? On one hand she's so worried about my health that she insists that I go to the emergency room even when it's not necessary, but then she turns right around and almost kills me to get me there.

I won't even describe the next few hours except to say that the day didn't get any better. Pam's kids, bless their hearts, are not at an age where it's easy to take them out, especially if they have nothing to do but sit in a dirty waiting room in a hospital.

Pam had them in the double stroller while I waited to be admitted, and neither of them wanted to stay in there. None of the toys and books kept them satisfied, and neither did the cups or bottles or crackers. So while Matthew and Sarah fussed, I tried to fill out paperwork, and Pam went back and forth helping me and the kids. Once I finally got in to be examined, I went through the usual tortures and tests, and the way it finally turned out was that they decided I should be admitted "for a day or two" to get my heart trouble under control. Turns out I really had messed up my medicines, so they had to put me on an IV to get it right.

Being admitted to the hospital and leaving Hugh by himself was the last thing I wanted, of course, but once you're in one of those places you're practically a prisoner, so there wasn't much I could do about it. As soon as I got settled, I called home to make sure Hugh was all right. Carolyn answered the phone. She said Pam had called her and asked if she could help out, so she took off work early to come and stay with her dad. I was so glad she was there, and I practically begged her to spend the night there so he wouldn't be alone.

She huffed and puffed and hemmed and hawed, but finally she said she would. She'd have to go get Brandon and stop somewhere to get them all something to eat, but then she would spend the night.

I said, "I should be home by tomorrow evening, but your dad really shouldn't be alone all day tomorrow."

"Mom, I really *have* to go to work tomorrow."

"I know. I was just wondering if maybe Brandon would be willing to stay with him till I get home."

"Oh, Mom," she whined. "I know he won't want to do that. I'm sure he's got plans of his own."

I wanted to ask, "Like what? I've never seen him do a thing but sit in front of the TV and flip channels. He could do that as easily at my house as he could at home."

Instead I said, "If it wasn't an emergency, I wouldn't ask. I hate to always be begging, but that's what it's come to. Maybe I'll have to call Pam again—"

"No, I'll see if Brandon will do it," she groaned. "Or what about Jackie?"

"I could call Jackie," I said, "but considering that Donna and Danny were just there last night, I hate to have her alone with your father, asking questions and—"

"No, you're right. Don't call Jackie. Brandon can do it."

Having solved that problem for the next day, at least, I tried to settle down and relax, but my brain wouldn't stop racing. No matter how hard I tried, and no matter how much medicine they gave me, I could not get to sleep that night. I stared at the ceiling, tired but wide-awake, and planned my next move. It was something I had been thinking about for a while, but this little hospital episode made me realize it was time to act.

When daylight finally came, I called Pam. "Are you coming to see me today?" I asked. "I need to talk to you about something important."

"I'm planning to come late this afternoon, once Cliff is free to watch the kids."

"Well, you know they'll probably release me this afternoon. Are you planning to stay till they do?"

"They won't necessarily release you today, Mom. The doctor said maybe two or three days."

"He said today!"

"He said *as early as* today, but he thought it would likely be a little longer."

"Well, it needs to be today. What will your dad do if I'm here three days?"

"I don't know. We'll have to figure that out. That's one of the problems with you two living there as sick as you are right now."

I wanted to get her off that subject right away before one of us uttered the words "nursing home." I said, "Well, anyway, Brandon's staying with him today, so I'll talk to the doctor and tell you what he said when you get here. Bye-bye, honey."

"Wait a minute," she said. "What's the important thing you want to talk to me about?"

"I'd rather talk about it in person. I can't hear you very well over this phone."

"Well, don't leave me hanging! What's it about?"

Pam doesn't have a lick of patience anymore. "I'll tell you when you get here. I've made a decision."

"Does it concern living arrangements?"

"No! Will you stop trying to—"

"All right," she said. "I know you love your secrets. I'll see you this afternoon. Bye."

When she got there later that day, she plopped down in the chair by my bed and said, "Okay, so what's the big decision?" Never mind that I was lying there looking half dead with tubes running in and out of me. She didn't have time to ask about my health.

I said, "As soon as I get out of here, I need you to take me to the lawyer. I want to change my will."

Her eyes got big, and I have to admit I kind of enjoyed being able to surprise her.

"Change it how?" she asked.

"What?"

"Change it *how*?" she yelled.

"I'd rather wait till we get to the lawyer's office to tell you the details. Will you take me?"

"No, Mom. I'm tired of these games. I won't take you unless you tell me what's going on."

I said, "It's not that I don't want you to know. I mean, obviously you're going to be right in there with the lawyer listening to what I say. But it's so hard to keep a secret in this family, and I just don't have the strength to try to explain this and justify it to everybody right now."

"So you want me to promise not to tell."

"I don't *want* to drag you into it at all."

"Does this have to do with those—children—of Dad's?"

"*No!*"

Pam had never talked about Donna and Danny to me, and I had hoped she wouldn't bring them up.

She said, "Well, I'm not going to let you get me into that lawyer's office and then surprise me with something I think is a horrible idea. I don't want some big argument in front of him. So either you tell me now what you're planning, or you'll have to get somebody else to take you."

I let out a big sigh, suddenly feeling so worn down that I was tempted to skip the whole thing. I'm tired of being treated like a child, blocked at every turn. Pam sat quietly and waited on me to speak. I decided to go ahead and tell her. She was going to find out eventually anyway. And if anyone besides me can keep a secret in this family (and I'm not sure anyone can), it would be Pam.

"All right," I said, "here's my plan. But if you tell a soul, I'll never speak to you again. I want to have a statement in the will indicating that if Hugh or I die, Carolyn has the right to live in our house as long as she wants to. Everything else will be split evenly between you three kids, but the house is not to be sold until Carolyn decides she no longer wants to live there. At that point, it will be sold and the money will be split among all three of you."

Pam nodded, thinking it over, trying to figure out what I was up to. "Does Carolyn know about this?"

"No, and I don't think I want her to. Not until one of us is dead. Or until I change my mind and decide to tell her."

"Why do you want to do this?"

"The rest of you have your own houses, but this might be Carolyn's only chance to own one."

"But you're not really *giving* it to her, right? She wouldn't really *own* it."

"It would sort of be hers, unless she decides to sell it, which she might never do."

"And Dad agrees with this?"

"Huh?"

"Dad agrees with this?" she shouted.

"Yes," I said, but the truth was I hadn't explained this exact plan to him. I knew he wanted Carolyn to live in our house, and I knew he would go along with my idea.

Pam asked, "How are you gonna get Dad to the lawyer? He'll have to sign this, too."

"I checked on that. We're gonna need a notary and two witnesses to come to the house. Nonfamily witnesses. Then your Dad can sign what the lawyer drafts."

"Do you really think Carolyn will live in your house?"

"I think she might. Once she realizes what a good deal it would be for her. No rent. A good neighborhood for Brandon."

Both of us were skirting around my real reason for changing the will, and I was hoping that either it wouldn't occur to Pam or that she at least wouldn't confront me with it. My real thinking was that if either Hugh or I died and Carolyn found out that the house was hers for as long as she wanted it, she would move in and prevent the remaining one of us from being shipped off to some awful place. I couldn't guarantee that she would go for it, but it was my only chance.

Pam said, "You realize Jackie's gonna be furious if you keep this from her."

I waved my hand and said, "By then I'll probably be dead. I absolutely do not want her to know. I want to do this quickly and quietly. Now there's one more tiny thing—actually a couple things—that I also want to put in the will. I don't like the way Jackie's been snooping around the house every time she comes over, looking for where I keep certain things that she'd love to get her paws on once I'm dead."

"What things?"

"One thing is that lamp in the dining room."

"What lamp in the dining room?"

"The lamp over the dining room table!"

"That old thing? It's been there for thirty years. Why would Jackie want that? It's all stained and—"

"It's a perfectly lovely lamp. Jackie already asked me if she could take it now and replace it with another one, but I told her under no circumstances could she touch it."

"Well, then that should take care of it. Don't put something like that in the will."

"Yes, I talked to my old friend Callie Manning on the phone about this the other day, and she said I should have the lawyer write that 'no permanent fixtures' should be removed from the house. She did the same thing in her will."

"Why are you talking to Callie about this?"

"She had to redo her will recently, too. She knows what I'm up against. And the other two things I want to put in there are my doll collection and my case of photographs, because Jackie's been sniffing around for those for years, and she's not gonna have them. I have them in a safe place, and that's where they'll stay. Only Carolyn knows where they are, and I'll kill her if she tells. Jackie tried to con me out of those pictures a few weeks ago, but I didn't fall for it. She said she wanted to make sure they weren't rotting, and she wanted to 'organize' them for me. But I know that 'organize' is French for 'steal,' and I won't let her get away with it."

"So what do you plan to say in the will?"

"I want to will the photos to Carolyn and the dolls to you."

"I don't want them," she said, just as rudely as if I had offered to will her a box of rattlesnakes.

"Fine," I said. "I'll will them to Carolyn, then."

"She doesn't want them, either. Don't do this, Mom."

"Why not? They're very valuable dolls. Lots of people would love—"

"When Carolyn was eight years old she might have wanted them, but now—"

"Lots of adults collect dolls!"

"Not Carolyn."

"Why are you taking this attitude?"

"Jackie's the only person who wants those dolls and those pictures. I don't see why, once you're gone, you won't just let her have them. What difference does it make?"

"I don't want her to have them, that's why. They're my dolls and I decide."

"Listen to yourself. You sound like a little girl. 'These are my dolls and you can't play with them. Na, na, na.'"

"It's not like that at all, Pam! You don't have to be so insulting. I'm merely trying to make a few simple changes to my will, which I have every right to do. Now, I called the lawyer, and he can see me next Monday morning. Will you take me?"

You would have thought I was asking her to drive me to China the way she sighed and hung her head down. "I guess so," she said. "But all these secrets from Jackie and Carolyn make me nervous."

"It's people *blabbing* the secrets that makes me nervous."

"Don't you think you should at least discuss this with Carolyn first? If she has no interest in ever moving to your house, then what's the point—"

"No, Pam. Now listen. Let me handle this my own way. It's my will, and your father's, and we have the right to divide up our things however we see fit. All right?"

She shrugged. To prevent more questions or argument, I got off that topic as fast as possible and instead told her what the doctor said, which was that I could go home the next morning. I had gotten Carolyn to agree to stay at the house one more night, and then Dad could be by himself for a few hours until I got home. Pam said she would come and pick me up, but she'd have to bring the kids.

Now my only worry was to keep the wrong people from finding out the wrong things. Pam now knew about the will, but she didn't know about Donna and Danny's visit earlier in the week. Carolyn knew about Donna and Danny's visit but not about the will. Jackie didn't know about either. Hugh didn't know about the will, and I didn't plan to tell him until I had a copy for him to sign. I knew it would be a miracle if I could keep all those lines from crossing, but I intended to try.

19 CAROLYN: SURPRISE, SURPRISE

I should have known it was all too good to be true. I was so optimistic after Donna and Danny came to see us. I really sensed an instant connection with Donna. Right away I felt like she was my sister. Everything about her—from the way she looked like us to the way she was so natural in talking to Mom and Dad to the way she jumped up and helped in the kitchen like she had known us all her life—made me think that all the secrecy and weirdness would soon be swept away and we could all get down to the business of being family. Donna and I both realized that the key to uniting all the family members was to follow up this first meeting with a bigger reunion where everybody could get to know one another. That's why we didn't leave it vague, but we set a *date* and a *place*.

Danny was nice, too, but he hung back more than Donna. He wasn't ready to run up and hug us and let the party begin. He wanted to look us over first, and I don't blame him. The important thing was that he *showed up,* and he was friendly. I figured it would take a few more times with us before he loosened up and began to see us as family.

That's why I was surprised when Donna called me a few days after they came and said that Danny wanted to see Dad alone. It worried me for a minute. I guess I had absorbed some of Mom's and Jackie's suspicions.

"Why does he want to see him?" I asked, afraid that Dad was too frail to handle some big confrontation if that's what Danny had in mind.

"Oh, he just wants to be able to talk more at ease. Danny told me that while we women were in the kitchen, he and Hugh were just starting to get to know each other, but they didn't have enough time to get into a real conversation. Hugh takes a while to get warmed up, I think."

"That's for sure. Especially since the stroke, he's forgetful and sometimes loses his train of thought. He was also nervous that night you were here. But if he's having a clear day, he's happy to talk for hours and mostly makes sense."

"Which is more than I can say for myself half the time," she joked. "Danny's been a little reluctant about this whole idea of meeting Hugh after all these years. But if he's going to do it, he really wants to make it meaningful. 'Hello-how-are-you' is not enough for him. So d'you think it would be all right for him to come?"

I told her I thought it would be fine and that I would find out from Mom and Dad when would be a good time. She said Danny would probably be starting a new job soon, but until then, his schedule was pretty open.

I called Mom and asked her if Danny could come. It felt a little strange that his request had to be funneled through Donna and then through me and then through Mom, but the relationship between the families was still at a delicate stage. Mom was playing especially hard of hearing that day, and she tried to find an excuse to say no to Danny, but finally I talked her into allowing it. She said she'd prefer a visit like that instead of a big get-together at Donna's with everyone invited. I didn't respond to this either/or proposition. I let it hang there, to be dealt with at another time. She insisted that if Danny came over, I was not to let Pam or Jackie or anyone else know about it. I said that was fine, and she said she didn't care which day he came.

Once we got off the phone, though, Mom called back about an hour later and said that, if possible, she'd like for Danny to come on Monday morning because Pam was going to take her to run some errands, and that way Dad wouldn't have to be alone.

"I thought you didn't want Pam to know about Danny."

"Well, ideally I'd prefer that, but she already knows he exists, so with a family full of blabbermouths, she's bound to meet him at some point. If he has to come here again, he might as well come when he can be useful. At least this way she can say hello and then take me and it's no big deal."

"Well, I certainly hope you're going to tell her ahead of time that he'll be there."

"I suppose."

"Well, you *have* to, Mom. You can't let her walk in and suddenly say, 'Oh, by the way, this is your brother.'"

"He's not *really* her *brother*."

"Yes, he is our brother. And if you don't tell her ahead of time, I will. That's not fair to Pam."

"You girls love to tell things, don't you? You'll probably blab to Jackie, too."

"No. Jackie didn't tell us about her call to Donna, so I don't think we need to tell her about Danny coming over. But Pam's different."

"Well, I'll tell her," said Mom.

So I called Donna and scheduled the visit for Monday. Little did I know that I had just unsettled the pebble that would let loose an avalanche.

When I went to work Monday morning, I wasn't even thinking about Danny going to see Dad that day. Once I had arranged everything with Donna the week before, I had no reason to think it wouldn't go as planned. So when I got out of a meeting in the middle of the afternoon that day and had a frantic message from Jackie on my voicemail, I had no idea what she would be calling about. She said it was an emergency and that I should call her immediately. My first thought was that Dad might have had another stroke or even that he might have died.

I took a deep breath and dialed her number. With Jackie, even the best of calls took courage on my part, and I could tell from her tone that this one would be rough.

She started yelling even before I finished the word "hello."

"I just want to know if you're in on it," she demanded.

"What happened?" I asked, my heart thumping so fast I thought I'd faint.

"Do you know what Mom was out doing today?"

"She . . . Pam was going to take her on some errands, I think."

"Ha! 'Errands'? Do you know what 'errand' specifically?"

"No. What?"

"You really don't know?"

"No, Jackie. Tell me."

"She was *changing her will!*"

My whole body went cold when I heard that, even before I had time to think through the implications of her words. A second or two later I thought about Danny being there that day, but I didn't know how to connect that fact with what Jackie was saying.

"Changing it to say what?" I asked.

"I don't know. Probably to take us out of it and to put those *new people* in it! Especially since that son from Los Angeles was *sitting there in Mom and Dad's living room* when I went over there this morning!"

She was snarling her words into the phone, and the chill I felt earlier had turned to sweat. This would have been a challenging conversation even under the best conditions, but what made it even worse was that I was at work. I sit in a cubicle where half a dozen people, including my boss, can hear my end of the conversation. We've been told to limit personal phone calls, which is not easy for me to do with Mom and Brandon calling me all the time. I have to yell so loud with Mom that people already laugh at me when I'm on the phone. Now I had a pile of work sitting in front of me, co-workers clicking away at their computers all around me, and a hysterical woman screaming at me on the phone.

Jackie was waiting to hear what I would say about the son from Los Angeles. Should I act surprised? Should I confess? Should I stall for time and tell her I wasn't allowed to talk at work?

She said, "Did you know he was over there?"

"What?" I asked, subconsciously resorting to Mom's stalling technique.

"You heard me. Did you know he was there?"

Just then my boss walked up with a folder in her hand. Instead of plopping it in my inbox, she hovered there, staring, waiting for me to hang up.

"Can I call you back?" I asked in my most businesslike tone. "I'm not able to talk right now."

"Just tell me. Did you know he was there?"

"It's a long story, and I'd rather talk about it once I get home."

"I knew it!" she screamed. "You're all a bunch of liars! I knew I couldn't trust any of you! You're not going to get away with it, I promise you that. I have legal rights, too. I know how to fight."

"Calm down, Jackie. Things are not what they seem. I'm sorry, but I'll have to call you when I get off work." I slid the phone into its cradle and looked up to my supervisor and smiled. She handed me the folder and said some words, but she might as well have been speaking Chinese. I nodded and smiled, and finally she went away. I opened the folder and leaned down over the paper as if the words were written in code and required my most intense concentration. I still hadn't even figured out what the folder was, and I wouldn't make sense of it for about half an hour, once the hurricane in my brain subsided.

I set my phone to automatically forward my calls into voice-mail for the rest of the day. We're allowed to do that when we're especially busy, which I was. Not that I got much done. Even the most trivial tasks took me three or four times longer to do than they normally would because I kept forgetting what I was doing. When I got home that night, I was planning to get myself something to eat, call Mom to get whatever information I could from her, devise a strategy for how to approach Jackie, and then call her back. But before I even set my purse down on the table, my phone started ringing. I stared at it for the first couple rings, wondering whether I should pretend to not be home yet and let the machine pick it up. Suddenly the ringing stopped. A few seconds later, Brandon sprang out of his room and announced, "Mom, it's Aunt Jackie on the phone."

"I thought you were supposed to be at practice!"

"They let us go early," he said and headed back into his room.

So much for pretending I wasn't here. I would have to face Jackie's wrath and somehow try to make her think I wasn't intimidated.

I picked up the phone in the kitchen. "Hi, Jackie. What have you found out?"

I thought that if I talked as if this was a dilemma we were *facing together,* she might be less hostile.

"I found out that I'm related to a bunch of liars," she said. "How long have you known Mom was gonna do this?"

"I didn't know she was going to do anything! I still don't even know what she's done."

"You didn't know that guy was going to be over there this morning?"

"I have met Danny, yes. And I knew he was planning to come over to see Dad. But I have never heard a single word about a will."

"Well, I wish I could believe you, but after what I've been through today, I can't assume that anything my family members say is true."

"Listen, Jackie," I said, hovering indecisively before taking the risk of speaking the next part, "I know that you called Donna a couple weeks ago and chewed her out without telling us, so don't get too self-righteous. You're the one who started concealing things."

There. I had said it. The danger of confronting Jackie with her own actions is that it sometimes backfires. Instead of bringing her down a notch, which is what I intended for it to do, it sometimes unhinges her and makes any rational conversation impossible. I did want to get some information from her about this whole will thing, but I couldn't do that if she was screaming at me for being a liar.

Jackie breathed these harsh little breaths into the phone. I could tell she was swaying between losing it entirely and calming down just enough to talk.

I filled the gap by saying, "Why don't you start from the beginning and tell me what happened, and then I promise I'll tell you everything I know."

"All right," she said, and I breathed a sigh of relief. Cease-fire. Over the next half hour, punctuated with a lot of huffing and puffing and occasional accusations of how devious we all were, Jackie told her story. She said that it started on Friday, when she called Mom to tell her she was planning to come and visit her and Dad on Monday morning. Normally Mom would have been really happy about that, since she usually blamed all her kids for not visiting enough. She also normally would have a list of errands that she'd ask Jackie to take care of for her. But on this day, Mom acted all nervous and told her not to come on Monday.

"Why not?" asked Jackie.

"Well, it's not good. . . . That nurse comes in the morning that day, and it's too much of a hassle. That always wears Dad out, and he doesn't like company on those days. So how about coming later in the week?"

Jackie didn't exactly buy this explanation, but Mom is no stranger to weird behavior, so Jackie let it go. But later in the day, it occurred to Jackie that Monday was *not* the nurse's day to come. The nurse comes on Tuesdays and Thursdays now. So Jackie called that home-health-care place and asked them when they were coming. Sure enough, it was Tuesday and Thursday. Then she picked up the phone to call Mom but put it down again before she dialed.

Instead of making Mom squirm around and come up with another lie, Jackie decided to wait till Monday and see what happened. So on Monday morning she called and Dad answered the phone. That's a little unusual, since Mom normally handles the phone these days. Jackie said he acted "real funny" and wouldn't tell her where Mom was. He said he didn't know, which she knew couldn't be true.

"Who took her?" asked Jackie.

"Pam."

"Well, where'd they say they were going?"

"Run a few errands, I guess. I don't remember. Want me to have her call you when she gets back?"

"It's an emergency, Dad," said Jackie, engaging in one of her own little lies. "Didn't she leave a number where she could be reached?"

That was a clever question. Mom always leaves a number for Dad when she goes anywhere without him. A couple weeks ago Pam took her to get her hair fixed and to lunch, and Mom insisted on leaving the phone numbers of the hair place and the restaurant.

"I don't know where that number is," said Dad.

"Find it. I need it."

Finally, "after about a week," as Jackie put it, she talked Dad into giving her the number.

"She'll be home any time, though," he said. "Why don't you wait and I'll have her call you? What's the big emergency, any-way?"

Jackie didn't answer him but instead asked another question of her own. "So did they take off and leave you there by yourself?"

"Well," he said, "I'm all right."

She got off the phone right away and called that number. As soon as they answered "Barnett and Associates," Jackie knew Mom must be there about the will.

I asked, "So what did you say?"

"I didn't say anything. I hung up and stormed around the room for a while."

"So you don't actually *know* that Mom was there about the will."

"What else would it be? That's the only thing she's ever seen that lawyer about. And if it was something else, why would it be a big secret? But if that wasn't proof enough, I got in the car and drove over there, and there sat this Danny guy with Dad."

"Were you mean to him? What did you say?"

"Not much. He didn't stay long after I got there. I'm sure

even *these* people don't have the gall to try to chitchat with me while they're stealing our inheritance."

"But Danny might not have even known they were *going* to the lawyer. Mom probably didn't tell—"

"Ha! Are you really that gullible? You think it's just a *coincidence* that this guy happens to show up at the same time our parents are changing their will? Come on, Carolyn."

"Well, if he was trying to force her to change the will, why wouldn't he take her to the lawyer himself rather than have Pam take her? I don't get it."

"I don't know. Maybe there's some legal reason why one of us had to be there."

"Then why would he need to be at Mom and Dad's house at all?"

"I don't know!" she huffed. "Maybe he was waiting for her to bring him a copy of the new will. Maybe he was buttering Dad up so he wouldn't change his mind. Maybe he was getting started on the next phase of his scam. For heaven's sake, why are you *defending* him?"

"I'm just trying to make sense of things. So what did you say to him?"

"Well, he introduced himself all nicey-nice, and I was civil to him, but I turned to Dad and asked him why Mom was at the lawyer's office. Dad played confused, like he didn't even know what a lawyer *was*. He said Mom had told him she and Pam were going to go run some errands. He said he didn't know that number was the lawyer's office and had no idea why she would go there. So then I turned to Danny and asked him if he knew anything about this. He claimed he didn't, but he certainly didn't want to stick around for more questions. He hightailed it out of there real quick."

"Did you insult him?"

"I didn't have time to. He took off."

I know enough about how Jackie operates to know that she was probably nastier to Danny than she was admitting. Whenever you hear Jackie's version of something, she's always the calm, reasonable one. But then when you hear it from someone else, Jackie comes off as rude and hostile. So if there was some innocent explanation to this will business, I dreaded to think what damage she might have done to our family's relationship with Danny.

Jackie said that after Danny left, she sat there with Dad and waited for Mom and Pam to come home. Dad stuck to his story that he didn't know what Mom was doing, so he was no help as far as providing any new information. When Jackie heard Pam's car drive up, she was ready for the big showdown, but she was shocked (and disappointed) when she looked out and saw Mom walking up the driveway alone and Pam driving off without a word.

"That coward!" said Jackie. "She was too ashamed of what she was doing to even face me."

Mom explained Pam's actions differently, of course. She said the kids had fallen asleep in the car, and Pam didn't want to go through all the hassle of getting them out of their car seats and taking them inside when she'd just have to get them packed up again a little while later. I know that Pam thinks it's a lot of work to take the kids into Mom and Dad's house right now, since she has to keep such a close eye on what they might get into, like pills or the remnants of one of Dad's accidents that might not have been cleaned up too well. But I also know that if she got there and saw that Danny's car had been replaced by Jackie's van, she probably figured she was in for a fight if she went inside.

Mom refused to explain anything to Jackie.

"It was a private matter between me and my lawyer," Mom

said. "It has nothing to do with you, and I'm not going to get into it."

When Jackie accused her of giving away our inheritance to Donna and Danny, Mom called her crazy and ordered her to leave the house.

"She said I was upsetting Dad too much and that if I kept it up, I'd send him into another stroke," said Jackie. "But I don't think Dad was even paying attention to us. He was looking toward the fireplace as if he was lost in thought. I told Mom I'd leave but that I wasn't going to let this drop. I told her we had legal rights and we weren't going to let these people march in here and make fools out of our parents. So I left, and that's when I called you."

Once again, I had to assume that she had upset Mom and Dad even more than she was admitting. She was probably more threatening than she had told me, and Dad was probably paying more attention than she realized. Even if the whole problem with the will turned out to be a misunderstanding, I foresaw many days or weeks of damage control with Danny and Donna. And if Mom really was playing some kind of funny game with her will, then this fiasco could last for years.

Jackie said, "I've been trying to get Pam, but she's either not home or not answering. She can't dodge me forever, but knowing her, she won't be much help against these people. So that's my story. Now tell me the secrets *you've* been keeping."

I told her about Donna and Danny's visit. I emphasized how nice they were and how well we got along and how unthreatening they seemed. "I think they've got more money than we do," I said. "I can't believe they're in this to scam Mom and Dad. If you spent some time with them, you'd see that they're not that kind of people."

"Look at the facts."

"We don't know the facts."

"Well, I intend to find out."

"Just don't overreact till we know more."

"What did they tell you about the relationship between Dad and their mother?"

"Nothing. We were friendly, but we didn't get into details of the past. We never will if we keep having these blowups."

"Well, it's not my fault! I'm not the one running to the lawyer to change my will or having these secret meetings behind people's backs."

"Will you do me one favor and let me try to get some information before you do anything else?"

"I'll give you a couple days, but then I'm thinking about contacting a lawyer myself to find out what our options are."

"Well, just *wait*. Please. I still think we're going to find an innocent explanation for all of this."

Jackie let out one of those awful cackles she uses for a laugh. "Yeah, right," she said.

I didn't even bother to tell her about the get-together Donna and I had planned. There wasn't much chance it would happen now, unless we could all bring our attorneys.

20 HUGH: WHAT I WISH I COULD SAY

I have imaginary conversations with Danny. The real Danny. The Danny I *know*. The Danny who has sat in my living room twice. The first time he was here, our conversation was interrupted by pie dishes and women's chatter, and the second time it was obliterated by the appearance of my mentally unbalanced daughter, Jackie. Danny left that second time without saying when or if he would come back, and who could blame him, given the fact that this is a house where a maniac might pop up at any moment and start flipping out for no reason.

But in spite of all the perfectly valid reasons for him not to return, I believe he will. Both times he was here, I saw the wariness in his face, but I also saw the curiosity. He wants to know who I am. He wants to ask questions. He wants to understand how much of me is in him. He wants to know why his mother would have fallen for me and why she would have fled from me.

He hasn't asked any of that yet. He knows, I think, that I could never construct a truthful answer to any of those questions so bluntly put. He knows that the truth lies at a deeper level, a level you can barely reach with words.

The first time I saw him, our conversation was mere politeness. I could see his curiosity but couldn't respond to it. The second time started out more promising. He told me about himself, and with each detail that he chose to reveal, I sensed that he was telling me, "Maybe you and I are not so different. I, too, have lived a life that contains incidents that even I would not try to justify. I am here to get to know you, not to call you to account."

He said, "I am divorced," and I heard, "I am not here to judge you for whatever caused your breakup with my mother. I, too, have known the defeat of losing the one you love to another man."

He said, "My son is in California with his mother and her new husband," and I heard, "I, too, have abandoned my son, and I understand that there can be reasons for it, that there can be circumstances beyond anyone's control."

I realize that I'm running the risk of overinterpreting him, reading into his words what I *need* to hear, but I really do believe he's trying to lay the groundwork for me to tell him my story without groveling. Right before Jackie burst in and sucked all the sanity out of the room, Danny was telling me about all the places where he had worked as an accountant. He said he got bored easily with his jobs and had trouble keeping them very long. What he really wants to do is start his own business, but it hasn't worked out yet.

When he asked me how long I worked at Brantwell and I told him almost forty years, he said, "I admire that kind of perseverance. You remind me of my dad. He worked at General Motors for over thirty years—even though it was in two separate cities—and he loved every minute of it."

His "dad." Barbara's third husband. Not the man she left me for. Don't think about Barbara now, I told myself. *Let it go.*

"You must have enjoyed it if you were willing to work there so long," Danny said.

"I did enjoy it, yes, in the long run. But when I was younger, I vowed I would never work there. It was where my father wanted me to work, so I was determined not to do it."

At that moment Jackie barged into the room. Almost fifty years of absence from my son was not enough punishment. Jackie had to prolong it. She came in red-faced and breathing heavy, glancing around like she was trying to figure out which piece of furniture to tear a leg off of so she could start busting up the place. Danny tried to be nice to her, but Jackie acted like it was all she could do to restrain herself from calling the police and having him hauled out of there. You would have thought she had caught him crawling through the window the way she hung back from him kind of half-scared and half-threatening.

She started ranting about the lawyer, and I had no idea what she was talking about. She turned on Danny and demanded that he tell her about this lawyer, as if he would know anything. It was so stupid and embarrassing that I was tempted to try to force myself up out of my chair and push her right out the door.

I couldn't have done it, of course. Jackie's built like a bull-dozer.

Finally she made enough sense to at least get across the idea that her mom was at the lawyer's office to change our will. That was news to me. Vonnie had told me that Pam was going to take her on some errands, and that's all I knew about it. She had told me that if anyone called, just tell them she'd be back that afternoon. She left an emergency number like she always does, but I didn't know whose number it was.

About the time that Jackie started screaming at me for being a liar and calling her mother and sisters liars and spewing out all sorts of other nonsense that I was too jangled to follow, Danny decided to leave. Who could blame him? I would have given anything to have been able to get in the car and go with him.

She kept it up after he left, but I shut her out. I'm able to do that now, even better than I used to. Sometimes I *have* to do it to avoid getting too upset, to keep from feeling like my head or my chest is going to explode. I've come to realize that when I'm confused, which I certainly was that day, it's often best to try to relax and think about other things until my brain clears up on its own and I'm able to deal with people again.

So once Danny was gone and Jackie was still yap-yap-yapping, I told her I thought she had made a fool of herself and that she was an embarrassment to our family, and then I tuned her out. I don't remember another word she said until Vonnie got home. I remember only a far-off braying voice, a sound similar to what I hear when the next-door neighbor has his lawn mower going.

While I ignored Jackie, I thought about Danny and continued our conversation in the way I wish it could have gone. I was thinking about his restlessness, his urge to move from job to job, his desire to start his own business. He said he admired me for working at Brantwell for forty years, but what I really wanted to tell him was, "My forty-year career is like so many other things. It's not what it seems. Nothing turned out the way it started. I was as restless as you are in the beginning. We're more alike than you would guess, Danny."

The first time I stepped onto the factory floor at Brantwell was the summer after I graduated from high school. The war was almost over, but I was to go into the army a few months later anyway. In the meantime, Dad got me a job at the factory, which at that time was still making parts for tanks and other military equipment. The pay was good. A guy could get all the overtime he wanted. Dad thought I should be thrilled with the job. He didn't even bother to ask me ahead of time whether I wanted it.

It was one of my high school graduation gifts. After my graduation ceremony, we had a little reception at our house, all the neighbors and relatives standing around eating cake and punch. Mom and Dad gave me a card and a present. A watch was in the package. An announcement was in the card: *You start work at Brantwell tomorrow. 7:00 a.m. Congratulations!*

I had to act grateful for this. Mom and Dad had their hearts set on it, and Dad had gone to a lot of trouble to work out the details with the personnel office. I thanked him and smiled and decided to make the best of it, but when I was alone in my room that night, I ground my teeth in frustration. For one thing, I was angry that I had to start *the next day*. I had already made plans to run around with my friends that day, to have our own celebration free of adults and punch bowls and polite conversation. Now I had to tell them I couldn't make it because I had graduated from the jail of high school to the prison of my father's factory.

I was also angry that I wasn't *offered* the job but was simply *ordered* to show up. It was the family factory. My dad had been there for nearly twenty years, and my two older brothers, Neil and Jim, ended up working for Brantwell for their entire careers except when they were in the military. Long ago I had made up my mind not to follow in their footsteps, but now my father, on the eve of my passage into adulthood, had simply appropriated my life as if it were his own. Furthermore, I was expected to thank him for it.

Considering how much I loved my work in later years, how the factory represented such a closed-off, safe, orderly place away from the tumult of the rest of my life, it's amazing for me to recall how much I hated it that first summer. I felt like I was turning into an old man overnight. I was instantly transforming into my father and my brothers. I hated the grind of factory life—punching in so early in the morning while my mind and body still craved sleep, dragging myself through the day, feeling each second of the clock's *tick-tick-tick* in slow motion before the bell would finally ring and I would be free. Then trudging toward home, smelling of oil and boredom, enjoying a few hours of pleasure with my friends until I had to grab four or five hours of sleep and do it all again.

The other workers made fun of me because as I stood at my workstation my foot never stopped tapping. The guys would say, "You trying to dance? You have to go to the bathroom?" But I couldn't keep my foot still. I was so restless that it was all I could do to keep the rest of my body still. At times it got so bad I could barely restrain myself from breaking into a run and escaping the factory forever.

Brantwell had guards at the door, and we had to show our passes as we came in each morning. We could bring in lunch pails, but we couldn't bring radios or books or newspapers. We got half an hour for lunch and two ten-minute breaks. The out-side world was not visible to anyone on the factory floor. The city around us could have been leveled by a tornado and we would never have known. Our supervisors enforced a strict dress code. No shorts, of course. No jeans. No T-shirts. We wore blue work pants and a blue button-down work shirt every day. The guards, the windowless walls, the uniforms, and the constant surveillance all made me feel like a prisoner. I looked forward to the army as if it were a Caribbean vacation. I knew it would be hard, but at least it would be *out there* in the world.

I couldn't have explained my frustration to Dad, of course, or to hardly anyone else in my life. My father would have said something like, "What more can you expect? Brantwell is the best factory in town! They have the best pay and the best bene-fits. It's also secure—they haven't laid off anybody in years."

Even worse, he would have taunted me with questions like, "What's the matter with you? Afraid to get your hands dirty?

Think you're too good for a little hard work?"

I never gave Dad the chance to fling that ridicule at me. I worked hard, and I didn't complain. A couple times Dad asked me why I looked so sullen all the time, but that was as close as we came to ever discussing my feelings. I was a good worker. I stifled my frustration and poured my energy into the work to try to make the time go faster. My bosses liked me and told me there'd be a job waiting for me when I got out of the military.

The job was waiting, but I didn't take it. I've never seen my dad as angry at me as when I came home from the army and told him I wasn't going back to Brantwell. He took my refusal to go back to that factory as a personal insult, almost as a rejection of him as a father. He said he had carefully laid the groundwork for my return, reminding the bosses of my discharge date and assuring them that I was eager to return. Now I made him look like a fool.

"You never bothered to ask me whether I wanted the job," I said. "This is not the Dark Ages. Sons are not required to spend their whole lives doing the same job their fathers did. Maybe I want to get out of here and try something different."

This was the first time I had directly challenged my father about the job (or much of anything else), and my mom and brothers had to join in, of course, and take his side. They called me "disrespectful" and "ungrateful" and "spoiled."

"So what are you gonna do?" Dad wanted to know. This conversation took place in the kitchen in the house on Green Street. Little could any of us have imagined that in a few years he would be dead, I would be working at Brantwell, and that house would be mine. He would win the argument in the end, but that night none of us knew it. My brother Neil and his wife, Betty, were there, and Mom was serving dinner. Neil and Dad still carried on their clothes the oily smell of the factory, where they had been working all day.

I told Dad that a friend in Lafayette had offered me a job as a house painter and that I intended to take it.

"A *painter*," scoffed Dad, as if I had chosen some exotic profession, like a belly dancer or a trapeze artist.

"*Lafayette*," said Mom in his same tone. Lafayette was sixty miles away from us. We had relatives there and had been there a few dozen times over the course of my life, but Mom pronounced it as if it were Baghdad or Bombay.

Neil put his head down and laughed into his creamed corn. He took on the patronizing attitude of a big brother listening to his more immature sibling describing his plan to build a space rocket to travel to the moon.

I glared at Neil, from whom I had dared to hope for a glimmer of support. He refused to look at me. Dad had already launched into his detailed critique of the life of a painter. "There is no security in it! You could be swamped with work one week and out of work the next. There are no benefits with it, right? No insurance, no pension plan. The pay probably stinks, too, right? How can you ever expect to support a wife and kids with a job like that?"

"I don't have a wife and kids," I said.

"You won't, either, if you keep making such stupid decisions."

"Lots of people are painters, Dad, and they live happy lives. Not everybody in the world has to work at your factory to be happy. Not everybody has to stay in Indianapolis. I want to go live my own life for a while and figure out what I want to do for a career. I don't want to get stuck at Brantwell the moment I get home from the army. Maybe later. I'm not saying I'll be a painter forever."

"There may not be any job openings later!"

"There'll be other factories to work at, then."

"Maybe not! You take everything for granted. You think everything's always going to be handed to you on a silver platter."

Whenever the words "silver platter" were brought into a conversation, I knew that any chance for rational discussion had come to an end. In my family, the worst attitude you could be accused of was thinking yourself to be superior to someone else or too good for hard work. Dad was trying to steer the conversation in that direction. I sensed that everyone at the table knew where he was headed. He was about to accuse me of being a prima donna. He'd say I thought I was too good for the hard factory work that he and my brothers did, so I was going to run away so I wouldn't have to lower myself to their lifestyle.

"Let's just forget it," I said. "I haven't even unpacked yet, and you're already expecting me to have the next thirty years of my life planned out."

Dad tapped his fork on his potatoes.

"What's wrong with the way your brother lives?" he asked, pointing at Neil, Exhibit A. "Isn't that good enough for you? He's got a good job, he's married, he just bought a little house."

I shrugged. I had no intention of participating in a competition with Neil. I already knew that in my father's eyes, both my brothers were way ahead of me. For me, it was a no-win argument. I couldn't say what I really felt, which was, *I'm happy for Neil, but I don't want his life. I don't want his boring job or his boxy little house or his pointy-nosed wife. I just want to get out of here and have some fun.*

If I had been like *my* daughters are now, I would have gone ahead and said those things. My daughters would tell me off and order me to mind my own business. But that's not how I operated with my dad. I was more used to *fleeing* arguments with him than *engaging* in them.

The answer I finally gave Dad was, "I don't know what I want to do as a career yet, but I've been thinking about maybe going to college."

Dad threw his hands in the air, and Neil smirked. I might as well have said I wanted to move to England and become a member of the royal family. Our family didn't go to college. We worked. Dad stuffed a big piece of pork chop into his mouth, but I could tell by his obsessional expression that he was planning an assault on the whole college idea. I didn't want to hear it. I finished my food as fast as I could and got out of there.

That conversation wasn't the final word on the subject. Before I left town three days later, I had individual confrontations with Neil, Jim, Mom, and even one of my former bosses at Brantwell. I suspected that Dad had put each of them up to it, but they didn't admit that, and I didn't ask. Dad didn't speak to me about it again, and when I left for Lafayette, he was at work. He avoided good-bye scenes. I'm sure he hoped that at the last minute I would come to my senses and plead with him to get me my job back.

My dad was a complete mystery to me back then, but now I understand him better. I've had a few decades to figure him out, and I've had kids of my own. I have also ended up living a life that is surprisingly similar to his. One of the stories we heard from Dad countless times was the story of his uncle Herb, who lost his job during the early years of the Depression and whose family fell into degrading poverty. This image of Herb coming to my father and begging for money to feed his family was seared into my dad's consciousness, and it motivated him to do whatever it took to keep his job and maintain financial stability.

Just as some kids grow up with the image of some boogeyman dangling as a vague threat at the edge of their lives, we grew up with the image of Herb and what could happen if you didn't do what your parents told you and work hard and get a good job and pay your bills on time. Dad helped Herb financially for much of the 1930s, but his beloved uncle still fell into alcoholism and died right around the start of World War II.

Even though Dad was laid off several times during the

Depression, sometimes for two or three months at a time, he was proud and grateful to God that he always managed to support his family. He wanted to make sure that we always did the same. By running off on my own and rejecting a job that offered security and decent pay, I was risking, in my father's eyes, falling into Herb's trap. Before long I might be an alcoholic roaming the streets and begging for food.

Dad overlearned the lesson of Herb. He didn't have much imagination about the many ways that a man could make a good living. But I know now, as I did not understand then, that he was motivated by more than simply a desire to control my life and shape me into the mold of himself and my brothers.

If Dad had seen my apartment in Lafayette (I invited him, but he and Mom never visited), he would have said, "I told you so." To Dad it would have looked like only one step up from Uncle Herb. To me, it represented freedom and simplicity. It was a furnished room that contained nothing but the basics—a bed, a tiny kitchen area, a table, a little chest of drawers, an old sofa. The bathroom, which I shared with another tenant, was down the hall. There was one clothes closet, covered by a curtain. There were no drapes on the window, just a pull-down shade. I could not have been happier with my accommodations. All of my possessions, which had easily fit into my car, were scattered around the room.

Does this sound familiar, Danny? I, too, knew the pleasure of reducing the clutter in my life so that I could concentrate on what I was experiencing rather than what I was accumulating. We are not so different!

Dad would not have seen the apartment the same way I did. He would have said something like, "It's dinky. It's ugly. You don't own it. You're just throwing away rent money on it. You could never bring a wife home to it or raise a family in it. You should get out of it as soon as you can."

Dad had no appreciation for the joy of simple living. For him, simplicity was nothing more than a euphemism for poverty. I hate to admit that the older I got, the more I started thinking like him.

During my first several months in that home I was happy to be in a space of my own, with no complications from my family and none of the regimentation the army had demanded. I worked hard every day that we were on a job, which was about three-fourths of the time. After work, I would stop off at a little cafeteria for dinner and then come home and do whatever I wanted—go out with friends, walk a few blocks downtown to see a movie, go out on a date, or sit by the window and read a book.

One of the things I liked best about that room was that it looked out onto a street that led to the downtown restaurants and movie theaters. My room was on the second floor, and it had a wide window ledge that I could sit on and watch the girls going to their jobs at the department stores and cafés, or the young couples walking hand in hand to the movie theater, or mothers taking their babies for a walk in a stroller after dinner. It seems like back then, before air conditioning, people were out on the streets more than they are nowadays, in the summer at least, and my street was always packed with people going about their lives.

Even though I enjoyed watching this daily parade outside my window, at times I felt strangely disconnected from it. After several months of living like this, I began to get the feeling that these people outside my window were the ones living *real* lives, and I was mainly *avoiding* life, somehow putting it on hold. In one sense I was enjoying my freedom from the chores that filled the lives of so many people I knew and saw—raising kids, mowing the lawn, visiting in-laws, and a thousand other responsibilities. But another feeling was growing in me, a *longing* for connection to the world outside me—to a woman, a family, a neighborhood. I envied the families I saw walking down my street, the kids squealing with excitement as they headed downtown to get ice cream or go shopping. I envied the couples walking arm in arm, unaware of me or anyone else watching them, lost in the intensity of their own relationship.

Is that how you felt, Danny, as you sat alone in your compact apartment in Los Angeles? Did you feel exhilarated one moment by the fact that the whole thrilling world lay just outside your window, while in the next moment you felt cut off from everything that would make it meaningful?

For the first year that I lived in that apartment, working and having fun and watching the world go by outside my window, I spent much of my time daydreaming about the kind of life I wanted to construct for myself. I still held on to the possibility of college. I lived just a few miles from Purdue University, where we sometimes did painting jobs, but I had no definite idea of what I wanted to study. My daydreams had to do with a certain lifestyle I wanted to acquire but not even the vaguest notion of the work that would go with it.

For instance, I wanted a job that would take me far away from Indiana. I wanted to wear expensive business suits and fly on airplanes or travel on luxurious ocean liners to the great cities of the world—London, Paris, Hong Kong—where I would celebrate big business deals by sipping champagne or martinis in fancy restaurants.

Can't you hear my dad's derisive laughter at such an idea? I never told him, of course, nor anyone else. I stayed in Lafayette, and I painted, and I waited for a more definite plan to emerge.

That's when Barbara showed up.

Oh, Danny, if I could sweep away the awkwardness and the guilt and the disaster that we're all still paying for, I would love to be able to tell you the thrill I felt when I first saw your mother.

I loved her so much that I probably would have fallen hard

for her no matter when she entered my life, but she was particularly irresistible that second summer of living in Lafayette. I was *waiting,* you see, for a plan or a person or *something* that I couldn't even identify. I had no doubt Barbara was it.

I saw her on a July afternoon when I had a day off between jobs. I was sitting in my window seat finishing my lunch when she walked by. She looked like a model walking down the runway—to me at least. She wore a blue dress, a little hat, and white gloves. She would have stood out no matter when she walked by, but at that time of day I was mostly used to seeing bedraggled housewives trying to corral their kids. I can still picture Barbara's face in that moment, the bright red lipstick, the half smile, the delicate chin.

I did something I had never done before. I got up and ran down the stairs to follow her. It had never occurred to me to go outside to get a closer look at the people who passed by my window. Even when I went out to see Barbara, I didn't consciously decide to do it. I just suddenly found myself on my way out to where she was. I could not bear to let this gorgeous woman simply walk away never to be seen again.

Once I got out to the sidewalk, I didn't know what to do next. She was still in view, headed toward downtown, and I could have run and caught up with her in no time. But what would I do when I reached her? Say, "I was staring at you from my window and decided to follow you"? Some men might have felt comfortable doing that, but it was not my style. With my luck, she would have screamed for help or run to tell the police.

Instead, I followed her from a discreet distance. When we got downtown, she walked into Marten's Department Store. I followed a few minutes later, and when I went through the revolving door, the first person I saw was her. She was behind the cosmetics counter, looking right at me. I could feel my face flush with embarrassment. Had she realized I was following her?

Why was she staring at me like that? I smiled, and she smiled back, and then I stumbled through the store, not knowing what I should do next. Finally I left the store after pretending to look at some socks and shirts in the men's department.

Over the next couple weeks, Marten's became my favorite store. I suddenly had a new passion for shopping. Barbara sometimes worked in cosmetics and sometimes in women's apparel. I first spoke to her about a week after my original sighting, when she caught me standing by the women's scarves and purses.

"May I help you, sir?" she asked, and once again I felt my face glow with embarrassment.

"I need . . . I'm looking for . . . a gift."

"For a girlfriend?" she asked with a smile.

"No!" I insisted, suddenly horrified that she might think I could love anyone but her. "For . . . my mother."

She helped me pick out a scarf, and then I paid for it and got out of there fast. In my embarrassment I feared she was laughing at me. She was so gorgeous that I figured this sort of thing must happen to her all the time, men pretending to want to buy something just so they'd have the chance to talk to her. I felt like an idiot. I promised myself not to make a fool of myself like this again.

The next day I was back, drawn irresistibly to the women's apparel section. I bought another scarf, and this time I tried a little conversation. "Did you know you pass by my apartment on the way to work? It must be a long walk in high heels. Does someone give you a ride if it rains?"

Two days later I was at the store again, not knowing what excuse I would make this time.

Barbara helped me out. She said, "How many scarves are you going to buy before you ask me out?"

The next night we went out on our first date, and she has

been part of my life—even during the decades when I never saw her—ever since.

I'd love to tell Danny all this, but I doubt I ever will. Conversations almost never move in the direction I want them to. For one thing, because of the strokes I get confused, and I'm so forgetful that I often can't come up with the words I need.

But even beyond that, there are other barriers. If you think about it, how often do fathers and sons really say what they want to say to each other? I could never tell my father what was really on my mind, and I'm sure my girls don't tell me their innermost thoughts, either. With my girls, it felt like from the moment they learned to walk, they were moving away from me, creating their own worlds, and turning to me only when they needed something. They don't really understand me now, even though they've known me all their lives. Why should I hope that Danny will be any different?

Still, I don't want to make myself content with imaginary conversations. I want to try to explain a few things. I want to see Danny again.

21

PAM:
I DON'T HAVE TIME
FOR THIS

Lots of people have told me I should treasure these days when the kids are so small because the time passes so quickly. It doesn't always feel like the days are passing quickly, especially when the kids get into trouble—like today when Sarah managed to get the bottle of baby powder open and was flinging it from side to side, screaming, "Nainin! Nainin," which means, "Raining." I keep the baby powder on the dressing table in the corner of the living room, so she managed to cover the table, the drapes, five or six stuffed animals, and the carpet. At least it smells good in there now.

But I do know what people mean when they say to cherish this time. It's hard to believe how much the kids have changed in a year. Last summer Sarah was an infant, bald and helpless, and now she runs and speaks a few words and flings baby powder. Matthew has changed just as much. He's gone from that babyish toddler look to the look of a little boy. He can speak full sentences now. Sometimes I don't even realize how much he's changed until I see pictures of him from six months or a year ago and realize he's hardly the same little boy.

Even though the kids drive me crazy at times and push me to the limits of my patience and energy, I love them fiercely and want to give them as much of my attention as possible. I love being a mother. It's so absorbing that it makes it harder for me to do the things I did before, like running over to Mom and Dad's all the time, responding to their every complaint. But I know they need me, too, and I feel bad when they want me to do something and I have to say no. For me, meeting the demands of each day is so challenging that I don't have time for extraneous conflict. Unfortunately, I'm caught in another tug-of-war between Carolyn and Jackie. Mom and Dad are certainly not helping the situation, either. Sometimes I feel like dropping out of this family and moving to Wyoming or some other place far away where I can concentrate on my kids and Cliff.

Mom picked the worst possible time to decide to change her will, with Jackie already so paranoid about these other kids of Dad's. And the situation Jackie found on Monday was enough to fuel the suspicion of even a more reasonable person than she is. It was bad enough for her to find out that Mom was at the lawyer's, but then for her to find Danny, whom she hadn't even met, at the house on the same morning . . . Well, that was all it took to convince her that we were all conspiring to disinherit her and give her portion of Mom and Dad's estate to these "new people," as she calls them.

It would help, of course, if I could simply tell her the clear and truthful story of what Mom *was* doing at the lawyer's. But in this family, there always has to be a secret hidden inside every action. So when Jackie called me at her angriest, I had to tell her that I wasn't allowed to say what Mom was doing. Jackie doesn't know how to react to me. She can't decide whether to treat me like an ally in her fight against the "new people" or whether she should assume that I'm one of the conspirators in this nasty scheme. If I hadn't been driving the car that took Mom to the lawyer, I might have been in the clear with Jackie, but now a cloud of suspicion hangs over me.

When she called me the night of the lawyer trip, I tried to reason with her, but I didn't get very far. I said, "Do you really think I'd be part of a plan to give away Mom and Dad's estate to people we don't even know?"

"I just look at the facts," she said. "Mom went to the lawyer. You took her. That man was in the living room with Dad."

"Well, I can assure you that what Mom did at the lawyer's office had nothing to do with the new people."

Jackie was silent for a moment, signaling her skepticism. "What *did* she do, then?"

"I can't tell you. You know how Mom is about these things."

Jackie's only answer was a big huff, her favorite sound. I hate hiding the truth from her and don't see why it's necessary. You'd think that by now Mom and Dad would have learned that the truth almost always comes out and that keeping secrets only prolongs the agony. Jackie kept pressing me to tell her the full story, so finally I compromised and told her that it had something to do with Carolyn. I hoped that wasn't saying too much, but I was sick of it all. Unfortunately, my revelation didn't quiet her, because then she started bugging me about *what* it had to do with Carolyn.

"Is Mom giving Carolyn those dolls?" she asked.

"Like I said, I really can't get into it."

"She'd do that, wouldn't she, just out of spite."

"I'm not saying she did."

"What about those photographs? She probably gave those to Carolyn, too, didn't she? Just because she knows I want them and Carolyn doesn't."

"I wish I had never even gotten involved in this."

The truth was that Mom had decided not to mention the dolls or photos in her will. I guess she figures it would be more fun to let us fight over them once she's dead.

Jackie said, "So what else did Mom—"

"I won't go any further," I said. "I promised Mom I wouldn't tell, so I have to honor that. But what she did is no threat to you, let me put it that way."

Even that statement might not have been the complete truth. If Carolyn did end up moving into Mom and Dad's house after they die, which I don't think she will, then that would reduce Jackie's part of their estate, or it would at least postpone when she would get it. But if Carolyn *doesn't* move into the house, then Mom's trip to the lawyer won't have any effect on anybody.

"Well," she said, "Mom hasn't heard the last of this from me. I have rights, too, and I don't intend to see them trampled."

I didn't respond.

Jackie asked, "So what did you think of this so-called son of Dad's?"

"Well, I barely talked to him. Mom rushed me out the door. Believe it or not, she actually had her purse and all that ready to go the minute I got there. Danny seemed like a nice guy, though." I couldn't resist adding, "He kind of looks like you in a way."

"Don't even say that!" she bellowed.

Once I got Jackie off the phone, not even half an hour went by before Carolyn called. She was frantic at first, too, having faced Jackie's fury. But Carolyn was a little easier to reassure. I told her what Mom had done was just a "technical" change in the will. I wish I had thought of that idea with Jackie. What I told her isn't exactly true, of course, so I don't feel comfortable with that. I guess I'm getting to be more like Mom and Dad, saying whatever keeps people calm for the moment. I don't want to be that way. I wish we could just lay everything out on the table and then learn to live with it. The truth is not so unbearable.

Now Carolyn is worried that Donna will cancel the "family reunion" cookout that the two of them were planning. Carolyn wants to go ahead with it and wants me to promise to come if Donna still has it. At first I told her no. I was too nervous to get involved in this whole predicament and just wanted to stay out of it. But then I talked to Cliff about it and changed my mind. I called Carolyn back and said we'd be happy to come. Like Cliff said, if these people are going to be involved in our lives in one way or another, then a fun setting like that might be the best way to get to know them and their families. It's better than surprising each other the way Danny surprised Jackie on Monday.

Besides, I miss the days when our own family used to have cookouts all the time in the summer. It seems like we were always getting together to celebrate one of the kids' birthdays or Memorial Day or the Fourth of July or nothing at all. I used to love watching the kids run around and relaxing in the shade and playing badminton. Now it's harder to get everybody together. We're either in a crisis or too busy with our own immediate families or working extra or something. I suggested that they have this get-together in Mom and Dad's backyard to make it easier for them, but Carolyn said Donna really wants us at her house. I guess we'll find a way to get Mom and Dad up there. Assuming, of course, that Danny and Donna don't decide to cancel it and get away from this crazy family while they still have a chance.

Carolyn was really happy when I told her we'd come to the cookout. When I hung up, I was feeling pretty good about how things might work out, but then a few minutes later the phone rang again. It was Carolyn. She warned me not to tell Jackie about the cookout. Carolyn hasn't decided whether Jackie should be invited, and she wants to talk to Donna about it before she makes any decision. She's afraid Jackie might come and disrupt everything.

"Great," I told her. "That's just what we need. Another secret."

22

DANNY:
TIME TO GET MY HANDS DIRTY

Hugh called me a couple days after my last visit and apologized for his daughter Jackie's bizarre behavior. He asked me to come and see him again, so I did. I don't know what Jackie's problem is with me, but I'm not going to let her scare me away.

I went back on Friday morning of that week, and at first I was afraid he was going to start apologizing again about how bad the house looks. He told me that the plumber had come the day before and had torn out part of the floor to fix the toilet. The toilet had flooded so many times over the years that the floor was rotting away underneath it. The plumber had put in new boards to fix it, but now that part of the floor was bare wood, with no tile.

"I'll have to get down there and put on some new floor tile when I feel better," said Hugh. "But in the meantime it looks horrible."

"You don't have anybody who could put that tile on for you?"

"No. I'll get to it."

"I could do that for you in no time," I said, not stopping to think about whether I should be getting involved in a home improvement project for a man I barely knew. "They have those tiles that you peel the back off of, and you can cut them with a razor blade around the edges. It's really pretty easy. If you wouldn't mind that kind of tile, I could have it done for you today."

"Oh no," he said. "I couldn't put you to that kind of trouble."

"Not at all. I'd really like to do it. We could talk while I work."

Vonnie stood at the corner of the room during this exchange, stopped in her tracks as she was heading from the bedroom to the kitchen. Hugh looked at her, and some signal that only they knew the meaning of passed between them. He turned to me and said he'd be grateful for me to do the work as long as it wasn't too much trouble.

Before I knew it I was on my hands and knees in Hugh's bathroom, measuring to see how much tile I would need. Then I left to buy the supplies, purchased with money that Vonnie pulled out of a little sack hidden behind some books in the bookshelf. The sack was rolled up and held in place with rubber bands, so with her arthritic hands it took her several minutes to get the money free.

When I got back with the tile and other supplies, Vonnie stopped me in their closed-in porch and whispered, "This is really too much work. It was nice of you to get this tile for us and be willing to help us out, but why don't you just leave it here and we'll get to it later? It'll be lunchtime pretty soon—I can fix you and Hugh something good to eat."

I suspect that what she was really saying was, "Why are you doing this? What ulterior motives do I need to worry about?"

I knew I wouldn't be able to explain my reasons in any way that would satisfy her, and I'm not even sure I fully knew the answer. All I knew was that doing something useful made this day much more bearable for me. I wanted to talk to Hugh, but I didn't want to sit like a statue all day in that stuffy living room and listen to the clock ticking. It's like whenever I've had an old friend come out to California to visit; we wouldn't just sit in a room and talk; we'd go out and play a round of golf or shoot some baskets or something. If I could *do* something while I talked to Hugh, it would feel less like an inquisition. It would be better than staring at him and wondering about all the things he must be hiding from me.

I assured Vonnie that I loved this kind of work and that it was no trouble at all. "Just bring me some water or iced tea every once in a while, and I'll be fine," I said.

"And lunch?"

"That would be great, thanks."

She offered no further objections. I think she was happy that, whatever strange reason I might have for wanting to crawl around in her bathroom, at least her floor would get fixed.

I'm not so great at home repair projects, and I had never actually laid floor tile before, but even for me this work was not too difficult. The bathroom was cramped and hot, but Vonnie kept me well supplied with lemonade and snacks. Except for our lunch break and her occasional interruptions to bring drinks, Vonnie left Hugh and me alone. It's possible that she was listening from the other room, but with her hearing problem, I doubt it.

For lunch she fixed hot dogs and baked beans. She needed my help to open the can of beans. She said she could never get the electric can opener to work, and her hands are too weak to use the manual can opener. Hugh said he can open a can with the manual opener, but it takes him a long time. "Another one of the humiliations of old age," he said. "One of hundreds."

Vonnie added that when her kids came over, she sometimes

lined up her cans for the next few meals and had one of them open them up for her. "The other day I asked the man next door to open a can. I saw him walking out to get his mail, and my girls hadn't been here in a few days, so I called him over here. He thought it was a funny thing for me to ask him to do, but he did it. We'll see how funny he thinks it is when he's my age."

Hugh watched me from a chair just outside the bathroom. He acted more alert than during my first visit, even though occasionally he would repeat the same question three or four times. On this day he was particularly interested in my accounting job that I was to start soon at a large restaurant supply company owned by one of Donna's friends. He wanted to know the name of the company (he asked this several times), the day I was to start, what I'd be doing, and so on. I dutifully answered these questions, but my lack of enthusiasm for the position must have shown through, because Hugh asked, "That sounds like a good job, doesn't it? Don't you want to do it?"

I set down the piece of tile I was cutting and looked up at him. For the first time, his words and tone sounded like they were coming from a father, from *my* father. I heard worry in his voice, as if he was afraid that I was going to sabotage myself in this job the way I had in so many others. Did he already understand me that well?

I decided to give him an honest answer. "It's a good job," I said. "I'm grateful to Donna for setting it up for me. But the truth is, it's not really my thing. I don't really want to do accounting anymore, even though I'm not qualified for much else. I guess a part of me was hoping to do something new once I moved away from California."

"Well, what would you do if you could choose anything?"

"I'd really like to start my own business."

"What kind?"

"A restaurant," I said and turned my attention back to the tiles.

"That doesn't strike me as such an impossible dream for a guy as smart as you."

This is my father talking, I thought. *My father.*

He asked, "Have you ever looked into it?"

"I did talk to some guys about it several years ago, but nothing came of it. It takes a ton of money. Plus, my ideas are a little too offbeat for some people."

"What do you mean?"

As he asked that, I had a sudden "Terri attack." My ex-wife bombarded my brain with statements like, *"Don't make a fool of yourself by telling him your stupid ideas. You're never going to do any of it anyway. You'll move from one dead-end job to another for the rest of your life. The least you could do is keep your mouth shut and accept that."*

Buster Flapjaw did his best to quiet her, but he didn't have much ammunition. I was in no mood to listen to their debate, so I went ahead and answered Hugh. "What I really want is to start not just *one* restaurant but a whole chain of them. I'd like to hit on that one perfect idea that could be replicated in thousands of identical restaurants all over the country. Like McDonald's. Or like Colonel Sanders did with Kentucky Fried Chicken. Except that I'd prefer something a little more upscale, not fast food."

I had even imagined how the business magazines would write about me someday: *Daniel Logan drifted from job to job in his early career, gathering ideas and learning how business works. Although he didn't fully realize it at the time, each position taught him valuable lessons that would ultimately help him create the Logan's chain of restaurants, one of the most successful restaurant companies in the world, now worth over three billion dollars. The chain has also brought its founder a personal fortune that would have been beyond his wildest dreams even a few years ago.*

Terri interrupted, *"You can console yourself with that fantasy all you want, but no investor in his right mind would give money to a man who can't even maintain his job at a car dealership or a rinky-dink hospital."*

Buster shot back, *"By the time this dream comes true, Danny will be married to a woman who understands and shares his belief that life should be about more than simply slaving away at some boring job. Life should be about finding one's calling and doing what is most meaningful."*

"Ha!" bellowed Terri. *"I hope this new woman is prepared to pay all the bills while her husband exercises nothing but his imagination."*

Once my restaurant chain was established and raking in untold millions or billions, I would eventually shock everyone by selling all my interest in it and devote the rest of my life to activities that were not work-related—helping charities, funding endowed chairs at universities, investing in the dreams of young entrepreneurs who would come to me with their ideas.

I would also spend lots of time traveling. I love cruises, and I would take as many different kinds as were available in the world—to Alaska, the Caribbean, the Amazon River. I would also leave myself vast amounts of unstructured time to do whatever I wanted to do at the moment—read, walk, watch movies, hike, daydream, drive across the country. I wouldn't let it worry me if noon came and I was still simply sitting on a balcony somewhere watching the waves crash onto some exotic beach. Or if I was staring at the mountains as I cupped my hands around a hot mug of coffee.

Hugh said, "Well, I guess before you started a *chain* of restaurants, you'd have to start *one* and see if it was popular, right? Isn't that how Colonel Sanders did it?"

"I suppose it is," I said.

"I guess the hardest part would be getting that first one up and running."

"Yeah. That's the point where I've always gotten stuck. I don't know, maybe I'm not cut out for business. Maybe I'd be better off in some other field entirely, something more creative or artistic."

Hugh answered with a skeptical "hmm" that could have been stolen straight from Terri.

I changed the subject by asking, "Did you always want to work at Brantwell?"

"No, no. I started out as a painter. A house painter, you know, not the artistic type. But I had other big ideas, too. I really wanted to be . . . I don't know . . . a traveling salesman, I guess, or some kind of big-time executive with a huge office and a big expense account who would fly all over the world and make business deals. I wanted to go to college. I was full of all kinds of notions."

"Why'd you go to Brantwell?"

"Well, it was . . ." He hesitated, shifted in his chair. He looked down the hall to see if Vonnie was close enough to hear. I knew even before I asked that taking a job at that factory must have had something to do with my mother. If he had worked there for close to forty years and had been retired for more than ten years, then he must have worked there while they were married.

He said, "It was a family circumstance. My father had worked there, and when he died, I moved to Indianapolis to take care of my mother and her house. The job was available, so I took it." He paused again and then added, "I was married to your mother at the time."

That was the first time Hugh had ever mentioned her to me, and even though his words were no revelation, it was strange to hear him refer to her. How bizarre it suddenly seemed to think that my mother had ever had anything to do with this old man in the chair. This man and my mother, along with Donna and me, had been a family. The mental picture of it would not form. What would life have been like if their marriage had worked out? What would my mother, or I, or Donna have turned out like if we had stayed connected to this man?

"Your mother never liked Indianapolis," said Hugh. "She hated the house we lived in. I don't know why. It wasn't that bad, really. Too dark, she always thought."

Is that why she left you, Hugh? Because the house was too dark? Tell me, Hugh. You've broken your silence about her; now keep it going.

He shifted in his chair again, and I imagined that he was about to change the subject. To keep him talking about my mother, I asked, "How long were you married to her?"

When I glanced up at him, his eyebrows were furrowed in confusion, or perhaps even anger or distress. Was he calculating the number of years? Had he forgotten? Was he angry that I had asked him a direct question about Mom? He stared at the wall and stayed silent and unmoving for an uncomfortably long time. I kept working on the floor.

Finally Hugh said, "We were married about four years. She left me, you know."

"She never told us the circumstances."

He sighed, leaned back in his chair, and said, "Well, things just didn't work out."

The famous lie, or evasion, about divorce. The explanation that does not explain. I've said it a hundred times myself, when I don't want to have to explain the complexities of why my marriage ended.

"She met another man," said Hugh.

Ah. Maybe we're finally getting somewhere. Still, what were the details? I waited for him to continue.

"Then they moved away," he said, "and they took you and Donna with them. There was a lot of ugliness—things that don't bear repeating, things that you would take as a slur on your dead mother, and I don't intend to drag her name through the mud—but eventually I didn't even know where she was living. She had you, but she wouldn't let me see you, and I let her get away with it. It's more complicated than it sounds. She had ways of keeping me away, certain threats she could hold over my head. You'll probably have trouble believing this, considering all that happened, but I deeply loved you two kids, and Barbara, too, and I just kept believing she would come back to me. I believed it long after it made any sense to believe it. Even after I met Vonnie."

Hugh stopped talking. He leaned his head back and ran his hand over his face, as if he were embarrassed by the words he had spoken and was trying to wipe them away.

His story was so sketchy that immediately a dozen questions came to mind, but I didn't know where to begin. What was the ugliness he referred to? I didn't buy the empty chivalry of this idea that he wouldn't say anything to slur Mom's name. It was too late for that little nicety. His actions had altered the entire course of my life, and I wanted to know everything, regardless of how ugly he might think it was.

His glossing over the details frustrated me, but on the other hand, he had just blurted out more than I expected him to. Although I was his son, I was also a stranger, and he was revealing facts he had apparently kept secret for almost half a century. So what was the hurry? Maybe I should keep quiet and let him keep dribbling out his story at his own pace.

As I slid another tile into place and tried to decide how hard to push him, he took in a big breath and exhaled the words, "Oh, mercy." It was a common expression for him. Hugh often punctuated his conversation with little groans and sighs. But this one, for some reason, brought the supposedly nearly deaf Vonnie shuffling in from the other room to see if he was all right.

"Of course I'm all right," he said. "Why shouldn't I be? Take a look at what a good job Danny's doing on that floor."

The moment had passed, and we did not get the chance to discuss my mother any more that day. Vonnie hovered more frequently, and the conversation turned to safer subjects. One thing Hugh talked about that afternoon was how much he missed going fishing. He said, "It's not even the *fishing* I miss so much as it is being *outdoors* by the lake or the river and seeing the trees and feeling the sun on my back. I get so sick of staring at these walls. I feel like a prisoner."

I said, "Why don't I come by one of these days and take you out to a lake where people are fishing? There must be places."

"They fish at Eagle Creek Park, which isn't very far at all."

"Let's go, then. Why not? I could wheel you in the wheelchair. You could fish if you want, or just sit and watch."

His face brightened. "You'd have to clear it with the warden," he said, pointing toward the kitchen where Vonnie was working.

"I'll talk to her. It's just as easy for you to sit out there as it is to sit here. Let's do it soon, before I start work."

Hugh agreed, and we settled on a day the week after Donna's picnic. Once we had set the day and time, he said, "Don't bother talking to Vonnie. I'll tell her myself. I'm busting out of here, and nobody's gonna stop me."

23 CAROLYN: ONE BIG HAPPY FAMILY

Donna refused to postpone her cookout because of the incident between Jackie and Danny, and she also rejected my request not to invite Jackie.

"No more games," said Donna a couple days after the episode. "Everybody's invited. We're gonna have fun."

I said, "I'm afraid she'll show up and make a fool of herself again. You don't know her. Once she gets an idea in her head, she can really go after people."

"Well, in the first place, nobody has done anything to her. I mean, Danny was just sitting there talking to Hugh that day, right? So what else could she say to him about it? Neither of us is any threat to her, so I see no reason to exclude her. Let her come and see for herself."

"You're brave."

"In the second place, let's say that we hide this get-together from her and then she finds out about it, which she's almost certain to do. How would she react then? She'd be furious and would probably imagine that we were all getting together to hatch some kind of conspiracy against her. Jackie is my sister, and I'm inviting her. There have been too many secrets keeping us apart already. If Jackie chooses to come and throw a fit, so be it. At least we'll have some entertainment."

I laughed and said, "Donna, I swear, you are exactly the breath of fresh air this family needs."

A few days later Donna sent out formal invitations to her gathering. Well, not *formal*, exactly, but at least *written* invitations, which is more than our family has ever done for a cookout. A few days after that I got a call from Jackie. As soon as I heard her voice, I expected her to say something about the get-together, but no, she had another grievance to bring up.

"Now they're *remodeling* Mom and Dad's house," she said, as if "remodeling" was synonymous with "filling with raw sewage."

I had no idea what she was talking about. "Who's remodeling it?"

"Those *people*."

"Remodeling it how?"

"That guy Danny put a new *floor* in the bathroom." Jackie spat out each of her answers as if the atrocity of what she was reporting should be obvious, but I still wasn't clear why I should be outraged.

"Have you seen it?" I asked.

"Of course I've seen it. I was just over there, and Dad was *bragging* about what a good job that guy did on it."

"Well, does it look good?"

"It looks fine, but that's not the point!"

"What *is* the point, Jackie?"

She roared out one of her groans. "As passive as you and Pam are, it's a wonder these people don't just go ahead and take over everything right now and get it over with. The point is that they're not even bothering to wait for Mom and Dad to die before they get their mitts on the house and change it around to the way they want it."

"Oh, come on. I wish you'd get off this. Mom and Dad are not going to give that house to them."

"You don't know that."

"Do you really think Danny wants to live in their house? He's a well-off businessman. He's not going to—"

"Oh, really? I thought he was unemployed and living with his sister. Maybe she wants him out. Maybe he'll even move in while Mom and Dad are still alive."

"Well, good! None of us are willing to move in and take care of them, so maybe he will."

"I do lots of things for them."

"We all do. But for the record, Danny does have a job. It just hasn't started yet. And he's only living with Donna until he gets settled. So he doesn't need our parents' broken-down house."

"Why are you defending him? He could be fixing up the house to sell it."

"Why are you accusing him of imaginary crimes? He wouldn't fix up a house to sell that he'll never own."

"I don't trust him or that Donna, either."

"You've never even met Donna."

"I talked to her on the phone. To me, it's just too weird that these people suddenly show up in our lives and start redoing our bathrooms and inviting us for cookouts."

"Well, we're related. They're curious about us."

"Hasn't it ever occurred to you that their mother might have put them up to this? As revenge? She could have told them, 'After I'm dead, go there and find Hugh Morris and his family and squeeze everything you can out of them. It all should have been yours in the first place.'"

I couldn't keep from laughing at that one. "You've been watching too many movies, Jackie. And you criticize me for reading gossip magazines and murder mysteries! Look, we haven't even found out the circumstances behind Dad's marriage to their mother. The breakup could have been all *her* fault for all we know. But if she wanted revenge, this would be about the most roundabout way of getting it imaginable. It's ridiculous."

"So I suppose you're going to her cookout," she said.

"Yes. Are you?"

"No. I have to work that day."

"Can't you get off?"

"No. You know how hard it is for me to get a day off. Especially on the weekend."

"You've done it before."

"And I practically had to sell my soul to do it. No. I can't come."

"You get off at two on Saturdays, right? You could come after work."

"I think I'll pass."

"You could at least have Tony and the kids go."

"They can go if they want, but I wouldn't count on it. Tony wonders why Mom and Dad didn't ask *him* to do the bathroom floor. He's done a good job on enough other projects at their house."

"I'm sure they would have been happy for Tony to do it. It's not like they've got people lined up wanting to work on their bathroom. If Tony wants to do some repairs, he can go over there any time day or night and get a long list from Mom and Dad."

That's where we left it. Jackie held on to her suspicions and refused to go to the get-together, so now I could only hope that at least she wouldn't talk Pam out of going. If Pam stayed home, then Mom might very likely use that as an excuse for her and Dad not to go, either, and that would leave just me and Brandon. Then who could blame Danny and Donna if they gave up on us once and for all.

Jackie said one other odd thing right before she hung up. We were talking about some clothes she bought for Mom at Wal-Mart, and out of the blue she said, "So I hear Mom's little trip to the lawyer was all about *you*."

"Oh, really? What do you mean?"

"You tell me."

"I have no idea. Mom wouldn't tell me what it was about. What did she tell you?"

"Nothing."

"Then what are you talking about?"

"Oh, nothing," she said in her singsong voice that she uses when she's playing one of her stupid games. "Maybe I got it wrong."

"Maybe you did."

She didn't reveal any other useful information, and I didn't press it. I was sick of hearing about that will, anyway. Even though I'm in no financial position to be so casual about the future, right at the moment I wouldn't care if Mom and Dad willed their stuff to some stranger off the street. At least we wouldn't have to hear about it anymore.

To my relief, Pam and Cliff and their kids went to Donna's cookout, and Mom and Dad went, too. Pam said Jackie had called and tried to get her all fired up about the bathroom floor, but she wasn't buying it. "He can tear the whole place down and start from scratch as far as I'm concerned. I'm sorry, but I just don't see floor-tile installation as a cause for alarm."

I took Mom and Dad in my car, which was no easy task. It was hard enough getting Dad in the wheelchair, down the steps, and out of the house, but getting him into the car was even worse. Brandon helped me, and before it was all over, we were practically lifting Dad's full weight and stuffing him in there like a bag of bricks. Dad was no help at all. He kept getting his feet stuck right at the door. When I tried to reach down and bend his legs more to push him in, he'd yell, "Stop! You're breaking my legs!" Mom was screaming, "Careful! Careful!" the whole time, as if that was really going to help us get him in there. I'm sure the neighbors loved the spectacle.

When we got to Donna's at midmorning, she immediately had her husband and two other guys run out to help me get Mom and Dad in the house. She had a perfect place picked out for Dad. It was a shaded spot on her big wooden deck in the backyard. From there he was only a few feet from the bathroom (one of three in her beautiful house), and he had a good view of all the activity on the lawn. He was a little rattled from the trip, so Donna gave him a glass of water and let him rest for a while before she started introducing people to him. She has a real gift for knowing when to draw people out and when to give them space. You can tell Donna is used to having get-togethers. The whole day was filled with lots of good food, activities for the kids, even a hired baby-sitter for the little ones so that their parents could sit and relax. I wish Jackie could have been there. She might have changed her mind about our new brother and sister.

The person who surprised me the most was Mom. She acted younger and happier than I've seen her in years, since before she and Dad starting having all their health problems. At first she hovered around Dad like she was witnessing his last moments of life, and I was afraid she was going to embarrass me by not even speaking to anyone else. But it didn't take her long to loosen up. That was thanks mostly to Donna, who turned all her attention on Mom and treated her like a queen.

Donna started out by offering Mom a tour of the house, which I know Mom was dying to see. It's a beautiful place, not a mansion or anything, but bigger than any of the rest of us have. Donna led her through each room as carefully as if Mom was a visiting head of state. Pam and I and a few other people joined in, but Donna directed everything toward Mom, who amazingly didn't ask for a single word to be repeated. When I'm talking to her, I can hardly get two sentences out without her having trouble hearing me.

Back outside, where most of the people were, Donna brought guests over individually and in couples to meet Mom as she sat on her "throne" (the plushest of the cushioned deck chairs) near Dad. Mom loved all the attention. You would have thought this whole party had been given in her honor. Later in the day, when I was off talking to other people, I even saw Mom *walking around* a little and laughing out loud as she talked to people. I couldn't believe it. I had expected her to be bound to her chair all day, huddling over Dad, saying "Huh?" and asking how soon we could go home. She didn't even look as stooped as she normally does! And the miracle of hearing that I had observed during the tour of the house continued throughout the whole day, as if someone had secretly implanted hearing aids.

Just before we ate I asked Pam whether she had noticed the change in Mom. She said, "Yes! I'm amazed. You'd think this party was Mom's idea the way she's been bopping around."

"You think she just likes it that Donna's making such a big fuss over her?"

"I think she's relieved that even though her age-old secret about Donna and Danny is finally out, the world hasn't come to an end."

"You think she'll be willing to tell us the whole story now?"

"I doubt it. She might be feeling pretty good today, but hiding things is pretty ingrained in her. She'll probably want us to leave well enough alone."

"I intend to find out more. Not today, but once I know Donna a little better, I want to piece together the whole story of Danny and Donna's mother."

"Do you think Donna knows?"

"Her mother must have at least told her more than our parents have told us. I figure if I find out what she knows, then I can confront Mom or Dad with it and get them to tell me the rest."

"You're sneaky."

"No, just curious. Aren't you?"

"Yes, but I'm too embarrassed to talk about it with Mom or Dad."

"Embarrassed? Why?"

"I don't know if 'embarrassed' is the right word. But the thought of Dad having loved another woman, having had children with her, having hidden it all these years . . . It's such a different image than I've always had of him that it makes me feel . . ."

"I know. It's almost like the feeling we'd have if we stumbled into a room and caught him *kissing* another woman."

"I wish Jackie had come," said Pam as a way to change the subject.

"So do I. It might have lessened her hostility. Last time I talked to her, she was still harping on that will."

Pam shook her head. "That will has nothing to do with all this."

"No. Jackie said the change in the will had to do with *me*."

Pam blushed, so I knew there must be some truth to the story. But what could it be? Were they cutting me out? Were they giving me everything? I couldn't imagine.

Pam said, "This is not the time or place to get into that."

"But the changes Mom made were about me?"

"Don't ask me about this, Carolyn."

"You said it was just technical changes."

"It was. It's nothing at all that you need to worry about, and if you make a big deal over it with Mom, you'll start another ruckus."

"Over *technical* changes?"

Pam said she had to check on the kids and wandered off. She needn't have run away from me. I certainly didn't plan to get into another big discussion over the will right there at the get-together, but if it was really so innocent, she could have just told me quickly and gotten it over with. Now I was left to imagine all kinds of possibilities.

I walked over to the deck, where Brandon and Donna's girls and a couple of their friends were splashing around in the hot tub. I was afraid Brandon might feel out of place among all these strangers, but he fit right in with the other teenagers. One of Donna's girls is about his age, and the other one is a two years older. I didn't get much of a chance to talk to Donna's husband, Phil, who spent most of the day at their gas grill that looked big enough for a restaurant. Phil is a bald, intelligent-looking man— some kind of engineer—and he lets Donna do most of the talking.

Beyond the deck, there was a grassy area where people played badminton, and then beyond that was a shady area with three or four huge oak trees and a wooden swing set. Donna's girls are too old for it now, but it was ideal for Pam's kids and the other little ones. Donna had brought out some of the little tricycles and balls and other toys that her girls used to play with.

Donna invited more than just our family that day. There were also some of Phil's relatives and some people from her church. I didn't count how many people came and went all day, but there must have been thirty or more. At first I had that awkward sense of being an outsider, and I wondered how much time would have to pass before I could politely leave, but as the day wore on, I settled in and got to know some people and felt more at ease. After lunch, I got a chance to talk to Danny alone. Mainly we talked about our divorces, an area of personal pain we share that made me feel closer to him than anything else we've discussed so far.

He told me all about his ex-wife, Terri, who was never satisfied with anything he did. "I think she thought she was marrying Donald Trump or Bill Gates or somebody like that, some entrepreneur who would suddenly surprise her and everybody else by bringing home megamillions from some big business venture. Under the right circumstances, I might have been able to do that. But I, well . . ." He shrugged.

I didn't expect him to continue his explanation, but then he added, "My mind wanders. I care about succeeding in my work, but I guess I don't have that totally focused drive that allows me to shut out distractions. I'm not lazy. But I can focus on work for only so long and then . . . I need something else. I . . . This probably makes no sense to you, does it? You're probably sitting there thinking, 'No wonder Terri left this guy. He's a loser!' "

I laughed and said, "Not at all. I know exactly what you're talking about."

He gave me a skeptical smile, as if he thought I was merely being polite, but I really did know what he was talking about, and I loved him for saying it—*"My mind wanders."* That sums up half my life.

I said, "My mind wanders, too. I sit in a cubicle at an insurance company all day. I'm known as a pretty good employee, and sometimes I actually enjoy the work. But some days I feel like someone has come along and smudged the ink on every piece of paper so that the words are nothing but random marks that even an archeologist couldn't decipher."

"Exactly! So you *do* know."

"There are so many other things to think about besides work!" I said. "Some days I don't even understand how everybody else can look so happy sitting still at their desks, when it's all I can do to keep from getting up and dancing around or throwing all the papers in the air like confetti or running out to the parking lot and never coming back."

"You *are* my sister!" he yelled, so loudly that people could hear it all the way across the lawn and up to the house. "Now would you please call my ex-wife and tell her exactly what you just said?"

I laughed. "I take it Terri didn't have much sympathy for your wandering mind."

"No. The only thing she sympathized with was making more money."

I thought about that for a minute. "Well, if your main concern about your spouse is whether he can make you a millionaire, you're almost certain to be disappointed."

"Yeah, but in all fairness to her, there were times when I'd be between jobs for several months, and once in a while the finances got tricky. Still, we stayed married for eleven years, which is about twice as long as we had a real marriage."

He told me a few more Terri stories and then asked me about my own marriage. My story was much simpler. "Paul had an affair with a woman who had been a friend of mine. They ran off together, and we got divorced. That was four years ago, and I've only seen him a couple times since then." Emotionally, as I'm sure Danny understood, it was infinitely more complicated than that, but those were the basic facts. I rarely discussed my divorce with anyone, and when I did, I almost never boiled down the story to a few sentences. To say it that way made it feel like I was talking about someone other than myself, the way strangers sometimes think they can sum you up in a few phrases, even though they really don't understand your complexities. But I trusted Danny to be able to fill in some of the details.

"Is your ex-husband still involved in Brandon's life?"

"No. He sent us money a few times, but not on any regular basis. And he's never had him come for a visit."

Danny sighed and looked off toward Donna's oak trees. "I'd love to get my son, Alex, out here. I'm going to try it even before this summer's over. I know he and Brandon would hit it off. Brandon reminds me of him."

"You should bring him. Would Terri fight you on that?"

"Of course! Do you think she'd pass up a perfectly good opportunity to make me squirm?"

I shook my head in sympathy. "I used to feel sorry for myself that my ex didn't even bother to check up on Brandon, but now I realize that there can be worse things than an ex-spouse who's uninvolved. At least we're beyond that game-playing stage."

"Well, no ex-spouse is a good ex-spouse. I mean, I wish it had worked out and we still had a solid marriage. Like Donna and Phil."

"Me too."

"But I'm gonna get Alex out here. I really think if he was here, it would give me enough incentive to make a go of it in Indianapolis. Maybe now that I'm about to turn fifty, I can finally grow up. Wouldn't that just burn Terri up?"

Donna's girls, Amy and Lisa, really seem to like having Danny living with them. In the middle of the afternoon, when a bunch of us gathered on the deck to eat homemade ice cream, Lisa told about the "battle of the bands" that she and her sister have with Danny. There are apparently two stereos in the house—one upstairs and one downstairs. Lisa and Amy like the same kind of MTV-type music that Brandon likes, and they sometimes play it loud on the stereo in their room.

"Then this one day," Lisa said, "we were sitting up there listening to some *normal* music when all of a sudden we hear this awful stuff playing downstairs, and it kept getting louder and *louder.* So we turned ours up a little more to try to drown out that *junk,* and then this other stuff goes up even more. So I ran downstairs and there was Uncle Danny, sort of *waltzing* or whatever around the room with his eyes closed and singing along."

"I wasn't waltzing," Danny said. "And it certainly wasn't junk. It was Frank Sinatra. Anybody ever heard of him? Hello? Probably the greatest voice of the twentieth century."

"Ha!" said Lisa.

"And what I was drowning out could not be considered *music* no matter how loosely you define that term. It was the hideous croakings of an insane asylum."

Phil said, "In the meantime, I was in the family room trying to read the newspaper. The walls were shaking!"

"So now every time we try to play anything good," said Lisa, "we're bombarded by Frank Sinatra or Neil Diamond or—I don't know—Barry Manilow or whoever."

"I have never played Barry Manilow," said Danny. "But if these young girls are ever to become civilized, which I have my doubts is possible, then they need to at least be exposed to *real* music, not the random depraved screaming of drug addicts and criminals."

"What's that song he goes around singing?" Lisa asked her sister.

"Don't get him started," said Amy.

" 'My Darling Clementine' or something like that?"

" 'Sweet Caroline,' " said Danny. "It happens to be one of Neil Diamond's greatest hits, which deservedly sold about a bazillion copies. Shall I go put it on so everybody can decide for themselves?"

"Please don't," Lisa said, but for the rest of the afternoon, Danny sang or hummed the song every time Lisa came near him. She responded by either covering her ears and running away or else singing right back at him with one of her own favorite songs.

Not long before we left (earlier than most of the others,

since Dad was getting tired), I heard Pam talking to Donna about how Mom and Dad were doing. Pam said, "Well, I have to give Dad credit. We didn't think he'd last a week at home after those last two strokes. In that rehab center he couldn't even walk across the room, and you've seen all the steps and obstacles Mom and Dad have in their house. But somehow they manage to squeak by day after day."

"Have they considered moving into an apartment or something that would be easier to maintain?" Donna asked.

Pam threw her hands in the air. "I've done everything but get down on my hands and knees and beg them to consider something like that. I've even made appointments for Mom to tour a beautiful assisted-living facility. They won't budge. Anything I try just gets twisted around into, 'You're just trying to dump us off in some nursing home to die.' "

"Oh, I've seen some lovely apartments for seniors."

"Well, you're welcome to try it out on them if you want. Maybe they would listen to an outsider. Not that you're an outsider, but—"

"I know what you mean."

"I know that living on their own in that house is not the best long-term solution, but what else can I do? They're stubborn. I guess they'll have to get to the place where they're completely helpless before they'll consider another option. I wish they'd at least *prepare* for what would happen if they couldn't live at home anymore."

"I'll talk with Vonnie about it if I get a chance."

"I wish you would."

"Well, Hugh and Vonnie sure seemed to have a good time today," said Donna. "I'm so glad they decided to come even though I know it's hard for them to get around."

At the moment she said that, Dad was a few feet away laughing and talking with some of Phil's relatives. I wandered over and joined in the conversation. Dad was telling stories with a vigor I hadn't seen from him in years. He was even, amazingly enough, telling things I had never heard.

"We had an aunt and uncle and two cousins who lived with us in Indianapolis during part of World War II," he was saying. "We were crammed in that house with us kids sleeping on couches and the floor and anywhere we could find. Didn't mind it, though. Families stuck together like that back in those days. But gas was rationed back then and my uncle had to drive from Indianapolis to Anderson to work. So he'd only be home with us on the weekends, but he didn't even have enough gas to get there and back. So he had to use a mixture of kerosene and gas. He'd pour gas into the carburetor to get it started, and then it would run on that mixture."

"I didn't think cars could run on kerosene," Phil's nephew commented.

"Well, let me tell you, it would smoke like crazy! I used to love to watch him drive away on Monday mornings just so I could see all that smoke. He'd pollute the whole neighborhood. But he always got there. He couldn't get tires for that car during the war, either, so he had to keep patching them and patching them. He didn't think anything of it. If a tire blew, he'd pull off to the side of the road without a word, fix the tire, and drive right on. People were tough back then. Nowadays people want everything now, now, now—they can't even go to the toilet without their cell phone in their hand. But in that generation we knew how to tough things out."

Dad went on like this for a while longer, but by about four in the afternoon, he showed signs of that vaguely hostile disconnection with reality that signals a meltdown might be coming. He kept calling me over to him and asking, "When are we going home? It's gonna be dark pretty soon." The sun wouldn't set for another four hours, and I don't know what darkness had to do with it anyway, but it was a bad sign. Then he told me he'd rather go inside now and sit in his recliner, and I had to remind him he was at Donna's house.

"Who?"

"Donna," I said, hoping I would not have to endure the embarrassment of explaining who Donna was with all those people sitting around listening. "Remember, we're here for the cookout with Danny and Donna and—"

"I know where we are!" he barked, and I knew it was time to head for home. Amazingly, we had gotten through the day without having to clean up any accidents, thanks in part to his reluctant willingness to wear one of the "diapers" he so despised. Some of the men helped me get him and Mom into the car without much trouble, and we were off.

I let out a sigh of relief as we drove away. All in all, it had been a day when I wished I could have stopped time and kept everything as it was—with a few exceptions, of course, like Jackie refusing to come. But Mom and Dad were in good spirits, everybody acted like a family, I got to know Danny better, Brandon liked his cousins, and Donna hugged me as we left and said she'd give me a call soon.

I should have been completely happy about it, but maybe as I'm getting older I'm starting to enter into Mom's pessimistic mind-set a little, because I couldn't keep myself from thinking that when things are this good in this family, you can almost bet they're about to get complicated again.

24 JACKIE: THE OUTCAST SPEAKS

Looks like once again I'm the bad guy, the outcast, all because I "boycotted" Donna's party, to use Carolyn's term. It carries no weight with her or the rest of them that I really did have to work that day in order to keep my job. I guess if these new people snap their fingers, I'm supposed to jump, even if it means getting fired. They ought to try working for my supervisor sometime. You can't just take a day off—especially on a Saturday, especially during back-to-school-sale time—just because some "relative" decides to cook burgers on the grill.

My punishment was that I had to listen to Carolyn on the phone raving about how wonderful it was, how by the end of the day they were practically all holding hands and frolicking around the yard while cherubs played music on their harps. She said it was time for me to drop my suspicions and join the rest of the family.

I'm still skeptical. I visited Mom and Dad a few days after the cookout, and Dad started in about this "son," Danny.

"He wants to start a restaurant," Dad said. "Maybe a whole

chain. He's gonna be big one of these days. I can just tell. He'll be rich. Maybe he'll make all of us rich."

That really got me. "Why would he?" I asked. "Even if he got rich, why would he give *us* his money?"

"We're family."

"Not really. Not in the sense that we should expect any money from them. And they shouldn't expect any from us. Anyway, I thought this guy was trying to get a job as an accountant."

"For now. You don't start a restaurant overnight. Takes money."

"And how's he gonna get it? From you?"

"I do wish I could help him."

I nearly threw the chair across the room at him! So here Dad goes. He can't even pay his own bills without help from us kids, and yet he's ready to give everything away just so this Danny can indulge in his fantasy of starting a restaurant. See what retiling that floor bought this guy? He'll get a whole restaurant out of it.

Dad certainly never talked this way about any of *our* business plans. What about when Tony wanted to start a business? Where was Dad then? He certainly didn't offer Tony any money or even encouragement. As I recall, his exact words were, "Don't do it, Tony. You'll lose your shirt."

Carolyn keeps focusing on how "nice" these people are, but I've been through enough to know that "nice" isn't all that matters. Carolyn and Pam are pretty naïve about people, and they haven't experienced half of what I've gone through. After Tony's mother died, his dad fell for this insurance scam that cost him most of his life savings. By the time he died, we had to dip into our own savings just to pay for the funeral. And I'm sure those insurance salesmen were "nice."

You've got to watch out for people even if they don't start out by intending to do you harm. Take this guy Danny. Let's say for the sake of argument that he showed up here with pure motives.

Just wanted to meet his biological father, later felt sorry for him, tiled his bathroom floor, expected nothing in return. Still, he could end up walking away with as much money as Dad can pull together for this restaurant deal and leave the rest of us in the lurch.

What if Dad decides to sell the house and invest most of the money in the restaurant? Then a couple months later he has another stroke and has to go to a nursing home. But he can't pay for it because he's already given his money away! And where is Danny then? Turns out he isn't such a swift businessman after all, the restaurant goes bust, he loses all the money, and he moves back to California. Whoops. Sorry. He wishes he could help, but he's out of cash. Still, he's awfully "nice" about it. In the meantime, the rest of us are going bankrupt trying to keep Mom and Dad alive.

Carolyn hints around that I'm all worried about Mom and Dad's money simply because I'm greedy and want to get my hands on it. That's not true at all. I have never asked them for a cent my whole adult life, and I don't intend to. Some parents *do* help their adult children through tough financial times, and Lord knows we could use the help right now, but I have never asked for it or even let it be known that we need it. I want that doll collection because it's *mine,* and I have every right to have those dolls in my possession. And I also have as much right to the photos as anybody, and I would do a *better* job than anyone in the family of taking care of them before they rot to pieces. Wanting those things doesn't make me greedy. I'm not trying to take something that doesn't belong to me or that someone else wants.

Anyhow, just for the principle of the thing if nothing else, I don't want to stand by and let some strangers cash in on Mom and Dad. I mean, I hope they live forever, but if they do pass away, I think we should be the ones to benefit from their estate since we're the ones who have taken care of them through their old age. We've made lots of sacrifices over the years. It's not just a matter of a quick bathroom repair project. Tony has often fixed up Mom and Dad's house and let our own slide for a while. He barely got any thanks for it, and he certainly never got an offer from Dad or anyone else in the family to buy him a business because of it.

I don't know what I can do to prevent these people from worming their way into Mom and Dad's life, but I'm tempted to contact a lawyer, at least to see what my legal options are. I'd like to be prepared for whatever tricks might come up. I don't really trust Mom after that little maneuver she pulled with her will.

I've also been thinking about hiring a private detective to investigate Donna or at least Danny, who seems the more suspicious one to me. Why does he suddenly show up in Indiana, jobless, homeless, remodeling the bathrooms of strangers? What's his real background? How many other old couples has he done this to? I know a guy that I went to high school with who has become a private detective. I saw him at our last high school reunion. My friend Janice, who was also in our class, hired him to find her ex-husband that she hadn't seen in almost ten years and who owed her child support. Manny, this detective, found him in *one day,* living in Kentucky, working at a convenience store. Janice didn't get much money out of him, because he hardly had anything. But that wasn't the detective's fault.

The problem for me is finding that detective. Manny's name isn't in the phone book, and Janice moved away and didn't keep in touch with me. What good is a private detective if you need a private detective just to find him? But wouldn't it be great if I hired him and he exposed this guy as a fraud? I have this fantasy of the police using me to set up a sting to have Danny show up somewhere and then they swoop in to arrest him. I wish I could have set up something like that in time for Donna's little get-together. That would have shown my family that I'm not just a troublemaker.

The only problem is, how am I supposed to pay for a private detective? Right now we can barely make it through the month without postponing payment on some bills or going further in debt. We shouldn't have taken that vacation earlier this summer. But we planned it when things were looking better, so part of it was already paid for. When we started making arrangements for it, Tony was getting quite a bit of overtime, and I was working extra during the Christmas rush. But now we've both been cut back, and there's even a chance that Tony could be laid off by the end of the year.

If one of us loses our job or if we have some emergency before the end of the year, I don't know what we'll do. We're skating on the edge of disaster. If Mom and Dad suddenly need money from us for moving to a retirement home or whatever, I don't see how we'll do it.

I haven't told anyone in the family what a mess we're in. Since they saw us take that vacation, they probably figure we're swimming in money. I'm not one to complain out loud, so I won't start now. Not that any of them are in any financial shape to help us much right now. Except maybe Pam and Cliff. I don't know. He's been a teacher for a long time, and she works part time, so maybe they have plenty of money. Anyway, I could never bring myself to ask Pam for money. I've learned that it's better never to say too much to my family about our financial problems. If they think you're broke, then somehow they believe that gives them the right to start giving you advice about how to live your life, and I don't need that.

One thing I do know is that if I could afford to quit my job, I'd be out of there in a second. My supervisor, Lucy, has gotten harder to deal with every day. I work my butt off, but she sneaks around watching me like she's afraid I'm gonna suddenly lie down on the clearance table and take a nap. Don't think I haven't been tempted to curl up there and do it. But the fact is that I do not sit down even once during my shift except for break time, and sometimes I don't even sit down then if I have to run out to my car for something or stand in line at the snack bar for something to eat.

Candy doesn't actually *complain* about my work, but she'll make little remarks all day that make it sound like she thinks I'm going too slow. She'll say, "Oh, you haven't had time to straighten out that rack of men's jeans yet?" or "You didn't forget that you have another cart full of clothes from the dressing room to reshelve, did you?"

Of course I didn't *forget,* which she well knows. What about the two other carts that I unloaded just before that? Did *she* forget about *those*? I try not to let it get to me, because I know she treats everybody that way. She thinks "management" means hounding people until you push them to the brink of quitting. Still, it sure would make the shift go faster if just once she would say something like, "Wow, Jackie, did you get that cart unloaded already? You're amazing!" But dream on; it's not gonna happen.

I try to be nice to the customers, since when I'm out shopping or go to a restaurant there's nothing I hate worse than a worker with a snarly attitude. I've never lost my cool with a customer, but I admit there are times when I'd like to wring their necks. On particularly bad days, the customers can seem like nothing more than demons sent to torture me. When I see these devil-women and their kids walking toward my department, it's hard to see them as anything but fat (not that I should talk) maniacs who give birth for the sole purpose of creating little monsters to run up and down the aisles throwing clothes on the floor so that I'll have to refold them and reshelve them.

I can't quit, though. We had to spend almost four hundred dollars on the car last month and nearly a thousand on Tony's truck. Plus there's something wrong with the air conditioner in the house, and both kids need clothes, especially Kevin, who has outgrown his pants. Every month since about Christmas, there has been some unexpected expense that kills any hope I have of catching up.

So maybe I *am* the cranky member of the family right now, but I can't help it. For a long time it seems like everything good has been flowing away from me, and now I'm ready for some of it to start flowing back.

25 PAM:
Near the Breaking Point

Here's the exact message Carolyn left on my machine: "Pam, there's been an emergency. I'm at the hospital, but I'll turn on my cell phone. Call me!"

My *second* thought was to be terribly worried, but my *first* thought was to be irritated. Did she think this was a telegram, where you pay per word? You'd have thought she'd at least take the time to tell me what the emergency *was*. Why does she play games like that? Is she afraid I won't call her back? Does she like the power of holding the secret until I manage to track her down?

When we were growing up, she did the same thing, always tantalizing us with some little secret until we were practically begging her (or bribing her with candy or an offer to do one of her chores) to tell what she knew.

When I got the message, I had just come into the house with the kids after going to the grocery store. It had been a harrowing experience. Sarah had been so restless that I almost gave up before I was even halfway through my list. But I persevered, using animal crackers as a sedative (for the kids and for me, too), and finally made it home. I wanted to call Carolyn right away, but Sarah was in dire need of a diaper change, Matthew was whining for juice, some of the groceries were melting in my trunk, and I didn't have Carolyn's cell phone number handy. She only uses that phone for emergencies, so I don't have the number memorized.

Since our family lives in a constant state of crisis anyway, I decided the emergency would have to wait, and I went about squaring away my children and my groceries. In a way her call shouldn't have surprised me, since Dad had been teetering on the edge of disaster since the strokes and Mom wasn't doing much better. But Dad's last doctor's appointment, a couple days after the get-together at Donna's, had lulled me into thinking maybe he was getting better. His periods of clarity were lasting a lot longer, and he was walking better. When we wheeled him out to the car, he was able to push himself up out of the wheelchair and get in without all the usual straining and yelling. He was still really forgetful, having to ask again where we were going even as we pulled up to the doctor's office, but at least he was getting through his days more easily. The doctor said he was doing about as well as could be expected (we drove all the way over there to hear *that*?) and sent him home with no new instructions or medicine.

By the time I got the kids settled and the groceries in, I was ready to face the emergency. I tried Carolyn's cell phone, but it wasn't on. I tried her home phone but no one answered. I tried her work number but was told she was out of the office on a family emergency. More mystery. *I'll give you the rest of my M&M's if you'll answer your phone, Carolyn.* I tried Mom and Dad's house. Busy signal.

An hour later Carolyn called from a hospital pay phone. She

said her phone battery had gone dead.

"How's Dad?" I asked.

"He's fine. It's not him. Mom had a heart attack."

I felt all the energy drain out of my body, leaving me tingling and weak. "How bad is she?"

"Bad. Can you come?"

"Cliff's at school. Let me call him home to watch the kids, and I'll be right there."

It took me two hours to get the kids settled with Cliff. By then Mom was out of the emergency room and in intensive care. When I first saw her, she looked pale and clammy. The first thing she said was, "Is somebody staying with your dad?"

"I think Carolyn's gonna take Brandon over there in a little while."

"He should go now. Your dad's been alone for quite a while."

"Well, she was waiting on me to get here so she wouldn't have to leave you alone. But I just talked to Dad on the phone on my way over. He's fine. He sends his love and says not to worry about him. He's planning to come and visit you as soon as he can, maybe tomorrow."

"No, no," she said. "It's too hard on him to come up here. Tell him to wait till I get home. There's no need for both of us to end up in this place."

"Well, we'll see. He's getting around a little better now, so—"

"It's not worth it. Tell him to stay home. Is Carolyn staying there tonight? I assume they won't let me go home yet."

"No, they certainly will *not* let you go home yet. You've had a bad heart attack, Mother. So the first thing you need to do to get better is to *relax* and let *us* take care of a few things."

"Well, is Carolyn gonna spend the night there?"

"I don't know! I just got here. But let us figure it out, will you? Now stop worrying or you'll make yourself worse. We'll take care of Dad, one way or another. All right?"

She leaned back into her pillow, and I thought maybe she was ready to calm down, but before I even had time to redirect the conversation, she started shifting around again and pulled herself up a little and said, "Don't you even *think* about carting him off somewhere while I'm in here."

Carolyn walked in during this last comment. "She's been like this from the minute I got here. It's all Dad, Dad, Dad. You wouldn't think she even realizes that she's the one who had the heart attack."

"Where's Brandon?" asked Mom.

"He's in the waiting room. I'm gonna drive him over to the house now to stay with Dad. So calm yourself before I have that nurse come in here and give you something that will knock you out for three or four days."

"That'd be all right with me," said Mom, settling back into her pillow again with a groan.

Carolyn motioned for me to come with her, and on my way out the door, Mom shook her head and said, "Plotting again. Always plotting."

On the way to the waiting room, Carolyn said, "So what do you think? Will she get out of here in a couple days like last time, or is she worse?"

"She's worse."

"I thought so, too. Do you think she'll make it?"

"Do the doctors?"

"The cardiologist talked to me, but Mom was making such a fuss right then that I didn't really grasp all of what he was saying, except that the heart attack was bad but that they'll keep trying things. Dr. Mandel hasn't been here yet, and he's the one I really trust. The other guy was kind of technical and, you know how some of those doctors are, kind of vague."

"We'll just have to pray for the best," I said, and Carolyn merely nodded. She probably thought that was an empty expression, but I really *had* been praying from the moment I heard Mom was in the hospital. I also planned to call some friends at church to have them pray, and I wanted to call Donna, too. Besides being my sister, I found out she is also a Christian, and I was glad to have someone else in the family actually *practicing* the faith we all to some degree profess. How I wish I had the courage to march right into Mom's room and ask if I could pray with her, but I always found it too awkward to talk to my parents about anything spiritual. The best I could hope to do was see if my pastor would come to visit her.

Carolyn said, "I knew it was bad when Mom called and said she had dialed 9-1-1 herself and asked for an ambulance. You know this aversion she and Dad have to ambulances. They'd almost rather *die* than to have somebody besides us take them to the hospital, and for Mom to *request* to go to the *emergency* room and to leave Dad behind is beyond belief."

"So when did she call you?"

"While she was waiting on the ambulance. She called me at work. She said she had this horrible tightness in her chest and she was sweating like a pig and could hardly breathe. She felt like she was going to die right there on the phone, and it scared me! I'm still scared. I've never seen her look this bad."

"I'm scared, too."

"I know she's had health problems all along, but I've been so focused on Dad that I keep forgetting how fragile *she* is. I never imagined she would die before Dad. If she doesn't make it, then what—"

"Well, she's still alive, so let's not jump to conclusions. Once they get that medicine in her and get her heart stabilized, maybe she'll be fine. She made it out of here last time, and she can do it again."

"I know. I'm just thinking *what if.*"

"I can't handle anything beyond getting through this day. So will you be able to stay with Dad tonight?"

"I guess I'll have to."

"I wish I could do it, but with the kids . . ."

"I know, Pam. That's all right."

"Did you call Jackie?"

"Yeah. She'll be here this evening."

I saw Brandon from the back as we walked into the waiting room. He was shaking his hands in the air as if playing the drums or simulating some exotic dance. Headphones piped in music only he could hear, but he also absently watched a soap opera that happened to be playing on the TV in front of him.

His mother tapped him on the head and said, "Time to go."

He stood up, said hi to me, and gave me a quick hug.

"Thanks for staying with Grandpa today," I told him. "I know it's not always the easiest way to spend an afternoon."

"It's okay," he said. "I just hope he won't start arguing about the TV."

"It takes two to argue," said Carolyn. "You know Grandpa can't stand MTV and that kind of stuff."

"All he wants to watch is the news. He'll watch it about seven times in a row. They tell the same things over and over, but he can't get enough of it! He forgets things so fast that he thinks it's new every time."

"I'll ask him if you can watch something for an hour or two, okay?" said Carolyn. "And then the rest of the time read your book or a magazine or listen to music or something."

"And he always wants me to get up and get him things. He can't stand for me to sit for more than about three minutes."

"He sounds like my kids, always wanting something," I said. "This will be good training for when you're a parent."

"Water, water, water. I bring him glass after glass. We oughta get a big barrel of water and attach it to a hose right next to him. Sometimes he forgets that I just brought him a glass, and he'll send me after another one. One time I finally looked over at the TV tray next to his recliner and realized he had three glasses of water he hadn't even touched!"

"Well, *anyway*," said Carolyn, "we're glad you're gonna be there with him, and I want you to make the best of it and be nice and don't get him all annoyed."

"Did you see Grandma?" I asked him.

"Yeah, I talked to her," he said, "and then they made me leave. Is she gonna live?"

"Yes," said Carolyn. "We think so. Now let's go so Dad doesn't get worried."

Mom was calmer that afternoon after I told her Carolyn would stay with Dad. Around suppertime Jackie and Tony and their kids came to visit. Dr. Mandel also came late in the day. His report was not encouraging. He said Mom's heart had sustained quite a bit of damage. He said they would try several treatments over the next few days and see how she responded. Even though he never said it, I got the distinct impression that he didn't think she would live.

Around eight that night I decided to leave so that I could be home to put the kids to bed. After all the stress of the day, I really felt the need to hold them in my arms and kiss them, maybe read a story or two and rock them. Right as I was about to leave Mom's room, Jackie said, "I think you and Carolyn and I should have a talk before you leave."

"Why?" asked Mom. "We're talking right here. What are you gonna do? Plan my funeral behind my back?"

"Yeah, Mom," said Jackie. "I thought I'd sing a solo."

"Well, then," said Mom, "I think I'll skip it."

I didn't want to have a talk with Jackie and Carolyn right then, but she wasn't really *asking*. So I led us down to the front lobby, where at least I could be close to an exit. I knew there were issues we should probably discuss, but if Jackie brought up that will again, I was afraid I'd strangle her.

She didn't mention the will. It was Dad she was worried about. What was our plan, she wanted to know (looking directly at me, not Carolyn), if Mom died? Had we made any arrangements for Dad? He certainly couldn't live alone anymore. Was the assisted-living apartment still an option, or would that take time to set up? Would the house have to be sold first? What would we do in the meantime?

I had held up pretty well that day, I thought. I had gotten the kids situated, made it to the hospital, got Mom settled down, talked to the doctors, made some phone calls to friends at church, called Donna, called my pastor, and explained Mom's situation to several people who called the hospital to ask about her. But for some reason, Jackie's question about what to do about Dad pushed me beyond my limit, and I fell in a chair— not sat in it, but sort of collapsed—and burst into tears.

I only cried for a few seconds. I'm not really prone to outbursts, but I couldn't help it. It felt like those horrible weeks of Dad's hospitalization and recovery from his strokes were about to be repeated with Mom—the danger of death, the uncertainty about what to do next, the eyes of my sisters bearing down on me to make the final decision.

Dear God, I prayed, *I can't go through all this again.*

Carolyn put her arm around me and said, "We've all been through a lot today. Go home to the kids. This is not the time for us to make any decisions about anything."

I got control of myself pretty quickly and stood up. "I do need to get home," I said. "We'll talk tomorrow."

Jackie kept quiet and decided not to push me.

I didn't expect to have any more of an answer about the future the next day than I did right then. All I knew was that any happy ending was hard to envision.

26 DANNY: GONE FISHING

I decided not to take that job with Jerry, Donna's friend at church. I know my decision disappointed Donna, but the closer I got to it, the more I dreaded it. I spent about half a day with Jerry as he showed me around the company and described the projects I'd be working on. It's boring work, and I can see why none of his regular people want to do it. He also indicated that he'd probably only need me for a year at most, a detail that had not come up before. So even if I took this job, I'd be looking for another one as early as six months from now.

Jerry is a nice enough guy, but everything about the place itself tells me I'd be climbing the walls within a few days. I know that for most people, the physical atmosphere of the office is a stupid reason for rejecting a solid, well-paying job, but my surroundings have a big impact on my state of mind. This office is located in an industrial park filled with rows of identical white buildings and some warehouses. My individual workstation would be a cubicle at the end of a row of four other cubicles. I'd have walls or partitions on three sides of me, and the fourth side opens to a narrow corridor that leads past the other cubicles. There is one narrow vertical window at the end of that hallway. It looks out onto the parking lot, but my own "office" is far enough away from it that I'd have to make a special effort even to get that view of the outdoors.

I still have enough money to go a few more months without work, but I'd like to get settled as soon as possible and find my own place to live. Donna and Phil and the girls have been great, but I don't want to wear out my welcome. They keep assuring me that they want me to stay as long as I'm willing to, but I'd rather leave with them still wanting me to stay rather than wanting me to leave.

I've been thinking about trying a different career altogether. The other day I drove by this construction site where they were building a new little shopping mall, and I was envious of those men out there hammering and sawing and measuring. I wondered whether I could get hired on a crew like that, whether I could learn the work, and whether it would pay enough for me to live on. The idea of *building* something, of being able to see it go up brick by brick and board by board and then to have it *standing* there once you're done, is very appealing. I know the work would be very hard physically, and I'm not at the greatest age to take on a job like that, but maybe the hard manual labor would sweat the restlessness out of me.

I've also thought about going back to school to train myself for something completely different from accounting. I saw an advertisement for a school that trains you how to be a court reporter. I would love that, I think, sitting there all day listening to trials and recording the words of the witnesses and attorneys and judges.

Needless to say, whenever I come up with one of these brainstorms, I also suffer an intense Terri attack. You should have heard her when I was debating the possibility of a construction job. *"You?"* she scoffed. *"You're almost fifty years old, and not a robust fifty, either, I'm sorry to say. Besides, at home you could barely change a light bulb. You didn't know a screwdriver from a potato peeler. You couldn't even . . ."*

On and on she went in that vein, with Buster Flapjaw defending me every step of the way, pointing out the fact that, even now, I'm in good enough shape to run two miles a day (though I haven't been very consistent about it), and I routinely beat men half my age at tennis and basketball. Well, maybe I don't do that "routinely," but it's happened more than once. And as Buster pointed out, not every job in construction involves swinging a sledgehammer. There might even be jobs that combine *some* of my physical skills with *some* of my accounting skills.

Terri also jumped all over the court reporter idea, saying I wasn't cut out for it, I'd make a fool of myself, modern technology would soon make court reporters obsolete anyway, blah, blah, blah. I stopped listening and let Buster make the necessary rebuttals. All I know is I don't want to go work for Jerry, so I'm going to have to tell him and Donna right away.

One effect of this decision will be to allow me to spend some more time with Hugh, and he can sure use me right now. On the day after Vonnie's heart attack, I volunteered to take him to the hospital to see her, which he very much wanted to do. We had to get "permission" from the daughters. Carolyn said it was fine with her if he wanted to go and if I thought I could get him in and out of the wheelchair and into the car and all that. I said it would be no problem, and even though it was a bit of a problem and I was wringing with sweat by the time I finally wheeled him into Vonnie's room, it was worth it.

Vonnie is not doing well, and I could tell that it was a comfort to each of them to be in the other's presence. Even though their marriage is troubled by every outside difficulty imaginable—illness, old age, money troubles, family difficulties, and so on—I have to admire their devotion. You can tell they're not just putting up with each other, despite their fussiness. They really would rather be with each other than with anyone else. What I wouldn't give for a marriage like that!

I couldn't help but wonder if Hugh had ever known such a close connection with my mother. It's still hard to picture Mom with him. She was nothing like Vonnie. She never doted on my dad (the one who raised me) the way Vonnie does with Hugh. My parents' behavior, when other people were around at least, was more formal, I guess you'd say. They respected each other, probably loved each other, but they weren't all that openly affectionate. They didn't argue much, but they didn't hold hands or kiss much, either. They each had their daily routines and their specified roles around the house, and they did their best to keep their lives orderly and quiet.

Mom must have been far more lively when she was younger. She *left* Hugh, an act that would be unthinkable for the mother I knew. I try to picture her and Hugh not only *young*, which is hard enough to do, but also energetic and passionate. I try to put into words and pictures the arguments they must have had, the accusations they must have hurled, the drama that must have surrounded their divorce.

I also try to imagine them earlier in their relationship, deeply in love. What brought them together? What was the attraction? I doubted that I would ever be able to ask Hugh those questions, or that he would ever be able to reach back through the years and put it into words.

Carolyn and Brandon were the only other visitors at the hospital that morning. Fortunately, Jackie was not supposed to come until later in the day. I agreed to stay with Hugh until early evening, when Carolyn would come to his house to spend the night. Brandon was particularly happy with me for freeing him from the responsibility of staying with his grandfather that day. We stayed at the hospital almost two hours. Vonnie looked shriveled, as if the IVs attached to her arms were sucking the life out of her rather than filling her with life-sustaining medicine. She and Hugh's fingers touched on the edge of her bed, but after the first few minutes, they didn't feel the need to say much to each other. You could almost have believed they were sending messages through those fingers.

We stayed until Hugh started sighing and repeating himself and showing other signs of agitation. Once I finally got him home and into his recliner, he leaned back and fell asleep even before I got a chance to get his lunch fixed and bring it out to him from the kitchen.

The "fishing trip" that Hugh and I had planned was scheduled for the next day, but after he woke up from his nap and ate his lunch, I told him we could cancel it and go see Vonnie again the next day instead. He said that was fine, but about ten o'clock that night I got a call at home from Carolyn saying that Vonnie was insisting that we go ahead with our original plans.

"Mom says that trip to the lake is all he's been talking about since you asked him to do it, and she's not about to stand in the way of it."

"Well, we could always do it another time. I mean, she's pretty bad off, isn't she?"

"She looked a little better this evening, actually, and she's certainly getting feisty again. She's called three times since I got here to Dad's house tonight. The doctor even said if she keeps improving, she might be able to go home in three or four days. I almost wish he hadn't said that, because now she's acting like he gave his *guarantee* that she wouldn't be there past the end of the week."

"Does Hugh still want to go to the lake?"

"Yes! He didn't feel like talking on the phone, so he asked me to call you. He said you two could always go to the park in the morning and then go see Vonnie later in the day."

"Can he handle that much activity?"

"I don't know. Maybe not. But you could always bring him to the hospital the next day—if you're available, of course. I don't want to impose on your time, but it's just—"

"No, that's all right. I could probably do that." I really didn't mind taking him, but it was remarkable how quickly the family's expectations for me were escalating. I worried a little about what they might ask of me next. Would Carolyn want me to start spending the night at Hugh's house until Vonnie came home?

As if she were reading my thoughts, Carolyn said, "I don't ever want to take advantage of you with this help that you're giving Mom and Dad. I know it's not your responsibility to do it, but Dad gets such a kick out of talking to you, and Mom has really loosened up a lot about you and Donna."

"Let me ask you something," I said. "Does Jackie know I took your dad to the hospital this morning and that I'm taking him to the lake tomorrow?"

She hesitated. "No," she admitted, "I didn't tell her. I didn't lie about it, but I think she thought Brandon was with Dad today. Mom didn't mention you to Jackie, at least not while I was there, so I didn't get into it with her."

"What do you think she'd say if she knew?"

"Honestly, she'd probably have some kind of hostile reaction, but that's just Jackie. Mom and Dad and the rest of us have every right to treat you and Donna like family. Jackie will get over it. So should I tell Dad your outing is still on for tomorrow?"

"All right. Tell him I'll be there."

———

As we were pulling out of Hugh's driveway the next morning, he startled me by yelling, "No! Not now! No!"

I stopped the car and looked over at him, but he shouted, "Don't stop! Go! Go! Go!"

I had no idea what was wrong with him, but I got the car moving again to pacify him. As we drove away from the house, I saw what he was reacting to. Coming toward us, and slowing down to stop in front of Hugh's house, was a big white pickup truck. The driver was a burly man with a flattop haircut. I had never seen him, but the woman sitting next to him was familiar. It was Jackie, and her mouth was in motion. She was straining to look inside my car, and Hugh was actually trying to put his head down between his legs as if to hide from her.

I said, "Should we stop and tell them—"

"No! No! No!" shouted Hugh. "Keep going! Go!"

I drove on, and in my last view of the pickup truck as we turned onto another street, I saw Jackie standing beside it, hands on her big hips, her mouth open, and her face contorted into an expression of baffled outrage.

Then Hugh started laughing. He reminded me of a teenager who had pulled off some devious prank. He slapped his knee and wheezed out his laughter. "Close call," he said. "You think she saw me?"

"From the look on her face as we turned that corner, I'd say yes. You didn't know she was coming over?"

"No. She's probably come to see if I wanted to go to the hospital."

"Well, this should make her hate my guts even more than she already does."

"Oh, don't worry about her," said Hugh. "We can't let the Jackies of the world control our lives. We're goin' fishin'!"

We didn't discuss the incident any further, but I couldn't help but imagine the horrible things Jackie was probably already saying about me to Carolyn and Pam or anyone else who would listen.

Lilly Lake at Eagle Creek Park was the perfect place to take Hugh because even though it was surrounded by tall trees that gave you the feeling of being out in some remote wilderness, it also possessed the amenities that made it possible for a man in Hugh's condition to go there in the first place—wide paths for wheelchairs, rest rooms that I could easily get him into, a parking lot that was only a few minutes' walk from the lake. I had offered to bring the supplies we'd need to actually fish in the lake, but Hugh said not to bother. He said just being near it would be enough for him right now.

The lake was visible from the parking lot, and as I wheeled Hugh down the gentle slope toward it, he kept saying, "Oh, Lord. Oh, Lord."

"You all right?" I asked.

"I haven't been anywhere like this in so long," he said. His mouth was wide open in wonder, as if he were entering an exotic paradise. I didn't want to ruin the moment for him by talking, so for ten or fifteen minutes I kept quiet and simply let him take in the view. I wheeled him down to a spot near the edge of the lake where we could see a group of teenagers pedaling their rented paddle boats and where we were just down the path from three or four fishermen. Behind us and up the hill just a few minutes' walk were a rest room and a shelter.

Hugh leaned back his head and listened to the sounds of the wind in the trees, the birds, the voices of the teenagers in the boats. Then he looked over at the fishermen, lost in his own thoughts as the men cast their lines and waited for a bite. "What kind of fish you reckon they have in this lake?" he asked.

I took out a brochure I had picked up on the way into the park. "It says they have bluegill, largemouth bass, carp, and channel catfish. We should bring a pole out here and let you fish one of these days. I could easily push your chair right out there close to the edge."

"I'd love it." He lifted his hands from his lap and clenched the arms of the wheelchair. It looked like he was about to stand up, and for a second I was alarmed, picturing him tumbling forward off the path and down into the lake. Then he loosened his grip and said, "Oh, Danny, I wish you had known me when I was younger."

"So do I."

He glanced up at me, wondering, I think, whether there was a hint of sarcasm or accusation in my response. He looked back out at the lake. He shook his head. He mumbled something incomprehensible. I didn't bother asking him to repeat it. I could tell he was in one of those phases where he was deep inside himself. Some of his words might eventually spill out into the open and others might not. After a while he said, "Look at those kids out there on those boats. They take all this for granted—this lake, the trees, the ability to paddle those things. For them, being out there is just a way to fill a few hours of a long summer. They'll get bored with it before long and run off to something else. I used to be the same way. I would come out here to fish for a few hours and would barely think about what a privilege it was. I just assumed that fishing was something I'd be able to do my whole life, whenever I wanted. Now, if we end up doing it, it'll be a major ordeal."

"There's no reason we can't do it." I unfolded the lawn chair I had brought and sat down next to him.

When I looked over at him again, he had lost his contented expression, and he now had that slack-jawed, vacant look of a man who had spent too many hours alone in the same room.

"What's the matter, Hugh? I thought you liked it out here."

He shook his head back and forth a few times, the way he does when he has something to say but can't locate the words.

"I do like it," he said. "But now that I'm old and sick, when

I come to a place like this, all I can think of is that the world has passed me by."

"What do you mean?"

He swept his hand toward the lake, the kids in the paddle boats, the fishermen on the bank. "All this goes on without me while I'm cooped up in my house wondering whether I can get to the bathroom without falling down. I don't even *exist* in this outside world. Not like I used to. I only exist in my family's eyes now, and to them I'm mainly a problem to be dealt with rather than someone to be—you know—reckoned with or loved or feared or all the other ways people treat you when you're part of the outside world."

He took out a handkerchief and sopped the sweat off his face. We were in the shade, but it was a humid day. I worried about him getting overheated, especially if he got agitated over what he was saying. He had a bottle of water sitting next to him in his chair, but he hadn't touched it.

"Take a drink," I suggested.

He ignored me and continued, "Back when I was working every day, there were people who liked me and people who hated me and people who were afraid of me, but I *mattered* to a lot of people, and if I hadn't shown up or hadn't done my job, lots of people would have noticed it. I knew it made a difference every day whether I was there or not. In those days, I was serving on the church board and was involved in all kinds of things, so even at home, the phone was always ringing and I was always rushing from place to place. I used to actually imagine I'd be happy when I could retire and give it all up and not have to worry about anybody but myself. But now my life is boiled down to just me and Vonnie and a few family members waiting on me to die."

"I don't think you give your daughters enough credit," I said. "They're not waiting for you to die. I know Carolyn better than the others, but I know she loves you very deeply. And even though Jackie comes off kind of hostile to me and Donna, maybe it's a sign that she cares about you and is trying to protect you."

"Protect me. You see? That's what I mean. That's what it's come down to, that they think I need to be protected like a child. That's why I've been confined to my house for so long, because my daughters think I need to be protected from everything."

"Well, with your strokes, they—"

"Take Jackie, for instance. I mean, I'm not *blaming* anybody, you understand? I blame myself. I blame myself, not for what I'm going through now, but for not enjoying all that I had when I had it. Do you see what I'm saying?"

"Yes . . ."

"When Jackie was a baby, she went through this period where she had lots of colds and ear infections. And there was this one week where she was so stopped up that she kept waking up in the night screaming because it was hard for her to breathe. This one night we had just gone to bed when Jackie started screaming. Vonnie turned to me and practically begged me to get the baby because she was just too exhausted from having been up with her almost nonstop for the last few days.

"So I got up with her and spent the night rocking her in the rocking chair in the living room until it was time for me to go to work the next morning. At the time, all I could think of was how annoyed I was that I would have to work the whole next day with practically no sleep. But now, I look back on that night as one of my best memories of Jackie. Isn't that strange? But it was just me and my girl, rocking back and forth in the darkness of that room, and all she needed was to sit up against my shoulder so she could breathe.

"All three of my girls were always wanting to climb all over me when they were little. Sometimes when I'd come home from work in the evening, I'd want nothing more than to sit in my recliner and read the newspaper. But I couldn't sit down without one or more of them jumping up there and wanting me to read them a book or go outside and play or fix something for them. And I usually did it, because I felt too guilty not to, but I didn't appreciate it most of the time. I would just hope they'd go to bed early so I could have some time to myself.

"But now I'd give anything to have those days back again. They certainly don't seek me out now, do they? Do they crave my attention? Squeal with delight when I come home from work? I know adults are different. I'm not saying I expect or even want those things from them now. It would be absurd, but I can hardly stand the fact that they merely patronize me. They're even embarrassed by me!"

"They also love you," I said. "That's the thing you shouldn't overlook. When they were kids, they showed that love one way, and now they show it another. And it's never perfect, just like your love for them wasn't perfect."

"Boy, that's for sure." He fumbled with the water bottle and took a drink. Staring at the kids on the paddle boats again, he asked, "Do people ever realize what they've got when they've got it?"

"Some do. Maybe you're not realizing what you've got right now."

Hugh grunted.

"You have Vonnie. She adores you. Do you know what some men would give for a wife as loving and devoted as she is to you? And you have three daughters who care about you. Three daughters in your life in a world in which many people your age are completely alone. And your grandkids. Doesn't it make you happy to see how Brandon's growing up? And Jackie's kids? And Pam's? You've lost a lot, but you haven't lost everything."

He sat completely still, and I didn't know whether he was ignoring what I said or whether he was thinking about it. After a long pause, he said, "And you and Donna."

"What?"

"I also have you and Donna now. I don't deserve anything but contempt from the two of you, but here you are."

"Here we are. Who could have predicted that? Life still holds surprises for all of us."

"Not too many more, I hope." He rubbed his hands over his face. "I'm worried about Vonnie."

"The doctor says she might be able to go home soon. Do you want to go see her today?"

"If we can."

"Let me know when you're ready to leave. Don't wear yourself out."

We stayed about another hour, and for most of that time I pushed him along the path that wound around the lake. When we drove home, I half expected to see Jackie still standing at the end of Hugh's driveway with her hands on her hips. Fortunately, the white pickup was nowhere in sight.

I managed to get Hugh out of the car, back into the wheelchair, into the house, in and out of the bathroom, and into his recliner, where he promptly fell asleep. Once he woke up, it was clear that this would not be a good day for a hospital visit. He was so tired and his mind was so fuzzy that he couldn't keep the facts straight about Vonnie. At least five times he asked, "Is Vonnie coming home today?" One time he even asked me if I would go to the kitchen and ask Vonnie to come and see him for a minute. He didn't seem to remember our plan to visit the hospital that afternoon, and I didn't bring it up.

I stayed with him until around five, when Carolyn came over after work. I told her about the trip to the park, omitting the part about Jackie. If Carolyn hadn't heard about it already, maybe that meant Jackie had decided not to make a fuss over it. I told Hugh good-bye and said that I'd call him in the morning to see if he wanted me to take him to see Vonnie.

He nodded. "Sorry I pooped out on you. I'm only good for about five or six hours a day, and then I'm wiped out again."

"That's all right. I'll call you tomorrow."

27 VONNIE:
WHATEVER MY LOT

First, the comical part. Until quite recently this would not have seemed funny to me, but I have traveled a great distance in the last few weeks. Danny took Hugh to Eagle Creek Park yesterday so they could enjoy the lake and watch the guys fishing. I didn't expect any visitors until around suppertime because I thought everybody else was either working or busy. But then not long before lunch, Jackie and Tony showed up. Jackie stormed in like she was warming up for a boxing match, but I didn't ask her what was wrong. I figured she'd pound me over the head with it soon enough.

"Is Dad coming up here?" she demanded.

"Maybe this afternoon," I said.

"Who's bringing him?"

"I don't know. You want to pick him up?"

She looked over at Tony, who wore his usual flat-faced look that indicated he wanted to be no more a part of this conversation than the wallpaper. He was there to drive the truck and smile until he could go back home and forget that he was even related to this family.

Jackie asked, "So have you *talked* to Dad this morning?"

"Yes, I talked to him first thing. He was feelin' good today."

"Why?"

"What do you mean why? Why not?" I knew what she was getting at, of course. She had somehow either found out about the trip to the lake or else she had gone to the house and found Dad gone. She was fishing to see how much I knew and how much I was willing to tell her, but I wasn't interested in playing that game. If she wanted to ask about Danny, she could come straight out with it.

She pressed me with a few more roundabout questions and then gave up. She went through the polite motions of finding out how I was feeling, but her visit was short. She went out in the same blustery, hip-swinging way as she came in.

About an hour later Pam called. She sounded harried. I could hear sweet little Matthew in the background pleading, "Wanna say hi! Wanna say hi!" He loves to talk to his grandma.

"Jackie says Dad's been kidnapped," said Pam. "What's this all about?"

"Kidnapped?" I had to laugh at that one. "Well, maybe we should call the police, then."

"Mom, what—"

"Oh, your dad's fine. Danny took him to Eagle Creek Park. They've been planning it for a long time. Hugh just wanted to get outside and watch people fishing. That's all."

"Why didn't you tell that to Jackie? Wasn't she just up there?"

"Yes, I don't know why I didn't tell her. Jackie just brings the mischief out in me for some reason. I can't get *every* streak of meanness out of me."

Pam directed her voice away from the phone for a few seconds to say something to Matthew, and then she came back on and said something that surprised me. "Well, Mom, lately you at least seem to have gotten rid of *some* of the meanness in you."

I laughed and said, "I don't know whether to take that as an insult or a compliment. What are you talking about?"

"I'm talking about Donna and Danny. You've gone from not even wanting to acknowledge that they exist to encouraging Danny to take Dad places, which you barely even let *us* do. Why the change?"

I thought about how best to phrase it.

"I realized they can't hurt me," I said.

"Well, I could have told you that all along."

"I was so scared what would happen if I ever had to face them as adults. But it hasn't been bad at all. I actually like them; don't you?"

"Yes."

"And the surprising thing is, they like me."

"Well, Mom, whatever happened all those years ago—which you still haven't explained to us, by the way—don't you see it was so long ago that everybody went on with their lives? There's no need to let it have so much power over you."

Easy for you to say, I thought. *I've been carrying this around for more years than you've even been alive.* I said, "Maybe so, but you know how you get a picture of a bad scene in your head, and you visualize it over and over until you'll do almost anything to keep it from happening? That's what this was like. I was determined to keep this all away from you girls."

"And you probably tormented yourself for years in the process."

"It reminds me of something I was thinking about you the other day. Remember when you were a real little girl and you loved me and your daddy to play hide-and-seek with you?"

"Yeah, barely."

"You could have played that all day long. And it was the funniest thing, because you'd get so excited—and so scared—when we'd go around the house or around the backyard looking for you. Half the time we already knew where you were, but we'd stretch it out and go real close to your hiding place but not look. Sometimes I'd hear you make these squealing noises, like you could hardly stand the suspense. But then when we'd find you, I remember you always had this disappointed look, this big letdown, like you expected more out of that part of the game. The fear was the only part you liked. The actual finding never lived up to the terror of the wait. That's how it's been with Donna and Danny. I spent all those years fearing them, but then when they actually appeared, they weren't so different from any other relative who might have shown up in our lives after a long time away."

"I'm glad you feel that way now, but I'm afraid Jackie's becoming even *more* scared of them as time goes by."

"What did she say?"

"She said that when she and Tony pulled up to your house this morning, Danny was backing out of the driveway. At first she figured he'd been visiting Dad and was leaving, but then she caught a glimpse of Dad sitting next to him. And Dad looked slumped over in the seat!"

I laughed and said, "He was probably hiding from them!"

"And she said Danny looked her right in the eye and knew who she was but then sped off as fast as he could like he felt guilty for what he was doing."

"Hugh was probably begging him not to stop."

"Well, I wish you'd talk to her, because this has her all riled up again, and she always comes to me with it. She already feels like you're trying to pull tricks on her with the will and some other things, and little incidents like this only prove it in her mind. She's threatened to turn her back on the family altogether, and I dread to think what bizarre things she might do if she's out there on her own with none of us there to drag her back to reality occasionally."

"I'm sorry, honey. I'll give her a call. I didn't really set out to keep their outing a secret—after all, there's not a thing wrong with them going—but when Jackie's here making such a big stink, I just don't know what comes over me."

That was yesterday. When I talked to Pam, I was feeling pretty good, better than I had since I've been in the hospital. I was even feeling almost lighthearted, if you can imagine that out of me.

But this morning, I woke up with the strangest feeling that I am going to die. It's the closest thing to a certainty that I can imagine, even though I could offer no facts to back it up. I do not believe I will leave this hospital.

It was the first thought I had this morning, even before I was able to get awake enough to fully realize how lousy I felt—so different from yesterday. I'm having trouble breathing again, and I have this sense, which is hard to describe to the doctors, that my body is *winding down*.

I haven't told anybody about this premonition. Not even Donna, who visited me today and who I told about something just as private—the prayers I've been praying these last few weeks.

Telling people I'm going to die sounds too melodramatic anyway, and if I'm wrong, then I'd feel pretty foolish once I went back home and picked up my life where I left off. But it has got me thinking. I'm not in a panic over it. I've been expecting it. Maybe I've even been dwelling on it too long. Mainly I worry about Hugh. What will happen when I'm not there to take care of him?

This one hymn, "It Is Well With My Soul," keeps going through my mind. I guess all these thoughts of death must have made me think of it, because I've heard it sung at a lot of funerals. It's a lovely hymn, though, not really a funeral song at all. *When peace like a river attendeth my way, when sorrows like sea billows roll; whatever my lot, thou hast taught me to say, it is well, it is well with my soul.*

Even though I've known that song my whole life, I could not bring to mind the words to the second verse. *My sin, oh, the bliss of this glorious thought ... my sin is ... nailed to the cross ... something or other.*

In the midst of trying to remember the words to this song, Donna showed up in my room.

I didn't expect her. I actually expected Hugh and Danny instead. Donna said they were planning to come later in the day. There was a time when Donna's sudden appearance would have sent me scurrying for the call button or fleeing from the room, but now she was exactly the person I wanted to see.

"All right," I said. "Here's a test for you, to see if you're really a Christian."

"Uh-oh. What is it?"

"You know the hymn 'It Is Well With My Soul'?"

"Yes! Do I pass?"

"Not so fast. For the life of me, I can't remember the second verse. It starts out 'My sin . . . .' "

In a beautiful voice, Donna, without any embarrassment, sang out, " 'My sin, oh, the bliss of this glorious thought! My sin, not in part, but the whole, is nailed to the cross, and I bear it no more, praise the Lord, praise the Lord, O my soul.' "

"Oh, honey," I said, "thank you for singing that. I haven't heard anybody sing that in years. I love that song."

"We still sing it in our church sometimes."

"They probably still sing it at ours, too."

"You're not able to go anymore?"

"Well, no, for the last ten years, since Hugh had his first

heart attack, we got out of the habit of going. But that song takes me way back to when I was a girl and we'd go to the camp meetings in the summer. They'd set up this huge tent at the campground and people would come for miles to attend a whole week of services. We'd sing song after song."

"That sounds wonderful. Our church still has a summer camp meeting like that. Not in a tent, though. They did away with that years ago. I've heard that the old-time camp meetings were pretty lively."

"I wish you could've been there. It's the music that sticks in my mind the most. We weren't just mouthing the words. It was really rejoicing. I can't even describe it anymore. It's too . . . I don't know. It's harder to talk about things like that these days. People are more embarrassed to talk about the Lord than they used to be."

Donna shrugged. "It depends on who you talk to. I'm not embarrassed by it. I'd like to hear about it. Did you become a Christian in that type of service?"

"Yes, I did. When I was ten years old. Let me tell you, there was nothing like the way the spirit of God filled that big tent. I mean, you could feel God's presence in the room. When I walked down to that altar to give my heart to the Lord, it was like His spirit was carrying me down there. And that forgiveness that washed over me . . . I'll never forget it. I could almost physically feel it. Like waves washing over me."

Donna sat there quiet, listening.

I said, "I don't know if things like that happen anymore. Everything seems different these days. So much more—"

"Of course it still happens! God hasn't changed. His spirit hasn't left the world."

"My faith has gone cold, then," I said, surprising myself with this admission.

"Well, maybe these memories are His way of drawing you back to Him."

"Maybe you're right. I've found myself praying so much lately. Maybe it's because I know I may never leave this hospital alive. I have a lot to answer for; I know that. Too much to even know where to begin. All I know is I've been praying to God for forgiveness."

"I believe that's a prayer He's eager to answer."

"I know my life can't go on much longer. The closer I get to the end, the more I feel this need to try to . . . How can I say it . . . set things straight? It's not really that. I think it's too late for that for the most part, and I don't have the power to straighten out the messes I've made, anyway. But at least I feel the need to ask God for forgiveness for those things. I suppose lots of people get this way when they see death staring them in the face."

"Some do, I guess, but not as many who really need to."

I leaned up in my bed and looked right at Donna. There was something I wanted to say to her, but up till then I had been too afraid. Now I felt the courage, so I decided to say it before I chickened out again. She sat there waiting. I said, "Donna, what I keep sensing is that I need to ask *you* for forgiveness first. You know that Scripture where Jesus says if you take your gift to the altar and remember that someone has something against you, put down the gift and first go be reconciled to that person? Well, every time I try to pray, that Scripture comes to mind, and I know I can't move forward until I talk to you."

She nodded but didn't speak yet. She could tell I had more to say.

"I could try to explain things to you. I could give reasons for what I did all those years ago and try to get you to see how things were. I didn't do what I did in order to hurt you and Danny. There were reasons. But you see . . . as soon as I start talking this way, it sounds like I'm trying to make excuses for myself, and that's not what I want to do. I know that what I did hurt you and Danny, and I'm sorry."

Donna didn't say anything at first, and I was afraid of how my words might have struck her. Then she surprised me by reaching over and taking my hand. She said, "I know it must not have been easy for you to say what you just said. I respect that, and I want you to know that I forgive you."

It's hard to describe what happened inside me once she said that. I felt like it was more than just Donna forgiving me. It's like somehow her words broke down a kind of dam that had been holding back a vast river of forgiveness, and I sat there too over-whelmed to speak as torrents of it washed over me. I actually kept my head down as the cleansing forgiveness flowed over me.

After a while I said, "I wish I could talk to my girls this way."

"Why can't you?"

"Oh, it's hard—"

"Tell them exactly what you told me. They would want to hear this. They need to. You know, Vonnie, maybe it's no accident that Danny and I popped up in your life when we did. Maybe it's the Lord's timing. I was thinking the other day that if you hadn't called me at just the time that Danny was moving out here to Indiana, he probably never would have come out here just to meet you and Hugh. This whole opportunity would have been lost."

I nodded. "During the last couple weeks I've kept wondering what if Hugh and I hadn't found you. What if you hadn't sent the letter, or what if Hugh had thrown it away? What if we had died before it came? I would have died with all this unresolved."

"I don't know whether you're aware of it, Vonnie, but my mother was a Christian during the last twenty years of her life, and I've sometimes wondered whether she told me about Hugh because she felt—even subconsciously—that some kind of reconciliation had to take place. I mean, she *told* me not to contact him, but I wonder whether deep down she knew I had to."

"That must have been it. She knew she was going to die, and she didn't want to leave all that unfinished business."

"That's right."

"You know, I always felt like I had to guard my world against your mother—even after Hugh and I had been married ten or twenty or thirty years! Isn't that ridiculous? And I hate to admit this, but when I first saw that letter you wrote to Hugh, part of me actually wished that I had already died so that I could avoid having to face all this. But then when I came to your house that day, and you hugged me like we were old friends, I finally realized I had been protecting myself against an imaginary enemy. I've been like a child afraid of some boogeyman under the bed who really isn't there!"

"Tell all this to Pam and Carolyn and Jackie. Don't let this opportunity slip away."

"I plan to, but will you . . . If something happens before I get the chance to talk to them . . ."

"You tell them. Don't put it off."

I nodded. "If I could get up out of this hospital bed and go home healthy, there's so much I'd do to make up for things."

"Maybe you will."

"Well, even if I don't get out of here, there are still a few things I can take care of. And I intend to."

I wish all three of my girls had been there right then so I could have hugged and kissed them. Strange, isn't it? The closer I get to dying, the fonder I am of them. I'm like a mother who's about to drop off her kids at the baby-sitter's. I have those last-minute pangs of regret.

Forgiveness.

Mercy.

I ask it not only from God but from all of them.

I have not been the mother I wanted to be.

I'd like to hug each one of them close to me. Tell them that I love them. I want to tell them that whatever joy I had in my life was what they brought. *I love you, Pam. I love you, Jackie. I love you, Carolyn. I love you, my grandchildren.*

And I don't forget the old man in the easy chair. *I love you, Hugh.*

Those pangs of . . . what?

Longing.

I love you all.

28

PAM:
ONE LAST REQUEST

I get nervous whenever Mom calls and says she wants to see me alone. To me that implies she's up to something secret, and secrets usually mean trouble. Still, when she called this morning and asked if I could come before anyone else got there to visit, there was such a tone of pleading in her voice that I decided I'd better go. Cliff watched the kids, and I drove over there before lunch.

Mom's been sick before, but she's never looked this frail. She shrivels up a little more each day and loses more of her color. Her main doctor still says she should be able to go home within a week, but I don't see how she'll be able to. I think she's getting weaker rather than stronger. When they brought her lunch to the room, she picked at a few things and then pushed the tray away.

Mom is also getting more like Dad in the way that she brings up topics you least expect. When I first sat down, instead of hitting me with some big request or announcement as I had expected, Mom said, "I've been thinking about that last day you and I spent shopping together."

At first I thought she was merely confused, the way Dad gets, because Mom and I haven't been out shopping together all year. She's always too afraid to leave Dad on his own and go with me, plus she doesn't like to walk too much.

"I'm not sure what you're thinking of," I said. "We haven't gone—"

"You don't remember, do you," she said. "I'm not talking about lately. This was maybe a year ago, before your dad's first stroke, when I needed some new shoes and you took me to the mall and we stayed away about twice as long as we had planned, till almost suppertime."

"Oh, yeah. That was the day you ate three pieces of pie!"

"That's right! And I remember every piece. For lunch, I had a piece of French silk and a piece of apple."

"*Sugar-free* apple."

"Well, I didn't want to eat too many calories! And then before we went home I had a delicious piece of banana cream."

"I couldn't believe it. And you were still so skinny."

"Well, at home I just didn't eat much. Not like I used to years ago."

"So what made you think about that day?"

She pulled herself up in her bed and leaned toward me a little. "I remember that as one of my almost perfect days. I mean, even though all we did was go to the mall and shop and gobble up pies, that was one of the best days you and I ever had together."

"Well, I had fun that day, too. I didn't even care if Dad and Cliff had to wait on us to get home."

"I really felt like you liked me that day."

"Of course I liked you, Mom. I like you *now*."

She waved her hand back and forth in that little dismissive gesture she uses, and then she leaned back into her pillow and looked out toward the window. "I'm not sure any of you girls like me anymore. And what's more, I'm not even sure I can entirely blame you. I know that lately I've mostly been a burden—"

"Oh, Mom—"

"No, please now, hear me out. I'm not saying that in a self-pitying way. I've been sitting here thinking and thinking about this, and I need to say it. It seems like lately, the past year or more, everybody in the family acts like I've never been anything but a fussy old woman and your dad has never been anything but a sick old man and we've never had much fun together or enjoyed each other much. And that's not the case. We've had lots of good times together, just like that day at the mall."

"Sure we have."

"So how did we ever stray so far off track?"

"Well, I don't know. I guess after Dad had his strokes and you got more feeble, it got harder to—"

"No, I mean so far off track in terms of how we treat each other, how we've moved away from each other, how we strayed from the church and from our faith . . ."

"I think you just said it. We *strayed*. We didn't intend for it to happen."

"Sometimes it seems like everything I've done has backfired and had the exact opposite effect of what I intended."

"What do you mean?"

"Like the way I dealt with Donna and Danny all those years. Or like what I did with my will. Making one simple change in it got you all annoyed at me, and Carolyn's about to bust wide open with curiosity, and Jackie's barely speaking to me."

"Well, Mom, you've got to realize that changing a will is a very sensitive issue. And if you act all secretive about it, it only makes people more suspicious. If you're gonna change the will, why not just tell everybody what you did?"

She shook her head. "What if I had told? Would that have pacified Jackie? No, it would only have thrown her into even more of an uproar because I'm giving Carolyn the option of keeping the house."

"Well, all right, then, let's talk about that deal with Carolyn and the house. You can't just . . . you can't . . ." I was groping for a way to finish my sentence without using the word "manipulate." "You can't try to control the way your grown children live their lives. I know why you changed your will. If you die, you want Carolyn to take your place and take care of Dad in your house. But Carolyn has her own life to live. If she chooses to move in there and take care of Dad, it's going to be because *she* decides that's what's best for her and Brandon. It won't be because you've turned over a *house* to her."

Mom threw up her hands. "I know! I know you're right. I'm not trying to defend myself. I'm just saying I never meant for everything to turn out this way. I love you girls so much! And I love your father so much! I wish I could set everything right. But maybe it's too late. Do you think it's too late?"

"Well, Mom . . ." I paused, not really knowing what she had in mind. "Nobody sets everything right, I suppose. You have to just move on from where you are and—"

"No, no, no." She shook her head some more. "There's one more thing I can do. It won't be enough, but it's something. I don't have time for anything more than that."

"What can you do?" I asked, fearful of what she might have in mind.

She sat up straighter and stared right at me again. "Pam," she said. Now I was really scared, because she was using that same determined tone she used when she asked me to take her to the lawyer to change the will. "I don't mean to try your patience, honey, but I may not have much time left in this world, and there is one more thing I have to ask you to do."

I took the deep breath of a weight lifter about to place his hands on the barbells and said, "All right, Mom. What is it?"

29 CAROLYN:
THE SUMMONS

In one way the scene in Mom's hospital room last night reminded me of the end of some Agatha Christie murder mystery, where all the suspects are gathered in the same room as the detective walks everyone through the crime before finally revealing the culprit.

I, like all my siblings, received Mom's summons to her bedside twenty-four hours before this strange family reunion was to begin. I didn't know the rest of them had also gotten the call. When I entered Mom's room, every eye in the room latched on to me. The atmosphere was as tense as if I had wandered into the wrong room and caught two lovers in the midst of an illicit rendezvous.

I pulled at my blouse and looked down to see if all my clothes were in their proper place. Pam said hello, as if speaking for the whole group, and then everyone relaxed a little. They clearly had expected someone else to walk through that door. Within a few seconds, I knew who that someone else was.

A quick sweep of the room showed me that the only person

missing was Jackie. Mom was in her bed, with Dad nearby in his wheelchair. Danny and Donna were next to him, and Pam sat in a chair at the foot of the bed. Two empty chairs remained on the other side of Mom's bed. One was mine, and I felt pretty certain the other one must be Jackie's.

I felt pinpricks of sweat all over me. What could the purpose of this be? Jackie was more suspicious of Donna and Danny than ever, especially since she had seen Danny "kidnap" Dad from the house. Mom and I had done our best to keep their hospital visits from coinciding with Jackie's. Maybe that extra chair wasn't for her. But if not, then why had Mom called everybody there *except* Jackie?

As strange as this collection of parents and siblings was, the room contained an even bigger mystery. About a dozen dolls from that doll collection that Jackie so covets were placed around the room—on the windowsill, at the foot of the bed, on a nightstand. These dolls, which are not even collector's items but are merely discarded baby dolls from our childhood, were in various stages of disintegration. One had what looked like a broken neck, one was naked and dotted with black smudges, and another was missing big chunks of hair. For years, Mom had kept these dolls locked away in a hiding place that only she and I knew about. Who had brought them here? And even more importantly, why on earth would Mom have them out where Jackie could see them? To taunt her?

I sat down and waited for an explanation, but instead everyone fussed about whether I wanted something to drink or whether I wanted some of the Oreo cookies from the package being passed around the room.

Before anybody got around to telling me what was going on, Jackie bounded in. As usual, she stormed in like a cop about to apprehend a dangerous criminal, but even she was reduced to frozen silence by the inexplicable assemblage of humans and dolls that awaited her.

"What's this?" she finally said, staring first at Danny and then at the dolls on the windowsill behind his left shoulder.

Mom, her voice shaky either from nervousness or weakness, said, "Go ahead and sit down, honey. I'm gonna tell you all about it."

Jackie, surprised into rare speechlessness, sat down meekly beside me.

All eyes were on Mom. She tried to pull herself up in the bed a little bit, but she was as weak as I had ever seen her. In a voice we had to strain to hear, she began, "I had so many things to say, but now most of it is jumbled up in my brain."

She stopped and took a long drink from the straw in the glass of water sitting next to her.

In a stronger voice, she said, "Maybe it's just as well. Words can't cover everything. I feel too horrible to give long speeches anyway. But I have a feeling—"

Dad coughed and hacked, and Mom stopped and looked at him to make sure he was all right. When he quieted down, she started again.

"I have a feeling I may not have much time left to do what I need to do, so I can't afford to wait till I'm out of the hospital." She let out a big sigh. "I know you all think you know me, and maybe in some ways you do know me even better than I wish you did. But when you get to be as old as I am, you'll find that most of who you really are is buried. It's buried in the past, and it's buried deep inside a body that you barely even recognize as your own."

She pulled her bathrobe more tightly around her. "I have not always been the shriveled-up prune you see in front of you. I can't explain everything that's happened. I can't justify every-thing I've done. Not much in my life has turned out the way I expected it to. I wish I could go back and change some of it. The other day when Donna was here, I asked for her forgiveness, and that's really what I need to do with all of you."

Mom looked at each one of us for a few seconds, and for a minute I thought she was going to cry. Instead, she said, "I can't set everything right. It's too late for that. I asked God for forgiveness, and I ask the same of each of you. I can't do everything. I can only straighten out a few details. If you look around the room, you'll see some dolls that have been packed away in our house for many years. I asked Pam to dig them out and bring them here today. I want to say in front of all of you, so there is never any confusion, that I have decided to give those dolls to Jackie."

Everybody looked at Jackie, who gave no visible reaction except to rock ever so slightly back and forth in her chair.

Mom continued, "Over by the doorway there, you'll also see that there's a box of photographs that Pam also brought up here. I want to make it clear that Jackie is to have those, too. There are more pictures that Pam couldn't find, but eventually we'll dig those out, too, and Jackie can divide them up among you or keep them as she sees fit. Your dad and I talked about this, and he's in agreement."

Mom took another sip from her cup and said, "There's one more thing your dad and I talked about, and I want to state it right now. Donna and Danny have never asked us for a thing, and I don't think they want anything from us, and our will makes no provision for them and doesn't even mention them. If we owe them anything materially, then I'm sorry, but we'll just have to fail them in that way. And that's all I have to say about the will. I wish I could leave more for everybody, but there isn't much left."

She looked over at Dad as if to give him a chance to add anything. He stayed quiet, looking down at his hands.

In a lighter tone, she said, "That's about it. If I get out of here alive, things are gonna be different. We're gonna have cookouts like the one Donna had at her house, and we're gonna enjoy each other during what time we have left."

After Mom finished, the room was silent for a few uncomfortable seconds, until Jackie stood up and said, "Thank you, Mom," and walked over and hugged her as best she could in Mom's frail condition.

Mom said, "Bring that box of pictures over here and I'll show you some things I bet you've forgotten."

For the next couple of hours we passed around pictures of a lifetime of Christmases, birthday parties, vacations, and backyard cookouts. I think Donna and Danny enjoyed it just as much as the rest of us. Anyone looking on from the outside would have assumed our family was plucked straight out of a commercial for Hallmark greeting cards. It was the best evening I've had with Mom in years.

30 HUGH: WHY NOT ME?

I've been on the brink of death for so long that I never thought it possible that Vonnie would go before me. I never prepared myself for what life would be like without her in it.

Vonnie went to be with the Lord three days ago.

A couple hours ago I heard her voice in the kitchen.

I wish I could say I am handling this well. I wish I could say I am stoic and tough. Sometimes the reality that she is dead wraps so tightly around me that I think I'll die from it, and sometimes I *want* to die from it. More than once I've prayed that God would take me before the funeral, because I don't know how I will ever get through it.

Pam picked out the casket, but she and the others wanted me to pick out the dress for Vonnie to be buried in. I did it, but even rifling through her clothes in the closet was almost more than I could bear. I have strange emotions at times. Yesterday I woke up from a nap—I sleep only in spurts—and I was furious with Vonnie, thinking things like, *Couldn't you have at least held out until I was gone? How could you leave me to face all this alone? What do you think our girls will do with me now that you've left me defenseless?*

Later, I was seized with guilt, wondering whether ultimately I was the one who pushed her into the grave. She worked so hard to keep both of us going that maybe her poor body couldn't stand it any longer. If I had died first, maybe that would have eased the pressure on her enough that she could have lived a few more years. Why didn't you take me instead of her, Lord? What's the point of my life without Vonnie in it?

My only consolation is that I know she went to her grave in peace. I don't say that lightly, the way people speak in polite terms about those who have died. She really *was* at peace. With all of us. With God, too. I wish I could say the same for myself, but I'm afraid I might still have a few more fights on my hands. You might expect that at least this week, leading up to the funeral, my daughters would be on their best behavior. But already I hear them whispering, conspiring, arguing. They've been here in the house for most of the time since Vonnie died. They try to have their secret conferences in the kitchen where I won't hear, but I pick up on the tones of treachery even when I can't make out the words.

I assume that most of what they're discussing in secret has to do with what they're going to do with me now that Vonnie's gone. It infuriates me that they don't even include me in the discussion. They'll toss me into some nursing home now for sure, just as fast as they can. I don't even know why they need to argue about it. They must be simply wrangling over the details—exactly where to dump me and how quickly they can sell the house out from under me to pay for the dump site.

Vonnie was able to thwart them, and I might be able to do the same, but it won't be easy without her. The only good thing about this is that my anger—and my vigilance, too, I guess—is all that is keeping me from being swallowed up by grief. It's all that gets me through those horrible moments of clarity when I realize I will never see my beautiful wife again.

Last night, right after I leaned back against my pillow for a mostly sleepless night in bed, I sensed Vonnie leaning over me, cupping my face in her hands, and kissing me on the forehead. I closed my eyes and felt the warmth of her hands on my skin. When I reached up to touch her, she was gone.

31 PAM: REST IN PEACE?

On the day Mom died, I actually believed we were going to get through this week without much turmoil, because when we all showed up at the hospital, everybody was hugging and crying and supporting one another. Mom would have been proud of us that day.

The problems started the next day, when we all gathered together again at the house. Carolyn had spent the night there and was edgy and depressed. She had gotten almost no sleep because she had stayed up talking to Dad. Cliff and the kids and I got there around ten in the morning, and Jackie showed up around one. By then, Carolyn, at my insistence, had tried to take a nap but still couldn't sleep. Sometimes when she's overly stressed like that, she likes to withdraw. The best thing to do is to leave her alone until she's ready to start talking again. When she's like that, she likes to read or watch TV, and when Jackie and Tony walked in, Carolyn was curled up on the couch reading an old *People* magazine.

I knew from the start there would be trouble. Carolyn didn't say hello or even look up at Jackie and Tony. She kept her eyes on the magazine. I doubt if she even realized she was snubbing them. I've seen her do things like this my whole life. When she's lost in thought, she forgets about the normal little courtesies.

Jackie could have smoothed it over by simply saying a quick hello and giving Carolyn her space for a while. She knows as well as I do how Carolyn deals with things. Instead, Jackie stood in the middle of the living room with her hands on her hips and stared at Carolyn, as if waiting for her to speak. Then she looked at Tony, gestured toward Carolyn, and shrugged, as if to say, "Look at this, won't you? Our mother is dead, and all Carolyn can do is sit and read a gossip magazine like she doesn't have a care in the world." I could almost read Jackie's mind, and I'd bet a thousand dollars she would have said something like that right out loud except that I intervened.

I said hi to Jackie and Tony and called them into Mom's bedroom to show her the dress Dad had picked out for Mom to wear. I thought that if anything would distract her from picking on Carolyn, surely that grim detail would. She was all right at first, but then she started firing all kinds of questions at me about when and where the funeral would be and who would sing and give the eulogy and all that.

Just as Carolyn often withdraws during a crisis, Jackie goes the opposite direction, wanting to take over and start bossing everybody around. I do have to say that, for the most part, Jackie's been much easier to get along with since that night that Mom gave her the dolls and the photos. That gesture had a big impact on Jackie. She's been much less hostile toward Donna and Danny, and she's been much nicer to me and Carolyn. Still, on this day, when most of us needed time to be quiet and grieve Mom's loss, Jackie wanted nothing but action, action, action. I had made a good start—so I thought—on planning the funeral, but Mom had been dead for less than twenty-four hours, and not every tiny item was nailed down. I was waiting for calls from the funeral home and the church.

Jackie said, "We really have to get the day and time of the funeral decided today. Otherwise, how are we going to let everybody know? We'll end up having to call everybody twice, once to tell them Mom passed away and once to tell them about the funeral. I've already told four or five people I'd have to call them back."

"I know. I'm trying to get it all worked out."

"At least the day and time, even if other things have to wait."

"I know, Jackie. I just told you—"

"I'd like to have a photo display of some of the highlights of Mom's life set up right in front of her casket. My friend Jeri at work did that for her dad when he died, and I thought it was so nice."

"Well, you can use the photos Mom gave you, right?"

"I don't have some of the ones I'd really like. I was hoping Carolyn would show me where the rest of them are."

My stomach twisted in dread at the mention of the pictures. When Mom had asked me to bring the dolls and photos to the hospital, I brought everything I could find in the place in the attic where she told me to look. When I lugged it all into the hospital, Mom said two big boxes of photos were missing. She told Jackie she'd give them to her later, but she never did remember where they were hidden. She had said that Carolyn (and maybe Dad) might know, but all Carolyn would say about it was that she'd have to look around. Dad couldn't even remember what pictures we were talking about.

At lunch on this day after Mom's death, Carolyn prophetically had said, "I bet we won't get through the next twenty-four hours without Jackie trying to get those other pictures again."

"There'll be plenty of time after the funeral to worry about those," I said.

"You just wait. She'll find some excuse for why she absolutely must have them right away."

"Well, please don't get into a fight with her over it. Can't you just find them and give them to her?"

"Not today I won't."

Now Carolyn wandered into the bedroom, but fortunately she didn't hear Jackie ask about the photos.

"Did you stay here last night?" asked Jackie.

"Yeah," said Carolyn.

"Are you gonna stay here tonight, too?"

"Probably."

"Well, it needs to be more than 'probably,' doesn't it? Dad still can't stay here by himself, can he?"

"No." Carolyn sat down on the bed and put her head down, letting her hair drape over her face as if to shut Jackie out.

Jackie said, "We're gonna have to figure out what to do with him for the long term."

"Then why don't you *tell* us what we should do, Jackie?" said Carolyn.

I know Carolyn's snarly tone was caused by nothing more than exhaustion and grief, but I saw Jackie's jaw clench immediately in that familiar sign of irritation. She said, "It's not that I want to *tell* you what we should do, but I think we should at least discuss it. We can't just bury our heads in magazines and pretend there isn't any problem."

Carolyn shook her head but didn't look up. "I was up with Dad all night."

"I know that. I'm not *saying* anything against you. Don't turn this into some . . ." She waved her hand in place of a word. "But we have to make some decisions."

"Well, *what*?" demanded Carolyn, her tone just short of frantic.

"Maybe Mom and Dad had some plan already worked out in

case she died before him," Jackie said. "I think the first thing to do is to take a look at her will and see if she made any provisions for this."

Carolyn looked up and stared defiantly into Jackie's eyes. "That will is Mom and Dad's. It's not to be opened until both of them are dead."

"I don't think that's true, is it?" asked Jackie.

"Well," I said, "obviously Mom left everything to Dad, so there's no need to bother with the will right now."

The truth was, I did need to open that will at some point and tell them about the provision that Carolyn would be allowed to live in the house for as long as she wanted to. And while I was at it, I'd have to mention the part about no "permanent fixtures" being removed from the house. Both of those would infuriate Jackie and might set her off in dangerous ways. I had no intention of getting into that battle until after the funeral.

"I think we should look at it anyway," said Jackie.

"Not now," said Carolyn. "We're not gonna use Mom's death as an excuse to satisfy your curiosity about the will."

"Why are you being so nasty?"

"I'm not, but don't march in here and start trying to find out things Mom didn't want you to know."

"Well, we can't figure out everything today," I said. "Let's go talk to Dad. Let's just get the funeral arranged and get through these next few tough days, and then we'll go from there."

Carolyn stood up and left. As she rounded the corner, Jackie declared in a loud voice, "When somebody dies, you look at their will. There's nothing so horrible about that."

"Let's leave it alone for now," I told her.

"You're gonna have to help me get those pictures for the funeral. I know she'll try to block it. Out of spite."

"I don't intend to make a huge uproar over it. Please just use the ones you have. There were some good photos of Mom in there."

"You and I have every right to those pictures. We're just as much Mom's daughter as Carolyn is. I'll ask Dad to get them for me if I have to."

"No, Jackie, please. Just wait. We don't need those pictures this very minute. Dad doesn't remember where to find things like that anymore, and Carolyn's distraught over Mom. She was up with Dad all night and has hardly slept at all. This is not the time to worry about pictures."

Jackie waited, but only for a few hours. By that evening the living room was full—with my kids, Cliff, Tony, Brandon, Carolyn, Jackie, and Dad. I thought the presence of all those people might restrain Jackie from saying anything that would lead to an argument, but without any warning she said to Dad, "I was hoping to put some pictures of Mom in front of the casket, so I was wondering if you could tell me where she keeps those other cases with the old photos in them. She said I could have them."

Carolyn, who was sitting on the floor holding Sarah by the hands and sort of rocking her back and forth, froze in place. Sarah hopped up and down, as if to jump-start her aunt, but neither Carolyn nor I could move until we heard Dad's answer.

"Old cases?" asked Dad, and for the first time since Mom's death I saw Carolyn smile.

"Yes, Dad. Where she keeps all those pictures from years ago."

He rubbed his hand over his chin. "I haven't seen any old cases."

Carolyn started rocking Sarah again, even singing a little song. I couldn't tell whether Dad was truly baffled by Jackie's question or he was simply using his "confusion" as a way of putting her off. Like Mom with her hearing problem, Dad's confusion is often real, but he also uses it selectively when it suits his purpose.

Jackie let out one of her big groans and walked out of the living room and down the hallway toward the bedrooms.

Carolyn called after her, "You'll never find them by scrounging around in there."

Jackie sprang back into the room. "Why don't you tell me where they are, then, instead of playing this stupid game?"

Little Sarah, startled by the sudden harsh tones, started to fuss. Carolyn hugged her close. "I think it's a disgrace that you're even trying to pull this little maneuver a day after Mom died."

"Well, I think it's a disgrace that you're blocking me from finding pictures for *our mother's funeral!*"

I interrupted. "This is not the time or place for this."

"When would be the time?" asked Jackie. "Will she act any different tomorrow, or next week? I think I have the right—"

"This is not about rights—"

"—to see my own dead mother's will and to look at her pictures. If I wanted to, I could get a lawyer to force you to give me access to those things."

"Always the lawyer threat," said Carolyn. "You'd really sue me over a box of old pictures?"

I said, "We're leaving if you two don't stop it."

"Don't bother," Jackie snarled, on the verge of tears. "Let's go, Tony. I've had enough of this."

Nobody spoke a word as she barreled out the door and Tony shuffled along behind her.

Dad broke the silence after her departure by asking, "Now what picture is she looking for?"

"Forget it," said Carolyn, and that's where we left it.

32 CAROLYN:
TIME TO MOVE

Even though Jackie and I didn't get along too well the first few days after Mom died, I have to admit she's done some helpful things to make up for it since then. Mom's death has hit all of us hard, but Jackie and I have reacted to it in opposite ways. I've been dragging myself around feeling depressed for the two plus weeks since the funeral, but Jackie's been a bundle of energy.

It's funny how moved she was by Mom giving her those musty old dolls and photos. The more I thought about it, even during Mom's funeral, the more I wondered what would have happened if Mom had simply given Jackie those things years ago, when she first asked for them. How much of Jackie's hostility during the past several years could we have avoided? Once a game like that—keeping something from somebody—gets started, it's hard to end it. I'm sorry now that I ever let Mom make me her accomplice in it. On the day after the funeral, I finally worked up the energy to scrounge around in the attic until I found those other boxes, and then I gave them to her as soon as she came over here to visit Dad the next day.

From then on, she's been over here every few days, making meals and cleaning and going through Mom's stuff, which I can barely bring myself to do. Until we come up with a more permanent arrangement for Dad, Brandon and I have been staying here with him. In order to make that easier for us and to allow us to get out every once in a while and get some things done, Pam and Jackie and even Donna and Danny and some of the other family members have been coming over here to stay with Dad and to help out in different ways. Jackie has taken charge of inviting people over and giving them assignments, whether it's doing a load of laundry for Dad or taking out the trash or going to the pharmacy to fill some of his prescriptions.

Nobody can accuse Jackie of not doing her share of the work. Most evenings when she comes over, she makes a big meal for everybody there. If she doesn't have time to cook, she has everybody chip in some money and she goes and buys a big dinner. It feels strange to say this in the aftermath of Mom's death, but these evenings have been some of the best times I've had with my family in years. Before she died, Mom said that if she ever made it out of the hospital, she was going to start having cookouts and family get-togethers again, and I think maybe this is Jackie's way of trying to fulfill that for her. Dad's old grill has been put to more use in the last two weeks than in the last two years.

Dad is really hurting over Mom's death, but I know he loves all the attention he's getting. His state of mind fluctuates more wildly than ever. Some evenings he's lost in his own thoughts and barely says a word, and some nights he's so confused that he doesn't make much sense. But every once in a while, more than ever before, he'll get into one of these moods where he displays the energy of a much younger version of himself and launches into a talking spree about the past in ways that we've never heard from him.

One night last week, when Donna and Danny were here, he even mentioned their mother by name, which I'd never heard him do. I walked into the living room to hear him say, "When I was married to Barbara, we thought nothing of staying out till two in the morning, even if I had to get up at six to go to work. Now I'm lucky if I can stay awake till nine in the evening."

After he said this, everyone in the room, which included Donna and Danny and Jackie and Tony and me, froze in place, hoping he would spill a few more details about this mysterious time in his life. How was it, I wondered, that he could have made it through our entire lives without ever once slipping up and saying the name Barbara out loud? Had he distanced himself from her so much that he never even thought about her? Or had the memory of her—and his need to stay silent about her—eaten away at him for all those years, as I imagine would have been the case for me if I had been in his shoes? Even now, after mentioning Barbara, Dad looked up embarrassed at our eager expressions and quickly changed the subject. He's still not comfortable talking about her, but I'm hoping that each time he refers to her, it will get easier for him to reveal more of the details of their life together.

Dad also talks about Mom quite a bit, in tones so tender and loving that I can hardly keep from crying every time I hear him. A couple nights ago, when I was walking back and forth through the living room carrying some boxes from Mom's room into the garage, I overheard him telling Pam about some trip that he and Mom had taken to Niagara Falls before any of us were born. I had never heard either of them mention such a vacation. A little later that evening I overheard another surprising bit of conversation between Dad and Pam.

Dad said, "We should have lived free and easy, but we didn't.

I guess it's easier to say that when you look back on your life. But ahead of time, you don't know what bad things could happen, so you kind of hunker down and try to protect yourself."

"What do you mean?" asked Pam.

"I mean we should have lived free and easy," he repeated. "But we were worried. Scared. Waiting for the catastrophe."

"What catastrophe?"

"It comes in the end, whether you live all hunkered down or not, so you might as well just stand up and *roar* out your life."

Pam listened intently, but her expression showed she was having trouble making sense of his words.

Dad said, "It's easy to see that now. I only wish I had more time to act on it. I tell you, if I had it to do over again, I never would have kept Donna and Danny secret from you. I would have had pictures of them right out there on the coffee table."

"Well, I wish you would have," said Pam, "but Mom might not have gone along with it."

"I would have *broken through* her worries. I would have shown her we had nothing to be afraid of. I would have opened up my life and said, 'Here I am, Lord. Here I am, family. Here I am, everybody.' But now it's almost too late."

Except for Dad, Pam has taken Mom's death the hardest. Sometimes she seems almost paralyzed by it, not wanting to tell us about the will or discuss what to do with Mom's things or take action on any kind of new living arrangement for Dad. Pam waited so long to say anything about the will that I assumed there was nothing to tell. I figured everything was left to Dad, so it was pointless to even pursue the issue with Pam. But then when I talked to her on the phone yesterday, she said something very mysterious.

"There is one detail in the will that I do need to discuss with you at some point," she said.

"What?"

"I don't want to get into it over the phone. There's no rush. After all we've gone through the last few weeks, I don't have the energy to deal with it right now. I wish I wasn't even involved. But before long, before we do anything further with Dad's situation, I'll have to tell you about it."

"Did Mom leave some kind of instructions about me?"

"Not now."

"Is it something she's leaving me?"

"Carolyn . . ."

"Well, don't do this! You're just like Mom. Dangling a secret in front of my face and then refusing to explain."

"I know. I'm sorry. I always hated when she did that, too. I should have kept my mouth shut. I'm not thinking clearly. It's just that before we do any more with Dad—"

"She left instructions about Dad?"

"No, not exactly."

I kept questioning her for a while but couldn't get anything else out of her. My imagination has been reeling with possibilities, of course. Did Mom leave instructions that Dad was not to be moved out of this house? Surely they wouldn't let her put something like that in a *will*, or at least they wouldn't have any power to enforce it. And she certainly wouldn't have the power to insist that I move in with Dad after her death. So I don't know what it would be.

Whatever we do with Dad, we're going to have to do it quickly, because Brandon and I can't go on functioning like this. It's been three weeks since Mom died, and we have yet to spend a night in our own apartment.

Pam said she'd call those retirement places that she had tried to get Mom and Dad to consider, but so far she hasn't done it. When I asked her about it again on the phone, she said, "I know I need to do it, but I just can't. Losing Mom took something out of me, and I cannot face the thought of going through that fight with Dad again about moving. Not yet. I know I need to. I'll do it."

"I don't see that we have any choice. Maybe you and Jackie and I should sit down with Dad and confront him about this once and for all. Let Donna and Danny come, too, if they want to get involved. I can't keep spending every night here. It's too hard on me and on Brandon, too. He doesn't even know where he lives anymore. It's—"

"I know. Nobody expects you to go on this way. I'm not arguing with you. None of us has the capability of taking care of Dad. When I pull myself together a little more, I'll be able to face it. I've been praying to God to give me the strength for this. But . . . maybe I'm not as strong as I used to be, I don't know. I just miss Mom so much, don't you?"

"Yes. I think about her all the time."

"I mean, I miss her even more than I could have imagined."

"So do I. I find myself storing things up to tell her when I see her again. You know what I keep imagining conversations with her about? This may sound weird, but it's true. Her funeral. I keep thinking about telling her who showed up and who didn't, what people were wearing, little pieces of conversation I overheard."

"I do the same thing. For the last couple years there have been so many emergencies to deal with all the time that I forgot how much I used to like just *talking* to Mom, at least when we weren't on the verge of an argument about Dad's care or the will or Donna and Danny or whatever."

"Dad talks to her now all the time. Sometimes I'll think he's calling me, but when I walk into the room, he's kind of mumbling to Mom. Sometimes he thinks I'm her at first, especially early in the morning or late at night, when it used to be just the two of them in the house."

"Has he mentioned anything about what he'll do once you go

back to staying in your own apartment?"

"No. The closest he comes is bragging about all the things he can do by himself now. He got to the kitchen using his walker the other day, and he made himself some lunch—a meatloaf sandwich and some applesauce. He does make it to the toilet without so many accidents now."

"Yeah, but one fall and it's all over."

"Which is why we need to take action."

"Give me till the end of the week to come up with something, all right?"

"Okay."

That's where we left it, as unresolved as ever. As long as people keep helping, I guess Brandon and I can stay here a while longer. But we can't put off a decision forever.

33

DANNY:
WHAT I CAME HERE FOR

Hugh was in a feisty mood when I picked him up for our next trip to the lake. It was about a month after Vonnie's funeral, and he was finally feeling like he wanted to get out again. Whenever I had picked him up before, I had helped him into his wheelchair right by his recliner and then wheeled him out of the living room, down into the enclosed porch, down the step to the driveway, and then out to the car. This time he said, "Take that wheelchair outside."

"What?"

"Let me show you. I can walk out to the car now. Help me out of this recliner."

I helped him up and got him balanced in front of his walker. From there, he took slow, determined steps all the way to the door. I opened the door to the porch and helped him step down into it. He crossed the porch, and I helped him out the door, down the steps, and to the door of the car.

Hugh raised his arms above his head as if he were an Olympic athlete acknowledging the cheers of the crowd. He said, "Put this walker in the trunk, will you? I might want to walk around a little bit at the park. I'm feeling strong today. I'm in training to show my daughters how tough I am."

When we got to the park, I talked him into letting me wheel him down to the lake. I was afraid he'd push his "training" program too far and end up hurting himself. The day's exertions already appeared to have sapped much of his energy. Once we got settled in a peaceful spot that overlooked the lake and the trees, he sat stone-faced, preoccupied.

"This has been a tough few weeks for you, hasn't it?" I asked, as a way of breaking through his silence.

He looked at me hard and said nothing at first. Then he stared back out at the lake. Finally, he spoke. "I only really loved two women in my entire life. Your mother. And Vonnie. Now both of them are dead."

I said nothing. I was surprised by his bluntness. I was afraid he might not be fully aware of what he was saying or who he was talking to. But I also suspected he was leading up to something, and I didn't want to get in the way.

"While Vonnie was alive, I never felt like I could even mention your mother's name. It seemed like a betrayal of Vonnie."

Hugh leaned his head back and stared at the sky, like a man getting ready to pray to God or speak to a ghost that he imagined was hovering in the heavens. I kept quiet.

He looked toward the trees and said, "You know, it's strange. When you marry someone, you say 'Till death do us part.' So I guess once your wife dies, you're not married anymore. Vonnie and I are no longer married. And yet I still feel as married to her as I ever did. It's strange, isn't it? Because I think that death doesn't really break that bond of marriage completely, any more than divorce does. Your mother and I divorced, and yet I always felt that the final thread that connected us was never fully severed, not even after I learned that she was dead. So now I have been married to two women, and I am no longer married to either of them, but neither do I feel completely cut off from them."

Come on, Hugh, I thought. *Where are you headed with this? Speak.*

He looked at me. "I feel that I owe it to you to explain what happened between me and your mother. I would have told you before, but like I said, with Vonnie there, I couldn't. I don't have to tell it if you don't want me to, but if I start, I plan to tell it all. The story doesn't put me in a good light. I won't tell it as a way to justify what I did. But you should know this, too—it doesn't put your mother in a good light, either. I will tell you things about her that you might not want to hear. It might be best that you don't. It's up to you. You don't have to decide right now if you need time to think about it."

So this is how I find out about Hugh and my mom, I thought. I had imagined that if he ever told me, it would be almost by accident, maybe during one of his hazier phases when the past and present danced around in his brain in an indistinguishable blur. But now I realized he had come here this day *planning* to tell me his story. In his mind, Vonnie's death had finally freed him to talk about the forbidden woman, my mother. As he probably understood, the story would be irresistible to me, no matter how angry I might later become about anything bad he might say about my mother.

I said, "I want to know everything you're willing to tell."

He looked at me and nodded. "Did Barbara tell you anything about us?"

"Not really. Not much."

"Well, I don't know what she was like during your growing-up years, but when she was young and we were first married, she was a very high-strung woman. Full of life. You felt like there was some kind of electricity that was turned on in her that most people didn't have. You wouldn't know it by looking at me now, but back then I was the same way. Restless. Nothing ever went fast enough to satisfy me. When the two of us got together, the atmosphere was always tense with some strong emotion—either love or anger or both of those and a few others mixed up together. I hope I don't embarrass you by talking this way."

"Not at all. Go on."

"So we got married and lived in Lafayette, and that's where Donna was born. It wasn't easy for Barbara to settle down to the life of a married pregnant woman or a mother of a baby, but she did the best she could. Then my father died, and we moved to Indianapolis to live with my mother in her house. That was not my idea. I didn't want to do it, and at first I told my brothers I would not do it. But Barbara thought it was a good idea, so we moved.

"It didn't work out well. She didn't get along with my mother, and she hated living in that house. You were born there. She loved you and Donna very much, of course. I want to make that clear to you. I have never accused her of being a bad mother."

I nodded, and Hugh shifted in his chair and continued.

"After a while she decided she wanted to get a job just to get out of the house a little bit. Most women stayed home with the kids back in those days, but Barbara was not one to sit at home all day and all night. I think she had planned on my mother doing lots of baby-sitting, but Mom wasn't really up to it by that point in her life, so we had a woman down the street baby-sit a few days a week while Barbara worked. She got a job at a shoe store. I was working at Brantwell."

Hugh stopped talking. He looked bewildered, stricken, as if his memory was jumping ahead to the more painful part of the story and he was struggling to find the words to use to describe it to me. "While she was working at the shoe store, she started fooling around—it hurts me to say this, even all these years later—she started messing around with this man there. He was the manager of the place.

"I found out about it when I showed up at the store one night around closing time and saw him kissing her. I was so stunned that I— What you've got to understand is that I *loved* this woman; I mean, I was *obsessed* with her. Nowadays you hear about men and women doing this sort of thing all the time. It sounds almost commonplace. But for me, that night, it was the worst jolt I had ever felt. I couldn't even make my feet move. I stood there outside the store, looking through the window, my feet stuck to the ground, for I don't know how long.

"Then I ran. I couldn't confront her at that moment. I would never have been able to make myself speak. I don't even know where I went for the next few hours, but eventually I ended up at home, and there she was in the living room reading a magazine. She acted like nothing was wrong. She asked me why I hadn't picked her up from work, and I made up some lame story about an emergency at the factory that I had to take care of. She told me I looked like I was coming down with something. I told her I thought it was the flu, and I went immediately and laid down on the sofa in this little back room. All night I laid there with my eyes wide open and my head almost exploding with rage.

"I stumbled through work the next day, hardly speaking to anyone, and by that night, after dinner, I was ready to face her. What I couldn't get over was how she could sit across the table from me and not betray the slightest hint that she was doing anything wrong. I even began to doubt what I had seen through that store window. My brain grasped for some innocent explanation, but it came up empty. I had seen what I had seen.

"After dinner I asked my mother to take you kids to her room at the other side of the house, and I told Barbara I had to talk to her in the bedroom. For the first time, I saw a spark of fear in her eyes. When we were alone in the bedroom, I felt so sick with humiliation that I could barely get my words out, but as I started talking, and as I realized from her expression that my accusations were true, my whole body was overcome with a fury toward her that I had never thought possible. I know that's no excuse for what ended up happening, but I'm just telling you how it was. I loved her so much that her betrayal was unbearable.

"Within minutes I was screaming at her, calling her horrible names, saying things so ugly that I can't even repeat them to you. At first she listened and even looked ashamed. I remember her sitting on the edge of the bed with her eyes averted downward and sideways, toward the floor. I expected she might sit that way through my whole tirade.

"But suddenly, she jumped up and started screaming back at me, accusing me of things, absurd accusations like that I was smothering her to death and that I had ruined her life by bringing her to live in this mausoleum and that she couldn't stand the sight of me anymore.

"Both of us were out of control, and before I knew what was happening, she slapped me hard on the face. Then she came after me with both hands. Her fingers were pointed toward me like the claws of a tiger. I was too shocked at first to even try to protect myself. In those days your mother liked to wear thick red lipstick and had bright red fingernails, and to this day I remember those fingernails slashing at me like she really wanted to kill me. All this happened so fast that I didn't even have time to think about what to do. My rage was beyond control. I swung back at her and knocked her down."

Hugh stopped his story and stared straight ahead, unseeing. He took weak, panting breaths. It was hard to imagine this old man, crumpled in his wheelchair, hitting my mother. It was also hard to imagine her—with red lipstick and red nails—attacking *anybody.* I felt like I was listening to a story about two people I had never met.

More quietly now, Hugh continued. "She ended up with a bruise on her face. Every time I saw that bruise, I thought, how could I have done that? I had never hit her before, or any other woman. I was as surprised by my own action as I was by her affair with the shoe-store man. I could hardly stand to look at Barbara for the next several days because I felt such shame.

"Later I found out that the next day she had one of her girl-friends take pictures of the bruises. A woman doing that nowadays wouldn't surprise me—you hear about cases like that all the time. But back then it was pretty unusual, believe me. She also wrote down the whole incident in her diary—inaccurately, in ways that made me look even worse than I had been.

"She was building up a file of dirt on me, and I was stupid enough to get snared in her trap. My blood runs cold even now at the thought of how calculating and merciless she was in her effort to cut me out of her life. She was like a surgeon slicing away a cancerous tumor."

As I listened to Hugh, I felt chills of my own. My mother, during my adult years, was nothing like what he was describing. She had been a rather meek woman, in fact. For much of my life, she had been a Christian, loving most of the time, rather reserved about her feelings. And yet, I could remember moments—maybe a dozen in my whole life—in which another more ruthless personality had shown through, at times when she was particularly incensed at my father or at us kids. I had stored those memories away, the way children are able to do, as if those incidents were almost make-believe and didn't really belong to my real mother.

As Hugh spoke, my mind flashed on a night when Mom and Dad had a horrible screaming argument and she threatened to leave him. She ended up not leaving, but the argument concluded with her flinging a suitcase at him. It missed and hit a mirror on the living room wall, sending it crashing to the floor. Mom went to their bedroom and slammed the door, and we heard nothing more from her that night. By the time we woke up the next morning, the mirror was cleaned up and she and my father were back to normal, behaving as if the incident had never happened. Nobody ever referred to it again.

Hugh started speaking again. "The morning after our fight, we didn't exactly make up, but we called a kind of cease-fire, mainly because you kids and my mother were scared half to death by what had happened. Barbara made a half-hearted promise to quit her job and never see the man again, but she made no effort to follow through. Instead, over the next few weeks she started flaunting her relationship with him, goading me to lash out again. One evening he actually brought her home in his car and kissed her before she walked up to the house.

"I may have been a little dense about the whole thing, but later it occurred to me that her whole strategy was to try to get me so outraged that I would do things I'd regret and then make her infidelity look not so bad by comparison. I mean, think about that first night when I looked through the window and saw her kissing him. It was closing time. She knew I'd be coming there. If she was trying to hide it, that would have been the worst time and place for her to kiss him. I think she *wanted* me to see them and cause a scene right there in the store. I didn't do that, but in the weeks to come I did plenty of other stupid things to make up for it.

"One thing I did was beat the guy up. I followed him home from his store one night when Barbara wasn't around, and I pounded the daylights out of him. He didn't call the cops or try to retaliate in any other way, but I found out later that, once again, Barbara took photos of him and had a neighbor write out a statement of what she had seen me do. You see, she was *using* her boyfriend, and he was so dumb he let her do it. She didn't care if he got beat up, as long as it gave her more ammunition to use against me.

"Barbara moved out after I beat up the boyfriend, and that pushed me to a new level of anger. She left you kids with me and my mom, and Lord only knows what she did all day and all night during those weeks. She stopped by the house to see you only when she knew I'd be at work. She wouldn't let me contact her. She acted like this was a situation that could continue this way forever and that there was no need to discuss anything.

"She didn't move in with the boyfriend right then. I don't know why. She moved in with this lady she was friends with. They didn't have a phone, and I usually couldn't find her there, so sometimes all I could do was write her letters. She saved the ones she considered threatening, which added more evidence to her nasty file against me. Several times when I showed up at the house where she was living, her roommate called the police and told them I was a Peeping Tom and was threatening her and Barbara. The cops told me to stop going over there or they'd arrest me.

"Before long I started feeling desperate. The whole thing was humiliating, and I felt like I had to find a way to sit her down and hash things out. By then the only place I could ever find her was the store, so one day I showed up at closing time and banged on the door so she would either let me in or come out and talk to me. The store had this big display window that looked out onto the street, and the boyfriend came from the back room and stood at that window and taunted me. It was so ridiculous when I think of it now. We must have looked like a couple of six-year-olds on the playground, calling each other names and shouting insults. I couldn't catch all the words he said, but the gestures were clear enough.

"After a few minutes of this, Barbara tiptoed out of the back room to catch the show. She sort of hid behind a display case at first, but then she started laughing at us and came and stood beside this boyfriend of hers. She pretended to try to quiet him down, but she was laughing the whole time. She wouldn't look at me. That guy might have been screaming at an empty side-walk for all you could tell from Barbara's expression.

"If I was smart, I would have walked away. I could have waited for them in back and talked to Barbara when she came out to go home. I'm not proud of what I did next, but you've got to understand I felt pushed to the brink. There was the woman I loved more than life itself laughing at me at that window, like I was some kind of monkey in a cage. And her idiot boyfriend was enjoying every minute of my humiliation. I felt trapped. I felt like I had no choice but to do something dramatic to show them I wasn't some weakling who would sit back and let them make a fool of me.

"There was a metal trash can sitting out on the sidewalk, and I picked it up and hurled it through that display window. Barbara immediately stopped laughing. She looked terrified. I remember thinking that no matter what happened to me—whether I got arrested or spent time in jail or whatever—it was worth it to change that expression on her face. That's how far off the deep end they had pushed me. Mr. Big Mouth shut his trap and started running toward the back of the store, not even bothering to see whether Barbara was following.

"I climbed in that window and chased both of them out the back door and to their car. I don't know what I would have done if I had caught them. All I wanted was to talk to her, but we were obviously beyond that point by then. They drove off, and a few minutes later I heard sirens. I thought about surrendering right then and getting it over with, but I decided not to make it any easier for them. I went home and waited for the cops to show up.

"But nothing happened. The next day, I went to work and expected not to make it through my shift without being called out and arrested. Nothing. I was supposed to pick up you and Donna from Mrs. Greiner's on the way home, but I went home first instead because I figured the police would be there waiting for me, and I didn't want you kids to see me get arrested. No police were there.

"I hadn't told Mom about smashing the window, so when I got home, I just asked her, 'Has anybody come by today?'

" 'No,' she said. 'Just Barbara.'

"That surprised me. I figured she would have stayed as far away from me and the house as she possibly could. 'What did she want?'

" 'Just to pick up some clothes,' Mom said. 'Where are the kids?'

" 'I haven't gone down to Mrs. Greiner's yet. First I wanted to see—'

" 'See whether anybody stopped by today? Who were you expecting?'

" 'Did Barbara say anything?'

" 'No. She threw some clothes in a some boxes and carted them away. You better go get those kids.'

"I ran all the way to Mrs. Greiner's. You and Donna were gone. Your mother had picked you up in the middle of the afternoon. Once again Barbara had made a fool of me. I told Mrs. Greiner, 'You had no right to let her take them. *I'm* paying you, not her.'

" 'Well, she *is* their mother,' she said, backing away from me like she was scared I might hit her or something. I wondered what Barbara might have told her about me. Mrs. Greiner said, 'Am I supposed to tell their own mother she can't have them? Am I supposed to become a kidnapper just because you and your wife can't get along?'

"I let it go. It wasn't Mrs. Greiner's fault. If anyone was a kidnapper, it was Barbara. I tried not to panic. There were lots of reasons why she might have taken you kids. I hoped that maybe by that night she would quietly return you. I thought maybe she had taken you away because she wanted to spare you getting caught up in anything surrounding my arrest.

"But why hadn't she told Mom what happened at the store? And why didn't the police come? I heard nothing from Barbara that night or the next day. That following evening after work, I drove past the shoe store. The window was boarded up, but the place was open. I saw no sign of Barbara or the man. I also drove by the house where she had been staying, hoping to catch a glimpse of you and Donna or your mother. I couldn't see anybody, but I didn't want to risk going up to the door. I drove by the boyfriend's place, but his car wasn't there and nobody appeared to be home.

"I was in agony that night and the next day. My brain was seized with such a tangle of emotions that I could barely function. I was outraged at Barbara, worried about you kids, looking over my shoulder every minute thinking I'd be hauled away. I went to work, which actually helped keep me sane, but I was nothing more than a robot.

"Barbara kept me in suspense for two more days, and then finally she called. 'Tom and I are leaving town,' she told me. 'I'm taking the kids. There's nothing you can do about it.'

" 'Yes, there is a great deal I can do about it,' I said. 'Do you think I'm gonna sit back and let you get away with this?'

"That's when she told me about her documentation of all the things I had done—the photos, the witness statements, and all that. She ran through a quick description of every piece in her dirty little file. She offered to send me copies if I wanted them. She said, 'You either agree to my arrangements or it's jail for you.' I was so surprised I couldn't even speak for a minute. The thought of how much she must have hated me to have compiled all that against me was almost paralyzing.

"Not wanting to let her think she could control me with her threats, I said, 'That's nonsense. You know none of that would ever hold up in court.' The truth was I didn't know whether a court would look at that evidence or not. I *was* guilty of smashing the window, assaulting the boyfriend, assaulting Barbara.

"She said, 'It *will* hold up. And even if it doesn't, which it will, I can use it anyway. To show your family. Your boss. Your mother. Her church friends.'

" 'Why, Barbara?' I asked her. 'How could you do this to me? How could it come to this after how much we loved each other?'

"She thought for a minute and then she said, 'I know you. You're the type that's hard to get rid of. But I intend to do it.'"

Hugh shook his head. "Can you believe it? That's all the explanation I ever got.

"I told her, 'I want to see the kids.'

"She said, 'I'll be in touch soon. About the divorce. You'll see the kids then. But I'm taking them, not you. Make no mistake about it.'

"She disappeared for three weeks after that, without a doubt the worst weeks of my life. I had no way of reaching her, no way to know when she'd show up again. No one would give me any information about her—not the people at the shoe store, not her family, not her roommate. I considered contacting the authorities, but what could I say? What would that lead to but more trouble?

"I was so depressed I could hardly get through the days. I missed days of work, and even when I did go, I made lots of mistakes and came close to getting fired.

"Barbara showed up unannounced on a Saturday afternoon. Somebody dropped her off at the house, and you and Donna were there with her. I was so relieved to see you I could hardly speak. Donna was confused by the whole thing and thought you had come back home to stay. You, of course, were too little to even know what was happening. The boyfriend was nowhere in sight."

Hugh stopped talking, lost again in his own memories. The sun had shifted enough to be in his eyes, so he asked me to push him farther down the path. We moved in silence. How I wished I could have heard my mother's version of what happened! How could she have kept silent about this my whole life? So much of what Hugh was saying sounded so unlike her that I wondered whether he had exaggerated it over the years to make her look worse and him look better. He might not even fully realize how he was twisting the facts. Still, I knew it was *possible* that the story had unfolded as he was describing it. I mean, as much as I hated to think about it, I could picture her in every one of those scenes.

When we got settled in a new spot, Hugh continued. "So anyway, that evening, while my mom watched you kids in the other room, I sat with Barbara at the kitchen table while she laid out her demands. She said she wanted a divorce right away. The only thing she was asking of me was that I leave her alone and no longer be a part of her life except for what was absolutely necessary for visitation with you kids. She would bring you and Donna for visits as often as possible, at least twice a month on weekends. She didn't want to be tied to any strict custody arrangement, but she would commit to maintaining at least that amount of contact. If I didn't agree to her conditions, she was prepared to fight me with every means at her disposal.

"I didn't agree to anything that night. She took you and Donna and disappeared again, violating *my* one demand, which was that she let me know how to get in touch with her. For a while, as we went through the divorce, she did bring you to stay with me every other weekend as we had agreed. She never did tell me where she lived the rest of the time. I got the impression from what one of her relatives said that she might be in Illinois, but I suspected she might be even closer, in Lafayette.

"When the divorce became final, Barbara vanished for good. She wrote to me and told me not to try to contact her. She said she would bring you kids only when it was convenient for her, but that she was planning to move farther away and that trips to Indianapolis would not be easy. She said if I tried to fight her, she would make my life hell.

"I thought about fighting her anyway. My life was already miserable, so what did I have to lose? But how would I find her? Go to the police? Threaten her relatives? Hire a private detective? And if I did find her, what would I do then? Launch a whole new battle for custody—a battle I would almost certainly lose?

"Every weekend I kept waiting for her to show up with you, but she never did. I was a mess. I couldn't sleep anymore. It was the strangest thing. I was so tired I was almost delusional, but my brain wouldn't let me sleep. I would lie awake at night stewing and worrying, unable to shut off the flow of thoughts. Sometimes I'd fall asleep for an hour or two here or there, but I'd wake up feeling totally unrested. I started drinking to help me sleep, even though the alcohol made me worse off than before. I lost my appetite, too, and lost a lot of weight. I got written up at work because I was too tired to function properly and because I was calling in sick too much. I was one reprimand away from getting fired.

"Only one thing kept me going during this whole period, and nothing else I say will make sense unless you understand it. Deep down I believed—against all the evidence—that Barbara would eventually come to her senses and come back to me. I was so obsessed with her, and so sure of our love in spite of all that had happened, that I was incapable of believing that she would take our children and stay with that man.

"I rehearsed dozens of scenes in my head where she would come back and apologize and beg me to take her back in and I would take her in my arms and forgive her. In some of those fantasies I was harsh with her and in others I was loving. In some she was crying and practically begging for forgiveness, and in others she was nearly silent as she slinked back home. It was crazy of me to think that way, I know, but in a way, it was all that got me through that first year. Even after Vonnie came along and we got married—I'm ashamed to say this—I didn't completely get rid of the possibility that Barbara would show up again and try to set things right between us.

"So Barbara did everything in her power to keep me away from you, and I was too paralyzed to fight back. Then I met Vonnie, who was related to one of my mother's friends at church. I fell in love with her, and before long I told her the whole story. She could see it was destroying me, and she pressed me to stop trying to fight Barbara and get on with a new life before I ruined myself. She knew it tore me apart to give up you kids, but she didn't see any other choice.

"It's easy to look back and blame her now, but I think she was motivated by two things. One was that she really did think I'd go off the deep end somehow if I didn't find a way to move on. The other motivation was that she was scared of the dirt that Barbara had on me and feared the scandal Barbara would drag us through if we took her on.

"Once I asked Vonnie to marry me, she made me promise that I would put my past behind me and never speak of it again. She meant well, I think, but even though she never mentioned you, she knew that what she was asking was that I give up any chance of getting you and Donna back in my life. At a better moment, I might not have agreed to her conditions. But I was at my lowest point, and here were the two most powerful women in my life—Barbara and Vonnie—both urging me to set my past aside, including my kids. I did it. I ached for you kids, yearned for you, but I did it."

Hugh stopped, refusing to look me in the face. I thought he might be at the end of his story, but after wiping his face with his handkerchief, he resumed.

"On the other hand," he said, "it was bearable. I say that to my shame, but it was. I started a new life with Vonnie. We moved across town, and I avoided my family for the next few years. Our girls started being born, and the longer we kept our secrets about the past, the harder it was to break out of that silence. The only sketchy information I ever received about you came from one of Barbara's relatives, who secretly called me once a year or so.

"And that's how I've lived my life, with the guilt of my decisions gnawing away at me. And I'm sorry. I am so very sorry."

Hugh and I sat silent for a long time after that. We heard kids in paddle boats laughing as they crossed the lake. We watched a couple of fishermen cast their lines into the water. When I next glanced over at Hugh, he looked like a statue, frozen. For a second it even occurred to me that he was dead, as if telling his story had been the one remaining task that had kept him alive and now his frail body had surrendered.

Then he raised his head slightly and sighed. "I'm not feeling so great. Could you take me home?"

Neither of us said much in the car. As I pulled into the driveway, Hugh surprised me by asking, "When's my grandson coming out here?"

He had never referred to Alex as his grandson. "Soon, I hope."

Just the night before I had talked to Terri about letting Alex fly out for a visit. I'm talking now about the real Terri, not the one in my brain. She was surprisingly cooperative, and when I talked to Alex about it, he sounded eager to come.

Driving home from Hugh's house that day, as pieces of his story flashed through my brain and his tone of regret sank deeply into my own spirit, I decided I would not rest until the plans for reuniting with my son were firmly in place.

34 PAM: THE TRUTH LEAKS OUT

Dad has been amazing us all with the stories he's been telling this week. I don't know how Danny did it, but when he took Dad to the lake a few days ago for one of their outings, he got Dad to tell him the whole story about his marriage to Danny and Donna's mother and how it broke up. Now, even though Dad isn't repeating the same account to the rest of us from beginning to end, he's letting plenty of it leak out.

When Dad talks, he reminds me of one of those little sippy cups that Matthew and Sarah use. Those cups have a little stopper that seals the lid so that no juice spills out when the cup is dropped. If the stopper wears out and starts to leak, there's no way to fix it. The spills get bigger and bigger until you have to just throw the stopper away. Dad kept his first marriage sealed as tight as the best sippy cup in the world for the last forty-five years, but now that he has started to leak the truth, the few little drips are turning into a flood.

Since Danny is the only one besides Dad who knows the whole story, we call him our "interpreter," because we often have to go to him to make sense of what Dad is telling us. Last time I was over there Dad said, "I should never have let Barbara control me. I should never have agreed to her conditions. She was the one who had the affair, not me. I should have straightened it all out right then and there, no matter how much mud she would have slung at me." I tried to ask him to clarify, but he went off on some other unhelpful tangent. Danny later explained what the "conditions" and the "affair" were all about. He says he can hardly picture his mother doing all the horrible things Hugh described, and I feel the same way about Dad. Mom and Dad always seemed so conventional and predictable, yet now I'm hearing about fights and affairs and broken windows and ugly secrets.

I've never seen Dad struggle so openly with guilt and regret. Has all of that been inside of him all these years, only to leak out now because of the strokes and the other events of the last few months? He talks about the future a lot, but not always in realistic ways. He said, "I'm gonna make it all up to you kids. As soon as I get back on my feet, things are gonna be different in this family. The way Vonnie wanted them to be at the end. I'm gonna . . . I'm gonna get us all to . . ." He left the sentence unfinished, as if he had no idea how to even begin to unravel the blunders of the past.

In the meantime, we "kids" are focused on the future. Jackie, Carolyn, and I are edging closer toward a "showdown" meeting with Dad to confront him with the obvious, which is that he needs to live somewhere where he can get some professional care. Danny and Donna have said they don't want to be part of the meeting, even though they've become as much a part of the family as the rest of us. Even Jackie treats them almost like a brother and a sister now, since she apparently finally got it through her head that they're not con artists after Mom and Dad's money. But they both feel this is one decision they shouldn't interfere with.

I talked to Donna about this meeting last week as I was

going through some of Mom's files. You might think we would have finished cleaning out all that stuff by now, but Mom saved everything, and she had a bizarre system of "organization," if you could even call it that. The closets are crammed to the ceiling with financial paperwork and old books and shoes and purses she bought decades ago and anything else you could think of. She must have saved every receipt and canceled check she ever had, and she stuffed them into old Kleenex boxes, our old school folders, even an old cereal box. Anyway, as I was scrounging through all this stuff, I told Donna that I didn't want to go to that meeting with Dad any more than she did. When she asked why, I said, "It's too embarrassing."

"Embarrassing?"

"I don't know if that's even the right word. It's just that he's my *father,* and for us to gang up on him like that, which is exactly how he'll see it, and try to force him to give up the house he has lived in for over forty years, and that he lived in with his *wife* who just died, it just feels too heavy-handed. I can understand why Carolyn wants us all to do it, because it'll show that we're united and that it's not just one of us having some crazy idea. And logically, moving to another place is almost certainly the best thing for him. But who are we to decide that for him? We might go through that and then he would still refuse, and what would we have accomplished but to make him hurt and furious at us? What I wish is that *he* would come to the conclusion on his own that he can't handle this living arrangement anymore."

"Is he absolutely incapable of caring for himself? He's doing better with that walker, isn't he? Maybe if he just had *some* help, he could make it. I know I'd be willing to keep coming over one or two evenings a week, maybe even more when school's not in session. I bet Danny would do the same. What if you, Jackie, and Carolyn were each responsible for one or two days a week of looking in on him?"

"Sure, but still—"

"And could he afford one or two days a week of some kind of professional in-home care? Surely that would be cheaper than a nursing home."

I thought about this as I rifled through an old shirt box marked *1978—Bills*. I said, "I bet Dad would even take Meals on Wheels. It was Mom who was against that because she didn't want more strangers traipsing through her home."

"I think he'd welcome the hot meal and the chance to talk to somebody."

"Of course any solution like this would only be temporary. Eventually, Dad's probably going to get so feeble again that he won't be able to live on his own. We'll have to face this later."

Donna nodded. "I don't mean this to sound insensitive, but anything you do at his age and in his condition is temporary. You never know how long you'll have him. If he deteriorates, maybe he'll eventually *want* to move out of the house. Maybe he'll ask for your help, and then it will go smoother."

"Well, we'll have to see. I'll have to talk to Carolyn and Jackie. I think they're pretty set on moving him somewhere. It's not fair to keep Carolyn and Brandon living here indefinitely."

Jackie, in fact, has already begun to take action in her not-too-subtle way. Some guy she knows is a real estate agent, and she invited him over to look through the house to give a ballpark figure of what he thought it might sell for. Dad immediately understood what was going on and told the man to leave. "This is *my* house," Dad said, "and it is not on the market. No offense, but my daughter is not authorized to invite real estate agents over to snoop around."

If that's any indication of the attitude Dad's going to take during our family meeting, then I wish I could join a different family.

35 CAROLYN: THE BIG SHOWDOWN

The closer we get to tonight's big showdown with Dad, the more nervous I get about confronting him. When Pam came over last night to visit Dad, I asked her if she minded if I took off by myself for a few hours to think things over. Brandon spent the night at his friend's house, so I had a rare evening alone. I bought a couple magazines and a new mystery novel and went to Burger King to enjoy the solitude.

Unfortunately, I couldn't concentrate on reading. I'd go over the same paragraph five times and still not have any idea what it said. I was thinking about Dad. Doesn't it just figure? Pam gives me the night off so that I can have a break from Dad, and then he's all I can think about.

I keep putting myself in Dad's place and trying to imagine the actual details of him moving out of that house for good. After staying with him during these weeks since Mom died, I can see what a comfort that house is to him, like an old sweater that he can wrap himself in to feel just a little less lonely. I know that reassuring feeling that a home can bring. Even my apartment, which I've lived in only a few years and which most people think is fairly unappealing, to me feels like a refuge.

Before I started staying with Dad, there were rough days at work when I longed to get back there and close the drapes and wrap myself up in a blanket in my big chair and shut out the world. I loved sitting there late at night, after Brandon had gone to bed, when there was only one lamp burning and the only sounds were the familiar ones—the refrigerator humming, the furnace turning on and off, a neighbor occasionally slamming a door or calling to someone outside. I'd make some hot tea and read my books and magazines until late into the night, feeling the happiest I'd been all day.

I know that this sense of refuge must be compounded for Dad, who has spent forty-five years in this one place. I can see why it would seem unbearable to him to leave the house, broken down though it may be, where his children went from being babies to little girls to teenagers to fully grown women, where he and his wife lived their entire marriage, where all his own personal dramas and hopes and fears played themselves out.

I can see why, especially in the aftermath of his wife's death, he would recoil at the idea of trading that home for the bare walls of a cold institution that smells of urine and death. A dark place like that rehab center where he stayed before, which had no more sense of home than a shopping mall parking lot. Even those assisted-living apartments that Pam looked into, with their perky wallpaper and stain-resistant carpet, would not be much better than camping out in the waiting room of a doctor's office.

I dread the thought of taking him to one of those places, the actual moments of leaving him alone there the first evening, with him knowing he has lost his home forever. Or the moment of knowing that the house has sold. Or the day when we move all the furniture and belongings out of his house—to a storage unit or our homes?—and close the door on that most important place of our past for the last time.

Right there in Burger King I was tempted to switch sides and support Dad's desire to stay at home no matter how hard it would become. But how could I do that? Pam and Jackie would be furious, since they both want to get him settled somewhere safe as soon as possible. The only way for him to be able to stay at home is if Brandon and I moved in there, and I don't know whether I could handle that or whether Brandon could, either.

Living there these last few weeks hasn't been easy. I'm not the tidiest housekeeper, but even for me, the place is a mess. I know Mom did her best to keep things presentable, but the house just overwhelmed her the last year or so. The carpets are dirty and even smelly in some rooms because of Dad's accidents. Even though I vacuum, I keep finding all kinds of things on the floor—pills, pill-bottle caps, hairpins, hair. It's as if this stuff keeps seeping up from deep underground. I don't see how there can be so much of it. Every faucet in the house leaks, and the toilet still clogs up a lot, and the oven barely works, and the window screens need to be replaced, and the water heater's making a funny noise, and on and on. I'd be crazy to move in there. It would take more money than I make just to keep it livable.

Dad's strokes have taken the edge off some of his grouchiness except for isolated episodes, but he's still not the easiest person to get along with. He's so forgetful that he can drive me crazy asking the same thing about a million times. It's not too relaxing to be in the same room with him. Last night after I got back to his house, I got him to the bathroom and gave him his nighttime medicines. I finally got him settled in his recliner again, and I was hoping to relax and read my book, but he interrupted me no less than five times with the same question: "When are you gonna bring me that medicine?" When I told him he had already taken it, he gave me this skeptical frown each time, like he thought I might be tricking him or I might be just too lazy to get up and get his pills. If I hadn't been there, he probably would have taken them five times without even realizing it. Finally I had to get up and go back to my bedroom to read because he was driving me insane.

I've been proud of Brandon for how he tries to get along with Dad, but it isn't always easy. I don't think either of them knows how to actually start a conversation with the other. I think Dad wants to talk to Brandon, but instead of asking him something nice, he'll say something that's kind of picking on him, like, "Why do you wear those shorts that are so baggy? Won't your mother buy you some clothes that *fit*?" Brandon doesn't really know how to steer Dad into a more productive line of conversation, so he usually withdraws into himself until they start talking to each other about something almost by accident.

When I picked up Brandon from his friend's house last night, I asked him what he would think if we ever ended up living with Grandpa permanently.

He shrugged. "Might as well. We're there all the time anyway."

"So you wouldn't mind giving up the apartment if it came to that?"

"Could I have the back bedroom at Grandpa's?"

"Yeah."

"Could I have my own TV?"

"Well, I don't know. I'm not—"

"He never wants to watch anything I like! It's just news, news, news. The same thing over and over—"

"I'm not saying we're *going* to move in there with him. I just wanted to see what you thought *if* we did."

Brandon shrugged again, and for him a shrug means "Fine with me."

So now I'm just a few hours away from the meeting, and I

still have no idea what to do. Maybe Jackie or Pam will be in one of their take-charge moods and will save me from having to do *anything*. Maybe they've got a place all worked out for Dad to go to, and I'll have to do nothing more than sit there and agree.

Donna called me here at work today to let me know that she and Danny were spending the day with Dad. She asked me, "How do you plan to start the conversation with Hugh tonight?"

"I have no idea," I said. "It'll be all I can do to force myself to *show up* to this meeting. I'm a nervous wreck."

36 DANNY: No Peace

For the past few weeks Hugh's mental and physical condition appeared to be improving slightly, but today there was a surliness about him that he had rarely shown during our previous times together. Part of the problem might have been that this is the day of the big meeting with his daughters that is supposed to determine his fate. They're probably meeting right this minute. Donna and I were at his house earlier today to fix him lunch and stay with him until Carolyn or one of the other daughters got there. Hugh isn't supposed to know what the gathering is about tonight, but I think he suspects what they're about to hit him with. His grouchiness with me was most likely his way of warming up for the fight to come.

Our visit started out okay, but while Donna was in the kitchen fixing lunch, he wandered into some discussion about the ways factories are run nowadays, and he got more and more hostile as he went. "Back in my day, the boss was the boss, buddy!" he declared. "He told you what to do and you did it. There wasn't any of this 'team management' or any crap like they have nowadays. He didn't worry about how you *felt* about things or what *opinions* you might have to contribute. But I'm telling you, things got done back in those days. Decisions got made and they got carried out. But by the time I retired, everything had changed. You couldn't even change a light bulb on the factory floor without about twenty people signing off on it. Industry in this country is going down the tubes!"

Thinking he wanted to have a friendly discussion on this topic, I offered, "But I've read that in many ways, industry is more efficient now. Workers are more productive, especially with some of the new technology that—"

"General Motors ruled the world in those days!" he bellowed. "Do you think in the 1950s people were driving cars made in Japan? No! They were driving Chevrolets and Pontiacs and Cadillacs!"

"Well, the Japanese were still rebuilding from the war back then, but—"

"Exactly!" he shouted. "And who do you think paid for that? We did! We gave it all away! We gave it all away to the Japanese and the Germans and the unions and the feminists and the homosexuals . . ."

I got the impression this list would have gotten a lot longer if he hadn't run short of breath and had to pause to suck in some air. I wasn't following him anyway. Hadn't he been a member of a union? And what did homosexuals have to do with Japan or General Motors?

"Back in the fifties," he said, speaking slowly as if he had already gone over this with me several times but I was too dense to understand it, "and up to about the late seventies, General Motors had a huge share of this country's car market. I don't even remember the numbers now, fifty percent or something like that. And now what is it? Just a piddly percentage. My company used to do business with them, so I know what I'm talking about."

Still trying to treat the conversation like a polite give-and-take, I said, "But you have to admit that even though that sector of the economy has changed, in other ways our economy is booming. It has expanded beyond the big corporations like—"

"Awww," Hugh growled, his face contorted into a grimace of derision. And then, in a voice so loud he sounded like he was addressing some kind of protest rally, he yelled, "It's expanded to what? People selling shoes in shopping malls! What do we *manufacture*? Tell me that. We manufacture *french fries*! Don't talk to me about a booming economy. I was there when—"

By this time Donna had bounced into the room to see what all the shouting was about. "What are you doing?" she asked me. "Are you trying to give him another stroke?"

"We were just talking about economic—" I began, but Hugh drowned me out.

"Think back to World War II!" he was saying. "Do you think the guys who run these factories today could have won it? Do you think Eisenhower used *team management* when he planned D-day?"

Yes, I thought, he may very well have used team management, considering that D-day was a combined effort of British, Canadian, and American soldiers. But I kept quiet because I knew Donna would kill me if I continued the argument.

Hugh declared, "He was the general, and he just ordered them in! He didn't consult everybody about their *feelings*."

Donna said, "Hugh, do you need me to help you into the bathroom before lunch?"

Helping Hugh to the bathroom was one of our purposes for staying with him, but Donna's question, coming in the midst of his tirade about Eisenhower and team management, was not well-timed.

"No, I do not need help into the bathroom!" he yelled. "Who said anything about the bathroom? Can't anybody around here ever have a normal conversation without fussing at me about peeing or taking my medicine or eating my vegetables? I feel like a child!"

"I'm sorry," said Donna. "It's just that—"

"It's humiliating! I'm not a two-year-old. Doesn't anybody realize that anymore?"

That was the tone of conversation throughout lunch, and as the time got closer for his daughters to arrive and the big meeting to convene, Hugh only got grouchier. Donna and I left before the meeting. Carolyn had invited us to participate, and Donna was open to the possibility, but I adamantly refused. Even though Hugh's daughters, including Jackie, have welcomed us into the family more lately, I still don't feel it's any of my business to decide where Hugh lives. Besides, I don't want to re-ignite Jackie's suspicions of me by taking any action that could be construed as an attempt to control Hugh's life or to edge out his daughters.

We left around four, which is when Hugh usually takes his afternoon nap. Brandon was there, and his mother was expected to come home within the hour.

On the way home, I told Donna, "When Vonnie came to terms with her past at the end of her life, it seemed to be liberating for her. But for Hugh, revealing what happened all those years ago doesn't seem to have brought him any contentment at all."

"No," said Donna. "He's making some progress with his children, but inside him, there is still no peace."

37   PAM:
ONE MORE HURDLE

I could have kissed Carolyn last night. In fact, I did. I had been so nervous before our big talk with Dad that I was hardly able to sleep the night before. I kept trying to think up excuses to skip the meeting, but I knew that would have been postponing the inevitable. I wanted to bring Cliff along for moral support, but Carolyn vetoed that idea. She said, "Frankly, the husbands have never been much help when it comes to Mom and Dad, so I see no reason to drag them into this now. Besides, I don't have one anymore, so I'd be outnumbered."

I imagined Dad accusing us of betraying him and not loving him and soiling Mom's memory and all sorts of horrible things. I imagined him refusing to ever leave the house voluntarily, vowing to stay there and die rather than let us cart him off. Who's to say how any of us would react to that kind of outburst? Would Carolyn go soft and side with Dad? Would Jackie go mean and say she'd drag him to the nursing home whether he wanted to go or not? It was hard to imagine a realistic scene that would not turn ugly.

I worried about Carolyn, too. I had seen her crumple in situations like this. It would not have surprised me if she had suddenly contracted some debilitating "illness" that would have forced her to cancel the meeting. Or, even worse, I could picture her showing up but crawling into her shell and making me do all the talking to Jackie and Dad.

She didn't do any of that. Instead, she did something far more surprising.

When I first got there, Carolyn was in the kitchen, washing some dishes. She kept scrubbing when I walked in, avoiding eye contact with me and making me fear that she had already begun the process of shutting us all out for the night.

"Hi," she said. "Go talk to Dad while I finish cleaning up the dishes. Jackie should be here any minute."

"Wait a minute," I said. "How are we gonna do this tonight?"

"I don't know. Have you already made arrangements for Dad to move somewhere?"

"No. I can't do anything definite until we're all in agreement."

As I said that, we heard Jackie coming through the door.

Jackie strode into the room and looked us over as if she were a boxer sizing up an opponent. "So what's the plan?" she asked. "Who's going to do the talking tonight?"

"All of us," said Carolyn, which didn't help at all.

Carolyn abandoned the unfinished dishes, dried her hands with a towel, took a deep breath, and led us into the living room, her head angled toward the floor. Dad was sitting in his recliner in the corner of the room. He stared off in front of him as if he didn't know we were there. He's often lost in his own world lately, but I wondered whether he was also using that aloofness as a strategy to shut us out if we tried to talk to him about issues he didn't want to hear.

The three of us took our seats on the sofa and chair closest to Dad, and then the room fell silent. Even though this room had been one of the most familiar places in the world for all of us for the past forty years, right then it felt no more like the home I had grown up in than the dungeon of some medieval castle.

Carolyn folded her arms and slumped down in the sofa, and I thought, *Oh no, it looks like I'm the one who will have to get this thing started.* Jackie's face was mellower than when she had come in, but her expression was guarded, as if she were a guest at this meeting rather than a participant in it.

Dad let out a huge sigh that may or may not have had anything to do with the distinctly awkward moment in which we found ourselves.

Carolyn surprised me by breaking the silence. "Dad," she said, "we need to talk to you about something. Since Mom died, the three of us have been worried about you living here alone. And we—"

"I'm fine!"

"And we understand that you don't want to move out of this house. We know how much it means to you, and we know how hard you and Mom tried to make it on your own even when your health was declining. But the fact is you need some help to be able to stay here. I talked to Brandon about this, and if it's all right with you, we'd like to move out of our apartment and move in here with you to help out."

For a long moment no one said a word, not because our minds weren't racing but because it felt like there was no air in the room left for us to breathe. Of all the scenarios I had imagined for that night, none of them included the possibility that Carolyn would volunteer to move in with Dad. Jackie looked just as astounded as I was, her eyebrows raised high and her mouth straining not to smile.

Dad had shed his vacant look and concentrated his entire

attention on Carolyn. It reminded me of that look he used to have when he helped us with our homework, a look of hopeful patience as he waited for us to "get it," as if he was rooting for us to understand whatever it was we were studying. He took his time responding to Carolyn. His eyes narrowed, as if he feared some kind of trick, either from his own brain or from this conspiracy of daughters who sat before him.

"You want to come and live here?"

"Yes. If you want us."

"Well, sure," he said. "Of course. You're always welcome here. You know that. You and Brandon? Live here?"

"Yes, Dad. That's what I'm thinking."

"Well, sure."

"Is that all right with you two?" Carolyn asked us.

"It's fine with me," said Jackie, "if you really want to do it."

I said, "You've really thought this through? I mean, this is a big commitment."

"I know it is. But it's what I want to do. It's what I think I should do."

Once again we were all reduced to uncomfortable silence, unsure of what to do with all the energy we had built up for this meeting.

Carolyn pushed herself up out of the sofa and said, "Now, I have some apple pie out there. Is everybody ready for some?"

I jumped up to help her with the pie, which I didn't know she had bought, happy to have an excuse for motion. I was too nervous to want anything to eat, but I ate the pie anyway, a celebration of Carolyn's great gift to all of us. As we ate, Dad asked at least three more times whether Carolyn really planned to move in for good. Jackie said little, but the words that did come from her were softer and less anxious than I've heard from her in ages. She didn't stay long after the pie. As she left, she gave each of us a big hug. "Call me, kid," she said to Carolyn. "If you need help moving, I can have Tony bring the truck."

Later, when I finally got Carolyn alone in the kitchen, I asked her what had made her change her mind about moving in, which she had always vowed she wouldn't do.

"Moving day," she said. "I know it sounds crazy, but when I thought of the moment when we would actually move Dad and all his stuff out of here, I just couldn't go through with it. I know he might get so bad that we'll eventually have no other choice, but I have to at least try this."

"Well, there's something I've been meaning to tell you," I said, "and I probably shouldn't put it off any longer."

I told her about the change in Mom and Dad's will that allowed her to keep the house for as long as she wanted to live there.

Once again, Carolyn surprised me, this time by looking unimpressed. She said, "That was just Mom's way of trying to manipulate me into moving in. I'm glad I didn't know about it before, because it probably would have kept me out of here. When Dad dies, Brandon and I—if Brandon's not grown up and gone by then—are moving out of here into our own place. I can promise you that. Nobody could have *bribed* me to move in here. I can't even really say that I *want* to do it. But I'm at peace about it, and that's a feeling I don't get very often."

38 HUGH: TALKY DAY

I think about Vonnie all the time. It's not only that I miss her, which of course I do. In fact, several times lately I've woken up from a nap thinking she's still here—not consciously thinking it, but simply assuming it the way I did when she was alive—and I wonder where she is and why I don't hear her shuffling around. Yesterday I went for ten minutes thinking she'd pop in the room any second, and then this horrible chill coursed through my body, this terrible realization that Vonnie was dead and would never walk into this room again.

How do people deal with the finality of death? How do they reconcile themselves to the fact that they will never again hear the voice of the one they love so much? All my senses search for her. I listen for her throughout the day. At night I reach toward her side of the bed. My eyes try to fill the blank space her death leaves in our home.

Nothing comforts the pain of her absence. Memories don't. Talking about her doesn't. Keeping quiet about her doesn't.

Mostly I do keep quiet about her, but sometimes, like this

afternoon, I talk about her when somebody else brings up her name. This time it was Donna. She was here for one of her "baby-sitting" sessions, which is what I (secretly) call these times when one or more of the kids comes over for several hours to make sure I get from my recliner to the toilet without killing myself.

Donna asked me whether I thought Vonnie had changed much during the last few weeks of her life. Of course she had, I said. She acted happier than I'd seen her in twenty years, in spite of her worries about me and her own health and everything else. I said, "You know that she said you and Danny coming into our lives was the best thing that had happened to her in a long time."

"Yes, she told me that, and it meant so much to me I almost cried."

"Well, I was shocked by her saying that because, frankly, keeping you and Danny and Barbara away had always been at the center of our marriage. Vonnie always refused to acknowledge that the world even existed before 1954. She refused to speak your mother's name. Or *your* names, either. The strange thing is, until this summer, I hadn't realized how weighed down she had been by all this. I always thought I carried most of that guilt myself."

"Really?"

"Well, with Vonnie, I figured that in her mind everything was more settled—she made sure you kids and Barbara were out of our lives, and that was the end of it. But for me, I was in an almost constant battle inside myself. I mean, sometimes I'd think about Barbara and you kids and tell myself what I was doing wasn't so bad. The fact that I never saw you or even acknowledged your existence was at least as much Barbara's fault as mine, probably more. In the end, she got what she wanted—a life apart from me, with no attempt on my part to complicate things for her or you. And she remarried, and you kids were taken care of. So who besides me was really hurt? But at other times, when I thought about the fact that I had turned my back on my own children and had promised never to see them again or even to speak to them again, I would feel such contempt for myself that I was almost incapacitated."

This was more than I had ever intended to say to Donna—or anyone else—but unfortunately the strokes sometimes make me talky, and this was one of my talky days. It's almost as if I forget I'm *saying* these things to someone and end up blurting things out that I usually would only *think* silently to myself.

Anyhow, Donna kept listening, and I kept going. "I can't tell you the number of nights I have woken up tormenting myself over this. It is always worse at night, because for some reason it is harder to keep my thoughts away then than during the day. But I would stare at the ceiling, arguing with myself about what I should have done and what I should do now. Even all that agonizing filled me with guilt because I knew I would never have the—what should I call it? Courage?—to step out and make things right. I mean, what if I had let myself come to the firm conclusion that what I was doing was wrong and that I should go to Vonnie and Barbara and tell them the deal was off—I wanted my children back in my life, and I wanted to stop keeping secrets?

"Would I have been willing to turn all our lives upside down—yours and Danny's included—for the chance to set things right? Would I have risked alienating Vonnie? Would I have been willing to face Barbara's wrath or her revenge? Would I have been willing to risk the possibility that you and Danny might hate me so much by the time it was over that all that upheaval would have been in vain anyway?

"A few times I came close to tossing aside all my reluctance and simply resigning myself to whatever consequences might come from acting. But each time, once harsh daylight arrived—once I looked into the face of Vonnie or one of my daughters and realized that keeping our family together was hard enough even in the best of circumstances—my resolve withered. I couldn't lob that bomb of the past into the middle of our living room. I delayed, and within a day or two my conscience would cloud up enough that I could let things slide awhile longer.

"The problem with having to keep everything secret was that I never even had anyone to talk to about this in order to get another person's perspective on it. I never told *anyone* about you kids and Barbara. And the people who knew about you already, like my brothers, I carefully avoided. So I only had my own guilt and second-guessing and dithering to go by. And I guess, until her last few months, Vonnie was the same way."

"You know that Vonnie talked to me toward the end, right? That she asked my forgiveness? That she asked God's forgiveness?"

"Yes. She told me."

"That's really what set her free toward the end, don't you think? Not just *telling* the story, but letting God's forgiveness wash over her."

"You're probably right, and I know you're going to tell me that I should do the same, but I can't."

"Why not?"

"I don't know. I can't explain it. After all these years, to simply turn to God to wash it all away seems too . . . simple."

"You'd rather *suffer* your way back to Him? *Deserve* your forgiveness?"

I shrugged.

She said, "You've been in the church for—"

"I know, for forty years, and I know that you can't earn your way back to God, but it's just that . . . I'm still working things out."

"Hugh, people have done worse things than you and been forgiven."

"I know that."

"And people have had worse things happen to them than what happened to me and Danny. If I can be blunt with you, I think it's arrogant of you to hang on to this as if it stands out from any wrong that anyone else has ever done."

I had no answer for her. I sat there thinking. After a while, I said, "I have nothing else to offer. I'm a broken-down old man with not much time left."

"That's what I'm saying," she said. "You have nothing else to offer, so you have to simply throw yourself at God's feet. Beg for His mercy. Accept His grace. That's what forgiveness is."

After that, she left me alone for a while, thank goodness. I fell into another nap, and when I woke up—or thought I woke up—I had the impression it was years ago when my daughters were little. I thought I was holding one of them as a baby in my arms. I could feel the weight of her. I pulled her up closer to my chest. I kissed her head.

When I woke up further and remembered my true reality, all I could think was, I don't want my life to end. In spite of everything I've lost, I want to go on and on. I want to know more, feel more, experience more. I want to go back and do it better this time.

I don't think I said any of that out loud, and I don't think Donna actually spoke to me any more about forgiveness. But I remember, or I imagine that I remember, her voice asking, "You're a Christian, aren't you? Don't you believe that your life *does* continue even after death? Don't you believe Vonnie is free now, enjoying eternity with her Lord?"

All I could answer was, "I hope so. I hope so. I hope so."

39 DANNY:
We All Need Mercy

Hugh died one week ago today. His death came only three months after Vonnie passed away. He died, as they say, peacefully in his sleep, but that expression is as false as most of what people say about death. He had been dying for a long time, and I didn't see much that was peaceful about it.

At the funeral home, I heard Donna say to Hugh's daughters, "I know that your father made his peace with God before the end, and in his own way, I think he tried to make amends with all of us. I have no doubt that he and Vonnie are celebrating together today in heaven."

I assumed this was nothing more than the bland reassurance that people like Donna give to a grief-stricken family, but I asked her about it later anyway. She insisted that she wasn't simply telling the family what they wanted to hear, but that she had based her conclusion about Hugh on specific bits of evidence she had either heard and seen herself or had been told about during Hugh's final weeks. I was with him quite a bit near the end, and I saw and heard some of this myself.

Hugh didn't feel well at all during those final days. He was preoccupied most of the time and could barely keep a conversation going. He'd launch into little bits of stories that had no beginning or end. He'd hold imaginary conversations with people he must have known years ago, but at the same time he couldn't quite place who the person was right in front of him. In the midst of all this, he repeated one sentence dozens of times. "We all need mercy. We all need mercy." It never seemed to connect to the rest of what he was saying. I took it to be some kind of random piece of data floating free in his brain, but Donna interpreted it as a call to God for forgiveness.

Another thing Hugh kept repeating was "Jesus, Jesus." One time I said to Carolyn that it almost sounded like Hugh was swearing, but she insisted, "No. Even at his angriest, Dad never used the Lord's name in vain. Whatever is going on in his brain, it's not that." Donna, of course, assumed that Hugh was simply calling out for Jesus, asking for mercy.

A few days before Hugh died, Carolyn said he reached out and held her hand one time when she brought him one of his bottles of water. It was a gesture of affection he almost never made. She said the look in his eyes made her think he was having a moment of clarity, even though it took him a long time to speak. When he did, he said, "I'm sorry."

"For what?" she asked, assuming he was referring to some trivial incident of that evening.

He struggled to answer. She had the feeling he had more to say than what he could put into words. She waited, and finally he said, "I love you girls. I loved your mother, and I love you and Pam and Jackie. You've got to believe that much. The strange thing is, I spent all those years feeling guilty for walking away from Danny and Donna, but it was you girls that I really ended up hurting. And now I'm so sorry."

I told Donna that a handful of sentences wasn't much to go

by, but she said, "They're plenty. The one sad thing about Hugh is that he ran out of time before he said and did everything he should have. He shouldn't have made his daughters interpret hints. He should have talked to them while he was still able. Hugh spent his whole life running from the Lord, but there at the very end, I think he was finally running *to* Him. I'm sure he regrets not having done it years ago. Coming back to God is not something any of us should put off."

I know that "any of us" meant me, but I guess I have to admit I'm still running. I'm more like my father than I ever could have dreamed.

After Hugh's funeral, Pam told me, "One of the last things Dad said to me was, 'First we live too long, and then we die too fast.' I asked him what he meant, but he couldn't tell me. I think there was so much more that he wanted to say to us, but by the end, he was simply incapable."

I feel bad that Carolyn uprooted her and Brandon's lives so soon before Hugh died. I asked her whether she planned to stay in the house since she had just moved there. "Oh no," she said. "We'll find our own place. I know the will says that I can stay as long as I want, but I have no intention of falling into that trap. No. Brandon and I will find another nice little manageable apartment. Freedom is what I'm after. I'm not taking anything with me from Mom and Dad's, unless there happens to be some money left over, which we could always use. I'm throwing the house wide open. Jackie or Pam—or you and Donna, for all I care—can come and take whatever you like. I'm finished with it."

"Well," I said, "I won't be taking anything, either, I promise you. Not even money. I'd like to hang on to my freedom, too."

What I did not tell her is that I've made another big decision. I'm leaving Indiana. I've decided to go back to California. Not to Los Angeles again, but to Sacramento, where Alex is. It never worked out for him to come and meet Hugh and the family, and I regret that. I've decided it's time for me to retire Buster Flapjaw and from now on to speak only to the real Terri, not the one who haunts my brain. I figure I can work (or be unemployed a little while longer) just as easily in Sacramento as I can here. And one thing this time with Hugh taught me is that I want to know my son. I don't want him to have to come and find me when I'm old and on the brink of death the way I did with Hugh. I don't want to run out of time.